ALSO BY
SCARLETT ST. CLAIR

When Stars Come Out

HADES X PERSEPHONE

A Touch of Darkness

A Touch of Ruin

A Touch of Malice

HADES SAGA

A Game of Fate

A Game of Retribution

ADRIAN X ISOLDE

King of Battle and Blood

Queen of Myth and Monsters

QUEEN OF MYTH AND MONSTERS

SCARLETT ST. CLAIR

Bloom books

Cover design by Regina Wamba/ReginaWamba.com
Cover images © Victor/Adobe Stock, wimage72/Adobe Stock, thawats/
Adobe Stock, 4 Girls 1 Boy/Adobe Stock, Yura/Adobe Stock

Published by Bloom Books, an imprint of Sourcebooks
P.O. Box 4410, Naperville, Illinois 60567-4410
(630) 961-3900
sourcebooks.com

Printed and bound in the United States of America.
WOZ 10 9 8 7 6 5 4 3 2

To those of us who have had to survive

ZENOVIA

VLASCA

AROTH

MOUNTAINS of AROTH

REVEKKA

The STARLESS FOREST

THE RED PALACE

CEL CEREDI

SADOVEA

HOUSE OF JOLA

HOUSE OF ELIN

ISTAS

VAIDA

THE NINE

HOUSE OF SIVA

HOUSE OF LARA

The GOLDEN SEA

HOUSE OF LITA

VIKO

HOUSE OF THEA

TIVA

SINTA

ISLANDS of ST. AMAND

The SILVER FOREST

MADOVEA
KEZIAH
FOREST of RAVENS
HOUSES
HOUSE OF VELA
ATOLL of NALANI
HOUSE OF HELA
ZUNI
OLATHE
ALO
The VIOLET SEA
MOUNTAINS of LAMIA
HOUSE OF ERIS
CORDOVA

CONTENT WARNING

This book contains violent themes such as rape, assault, torture, and infant loss. If you or someone you know is struggling, please reach out for help.

Here are just a few resources:

National Sexual Assault Hotline
(800) 656-4673

National Suicide and Crisis Lifeline
988

National Suicide Prevention Lifeline (Options for Deaf and Hard of Hearing)
For TTY Users: Use your preferred relay service or dial 711 then 988

Substance Abuse and Mental Health Services Administration National Helpline
(800) 662-4357

QUEEN OF MYTH AND MONSTERS

ONE
Isolde

Nine corpses were impaled outside the gates of the red palace.

I could see them now from the library window, aglow in the torchlight. Over the last two days, I had learned a lot about the process of impalement. Namely, that if done well, it could take hours, even days for the prisoner to die. It was a horrific death, and even more horrific to watch as each body slid slowly down, their weight inevitably driving the end of the spear through their mouth or throat or chest.

All the while, they begged any who passed to kill them faster, but no one came to their aid, not even me.

In the aftermath of Ravena's attack, those who had betrayed our kingdom fled, but my husband was a merciless king. He had ordered his loyal noblesse to hunt, and he had joined them. In a day, they had captured the vassals who had supported Adrian's former noblesse in their rebellion, and now they were a gruesome warning to anyone considering treason.

I wondered what it said about me and who I had become that I was not appalled by Adrian's choice of punishment.

Even now, as I stared, I felt nothing but anger—anger toward those who had tried to hurt me, who had attempted to take away my power, who perceived me as weak.

Among them, my father, whose death had occurred by my hand.

You are worth every star in the sky, he'd said in the throne room of Lara when Adrian had asked for my hand. My father had been willing to go to war with the Blood King for me.

And perhaps he had meant it then, until I had given him another way to reclaim his kingdom and the rest of Cordova.

I still could not fathom it, could not come to terms with how everything had ended. My mind was a whirlwind of feelings, the greatest among them shock. My body was heavy with it, my chest tight with it, my eyes blind with it. Through my numbness, there were bursts of anger and sadness, each of them shaking my body, violent tremors that left me exhausted. Yet I could not sleep, because each time I closed my eyes, all I saw was my father, his face drained of affection, possessed by a determination to end my life because it would end Adrian's too.

That haunting memory was how I'd found myself in the library before sunrise.

If I couldn't sleep, I might as well research. Usually,

I preferred the company of the librarian Lothian and his lover, Zann, but tonight I was glad for the quiet as I leafed through books on the history of witches.

Ravena had escaped with *The Book of Dis*, which she believed would give her the power she always wanted, though it likely would come at a grave price.

All spells cost something, but the toll for dark magic was life.

And yet I had been willing to pay that price two hundred years ago. Now I wondered why. I could not remember, just as I could not remember any of the spells I'd written in the book. I came here now to search the library's archives in hopes that something from those texts would spur memories from my life as Yesenia.

So far, I'd only recalled a few things. I remembered High Coven and most of the relationships I'd formed with my sisters. I remembered Ravena, her betrayal, and her allegiance with King Dragos. Mostly, I remembered Adrian and the quiet way we fell in love, but those memories did not compare to the feeling of relief, the strange peace that came with knowing exactly who I was.

I had no conflict over my two lives—Yesenia was of the past, a life once lived. Now, I was Isolde Vasiliev, queen of Revekka, future queen of Cordova, and I was here to conquer.

"I do not particularly like waking alone," Adrian said.

I turned to find him leaning against one of the ebony shelves lined with black-bound books. He wore a long robe, red and patterned in gold. His hair was unbound, falling in loose waves around his shoulders. His arms were crossed, and while he teased, I knew something more had driven him from bed—worry.

"I couldn't sleep," I said.

He frowned, and my gaze lingered on his mouth before rising to meet his eyes. That was one thing that had changed in the two hundred years we had been apart—his eyes. Once, they had been blue, but now they were rimmed in white. I always assumed it had happened after he was turned, but then, no other vampire I had met since coming to Revekka had those eyes.

"Couldn't sleep," he said, tilting his head. "Or wouldn't?"

He knew the answer, so I asked a different question.

"Did I ever tell you about *The Book of Dis*?"

He shook his head. "No. You never told me about Dragos either."

I had not told him of the former king's abuse. A strange guilt blossomed in my chest, though I knew that was not what he intended.

It was my turn to frown as I searched for a reason for my silence.

"Though why would you?" he asked, and I met his gaze as he approached, his hand pressed against my cheek. "You were so far above me then."

"Stop," I said, the knot of guilt growing. It had not been about status at all. If Adrian had known, he would have killed Dragos, and while he had ultimately done so, it was in the aftermath of his victory over Revekka. "You know that isn't true."

"Ah, but it was," he said, taking a step closer. His hand moved to my neck, his body flush with mine. I tilted my head all the way back to keep his gaze. "I was nothing but a glorified guard, but you—you were something more."

I wrapped my hand around his wrist, not to push him away but to keep him close.

I shook my head, feeling something thick gathering in my throat. I could not help hearing the screams of my sisters—my coven—the night of their burning. It had been the first day of what would become the reaping and a complete decimation of every witch in Cordova.

I took a deep, shuddering breath.

"I got everyone killed," I said.

"Dragos needed power, so he turned on the only people who had it," Adrian said. "You were just a way to shift responsibility."

I could barely breathe. When Adrian had taken my blood, I'd only known the consequences of the curse Dis had cast on him—that tasting my blood meant our lives were tied. If I died, he died. I did not know that the traumas of my past would also haunt me.

"Tell me how you killed him," I whispered, searching his eyes.

Adrian tensed, his fingers pressing slightly into my skin. I wondered if he thought I would run, if he wasn't quite convinced I was firmly rooted by his side, but there was nothing that would drive me away, save death.

"Will it help you to know?" he asked.

In truth, I did not know, but I answered anyway. "Yes."

Still, he was quiet, but when he spoke, his gaze did not waver from mine, like he wanted to see how I changed with the knowledge of his execution of Dragos.

"I cut off his head. The blade was dull."

I was not surprised by his choice of weapon or the brutal way in which he'd chosen to execute the former king of Revekka, and because of the last two days, I had no trouble imagining him hacking away at Dragos's neck until his head rolled.

"And I kept it on a pike outside the gates where our treasonous dead are now. His body lay beneath it, and it was picked apart until it was nothing more than bones."

"And the bones?" I had not imagined he would give Dragos the satisfaction of a burial in any form.

"Look closer at my throne the next time we hold court," he said.

Something in the pit of my stomach twisted sharply. Adrian had built an empire on the bones of his greatest enemy. A month ago, I would have been disgusted, but life at Adrian's court had changed my opinion on his brutality. There was no room for vulnerability here, no room for forgiveness. It was conquer or be killed.

Dragos had taught us that, and he had taken everything.

So had Ravena.

"What are you thinking?" he asked.

I raised a brow. Adrian could hear my thoughts, but not always. I think it had become harder to break through the numbness that overwhelmed me since my father's death. "You cannot tell?"

"Your emotions are quite tame," he replied.

I didn't believe him. I felt like chaos, but I respected that he asked.

"I am thinking about how I will fashion a throne from Ravena's bones."

The corners of Adrian's lips curled, and he leaned closer, his breath on my lips as he spoke. "If that is your wish, I shall build it myself."

Then his warm mouth was on mine, and his arm tightened around my waist. He was an anchor I grasped in the darkness of my grief, the only thing that brought feeling, and I craved this—his heat, our madness, the distraction.

I clung to him, my fingers digging into his biceps as his mouth left mine, lips trailing over my jaw and neck, his tongue caressing my skin, and I ceased to breathe when I felt the scrape of his teeth there. He seemed to notice and pulled away.

"I do not have to feed," he said, his hand lifting to brush my cheek. "But I do want you."

Adrian had not taken my blood since the night he had first fed from me. When I asked him, he said, "I need you strong." And yet when dawn broke in a few hours, he would leave once more to hunt for the last two rebels—his former noblesse, Gesalac and Julian.

I needed him strong for that.

"I am well enough," I said.

"You aren't sleeping," he said.

"Who needs sleep," I said, rising on the tips of my toes and lacing my arms around his neck, "when there is so much we could do?"

His hands were on my hips, but he was still.

"Adrian," I said, his name a breathless whisper, and my eyes fell to his lips once more, my fingers trailing his cheek. "Please."

It wasn't until I looked into his eyes that he caved, and his mouth collided with mine. I basked in the way my mind went blank, the horror and the anger of these last few days replaced by a blissful heat that seemed to swell, filling me to bursting, but making me aware of how much I needed this, needed him.

Adrian's fingers dug into my skin, and he guided me until my back hit the wall where he pinned my wrists so he could kiss me uninhibited, lips tracing a path to my breasts, which he lavished with attention. Even through the fabric of my nightdress, the teasing was exquisite, and my hands were soon free to rake through his hair and drag his mouth back to mine.

Between us, Adrian untied his robe and hiked my shift up before lifting my leg, cradling the back of my knee over his arm, his erection pressed into my heat. I sucked in a sharp breath, my head falling back on a moan, exposing my neck, where he kissed and nipped at my skin, his voice a heady rumble.

"I love the way you taste," he said, grinding into me until I felt too hollow, too empty.

"I need you inside me," I said, my hands on his shoulders, ready to give him the leverage he needed to cure my desperation. "Give me your come and you can have my blood."

He chuckled breathlessly. "Oh, Sparrow. I will fill you to bursting."

Our position against the wall did not give me the opportunity to watch as he guided himself inside me, but I felt him, exhaling as he slid deeper and began to thrust. I couldn't catch my breath as each wave of pleasure rose higher than the last. I was drowning in this and I never wanted to resurface.

"Isolde," Adrian said, and I opened my eyes. He stared back, gaze fierce and lustful. "Look at me."

He cupped the back of my neck, his other hand pressed flat to the wall, and he moved deeper, ground against me harder. I lost control of my expression, my mouth caught between moans, grinding my teeth, and biting my lip. When the first keening cry bubbled from my lips, Adrian descended, his sharp teeth cutting into my skin.

I clung to him, nails digging into his flesh. He still moved inside me, but slower, timing the pull of his lips with the thrust of his hips. He drew back once to kiss my mouth before returning to the wound he'd made, and with the taste of my blood on my lips, I followed each wave of pain and pleasure until it dragged me into darkness.

I woke with the memory of how Adrian had filled me and fucked me and bit me, and I had ascended into something ethereal and divine—something that had taken me from sorrow to bliss. I wanted to go back, to reclaim that power, but I was once more in this mournful body and confused.

How had I gotten to bed?

There was movement to my right, and I shifted to find Adrian standing near the window, bathed in the bloodred light of Revekka's dawn. He wore armor that glinted gold and silver as he turned to look at me. He had pulled his hair back, and the angles of his face showed sharply, contoured by shadow.

He was fierce, frighteningly beautiful, and already bathed in red.

"Do you expect to be injured?" I asked as I sat up, pushing the blankets from my body, already feeling better without their weight. I had never seen Adrian wear armor, not when he came to claim my kingdom and not when we made our return to Revekka.

It startled me, and I had to work to swallow the panic that rose into my throat, knowing I could not protest his departure. This was necessary to the survival of our kingdom—to what Adrian had built and what we would continue to build together.

Adrian offered a small smile, as if he thought my concern was cute rather than valid.

"It's merely a precaution," he said. "I am no longer hunting mortals."

Today he would search for Gesalac and Julian, whom Sorin had not been able to track beyond the borders of our land, which meant they were likely hiding, harbored by Revekkians. Or were they relying on the land for shelter until they could begin the next phase of their plan?

And what *was* that plan?

Of the two, I feared Gesalac more. He was the most outspoken and perhaps had the greatest vendetta against Adrian, as he had killed Gesalac's son after I had grown annoyed by his continued harassment. I'd snapped when he'd touched me and drove a knife into his neck.

Adrian had finished the job.

Julian was less imposing, but he, like Gesalac, saw me as the enemy, and it was his opinion of me that had cost him his eye.

"Do you think you will find them?" I asked.

My lungs felt heavy in my chest, my breathing far too shallow.

I was afraid of what would happen if they managed to escape.

"Perhaps," Adrian said. "They will likely seek refuge with kings whose petitions to become immortal I denied."

Kings like Gheroghe of Vela, the slave king who conquered my mother's people.

I rose to my feet.

"Can either of them sire vampires?" I asked.

"They can," he said. "And they likely will."

Under Adrian's rule, only he held the authority to decide who became immortal. Anyone who disobeyed was executed, but Gesalac and Julian had signed their death warrants already. They had nothing to lose.

"What happens then?"

Adrian's fingers tilted my chin as he answered, "I will kill them all."

I should draw comfort from his confidence, and I had no doubt he would exact revenge, but would it come too late?

Adrian drew me from my thoughts with a kiss, a soft brush of his lips before he pulled me close. With our bodies pressed together, there was a shift in his behavior and his tongue drove into my mouth, hand tightening into my hair, knee coaxing my willing thighs apart. A moan caught in my throat as the friction of our bodies sparked a fever in my blood, filling, tightening, drenching.

I wanted to touch him, but my hands were barred by his armor. I questioned my power and his restraint. Could I convince him to delay?

But I also wanted this over. I wanted Gesalac and Julian caught. I wanted to watch their torture and their deaths.

Adrian must have sensed the change in my thoughts because he pulled away, mouth tense, eyes alight.

"You will rest today," he said.

My lips flattened at his command, and very gently, he pulled my hair, guiding my head back, exposing my neck. He pressed his lips to the spot he had bitten in the library. It was healed now, but the memory lived on my skin.

I held my breath and shivered at the soft caress of his mouth. A wave of heat blossomed in my chest and made me light-headed.

As he pulled away, he studied me, twisting a piece of my hair around his lithe finger.

"You will rest today," he said again. "If you want me tonight."

"Are you attempting to bribe me?" I asked.

"I should not have taken your blood," he said. "You could not handle it."

"I feel fine," I said.

"It doesn't matter that you feel fine," he said. "You lost consciousness."

I frowned. "Why is that…bad?"

His hand loosened in my hair, and he brushed his thumb along my lips.

"You should always be alert when we are together," he said. "When I took your blood, I was inside you. You went limp. You were gone. So yes, it is bad."

I dropped my gaze. I couldn't help feeling a little guilty, even a little embarrassed. I hadn't thought of what Adrian had experienced after I blacked out. Now I considered just how unnerved he must have been.

"Isolde," he said in an attempt to draw my attention, but still I looked away, swallowing.

"I will rest," I said, my tone far more cross than I intended.

"Isolde," he repeated quietly, and when I finally met his gaze, his stare was gentle. "You are my light."

I took his face between my hands.

"You are my darkness," I said and kissed him.

We stared at each other for a long moment, and then he took a step away, and I felt the distance sink into my heart.

"Will you see me off?" he asked.

"Of course."

I was still wearing my shift and did not want to delay Adrian by returning to my room to dress. Instead, he offered a woolen overcoat. The fabric was heavy, the sleeves too long, but it was warm and smelled like him.

We walked in silence, my hand on Adrian's arm, and when the doors opened to the courtyard, a wave of cold air stole my breath. Frost had settled on the stones, gleaming like bloody webs beneath the sun's light.

Adrian's men were gathered there with their horses, and at our appearance, they knelt, rising at his command. Some were soldiers, others noblesse, and while none here had aligned themselves with Gesalac and Julian, I couldn't help questioning their loyalty to Adrian. Since I'd joined him here, he had lost four of the nine noblesse.

Were the rest merely biding their time before they struck?

Suddenly my stomach churned. If they chose today to attack, could Adrian take them?

My gaze shifted to Daroc, Adrian's general, and Sorin, his lover. Visually, the two made a stunning pair, but they could not be more different. Daroc, with his strong and angled features, always looked severe, his eyes piercing, as if he were trying to read everyone's mind, and perhaps he could, but I'd learned from the start that vampires did not willingly tell their abilities. Even Sorin, who was the most forthright, had not told me he could shift into the form of a falcon. I'd learned that by chance when he had come to my rescue in the woods after being attacked by Ravena and mist-possessed Ciro. Looking at him now with his soft features and dimpled smile, I found it hard to believe he could be anything but good.

And yet someone had told Ravena that Adrian had tasted my blood. The act made me his greatest weakness—our lives were bound.

I have waited centuries for this. For you, Adrian had said. He had been so willing, comforted in the knowledge that he could trust the four who knew the consequences of the bloodletting—Daroc, Sorin, Adrian's cousin Ana Maria, and his viceroy, Tanaka—and yet as it turned out, we could trust no one.

I took a deep breath, attempting to release the tension tightening my chest at having such a weakness known to my greatest enemy, and faced Adrian, who drew my hand to his lips, his eyes burning into mine.

"We will return at sundown."

The words were a fierce promise, and I held them close to my heart. He claimed my mouth in a searing kiss, drawing his thumb over my bottom lip as he pulled away.

"See that you do," I said, and he turned and mounted Shadow. I wanted him back already, but I also wanted him to return tonight, triumphant, with Gesalac and Julian as our prisoners.

With a final look, he rode out, his men falling into step behind him. They left through the gate, and I followed, watching as they cut a path through the nine impaled bodies that decorated our doorstep.

Not even the cold air could keep the smell of decay at bay. It tinged the air—subtle but sour—and it turned my stomach. Still, I kept watch until I could no longer see Adrian descending the sheer pathway into the valley of Cel Ceredi. Only then did I move, climbing to the tower wall where I tracked them, racing through the city, to the outer wall—a streak of shadows cloaked in red as they dashed into the darkened forest. Even when they left my sight, I lingered.

"Come inside, my queen," said Tanaka, breathless from toiling his way up the stone steps behind me. I wondered when he'd joined us in the courtyard. I had not noticed him before.

Tanaka, Adrian's viceroy, was older than any other vampire I had met. His skin was white and wrinkled, even on his cheeks, and while his hair was still dark, it had receded nearly to the back of his head.

I wondered at his age and why he was changed so late in his life. Despite having a few memories from my past life as Yesenia, I did not remember this man or his connection to Adrian, though it was possible he grown closer to Adrian in the two hundred years since my death.

A lot had happened in my absence.

"My queen?" Tanaka asked.

"I am not quite ready," I said, not looking at the old man.

"But it is cold," he said.

I did not mind the cold. It, at least, allowed me to feel something beyond the strange, distant numbness that had consumed my body since my father's death.

"If you are uncomfortable, you may return to the palace," I replied.

He huffed out a breath and tried once more. "Adrian will be very cross with me if you were to catch a cold."

"Then I will be sure to protect you from his wrath," I said, though my reply felt distant, even to my ears. I was distracted, but by nothing in particular, truly unable to focus on one line of thinking. It was as if my mind were a puzzle, and since the bloodletting and betrayal, I had been trying to piece together a picture of my world—its truths and its lies.

I lingered on the tower wall for a few minutes longer. Tanaka did not try to convince me to return to the palace again, and he did not leave my side. I wondered why he stayed. Was it out of true loyalty to Adrian or a ruse?

"Winter is upon us," said Tanaka, his voice quiet, almost as if he were speaking to himself.

I glanced at him, and he nodded toward the eastern sky where clouds gathered, thick and heavy, full of a coming storm.

"It will be snowing by sundown."

I frowned. Winters in Revekka were harsh, and while I doubted it would affect Adrian, I worried for those outside our city.

"Is Revekka prepared?"

The blood mist was still a threat, and with fewer noblesse, could the others survive?

"We will do the best we can," he replied.

"What is your best?" I asked, and when I looked at Tanaka, he had frozen, mouth ajar as if his answer was stuck in his throat, or perhaps he did not have one at all. After a moment, he composed himself.

"These are winter folk, my queen. They know how to survive."

As much as I desired to remain outside awaiting Adrian's return, I was queen of Revekka, and while my husband hunted, I would plan.

This world thought they knew a conqueror when Adrian had been born, but they had yet to feel my wrath.

"I must speak with Gavriel," I said, determined to gather information about Lara. Unfortunately for Adrian, I had no intention of resting. "Summon him to the garden."

With a final look at the horizon, I left the wall.

TWO
Isolde

I returned to my quarters, parting ways with Tanaka at the base of the stairs. I was chilled to my core, my skin so cold it felt tight over my bones and my long hair tangled after spending so much time in the wind, but with each step, my body thawed and I continued to plan.

I would have to return to Lara eventually, along with Killian, and preferably before news of my father's death spread. I had little faith that I would be welcomed by my people and even less faith that the Nine Houses—or what remained of them—would allow my coronation to take place. And while I knew Adrian could force anything I desired, I did not wish to conquer that way.

Becoming the first queen of Lara mattered. It was how I had always imagined my life, and even though it was unfolding differently, I wanted it no less. And it was not only Lara I wished to possess. I wanted Vela. I wanted to watch the life drain from King Gheorghe's face as I conquered his kingdom, reclaimed my mother's homeland, and freed her people—*my* people. As badly as I would have liked to leave tomorrow, I knew the consequences would be disastrous. Things had to settle in Revekka, and I hoped in that time I would learn Ravena's intentions with *The Book of Dis*.

By the time I crested the steps that led to my private room, my heart was filled with fire and vengeance.

As I approached, I heard Violeta and Vesna, my ladies-in-waiting. I paused for a moment, trying to catch pieces of their conversation, but their voices filtered through my closed door, a low murmur of unintelligible words. There was a part of me that felt guilty that I would seek to spy, and yet my trust in others had been crushed and I no longer felt confident in my ability to discern friend from enemy, no matter their role or age.

So I listened a while longer and only caught a few words.

Mother. Jasenka. Kseniya.

Vesna was talking about her family, likely that they were making the move from their small village in Jovea to Cel Ceredi this week. Adrian had appointed Tanaka to find them a small space to rent after I had asked to relocate them. I had many reasons for the request—I did not like seeing Vesna so sad and preferred that she was able to return home to her sisters nightly, and perhaps I felt just the slightest bit of guilt given that I was the reason they were fatherless, but I had not thought beyond the knife in my hand when the man had come to my court, offering his daughter to my husband as a concubine in exchange for immortality.

So I'd taken Vesna and offered him the opposite.

While I knew how Vesna was handling the situation, I was not so certain about her mother or her two younger sisters. I had taken a husband and a father, and despite his abusive nature, emotions always complicated truths.

Would they see me as their liberator or a murderer?

And did it even matter? I was their queen.

I pushed those thoughts aside and entered my chambers. Violeta and Vesna stopped speaking and stood immediately. I could not help the suspicion that clawed at my stomach with their sudden silence.

"My queen," they said in unison, dipping into curtsies.

"I have much to attend to today," I said, crossing to my armoire to choose a dress. I had no intention of languidly preparing for the day. I felt as though that luxury was gone, suitable only for a queen who did not intend to rule.

"Of course," Violeta said. "Will you not eat first, my queen?"

"No," I said. Even at the mention of food, my stomach twisted. Everything I had consumed since my father's death tasted burnt, but I offered no explanation.

I had no doubt that the two were attempting to abide by orders Adrian had given, but little could be done when I refused.

I chose a dress—light blue with gold threading. The neckline was scooped, the skirt, though tulle, was sleek, and the sleeves were long, which would keep me warm enough within the castle walls as the storm moved in.

Once I was changed, I smoothed my hair in the mirror. Normally, Violeta would attempt some sort of braid or twist, but I only needed it tame enough to wear my mother's pearl tiara. It seemed fitting, on the heels of my father's betrayal, to honor her memory instead. Though it did not feel sufficient, I had little else. My attachment to her and her people was an ache I felt deep in my bones. It was part of my soul that had fractured at birth and would never heal.

I would always mourn what could have been had my mother survived, had she taught me the ways of her world. I knew even if I managed to free the Nalani, I would always be different—never one of them but *other*. That was how it was when I had been princess of Lara, and it was the same now as queen of Revekka.

And even if I managed to free them, would I be seen as just another conqueror, or would they see me as one of them?

Violeta brought over my tiara. I'd last worn it the day my kingdom had fallen under Adrian's rule, the day he had asked to marry me. It was a simple piece, a silver band set with fresh pearls. Of the items left from my mother, this was my favorite. It was the crown she had worn in her wedding portrait.

I now wondered under what circumstances it had been given to her. Was it a gift from her mother and father, offered with understanding that her marriage to my father would mean a peaceful alliance? Or was it one of the few possessions she had managed to bring with her when my father had taken her as a prisoner?

I turned to the mirror and placed the crown on my head, searching my face for my mother's features, but all that reflected back were my father's—his deep frown, his hollow cheeks, his troubled brow.

I looked miserable.

I turned from the mirror to find Violeta holding a pair of pearl earrings.

"You should wear these, my queen," Violeta said.

They had also been my mother's, and despite how many times I had worn them, seeing them now brought tears to my eyes. I took a deep breath, swallowing the strange wave of emotion that welled in my blood.

"Thank you, Violeta."

I took the earrings and refused to look in the mirror as I hooked them in place. When a knock sounded at the door, I stiffened, my body tense with frustration.

Violeta and Vesna looked at me.

"We can tell them you are busy," Vesna said. "It is not untrue."

It wasn't, but no matter how quickly I got to my agenda today, the events I had planned would take time to unfold. Besides, what if Ana had come to speak with me? I did not want to miss the chance to see her, especially given that I had much to discuss with her, including her use of magic.

"Answer it," I said.

Vesna obeyed, and when she opened the door, I recognized the voice on the other side.

I sighed, and before Vesna could announce his presence, I said, "Come in, Killian."

The commander of Lara's military—and one of my former lovers—entered my quarters. He was dressed in black—not because he was mourning but because he could not bring himself to wear the blue of Lara, nor the red of Revekka. Despite how my father's betrayal had hurt him, he was not yet ready to embrace my kingdom even though he had fought at my side against Gesalac and the crimson mist.

"My queen," he said and bowed.

"You shaved," I said, surprised to see that his long beard was trimmed close to his skin. He had not shaved since he had started growing facial hair. I had never cared for his beard, but I thought that perhaps he kept it because his father had kept one too. I wondered if this was his way of distancing himself from the loyalty he had to King Henri.

"Y-yes," he said and ran a hand over the back of his head. "I hoped for a moment of your time today."

"By today, I'm assuming you mean now."

His eyes shifted to Violeta and Vesna. "A moment… alone."

Alone. The word straightened my spine and sent my heart racing. I did not wish to be alone with anyone but Adrian. At the same time, my chest tightened with guilt. Killian had helped me and was just as devastated by my father's betrayal. But while I knew he was loyal to me, would he also be loyal to my husband?

"I am afraid I have no time this morning," I said. "I must meet with Gavriel."

Killian's shoulders stiffened. "Why?"

The word tumbled out of his mouth unceremoniously.

"I have questions about Lara," I said.

He was quiet for a moment, likely wishing to contain his initial reaction, but he did not need to because I knew how he felt. It was the same way I had felt any time he had minimized my concerns regarding Lara's politics or defenses.

"Do you not trust me?" Killian asked.

"This has nothing to do with trust."

"Then why not ask me?" he said.

"Because you are too close," I said. "I need the truth."

"Are you calling me a liar?" he asked.

I clenched my fist to keep from rolling my eyes. "No," I said. "Unless you knew my father intended to kill me when he arrived here. Then I would call you a liar. Then I would call you a traitor."

Killian paled, and when he spoke, his voice was a quiet rumble. It hinted at the pain I had caused with those few words. "You cannot think I would have let him hurt you." When I did not speak, he continued. "If I had known his intentions, he would not have made it beyond the borders of Lara."

There was a part of me that had expected Killian to justify my father's decision because he had been just as upset when he'd come to Revekka and discovered that not only did the Blood King still live, I was in love with him. Instead, Killian attempted to protect me.

"I wish I had known," he added. "I would have liked to spare you this agony."

There was a lot to say about Killian and the complicated nature of our friendship, but perhaps his greatest attribute was his loyalty—not to crown or title but to me.

"I do not doubt you," I said. "But it is for that reason I must speak with Gavriel. Your view of Lara was influenced by my father. How are either of us to know the truth?"

"Is that an invitation to join you?" he asked.

I studied him briefly and then said, "Only if you agree to wear my colors."

His jaw tightened. "Which colors?"

"Red for Revekka, blue for Lara, and gray…for when I conquer Vela and free my mother's people."

"You wish to conquer Vela?" he asked, his brows raising.

"I *will* conquer Vela," I said. "I will burn it to the ground."

Killian waited outside my door while Violeta helped lace up my boots and clasped a blue, fur-lined cloak around my shoulders. Despite the cold, I did not wish to meet Gavriel within the castle. I did not trust its walls with their hidden passages and concealed doors—anyone might happen upon us; anyone might listen. At least in the garden, it was harder to hide. More than that, however, it was a place from which I drew comfort and strength because it was where I felt closest to my mother, though I was miles away from her gardens in Lara—the ones my father had made certain survived long after her untimely death.

Once more, I found myself at odds with my father, whose love allowed for altars dedicated to my mother's memory but no action toward what mattered most—the freedom of her people and the life of her daughter.

I led Killian outside through the entrance of the Red Palace, following a path that cut between green hedges and a set of stone steps that descended into the extensive gardens. It had grown colder since I'd seen Adrian off this morning, and I briefly wondered where he was now, if he had any luck locating Gesalac or Julian, and when he would be home.

"Everything is still alive," Killian said.

It was true—trees were still lush, flowers were still blooming, the hedges were thick—and yet snow whirled in the air, gathering in the crevices of leaves and petals, glittering red beneath the heavy sky.

"Winter falls upon us fast," said a voice, and I whirled to find Gavriel pushing away from the castle wall on which he had been leaning. He was an imposing figure, both because of his build and his height. As he approached, he scanned the landscape, eyes squinted, adding, "Everything will die soon."

His words felt ominous and sent a chill up my spine.

I'd only had one interaction with Gavriel before today and it had been after I had discovered the desecration of Vaida in Lara. Adrian had assigned him to stay at Castle Fiora, and there he had remained until my father made the journey to Revekka for my coronation.

Now I wondered what would have happened had they not come at all.

Gavriel bowed low before me.

"My queen, Commander Killian," he said and straightened. "I apologize. I did not mean to startle you."

"I did not expect you so early," I said.

He grinned. "It would have been in poor taste to be late for a meeting with my queen."

I studied the vampire, curious about his speech.

"Where are you from, Gavriel?"

"Keziah," he said.

I did not know much about Keziah, save that their ruler had refused to join the nine kings who would make up the Nine Houses of Cordova. They had not been the only country in Cordova to do so, preferring not to organize against the Blood King or take his side. Among the Nine Houses, their choice was perceived as indecision—a weakness that needed to be eradicated. And yet when the Nine Houses organized an army to move against Keziah, they found its people were anything but weak. They had fought ruthlessly to maintain control over their land and the kings of the Nine Houses were forced to retreat.

Every year, the kings would meet for assembly to discuss their so-called unified approach to ruling the houses. To the disdain of most in attendance, my father brought me along after I turned sixteen, and it was there I learned the true fears of men—anything more powerful than them.

The kings would malign Keziah, embarrassed by how they had been beaten so brutally, but they never approached the subject of invasion again.

I recalled deciding then that if I were ever going to go to war against the vampires, I wanted Keziah on my side.

How time had changed things.

"How long have you served my husband?"

"Ten years," he replied.

"So little?"

He chuckled. "Not all of us were born centuries ago. I left for Revekka as soon as I came of age to swear allegiance to King Adrian."

"I did not think Keziah wanted vampire rule," I said.

"My people are proud and very brave, but even they are not strong enough to survive what this world has become."

I wondered what he would do if Adrian failed to protect Keziah.

"If you are trying to determine the depth of my

loyalty, perhaps you should ask me. It would save us both time, given that we have so very little of it."

"It is not your loyalty to Adrian I wish to assess," I said. "It is your loyalty to me."

"You are one and the same."

His statement did not put me at ease. Rather, disappointment blossomed in my chest. I wished to be Adrian's equal, but equality did not mean we were the same.

"How wrong you are," I said. I took a breath and asked, "How are my people?"

"Agitated, uncertain," he said.

I had expected such news, but hearing it was disheartening.

"The news about the destruction of Vaida spread quickly, and on the heels of your marriage to Adrian, some of your people believe he broke his promise to protect them."

I glanced at Killian, who had once assumed the same.

"And the Sanctuary of Asha is not helping," Gavriel added.

My gaze snapped back to him. "The sanctuary?"

"You've a priestess there who claims Asha has sent their salvation."

Despite the strong presence of goddesses within my life, in the lives of everyone in Cordova, I had never been religious. I could not fathom worshipping anyone who had taken my mother from me so young, but I would be stupid if I did not acknowledge either of the goddesses' power. And true power it was, because it was strong enough to have created Adrian.

"Have you heard this?" I asked Killian, who shrugged, then shook his head.

"A few whispers here and there," he said. "Nothing more. I certainly have not seen any evidence that it is true."

"You don't need evidence when people have faith," I said. The mere fact that anyone would believe the priestess or trust the veracity of her words was dangerous—especially to my rule.

"How do we know this isn't some falsehood spread by the priestess?" I asked.

"We don't," said Gavriel.

"Find out," I said.

"As you wish," he said. "Anything more, my queen?"

"Return to Lara tomorrow," I said. "Tell the court my father has decided to extend his stay in Revekka."

I thought about embellishing, adding that King Henri had missed his daughter too much to stay only a week, but I could not manage to speak the words.

"My loyalty is to you, my queen." Gavriel bowed, accepting my orders, and left.

With Gavriel's departure, I remained silent for a long moment, considering his words. I'd known returning to Lara would not be easy, given how I had been treated upon my departure, but this certainly complicated my plans.

"With rumors of the salvation of Asha, what of Nadia?" I asked Killian, my voice hushed.

Nadia, my maid, the woman who had helped raise me, was a passionate follower of Asha, and I could not help hearing her voice as Gavriel's warning played through my mind.

Asha is our savior, she would say. *She will send our salvation.*

When? I asked. *After we are all dead?*

Insolent child, the goddess gave you life!

My mother gave me life, I said. *She died for me too.*

When Killian did not answer, I met his gaze. I knew what he would say before the words left his mouth, and yet I could not protect myself from the pain, the heartache, of knowing she would never choose me.

"Nadia loves you," he said. "But she loves her goddess more."

I might have flinched had it not been for a bell signaling, sharp and frantic, so loud it echoed in my bones.

"What is that?" Killian asked, and though I had never heard the sound before, my heart raced with it, frenzied and panicked.

"Something horrible," I said, a sudden lump forming in the back of my throat.

THREE
Isolde

I gathered my skirts in hand and raced through the garden. Killian followed, and once we had topped the stairs, the ringing had ceased, replaced by dreadful, deafening screams.

A crowd had gathered in the courtyard. I pushed my way through to the front in time to see Miha and Isac leading a small party of soldiers into Cel Ceredi on their horses where giant, black dogs chased, mauled, and mangled my people in the streets of the village.

These creatures were aufhockers, drawn to life and driven to end it. When Nadia could no longer scare me with stories of witches, she had used aufhockers to try and keep me from sneaking out of the walls of High City at night.

"You know they look for girls like you," she would say. "Troublemakers who disobey the rules, and when you are alone in the woods, they will hop upon your back and tear your throat!"

"How can they tear out my throat when they are on my back?" I'd asked.

"Do not ask questions, insolent child!" she would say, and though we laughed, I knew there was truth to some of what she said. Aufhockers would rip out your throat, but they did not care if you were trouble or not—anyone with blood was prey.

Adrian would have never left me if he had thought they were going to attack. He had likely believed as I had—that monsters did not venture within the bounds of Revekka—and though I knew differently now, I certainly never expected a pack of twelve or more hounds to approach a city during the day. Not even the fires raging at the gates had kept them at bay.

"What is this madness?" Killian whispered.

It was more than madness. It was chaos, and it would soon be complete carnage if we did not help.

"You will stay here," Killian said, drawing his blade.

I glared. "How many times, Killian—"

"I can't lose you," he said, cutting me off. I stared at him, not so much surprised by his words but the sincerity of them—the desperation of them. His eyes were hard, his jaw tight as he spoke. "I won't."

He took a step away.

"Stay," he said again. "Please."

Then he turned and charged through the gates.

I did not watch him go because I had no intention of listening to his plea, but I could not join the fight without my weapons. As I turned, I looked upon those who had assembled here, high on the hill, with no intention of helping those at our feet.

"Prepare the great hall to receive the wounded," I

said. "Those of you who can fight will take up arms and follow me. Someone get me a horse."

I cut through the crowd once more and entered the castle, hurrying upstairs. Bursting into my room, I raced to my nightstand where I kept my knives. Usually, I would sheath them in braces around my wrists, but I hoped to use them more like darts in an effort to keep as much distance between myself and the rabid hellhounds as possible.

I found my sword in the chest at the end of my bed and belted it around my waist. Once I was finished, I removed my mother's crown and my cloak, which would only get in the way.

Taking one of my knives, I quickly cut away at my long skirt until it fell just above my boots, then sheathed my knives—one at my waist and one between my breasts.

I rushed downstairs and found Tanaka waiting, barring the way, his expression severe.

"You cannot go into battle, my queen," said Tanaka.

I tilted my head, eyes narrowed and full of anger. When would my wishes stop being met with Adrian's will?

"I did not become queen to watch my people die from the safety of a tower."

"King Adrian—"

"Is not here, so I will lead my people in battle. You may stay here in the comfort of my castle."

I moved past the old man.

"You defy his orders," Tanaka said, continuing to speak even as I retreated. "And yet it is not you who will pay the price."

I ignored him.

I did not care that Adrian had left orders.

The consequences of disobeying his wishes would never weigh on my conscience as heavily as the deaths of our people.

As I left the castle, I found Violeta standing with a large steed. The horse, Reverie, was white and black-spotted, and her mane almost looked silvery, even beneath this strange, red-tinged light. As I mounted her, I met Violeta's gaze.

"Find Ana. If she is not already aware, she must be prepared to help the wounded. Do whatever she says."

With that, I left, spurring Reverie down the steep hill on which the Red Palace stood and into the city below. I did not look to see who followed, worried I was already too late. Even from here, I could see blood staining the thin layer of snow that had gathered on the ground and pooled beside lifeless bodies. All the while, the hounds continued their vicious attack against mortals and vampires.

As I spurred my horse on, something flew past me, narrowly missing my head. I ducked, thinking it had been an arrow, but watched instead as Gavriel shifted midflight from the form of a crow, knocking into one of the aufhockers and piercing it with his blade. The creature gave a cry but was soon silenced by a blow to the neck that severed its head.

More hounds descended on Gavriel while a few turned toward me, as if drawn by the sound of hooves.

I drew my blade, preparing to clash with the creatures, but as we came nearer, my horse reared up, snorting and throwing back her head. She turned sharply, and I tumbled to the ground as she sped off. A few hounds raced after her while two others faced me. I rose to my feet and gripped my blade. I felt so small opposite them, their demonic eyes glowing red, their sharpened teeth dripping with blood that pooled at their feet.

The hounds didn't stop to assess if I was a threat; they just charged. I knew I could not take on both at once, so I focused on the one to the right, moving so I was in its direct line of attack. As it neared, I swung my blade down on its muzzle, creating a deep cut, but it did little to stop the hound as it bit down on the sword and wrested it from my grasp, jerking me forward.

Frantic, I reached for the dagger at my side just as the creature moved to attack me again. I shoved my blade into its head, right between its eyes.

The hound roared and bit down on my arm. I screamed, but only a shock of pain registered before I drew my second knife from between my breasts and drove into his head once more. This time, the hound groaned, and before it could collapse to the ground, I was thrown back as the second creature rammed into me.

The impact stole my breath, and as I fought to fill my lungs with air, I struggled to my feet and ran. I only made it a few steps before a set of claws bit into my back. I screamed and fell, rolling on to my back in time to watch the aufhocker pounce, claws and fangs bared, when a spear cut through the air and lodged in its eye.

The hound continued its flight through the air and landed near me, dead.

"Are you all right, my queen?"

For a moment, my vision blurred, but I knew Gavriel stood over me.

"Yes," I said, and I took the hand he offered.

"You should not have come," he said once I was on my feet.

"I had to," I said. It was the only response I could offer. Gavriel would not understand why I had to come. I had not wished to be queen so I could sit on a throne. I wished to become queen to protect my people, which meant if they went into battle, I would lead.

"You are mortal," he said, his voice gentle. "You were not made to fight these monsters."

I did not speak because I had nothing to say. Sluggishly, I moved to retrieve my blades—each one completely covered in slick blood.

With my daggers sheathed and my sword in hand, I looked to Cel Ceredi and stumbled toward the village. Gavriel followed as the carnage unfolded before us.

Many people lay dead, bodies torn open by teeth and claws. Those who had yet to die and were injured lay screaming and writhing on the ground—some with deep gashes, some with missing limbs. The bodies of several aufhockers lay still upon the ground, and while they appeared motionless, I found myself gripping my blade.

A terrible howl erupted from behind me, and I turned in time to see Isac and two other vampires taking down what seemed to be the final aufhocker. It was shaking its head vigorously, trying desperately—and hopelessly—to dislodge the blade impaling his skull.

With a groan, the creature finally crashed to the ground.

The battle was over.

It was over and I had only managed to kill one monster. The second had almost killed me.

Gavriel was right in a way—I was not made for this world—but neither was he. He had been *created.* As the pain from my wounds coiled through my body, I thought that perhaps I should be too.

FOUR
Adrian

I heard the voices even before we entered the Starless Forest.

They were the cries of witches who had been murdered here. They were not always so loud, most whispered in the language of magic, not spells but prayers for peace. Today, they wailed—a keen and haunting refrain.

Something was wrong, something beyond the traitors who roamed my country.

I was not unfamiliar with the feeling, the constant gnawing in my gut. It was a restlessness I felt deep, an ache that had not gone away even with Isolde's return.

I had never thrived on peace. I was a creature forged by violence, honed by hate.

I wanted blood.

I had always thought that finding my lover—the one who had spurred my desire to conquer the world—would ease this rage. It had proven to be a fire that not even she could quell.

She had only made it worse.

It did not matter that she had returned to me, soft and full and smelling of jasmine. The nightmare of her death clung to me, my constant companion, my greatest fear. It did not matter how many years passed or how much time separated me from the night she died; it would always feel like yesterday. My mouth always tasted of her ashes. The scent of her burning flesh and singed hair undercut every smell I inhaled.

Leaving her behind today only fueled the anger in my blood.

I had no trust that anyone would guard her as I did, but I knew just as well that Isolde would dislike having her freedom impeded. I could not bar her from leaving her room, the castle, or Cel Ceredi without consequences. I had to grant her space and hope her trust extended to no one save me.

We had no one.

Nothing had been more obvious after Ravena's attack when two of my noblesse and another yet unknown individual among my inner circle betrayed me—betrayed *us*.

My fingers tightened on Shadow's reins as I waited, impatient for Sorin and Dracul's return. They had flown ahead to scout once more. I was certain the traitor noblesse were intent on reaching another kingdom, but escaping the boundaries of Revekka was not so easy with our armies scouting and marching across the land.

"The queen is safe with Tanaka," Daroc said, guessing my thoughts as he rode beside me.

"My queen would take up a blade before Tanaka could draw enough breath to tell her to hide."

Tanaka was not a warrior. He never had been. He was a statesman; his eternal love was politics. If anything, Isolde would ensure *his* safety.

"Miha and Isac are there," said Daroc. "Gavriel too."

I clenched my jaw, uncomfortable at the thought of anything happening in my absence, but Isolde had survived despite the odds, fighting vampires, the crimson mist, a witch, even her father.

She was resilient. She was my queen.

I would not fail to protect her again.

"Isolde is not safe until Gesalac and Julian are dead," I said.

"Even with their deaths, she is not safe. She will always be in danger as long as she is mortal." Daroc paused.

I knew what he would say next. I could feel it in the air between us where hostility built.

"As are—"

"I am well aware, General," I cut him off. I was never eager to be reminded of my weakness, but I was even less eager to hear Isolde continuously targeted as one.

Daroc had never been fond of my fixation with Yesenia's return.

In some ways, he was no different than Gesalac and Julian, who seemed to think she was a distraction.

"If you did not deem emotions outside disfavor and anger as weaknesses, perhaps you'd have an easier time with Sorin."

Daroc worked his jaw, and his frustration only fueled my need to fight. Since I'd found Isolde atop my palace, injured and exhausted, the desire had vibrated my very bones. I wanted to level kingdoms and end bloodlines. I could feel it in my blood, rushing through my veins, a demand, a vicious need to expend my rage.

It was a demon that had clung to me, even two hundred years later. It had even been there at my birth, and it had been coddled by neglect and abuse.

"I *meant*," Daroc managed, clinging to his control, "that you should consider turning her as soon as possible."

"As if I have not considered it," I snapped.

As if I had not fantasized about it every time I took her blood. It would take only a deeper bite and a taste of my blood. She could feed from me once the ritual was complete. A dizzying wave of lust fired from the bottom of my stomach to my head.

My cock grew uncomfortably hard.

I wanted her bite. I wanted to feel her teeth sink into my skin. It would be just as intoxicating as being inside her.

I felt the groan gathering in the back of my throat.

"Fuck," I grumbled.

This was not the time for fantasies.

"Whatever is holding you back is irrelevant," Daroc said. "You should have turned her the moment you took her blood. You knew the consequences."

While he condescended, I knew my worth to Dis.

I was her power on earth.

I was how she conquered.

If Isolde died, I died, and Dis lost everything.

"Remember your place, General."

"Shall I remind you of yours? You are a king. A conqueror. Not a star-crossed lover."

I drew my blade, and the point came within a hair of Daroc's neck. He didn't flinch, did not move to take up his own weapon. He only glared back at me.

There was a long stretch of silence.

"My decisions regarding my queen are of no concern to you."

I expected him to reply, to inform me that my link to Isolde made her everyone's concern, but he maintained a stern expression. Before he could speak, two shadows passed overhead—a falcon and a black bat.

Sorin and Dracul had returned.

Of my noblesse, only those two could shape-shift, and they commanded among the ranks of my army several others who had the same ability.

"Is everything all right?" Sorin asked.

Neither of us moved, and our eyes did not leave the other's. I waited for Daroc to surrender to my command, knowing that he too raged inside. We were not so different, he and I, but where he would exercise control, I unleashed violence.

It was the reason I conquered and he followed.

Finally, he nodded, narrowly missing my blade.

I left the end pointed at his throat a second longer before sheathing the weapon and turning my attention to Sorin and Dracul.

"You have news?" I asked.

Sorin's eyes were locked with Daroc's but soon shifted to mine, and while there was tension there, I could not tell what the tracker was thinking.

"We have tracked Julian east, beyond the borders of Revekka," Dracul said when Sorin did not speak.

I ground my teeth at the knowledge, despite

expecting this. Vela lay east, and King Gheroghe had recently petitioned me, hoping to become immortal in exchange for his surrender. In doing so, the human king had offered the perfect refuge to the traitor noblesse. He was also stupid enough to accept if Julian suggested turning him—stupid not only because I would kill him when I found him, but also because he trusted Julian, a vampire who wanted power and would use Gheroghe's kingdom to rise against me.

Likely, Gheroghe would not survive the bloodletting.

"We could not track Gesalac beyond your realm."

Which meant he had likely taken refuge in a village, but where? More importantly, who was protecting him? One misguided Revekkian? Or a whole town?

"Dracul, take your men. Hunt for Julian. You are to kill anyone he turns."

The noblesse bowed in acceptance of his charge.

"And Julian? How do you wish for this traitor to be returned to you?"

I considered his question, though I knew the answer. I wanted him alive. I wanted him to die by my hand, but that did not mean he should not suffer until his fate.

"Flayed," I replied.

None in my company balked at the request, but I wondered what Isolde would have said had she heard my command. She knew my reputation and was not averse to violence, unflinching as she watched the impalement of our prisoners. But was there a limit to her ruthlessness?

"As you command, my king," Dracul said, and in a blur of black wings, he was gone. A few others from our company followed, transforming into similar animals—bats, crows, even owls, whose presence had taken on a different meaning since Isolde's attack in the woods during the Great Hunt.

Owls are an omen of death, she'd said, and death had followed those words.

Still, I let them go despite the dread.

I turned my attention to Sorin. "You saw no trace of Gesalac?"

"None, my king," he replied.

"Then we will search the whole of Revekka until he is found," I said and paused, gaze sliding over each expressionless face of my remaining noblesse. "And when we find him, none who have harbored him will be spared."

My noblesse dispersed to call their men to arms and search their respective territories. Razan and Iosif went north, Vlad and Iker to the west, Sorin and Daroc to the south, and I would take the east. Mostly forest and mountains, there were few villages, and those who inhabited the eastern cradle were hardened. It was a haunted land, born from the blood and turmoil of its ancestors.

I knew this because I was one of them.

Now alone, I closed my eyes and focused on the way the earth moved and breathed.

If you are quiet, she will speak, Yesenia had said.

The earth had a heartbeat, a steady thrum, disturbed only by the thundering of hooves, the burning of fires, and...the screams of a dying woman.

Strange, I thought. Monsters did not usually attack in the daylight, even beneath the red sky.

I opened my eyes.

"Shadow," I commanded, spurring him on toward the violent attack. By the time I arrived, the woman would likely be dead, but it was better to lose one mortal than a village.

Shadow's feet hit the earth hard, jarring my body as I sat forward in my seat, the fingers of my left hand tangled in his mane. The wind was deafening as he raced around trees, heedless as lower branches whipped my face, stinging like small blades. The cuts healed quickly, even before the blood could dry on my face, but I did not ease our pace until we were within view of the monster and its victim.

Through a line of naked trees, I could see the creature—large, black, with fur standing on end down its back. It growled as it looked up from its prey, a woman with a swath of dark hair spread out over the leafy ground and skin so pale, the blood that stained it shone like the sun behind the red sky.

The creature was an aufhocker. Once a dog, it had likely been bitten or killed by another of its kind. Normally, they hunted at night, but this one bared bloody, razor teeth, its eyes aglow as it watched me approach.

Shadow snorted, shifting on his feet. He was not fond of dogs, least of all ones willing to rip out his throat.

"It's all right," I said, smoothing a hand over his mane before dismounting. As my feet thudded against the ground, the aufhocker growled and crouched, prepared for attack.

It knew, despite presenting as mortal, I was no such thing. In the aftermath of my creation, the goddess Asha sought to make something as powerful. The results were monsters with a thirst for blood that, while never obtaining my strength, were still deadly to humans.

I drew my blade.

The aufhocker's growl deepened, and it launched itself at me with two powerful leaps that dug fissures into the ground. It came at me with its mouth open, and I lifted my sword, hilt poised in my hand like a spear, before hurling it at the monster, which roared as the blade lodged in the back of its throat. As it landed, it shook its head in an attempt to dislodge the weapon, slinging blood and drool.

I watched for a moment before approaching as it pawed at the hilt. The creature growled, though it was more of a gurgle. I gripped the slick blade and pulled it free, only to jam it farther into its throat before taking hold of its snout and snapping its jaw. The creature gave a final, mournful moan before going limp at my feet.

Its blood pooled on the ground, dark and glossy. I had done this so often, I felt nothing—no remorse, no thrill. This was the way of the world, and I had been the catalyst.

My only concern was that the creature had gone against its nature and roamed in the daylight. Was this the disturbance that had the witches wailing?

In the silence that followed, my gaze shifted to the woman who still lay motionless except for the hurried rise and fall of her rattling chest. I bent and took up my sword once more, blade dripping with crimson.

As I came toward the woman, I saw her eyes were open and her throat shredded. During the attack, she had fallen on her cloak and was framed in a sea of royal blue. It made her look even paler, her blood an angry contrast.

She was far younger than I expected, and I wondered what had brought her to the woods until my eyes fell on an overturned basket some distance away, a handful of mushrooms and herbs scattered on the ground. I recalled how Yesenia would wander the grounds outside the Red Palace two hundred years ago for the very same supplies.

A sudden wave of unease straightened my spine, and my wish to return to Isolde renewed.

I knelt and the girl met my gaze. She seemed to breathe harder as I hovered, and whether out of fear or her approaching death, I did not know.

"This is a mercy," I said and leaned nearer as I whispered, "Close your eyes."

It took her a moment, but she obeyed, and I rose, lifting my blade overhead, only to bring it down on her ruined neck. The head separated from the body cleanly, and despite the decapitation, I knew it was not enough to keep resurrection at bay after an aufhocker bite.

She would have to be burned.

I used the woman's cloak to clean my blade and, once sheathed, leaned down to pick up her head by her dark, silken hair when I caught movement in the tree line.

A young boy stared back at me, wide-eyed and shaken. I wondered if he was this woman's son, maybe her brother. I did not ask, couldn't, even if I had wanted to, because as soon as I noticed him, he turned and fled in the direction of the village of Volkair.

I followed, head in hand, knowing they would have fire to burn it.

The trek through the surrounding woods was short, though the voices of the dead grew incessant. I did not understand their language, but their words prodded my mind and warped my reality, and in an instant, I was no longer trudging over the rugged floor of the Starless

Forest but sinking into a soft bed, my hands and knees framing Yesenia's body. She stared back at me, eyes hooded, hair spilling over her pillow. I had little hope that we would be together beyond this day, and even as I moved inside her, I could not fully commit to this moment, too desperate and anxious to give her every part of me as she deserved.

Had Isolde recalled our time together in the hours before Yesenia's death? I would never ask for fear of causing her pain, and in the end, it did not really matter. She did not need these memories to fuel her vengeance.

I stepped out of the tree line, shaking off the memories clinging to me, once more fully present in the reality of my bloodied world.

Goddamn witches. Even from their high graves, they still cast spells.

My teeth were set, my fist wrapped tight in the girl's hair, her head hanging at my side as I entered Volkair. A main road snaked through a ragged village, flanked by worn homes and shops, their thatched roofs dusted with snow. A few farm animals ran loose, prey for the monsters that lurked in the nearby forest.

I headed toward a fire blazing in the center of the road. My boots became heavy, caked with mud, and as I threw the girl's head into the fire, I looked to find the townspeople had come out of their homes, gathering beneath what little outdoor shelter they had.

The boy had likely alerted them to my presence—and the death of the nameless girl. I could not be certain what he had said or if they believed him, since it was unusual for monsters to venture out in the daylight.

All monsters except for me.

I turned fully toward them.

None of them bowed; none of them so much as nodded. They stood, solemn and staring.

"Have you forgotten your king?" I called, a warning and a chance to show respect, but the only movement came from one man who stepped apart from those who cowered.

To my disappointment, it was not Gesalac. This man was mortal.

He was thin, and age had bent his tall frame so that he stood almost like a crumbling oak—hunched at the shoulders, skin perpetually weathered by the red sun.

The land and this village had nursed this man as it had me, and he faced me, unafraid.

"Or have you found a new one?" I muttered, narrowing my eyes.

"Our king left us to die on the edge of his kingdom," the man said, his voice just as scarred as his body. "If that is the title you claim, then you may have it, along with the souls of our dead."

I tilted my head to the side. "The dead have always burdened me. What are a few more?"

The mortal stared and then spoke quietly to the others. "The Blood King mocks our grief."

I straightened my neck, the corner of my mouth lifting.

I knew this game. This brave, stupid mortal wanted to be a martyr. I wondered what spurred his sacrifice. Who had offered something more to believe in than the safety of my rule?

"If you wanted your death to mean something, you should have chosen to fight the monsters in your woods."

"They only exist because of you," he said. "Perhaps if you die, they would too."

I chuckled at his ignorant response. It was a common belief among the people of Cordova, and many had attempted to assassinate me, believing that if I died, other monsters would follow, but I was a creation of Dis, and the monsters were creations of Asha. We were not the same, though we were all eager for the blood of mortals.

"I cannot die," I said.

This time, the man smirked. "We do not need to take *your* life to end you."

This response tightened every muscle in my body. Until this moment, I admired this man's courage, but his words were dangerous and a direct threat to my queen. Despite this, I did not think he knew about my weakness; rather, he threatened Isolde because he knew I loved her.

"Is that a thread of humanity I see in your eyes?" the man asked, offering a raspy chuckle.

I moved at an imperceptible speed, appearing behind the martyr, striking his ankles. He cried out and collapsed to the muddy ground as I placed my palm against his forehead and jerked his head back.

"I am certain you wished to die quickly," I said near his ear. "But threats against my queen deserve an agonizing end."

Once more, he laughed. "I do not care how I die. I shall join my goddess in the sky."

"Your goddess?" I seethed, truly mocking him. Asha did not protect her mortals in life, so why would she protect them in death? "Have you forgotten that all the dead belong to Dis?"

"Not anymore," he said. "The light is coming, and

she will cast out your darkness. It happened once before and it will happen again. Only we will not leave ash and bone behind."

I was used to my rage, but his words took me a step beyond, past a point where I could extend death. As I moved to drag my blade across his neck, the creak of a bow drew my attention, but before I could rise to my feet, the arrow had lodged in the old man's head.

I pulled it free with a jerk, twisting it in my hand. I reared back and sent it flying in the direction it came, satisfied with the groan that sounded from the shadows as I hit my target.

In the next second, a hooded man fell face-first in the mud, dead, and I wondered how many more would die by my hand today.

Finally, Gesalac appeared.

He had exited one of the run-down buildings, dressed in gold armor. His finery was misplaced here among the worn and ruined village, though it seemed he had managed to gain their trust. I wondered how many years it had taken. Had he worked the land beside them? Had he helped repair roofs and gathered wheat to knead bread?

Those were the actions that would gain their devotion.

I stepped around the mortal at my feet.

"Once again, you choose your queen over your people," said Gesalac.

"Is my love for Isolde your only critique of my reign? If so, I will have to assume you are jealous," I said. "Are you in love with me, Gesalac?"

The vampire's eyes narrowed.

"You murdered my son."

"He is not the first son I have murdered, nor, I imagine, the last, but let us not pretend that your vengeance is fueled by fatherly devotion. You want my throne, my empire."

He chuckled. "What empire? What kingdoms have you conquered since you began fucking that woman?"

I managed a smile despite how hard I clenched my teeth.

"My queen and I will conquer this world, and when we have our empire, we will fuck on a bed of your bones."

Gesalac smirked and began to circle. "You may need a queen to rule your kingdom, but Isolde needs no king. You will make her into a monster."

"You say that as if it is a bad thing."

Gesalac's blade came down hard on my own, but I was far quicker and struck him in the chest with my hand. The push sent him a few feet down the road. He landed on his back, his golden armor covered in mud.

I followed as he got to his feet, dark eyes gleaming. Once more, he circled.

"Do you recall this place?" Gesalac asked.

I did not answer, though I knew it well. It had been my home. This was the earth I had worked, the fields I had plowed, the roofs I had once repaired. It was the village that raised me, where the anger that fueled me had taken root.

I had always been a monster.

Yesenia's death merely uncaged me.

He continued but stopped circling, and as he spoke, his gaze never left mine. "You are merely a farm boy whose father was a broken soldier and whose mother whored herself for alcohol."

I imagined Gesalac was aware of the wound he probed—it was open and gaping, never cared for, never healed. I'd used it to go to dark places where I did violent things, but if he thought it made me weak, he was wrong.

My past gave me the strength to do what no one else had done—endure.

I managed a laugh.

"Merely a farm boy," I said, eyes falling to the cold ground where snow had yet to gather, and in the quiet, my body burned. I only moved to attack when I could no longer stand the throbbing in my head and hands. As my blade met Gesalac's midswing, the sound was like lightning crackling across the sky, a vibration that went to my bones.

It felt like life, like breathing once again.

"I was your beginning," I said. "And I will be your end!"

Our blades clashed, the force behind each strike growing harder and faster until our swords locked, neither of us relenting in our determination to see the other fall. Finally, I moved, punching Gesalac in the side over and over until his armor bowed, cutting into his skin. He stumbled back and I followed, blade lifted over my head. But as I drew my weapon down upon him, he grabbed both of my wrists, his head knocking into mine.

The blow was dizzying, and this time I stumbled back.

Before me, Gesalac laughed.

"And to think you are supposed to be the most powerful among us."

I laughed too.

"My greatest strength is that you do not even know what I am capable of."

His smile faltered, and I shifted, invisible, reappearing behind the vampire. I shoved my blade into his back. It exploded through the middle of his chest and he screamed as I twisted it. Then I kicked him, and he flew across the small village, landing against a wooden fence that buckled beneath his weight. I followed, launching myself at him.

As I landed on the traitor, he twisted, using one of the fence poles as a weapon. Its sharpened end slammed into me, piercing my armor, sinking deep into my chest. My scream was more of a roar as my body seized, shaking from the shock of my injury. Gesalac threw me back and I struck the ground hard. But I was already working the wood free, and once the stake was out, I threw it aside, hands covered in my own blood.

I curled them into fists, my eyes locked with Gesalac's. He had managed to get to his feet, hands clasped around the end of my blade, which protruded from his chest as he attempted, in vain, to pull it from his body.

"I'm finished here," I said. "It is time for you to kneel."

At my command, the traitor's knees struck so hard, the ground shook. His eyes widened as I approached.

"H-how did you—"

"When I stand before them, I can control the mind of any vampire I've turned," I said, gripping the hilt of my blade. "Pity you did not know."

He cried out as I pulled my sword free and then shoved it into him again—and again and again, even as he lay facedown in the mud. Though I knew the wounds would heal soon after they were free of my blade, all that mattered was that he felt pain.

"My king," said a voice, and I recognized it as Daroc.

I ignored him a second longer so that I could shove my blade once more into Gesalac's back. Once it sunk to the hilt, I stepped back, coming face-to-face with my general.

"Restrain and mask him," I said, breathless. "Tonight we will celebrate a traitor's demise."

I turned away and found the inhabitants of Volkair staring back. Their expressions were mixed. Some were angry, and some were afraid. Their thoughts screamed at me—*monster, murderer, mongrel.*

"And the village?" Daroc asked.

"What?" I looked at him, now aware that all my noblesse had returned, mounted on their horses, even Sorin, who held Shadow's reins in hand.

"The village, my king," Daroc said again.

I looked at the villagers and knew their loyalty had shifted. It was in their movements and their expressions, their thoughts and their actions. They had harbored a man who attempted to kill my queen, and they had allowed a mortal who also threatened her to speak for them.

More importantly, they were witnesses to my abilities.

I met Daroc's gaze again.

"Burn it," I said.

Thick smoke billowed above the trees, smelling of pine and flesh. We waited just outside the borders of Volkair for Sorin's return as he scouted the woods for survivors.

I stood apart from my noblesse, staring into the forest, listening. The dead still spoke, quieter now than before, and as I listened, it wasn't Gesalac's voice that rang in my ears but the farmer's.

The light is coming, and she will cast out your darkness.

The words did not bother me as much as the way he spoke them—with the conviction of a follower who had been shown a glimpse of the future. What had he seen or heard that had given him such hope? And how would I destroy it?

"Are you all right?" Daroc asked, coming to stand beside me. I did not look at him as I answered.

"No."

I had yet to feel calm since the betrayal of my noblesse, and I would likely rage until I returned to the Red Palace. I wanted to see Gesalac suffer at the end of a metal spear. I wanted Isolde to watch him die beside me, and after, I wanted to take her to bed.

I wondered if she had rested today. Would I be able to drink her blood?

My hunger for her made my stomach hollow.

"Gesalac knew of my childhood," I said, and when I looked at Daroc, he stared back, surprised, and then his brows lowered.

"Who told him?"

"Only three of you know," I said and turned my head to meet his gaze. "You, Tanaka...and Ana Maria."

Overhead, the dark outline of a falcon flew into view, and we turned as Sorin shifted, landing in the clearing before us.

"My king, you have to see this."

Daroc stiffened beside me, and I knew it was because of his lover's expression. His eyes were wide, his breathing heavy, as if he had fled wherever he'd been.

Daroc took a step toward him but halted.

"What is it?" I asked.

"I…don't have words," Sorin said.

I frowned and thought only of the crimson mist, though that would hardly shock him. I exchanged a look with Daroc.

"Stay," I said.

"My king—"

"Watch Gesalac," I said, each word slipping between my teeth. It was as much a show of trust as it was a command. I trusted Daroc with my fugitive.

It took Daroc a moment, but he soon relaxed, nodding once.

As I mounted Shadow, Sorin shifted and flew north. I followed, watching as the falcon cut across the sky. It did not take me long to recognize this path—memories were attached to it, and they smelled like burning flesh and tasted of ash. Suddenly, I had no strength. A cold weakness consumed my entire body.

I knew where Sorin was leading me.

When he dove out of sight, I slowed and entered a clearing, bringing Shadow to a stop. I slid off my horse and took a few steps toward an ancient tree. It had a wide trunk and many branches and twisted roots that jutted in and out of the ground like serpents.

At the base of the tree was a large stone wrapped in dead vines, and at the base of that stone was an empty hole.

This was the gravesite of High Coven, and it was empty.

We will not leave ash and bone behind, the old man had said, and I wondered what had the people of Volkair done.

FIVE
Isolde

In the aftermath of the battle, I walked through the streets of Cel Ceredi as survivors emerged from their homes and a new kind of horror took place as they ran to their dead, wailing over still and bleeding corpses. The deceased were only part of the destruction—pyres had collapsed, and embers were scattered across the snow. The aufhockers had torn into homes with their lethal claws. They had not only killed people, but animals, and their remains were among the dead.

"You are injured," Killian said.

I turned to look at him, his expression severe. He had a cut on his cheek and a gash on his shoulder but was otherwise okay.

"We should help the wounded," I said.

"*You* are wounded," he said.

"I will be okay," I said because I had Adrian, but even

as I spoke, my wrist began to throb. It was swelling and the bite marks were growing red and angry.

I hoped he would arrive soon.

Miha and Isac approached, Gavriel following. They said nothing about my presence, nor did they comment on my injuries, though I knew they were concerned. I could tell by the glances they exchanged, but I could not help wondering if their worry was more for Adrian's reaction than my health.

"My queen," they said, bowing.

"Has this ever happened before?" I asked.

Miha shook her head. "Aufhockers never come out during the day."

"Even beneath this sky?" Killian asked.

"They are nocturnal," said Isac. "They wake at sundown."

We were all quiet as I scanned the town once more, pausing to stare at each large mound of black fur. A part of me did not trust that any of them were dead.

"We have to burn them," I said.

Everyone, even the animals. Like many of Asha's monsters, an aufhocker bite just created more of their kind. I ground my teeth hard, ignoring the dizzying pain in my own arm.

"You must return to the castle," said Killian. "We can care for the wounded and the dead."

"Killian is right," Gavriel said, and he turned to look west, where the sun sat in the sky, bright and red. "Our king should arrive soon."

I did not argue because there was nothing I could do. My back burned from the monster's claws so I could not bend, and even if I tried, I could not pull or lift with my arm and its angry bite. Also, I did not think I could walk the distance.

"I will find a horse," Gavriel said, and with a bow, he left to search. Miha and Isac began to gather bodies, choosing to begin with the aufhockers first.

"Are you sure you are all right?" Killian asked. His gray eyes were stormy, and I thought about how he had begged me not to come.

"I will be," I said.

He studied me, silent, and then said, "I know you wish to lead by example. I know you wish to protect your people, but battle isn't the only way to fight for them."

I did not respond, did not really wish to speak at all, and it seemed that he did not wish to hear an answer, because he left, crossing to kneel beside a woman who sobbed over the body of a man.

Gavriel returned, leading Reverie, and my heart rose seeing that she was okay until I came around to mount her and saw four deep, bleeding gashes on her hip. I met Gavriel's gaze.

"Will she be okay?"

"So long as her wound does not become infected." Then his eyes fell to my arm. He frowned deeply but did not comment on it. "Can you mount on your own?"

I did, though the movements jarred my back and arm. Once I was firmly seated, Gavriel kept hold of the reins, leading Reverie up the steep hill to the Red Palace.

We did not speak, not until we were in the crowded courtyard. Tanaka was among those gathered. He looked older, angrier, his mouth set in a hard line as he glared at me. I threw my foot over and slid off my horse, surprised when a set of hands grasped my waist before my foot could touch the ground.

I spun, facing Gavriel, who dropped his hands to his sides.

"My apologies, Your Majesty," he said. "I only wished to help."

"If I wanted your help, I would have asked."

He held my gaze and then nodded. "My queen."

I left the courtyard, passing Tanaka without a glance, and headed to my chambers. On the way, I passed Violeta, whose eyes widened with shock at my appearance.

"I need a bath brought to my room," I said.

"Right away, my queen," she said and fled in the direction of the kitchens.

Once in my room, I began to peel off my ruined dress. Parts of it stuck to me, dried in the blood that covered my skin. I pulled on a robe, and while the fabric was soft, it felt uncomfortable against my wounds.

It did not take long for Violeta to arrive. A set of servants positioned the bath near the window as usual, and then they took turns filling it with steaming water. When they were finished, Violeta lingered, and though she was quiet, I could feel her eyes on me.

"Do you need anything, my queen?" she asked.

"I'd like to be alone," I said.

"Of course," she said, and as she made her way to the door, I spoke.

"Thank you, Violeta."

When the door closed, I shed the robe and lowered myself into the hot bath, gritting my teeth as the water burned my wounds. I focused primarily on the bite on my arm, scrubbing the marks with soap despite the pain. The redness had now spread from the marks, consuming my entire forearm. It was swollen and tender, the slightest pressure sending a wave of nausea roiling inside my stomach, which only served to make my anxiety worse.

There were always consequences when monsters bit or scratched—infection often set in quickly, and the longer it was allowed to stay in the blood, the more dangerous it became. Sometimes it created monsters, sometimes it killed, and while I knew Adrian could heal, was there a point when it would be too late?

There was a knock at my door, and before I could speak, Ana entered. Though pale, her cheeks were flushed, and she looked frustrated. As Adrian's cousin, she shared his features—pale hair and skin and the same eye shape—though their coloring, while striking, was different. Ana's eyes blazed green and looked hard at me as I sat in the rapidly cooling water.

"Gavriel tells me you are injured," she said.

"Yes," I said. It was not as if I were trying to hide it.

Ana crossed the room, her eyes falling to my arm.

"You were bitten," she said and fell to her knees beside me, demanding, "Why did you not say anything?"

I stiffened, preparing for her to touch my arm, but she didn't. She only stared.

"We both know there is nothing you can do," I said, and Ana met my gaze. Perhaps that was why she was angry, because she had no control here.

She pressed her hand to my forehead.

"You are feverish," she said and then rose to her feet. As she did, she gave a sharp inhale, and I knew she had caught sight of my back. "You must let me treat you," she said. "Let me do something until Adrian arrives."

"Do whatever you wish," I said. "But I will greet Adrian at the gates."

"He will be furious," she said.

"He always is," I said, and she shook her head.

"You have never seen his fury," she said.

I rose from the bath and dried off, lying naked on the bed, back exposed, my arm extended to the side. I tried to prepare for the pain of her treatment but could not stop from curling into myself when she began her work, starting with the medicine she poured on my arm and back. The odor was sharp and foul, and I groaned, burying my face in the covers. After, she smoothed something thick over each wound and wrapped them.

When she was finished, she pressed her hand to my forehead again. I avoided her gaze, not wishing to see her concern. As she cleaned her hands on her dress, she spoke.

"I do not know that anything I have done will slow the infection," she said. "We will have to hope Adrian can." Ana left with instructions to wear something loose. "And take off the binding as soon as you are able."

Outside my robe, I only had one loose gown and it was white. The neckline hung off my shoulders, embellished with crystals. The sleeves were like wings, covering my arms and the bite, which had gone numb since Ana's treatment. Once I was dressed, I headed downstairs to the great hall where the wounded had been taken. Ana had begun her work and moved from patient to patient.

They lay beside one another, row upon row, all in various states of unease. Some moaned in pain, others were unconscious, and all the wounds were horrific. I paused before one, a young boy who writhed on the floor, his face swollen and red with the bite of an aufhocker. The woman beside him was still, though breathing, her shoulder mangled, but I could not tell if it was from teeth or claws. A man sat propped against the wall with his bloodied leg stretched out, a thick flap of skin and muscle splayed open on the floor.

Finally, I made my way over to Ana, who knelt beside a child, prodding a bite that looked a lot like mine. After a moment, she sighed and rose to her feet, rubbing her forehead with the back of her hand.

"Most will not survive this," she said.

I knew what she meant. Those with bites would have to be executed. I looked back at the bodies—so many bodies—lining the floor of the hall.

"How will you do it?" I asked, quiet.

"Poison," she said and looked at me. "I will give them poison."

"Is that truly merciful?" I asked.

"It is better than burning them alive," she said.

Just then, a horn blasted from outside.

"Adrian," I breathed and ran from the palace, halting when I saw my husband burst into the courtyard mounted on Shadow. I knew by the violence in his eyes that he had seen the carnage in Cel Ceredi, and I felt his relief shudder through my own body when he finally met my gaze. He dismounted his horse and strode toward me with determined steps, closing the distance between us.

He did not speak as he curled an arm around my waist, pulling me flush against his body. I swallowed the pain ricocheting through my body as he kissed me, his tongue sliding across my mouth, but when he found my teeth clenched, he pulled away, studying me. Then he pressed a hand against my skin, eyes ablaze.

"You're on fire."

His grip on me tightened and my body went rigid, my fists clenching against his chest. He seemed to realize that his hold was the source of my discomfort and released me.

"What happened?" he demanded, but this was not the place to reveal my injuries, especially the bite—not with the crowd who had gathered around to witness Adrian's return.

"Later, Adrian," I said and leaned forward, pressing my lips to his—a soft kiss, a promise. As I pulled away, I asked, "Who have you brought me?"

Adrian studied me and then brushed his thumb over my cheek.

"I have brought you a pig to slaughter," he said and stepped away, turning as Daroc and Sorin led a prisoner forward. His hands were bound behind his back, and yet I knew if he wanted, he could break those bonds, though the move would be futile given that his head was enclosed in an iron cage. It was eyeless and the weight of it kept his chin to his chest.

Despite this, I did not need to see his face to know that this was Gesalac—he was tall, and his shoulders were broad and stacked with muscle, unlike his thin counterpart, Julian, who was nowhere in sight.

Daroc and Sorin pushed Gesalac to the ground and removed the iron hood, revealing the traitor noblesse's cruel face. His hair was soaked with sweat, pieces of it falling into his bloodred eyes, and as he looked at me from his knees, he shook—not from fear but from hate. I could feel it radiating from his body, see it in his soulless eyes. It felt like a physical blow.

It was the kind of hate that fueled vengeance and conquered kingdoms.

I knew it because I felt it too.

And Gesalac's was about to be smothered.

"You are still a witch." He scowled at me, and Adrian kicked him in the ribs. He arched, throwing his head back as a pained whine escaped his mouth.

"Do not speak to her," Adrian said. "You are not worthy."

I took pleasure in Gesalac's few ragged breaths before he continued to speak. "She fucks you and you make her a goddess, such is her power."

Adrian drew his blade.

"You cannot even see, so blinded by her magic."

I found it strange and unnerving that Gesalac was accusing me of witchcraft, especially when I had no magic.

Adrian reared back and swung even as Gesalac continued to speak.

"She will be your death—"

He was silenced with a clean blow to the neck, his head dropping to the ground with a wet thud. His body followed. In the aftermath, there were no cheers like yesterday when the vassals were impaled, only a melancholy quiet.

There had been enough death today.

"Impale his body," Adrian ordered, and he seized Gesalac's head by the hair, tossing it into the blazing fire at the center of the courtyard before approaching me. "Have I pleased you?" he asked.

"Yes," I said. "Where is Julian?"

His eyes grew dark at my question, and I knew he felt shame at not having found the second noblesse.

"Dracul is tracking him."

I had questions, namely, what happened if he managed to seek refuge in Vela with King Gheroghe?

But Adrian already knew what I wanted to know and leaned forward, whispering, "Patience, my sweet."

As he placed a kiss to my forehead, he pressed his hand into my back, a move that made me cry out in pain. He drew back and looked at his hand—it was covered in blood. His eyes met mine, and all he could say was my name.

"Isolde."

"Adrian," I whispered. "Let's go upstairs."

I entered the castle ahead of Adrian, his eyes pinned to my back, and I could feel the blood soaking through the fabric of my dress. When we made it to his room, he reached around me, throwing open the door and ushering me inside. I crossed the room to stand near the bed, putting distance between us.

"You were injured," he said, his voice trembling, but I could not tell if it was from fear or anger—perhaps both.

"Yes," I said, quiet.

"Let me see."

I stared at him, knowing he was not prepared for this, and yet I obeyed, sliding the dress down my body. It puddled at my feet, and I stood naked before him. The wound on my arm throbbed painfully. Ana's medicine had long worn off.

Adrian's eyes narrowed on it quickly, and then I turned so he could see my back.

"I told you to rest," he said, his voice rising.

"And how noble that would have been—sleeping while our people die?"

"Who did you save?" he demanded, bitter. "No one! But I almost lost a wife."

Hot shame washed over me, and I knelt to retrieve my dress, clutching it to my chest.

"Are you angrier that I was hurt or that if I had died, you would have too?"

He took a step toward me, bending over me, a towering god radiating with anger.

"How dare you."

The words slipped between his teeth, but they shuddered through him, a wound unhealed,, and right now, I wanted to stab it.

"Did that hurt?" I asked, tilting my head back to meet his gaze.

"I did not spend two hundred years yearning for you, killing for you, conquering for you, to watch you make stupid decisions. You are *mortal*."

"Then maybe I shouldn't be."

Adrian was still, then he canted his head to the side, a strange spark in his eyes that was no longer angry but hungry.

"Is that what you want?" he asked. "To be like me?"

I had thought I would say yes, but when faced with the question, I truly could not say.

Becoming a vampire would mean no longer being Adrian's weakness, but more than that, it would mean I would no longer be vulnerable, and that was something

I *did* want. And yet with the news from Lara about my people and their hope in Asha's salvation, I knew they would never follow me as queen if I became like Adrian.

Likely, he would say it did not matter, but I did not wish to force my rule on them. I did not wish to rule through fear—not completely, anyway. I wanted loyalty, adoration, and love from my people.

Becoming a vampire would be a betrayal.

Adrian's brows slammed down over his eyes, and I knew he had been listening to my thoughts.

"Do I not give you loyalty, adoration, love?"

I glared. "Am I only allowed to receive such affection from you?"

"I should be enough," he said, gripping my shoulders.

"Don't sound so insecure, my king."

Adrian gripped my chin and kissed me hard before pulling away.

"I should turn you," he said, his hand falling to my neck. "I want to because I know you, and you will do something like this again."

I held my breath, waiting as his lips brushed my skin, his teeth and tongue teasing. It wasn't until he pulled away that I realized how hard I had been holding him. He studied me, my eyes and my lips, and then released me.

"Lie on your stomach," he said, stepping away.

I stood for a moment, dizzy, uncertain if it was from my injuries or the anticipation of his bite that never came.

Adrian began to remove his armor, and I shifted to the bed, lowering myself onto my stomach, much as I had done earlier with Ana.

I watched as Adrian undressed, and as he went to

remove his breastplate, my eyes settled on the large puncture at the center of it.

"You were hurt," I said.

Adrian's eyes found mine.

"Were you worried for me?"

His question made me angry.

"Of course. You are not the only one who fears losing someone."

Adrian said nothing, and I watched as he set his teeth, jerking the remaining armor from his body. As it fell to the floor, I saw that the skin on his chest was shredded. His body had healed around the metal of the plate, and even as it bled before my eyes, it healed again.

Adrian did not clean the blood away. Instead, he pressed his hand into it and approached me, naked, smoothing it over my back. I drew in a breath. It wasn't painful but also not pleasant—it felt as though my skin was prickling—so I focused on the way Adrian's fingers moved down my back, slow and sensual.

When he bent to kiss my shoulder, I knew my wounds had healed. I rolled onto my back, facing Adrian. His eyes burned as they trailed down my body.

When he met my gaze again, he spoke.

"This will hurt," he said.

I rose to sit and gave him my arm.

"I trust you," I said.

He kissed me and then anchored his hands beneath my knees, pulling me closer. I wrapped my legs around his waist, tight, focusing on the feel of his cock nestled against my heat, hoping that would distract me enough.

"Rest your head against my shoulder," he said as he held my injured arm. "And if you need to, bite me."

It was the only warning he gave before he sank his teeth into the hound's wound.

I screamed.

I had not been prepared for the pain, though I did not know how I could have prepared for it. It was acute, sharp, burning. With each pull, Adrian filled his mouth, then he would release me and spit the blood and venom on the floor. I tightened my hold on him, digging my nails into his skin, and each time he bit into me, I bit him, though I did not break skin.

I didn't know how long he worked, but eventually I felt nothing beyond the pain in my head. When Adrian finished, he dropped my arm and tangled his hand in my hair, kissing my face and holding me close.

The last thing I remembered was how he looked at me as he guided me to my back—completely and utterly haunted.

Later I woke, my wounds no longer hurting, but I was covered in sweat and desperate to fuck.

I arched my back, parted my legs, and slid my fingers into my heat. A strangled sound escaped my mouth, my head pressing hard into the pillow. I was so hot, so wet, my fingers did nothing to bring pleasure.

Frustrated, I rose and rolled onto Adrian. I straddled him, sliding my heat over his swollen length. He groaned, his hands going to my thighs as I kissed him, driving my tongue into his mouth while he helped me move over his cock.

"I need you," I said, releasing his mouth and guiding him inside me.

As he drove into my heat, he drew in a sharp breath. "Fuck!" His hands dug into my skin. "Yes."

He rose, one arm around my waist, the other on my shoulder. He used the leverage to set a pace that made my muscles tighten around him. I moaned deep and guttural. My hands threaded into his hair and pulled, forcing his head back so I could mold my mouth to his.

When he broke free, he spoke. "Your skin is on fire."

"Don't stop," I begged, kissing him again.

I was hot, but so was Adrian. Our bodies had grown slick together in our desperation to find release.

Adrian shifted, and I found myself on my back with his fingers curled inside me, stroking. I rose onto my elbows, letting my legs fall open as far as they would go, digging my heels into the bed, every muscle inside my body bunched as a sweet and heady pleasure built.

I couldn't think, couldn't breathe. I made desperate attempts to draw air into my lungs, only to sob from the pleasure of him.

My body released suddenly, and a stream of liquid left me. Adrian bent to place his mouth over my clit, sucking and licking my heat before pulling out, only to fill me with himself once more.

"Yes, yes, yes," I urged him on, lifting my hips. He gripped me and pulled me up, my ass resting on his bent knees. His pace was steady, building pressure in the bottom of my stomach. He leaned over me, roughly kissing my mouth.

"Let me come while I ride you," I said, and all he managed to do was offer a short laugh before he rolled onto his back and let me mount him once more.

We moved in tandem, our wet bodies slamming together, our breaths ragged. I could not help the keening cries that escaped my mouth or the string of words I repeated, a desperate chant, a bewitching spell, holding on to this rhythm until I came with a guttural cry.

Adrian's final thrust had him pulsing inside me, and as he groaned, I bent to kiss his warm mouth.

"It's hot," I said, breathing hard, my heart racing.

"You have a fever," he said, his hands splayed across my waist.

"A fever," I repeated.

My head was on fire, burning from the inside out.

I stood, leaving Adrian on the bed.

"Where are you going?" he asked.

"It's hot," I said again and turned. I crossed the room to where the metal bath sat before the fireplace—empty. "I want to swim," I said.

"Isolde," Adrian said, rising from the bed. "It's freezing outside. You cannot swim."

I ignored him and headed for the door.

Adrian's arm hooked around me, driving my back to his chest.

"I will order you a bath," he said near my ear.

"I don't want a bath," I said.

"Isolde—"

"I need to go outside, Adrian."

Something in my voice must have convinced him to let me go, and as soon as his arm fell from me, I bolted from his room. I raced down the stairs, only slightly aware that people were around and watching. None of them tried to stop me. Instead, they pressed themselves into the walls. I assumed that had to do with Adrian, who I could feel at my back, stalking like a shadow.

I ran into the cold night, my bare feet sinking into the snow—and I was still so hot.

My body was changing. I could feel it in my bones, which ached in a way that caused my insides to throb.

"Isolde."

I turned my head and looked at Adrian. He stood naked on the stairs of his palace.

"Tell me what is wrong."

"I don't know," I said, frowning. Then I turned and looked toward the garden, bolting again. As my feet carried me at what felt like an abnormally fast pace, my bones broke.

It was the only way I could describe it.

The pain sent me to the ground, and I screamed. Tears welled in my eyes and spilled down my cheeks, and as strange as it was, the only thing I could think about was water.

Water is rebirth.

You will survive in the water.

And it was *near*. I could smell it.

I reached out with my hand to crawl when a set of claws burst from my fingertips. Blood dripped onto the snow and while I screamed, I dug into the earth, using my claws to pull myself forward, propelled by my one and only goal—water.

Even as I crawled, my bones moved, fusing into something that made me feel completely *other*. The knowledge that I was no longer human passed through my mind before I rose to my feet with what energy remained in my body and staggered into the grotto.

My vision was blurry, but I knew where I was because of the lingering scent of jasmine in the air. I came to the edge of the pool and broke the ice layer on top as I waded into the depths. The water cradled my body in a cold embrace, and the burning in my blood and the ache in my bones ceased.

"Isolde."

Adrian stood on the bank, and even in the dark, his eyes glittered.

"Stay," I said. "I will be back."

Then I submerged myself beneath the water, and there was no pain as I felt my body transform and become a foreign thing—an animal, covered in thick black fur.

Reemerging, I crept to the shore on all fours, holding Adrian's gaze as I sat, allowing a long, black tail to curl around my feet.

The corner of my husband's lips lifted.

"Aren't you a beautiful beast?" he said.

I narrowed my eyes at him, allowing a growl to escape my mouth. I did not appreciate his humor so shortly after becoming the very same creature that had killed so many of my people.

I had become an aufhocker.

I was an omen of death.

SIX
Isolde

When I woke, it was cold.

I sat up, holding my blankets to my chest, noticing the shutters were open. Snow had gathered on the ledge while flurries fell, languid and delicate, to the floor.

I rose, naked, and crossed to the window.

Adrian's room overlooked part of the palace gardens. Yesterday, everything had glittered with a dusting of icy crystals. Today, nothing was visible above heavy drifts of red-stained snow.

Gavriel had been right. Winter did come fast.

I should close the shutters, but I couldn't look away from the garden below as I remembered toiling through the snow to reach water, and when I had emerged, I had been something monstrous.

A darkness gathered in my chest, as I recalled that I had become an aufhocker.

The very thing that had killed my people in Cel Ceredi.

And while I was somehow once again in my human form, I felt different, altered. I looked at my arm, where the aufhocker had bit me, where Adrian had bit me—it was fully healed. I looked at my hands, spreading my fingers wide—fingers that had sprouted claws last night. Something gathered in my throat, a hysteria I wasn't certain I could quell.

I did not want to be this—whatever *this* was. A shifter. A creature that craved extinguishing life.

The door opened and I turned as Adrian entered the room.

He stared at me, his eyes like embers, and as his gaze trailed my body, I warmed beneath it despite the winter air.

He was dressed in black, with gold accenting the clasps of his surcoat and securing his cloak, which draped over his right arm in a pool of deep red. There was always a sharpness to his features, but this morning they seemed far more menacing.

"Am I a monster?" I asked.

He chuckled, amused by my question, but his response only made me angry. "It would seem so," he said.

"So you failed," I said. It wasn't a fair thing to say, but I felt like fighting because he had laughed and I…I was afraid.

Adrian narrowed his eyes and tilted his head to the side. It was as if I had slapped him. "If I had failed, you would not be here now in human skin."

I cringed at his words.

"I *am* human."

His smile twisted my stomach.

"Not anymore."

"What is this pride you have?" I demanded. "I am a *monster*."

"So am I," he said. "Does it make you sick to be like me?"

"But I am not like you!" I snarled. "I am a creature, an *animal*! I do not even know who I will be when I shift. What if I murder innocent people? What if I am murdered by *your* people?"

It was a fair question. I would look just like every other black hound in a pack.

Adrian's mouth tightened. "You will not be killed," he said.

"And you can control that?"

"I will," he said.

We glared at each other for a moment. I was the first to turn away, closing the shutters. I crossed to the bed where Adrian's robe lay folded on a chair, pulling it on.

"You are failing to see the potential in this power," Adrian said.

"It is hard to do so when I do not know what this means for me," I said. I had already expressed my fears. Did I need to repeat myself?

"What happened last night?" I asked. "After I turned."

"You came out of the water and collapsed and turned back into...you," he said. "I brought you inside, and you were still feverish, so I opened the window while you slept."

I did not know what to say, so I remained silent, attempting to process everything that had occurred.

"Do you think I will leave you to figure this out on your own?"

The angry part of me did not want to figure this out because I did not want to *be* this.

"And how will we do that?" I asked.

"You are not the only shifter in this kingdom, Isolde," Adrian said. "There are others like you."

"Sorin is a falcon, not a—"

"Monster?" Adrian cut me off. "But he is a monster. We all are, and we all have sides of us we must learn to control. You are no different. You never have been."

I clenched my jaw hard. Right now, I did not feel like controlling myself. I wanted to tear him to shreds. I wanted to eviscerate him with my words. I wanted to lash him with my tongue.

And he must have been listening to my thoughts because he laughed. "I would take the tongue-lashing," he said, "if it meant I could fuck you on your stomach."

"You haven't even tried to understand my fear," I said. "What makes you think I would let you touch me?"

Adrian's gaze hardened, and it was my turn to smile, though there was nothing entertaining about this.

"Get dressed," he said, and I bristled at the order. "High Council is in an hour."

He left, and I flinched as he slammed the door behind him. I took that as a sign I had succeeded in my goal to hurt him, though to my own detriment, because I did not like that he had left before we could discuss High Council. I wanted to know his agenda, and I wished to communicate mine without the noblesse present. I did not trust that they would support me. Though it was not as if I wanted something that did not align with Adrian's goal of conquering Cordova.

I wanted to return to Lara, and I wanted to invade Vela to rescue my mother's people. And nothing about my current situation felt like it would make those things easy.

I left Adrian's room for my own and summoned Violeta and Vesna with a pull of the servant's bell. I wanted to get ready as soon as possible, hoping to check on the wounded in the great hall before High Council. Grimly, I wondered if anyone had survived.

Violeta arrived, followed shortly by Vesna, who carried a tray with tea and toast.

"Good morning, my queen," said Violeta. "Are you well?"

"I am all right," I said, unable to lie completely. In truth, I did not know. As I had so many times in my life, I was faced with something I had never expected, never wanted, and while marriage to Adrian had become something far more passionate and meaningful than I had ever believed, I failed to see the value in the ability to shift into the form of an aufhocker. I'd have much rather been a falcon or crow—something with wings so that I might collect my own intel on Lara and Vela.

Instead, I was a mindless creature with a thirst for blood.

And I was angry with Adrian for dismissing my fear.

"I wish to get ready quickly," I said. "I would like to check on the wounded."

Violeta did not speak, and her silence somehow seemed far more unsettling. My gaze shifted to Vesna, who was pouring tea.

"Are your sisters and mother well, Vesna?"

"They are," she said, though her voice trembled. She cleared her throat and added, "Just shaken."

"I think we all are," I said.

"Do you think it will happen again?" she asked.

"I cannot say," I said. As badly as I wished to promise it would never happen again, I couldn't. We did not know why the creatures had attacked anyway. Even in the night, we had never worried about an entire pack ravaging a village. In fact, it was far more usual for aufhockers to remain hidden, feasting on small prey unless a villager or two wandered into their territory.

But these had seemed possessed.

"A preference on dress?" Violeta asked.

I often let her choose my outfits, but today I intended to draw attention.

"I'd like to wear red," I said, and after a short audit of my wardrobe, she chose a gown. The sleeves were long and loose but gathered at the wrist, and the skirt was layered and warm. The only embellishment was a long gold belt clasped at my waist, the remaining length left to hang down the front of my dress.

The color was stunning and ignited like fire against my brown skin and black hair, which was down, only parted to the side to better accommodate the gold crown Violeta brought to me. While there was nothing simple about its workmanship, it was not embellished with gems or pearls. Instead, the metal had been fashioned into a series of fleurs-de-lis and delicate filigree. The final touch was a set of simple, gold earrings.

When I finished dressing, I chose to look in the mirror, which I had taken to turning toward the wall given that Ravena used them to spy and travel. Despite this, I could not bring myself to destroy it or take it from my room. There was a part of me that wanted a way to communicate with her, as dangerous as it was. Adrian had not been pleased with my decision but had reluctantly agreed. We both knew I was the only potential link to finding her, and I knew eventually she would seek me out. When that time came, I needed a plan, so that I could find *The Book of Dis*.

There was movement in the mirror, and for a brief moment, I thought Ravena had returned, but it was only Vesna moving into the frame.

"You look beautiful, my queen," she said.

I looked down at the dress, hoping it would serve the purpose I wished—to capture attention throughout High Council.

I had only attended once, and I had been unimpressed with Adrian's chosen advisors—all men, save Ana. His men tended to ignore me whenever I was present, or perhaps they presumed as Gavriel had that we were one and the same. In some ways, I understood Adrian was their king and he had chosen them to serve him, but I was their queen, and I intended to be heard, separate from my husband.

I turned my back to the mirror.

"Will you not sit and eat, my queen?" Vesna asked.

"No," I said. I still wished to find Ana before High Council, and in truth, I was not hungry, and everything she brought still smelled burnt. I did not know if it was grief or if the memory of being burned so long ago lived in the back of my throat.

Despite this, I took a piece of the bread she had sliced open.

"I will eat as I walk," I said and dismissed them, leaving my room for the great hall, finding the foyer quiet and cold. The doors of the palace were open and overlooked a raging fire. For a moment, my stomach soured, thinking that perhaps they'd begun to burn bodies in the night, but there were no corpses in the flames.

As I entered the hall, I halted in my tracks, and my earlier relief about the fire evaporated. Nearly half of the wounded were gone. Those who remained appeared to be villagers who had only been scratched or hurt themselves fleeing the aufhockers.

"My queen," said a voice, and I turned my head to find Isac standing nearby. He bowed and moved to stand beside me.

"So few are left," I said.

"Many were bitten."

I swallowed hard. I had been bitten too, and I was still alive though very much changed.

"Was there no hope for any of them?"

"Aufhocker bites infect fast," he said. "There comes a point where there is no coming back. Perhaps if the battle had not lasted as long…"

His voice trailed away.

"Where are the bodies?"

"The last of them were just moved to the sanctuary," he said.

"Is Lady Ana there?" I wondered how she was doing, knowing she had been the one to administer the poison that had taken their lives.

"I believe so," he said. "She must prepare them for burial."

I thought it was strange that Ana had the task, but perhaps she had insisted.

"Thank you, Isac," I said.

He offered a small smile. "Of course, Your Majesty," he said and bowed. "I am glad to see you are well."

He had no idea how much guilt his words would create within me, but as I left for the sanctuary, it only grew.

The sanctuary was technically part of the castle, though only accessible from the outside. It was from Dragos's reign, back when the old gods were worshipped, though it had been clear Asha was the center of worship within. Initially, I'd been surprised to learn that the space still existed within Adrian's castle, given his contempt for the gods, even Dis, who created him, but Adrian had seen that no iconography dedicated to the goddess of life remained within the cavernous room. It was merely a quiet place to mourn the dead with no allegiance to any god.

I paused outside the doors of the sanctuary. They were slightly ajar, and I hesitated, choosing to peer through the small opening into the cavernous room. There were no windows, just great, arched alcoves where paintings of the old goddesses once hung. Clusters of tall, wax candles provided pockets of dim light, enough to illuminate several still bodies that rested among the shadows of the floor.

One body remained separate from the others, elevated on a stone altar. It was Isla, Ana's vassal and lover, who had been corrupted by the crimson mist and killed during the attack on my coronation day.

A wave of emotion raced from my chest to my throat as I watched her. I felt guilty for my own thoughts when faced with Ana's unbearable pain, but I was grateful I had not lost Adrian. It was selfish and not becoming of a queen. I needed to focus on finding a way to fight the mist.

Ana stood among the dead, her back to me, and as I slipped through the door, she turned to face me, brushing tears from her cheeks.

"Oh, Ana," I said, embracing her.

She took a deep breath and then looked around the room, her eyes continuing to water.

"Did you…did you have to do this by yourself?" I asked.

She shook her head and swallowed. "Killian helped."

A thickness gathered in my throat. I would have to check on him today.

"It was awful," she said, wiping her sleeve across her eyes. "If we could, we held them until they passed."

I was quiet for a moment, but I could not help asking, "Could Adrian have saved them?"

I feared her answer because there was a part of me that knew I could not forgive Adrian if he possessed the ability to save our people and chose not to.

She shook her head. "There were so many injured. By the time I managed to examine them, they had already developed fangs. It is the first sign the change has taken root. There would have been no stopping it, even with his bite."

My fear dissolved once more into guilt. I hated that I had even questioned him, but I was still coming to terms with what I had become, and I did not understand it.

"We should go," I said. "High Council begins soon."

Ana and I left the sanctuary for the west wing.

With each set of stairs we climbed, I felt more and

more dread—not because of the upcoming meeting but because Adrian's council chamber was located just beyond the mirrored hall where I had killed my father.

I'd had no intention of letting this bother me, had told myself it was just a room, but as I found myself standing before it, I was unable to move.

It was not as if the hall had not been cleaned. In fact, it looked much like it had before Ravena's attack, minus the mirrors I had destroyed, but that was just it. I could not exist in this space and not think about the horror of what had happened—where I had landed after my father had pushed me down the stairs, where I had been when he had tried to convince me that dying would be worth the honor of having saved a world that cared nothing for me.

Then I felt Ana's hand in mine, and when I looked at her, she seemed just as sad.

"It's all right," she said, her voice hushed, as if she did not wish to disturb the nightmares that lingered there. Perhaps she feared they might come alive too. "I am with you."

I took a deep breath and walked with her down the hall, my hand tightening the farther we walked. I did not let go until we were in the council room, and even then, I think I would have held on had it not been for Adrian, who seemed to be trained to find me the moment I entered a room.

Ana released my hand just as Adrian extended his, an invitation to join him at the head of the oval table around which the men had gathered, among them his usual advisors, Daroc, Sorin, and Tanaka, and his remaining noblesse, Razan, Iosif, Vlad, and Iker. When they realized I was present, they rose, bowing, and despite our earlier argument, I went to Adrian.

When my fingers touched his palm, his closed around mine.

"My queen," he said, pressing his lips to my skin.

His frustration had ebbed since we parted, and while mine had not, I could not deny the comfort his touch brought after walking through the hall and seeing the bodies in the sanctuary. There was a part of me that wanted to collapse in his arms and cry, but I couldn't, not here in front of these men who likely would not listen to me without Adrian by my side. I hated the thought that these people might value me more for apathy, which would certainly be misinterpreted as strength, rather than my grief.

I felt Adrian's fingers beneath my chin, and as he tilted my head back, he kissed the corner of my mouth.

"How are you feeling?" he breathed, a quiet question meant only for me to hear.

"Mournful," I said, and once more I felt the emotion building in the back of my throat. I had not anticipated this—to feel so much so keenly in this moment.

Adrian said nothing, only smoothed his thumb over my cheek. I knew he would take this from me if he could, but there were few ways to relieve this kind of pain, among them time or magic, and since I did not have control over magic, I had to rely on time.

"You are my light, Sparrow," he said. It was not a direct apology, but in the aftermath of our disagreement, I needed the assurance of his love.

"You are my darkness," I said. I expected him to let me go quickly, given that we had an audience, but he didn't. He held me a moment longer, studying my face before guiding me to sit. The members of the council followed, though Adrian remained standing beside me. Ana too chose not to join the table, preferring to stand apart like a ghost, haunting the room.

"Shall we begin with our most pressing matter?" Tanaka asked.

"Are they not all pressing?" Adrian asked. "We have a witch on the run who has stolen a spell book, and we have no inkling of her plans. Yesterday, Cel Ceredi was attacked by a pack of aufhockers, and nearly thirty of our people are dead."

"Forgive me, my king," said Tanaka. "I assumed you wished to speak of the traitor."

"Dracul is hunting Julian," Adrian replied. "Unless you speak of another?"

I studied Daroc and Sorin, Ana and Tanaka, but none of them tensed at Adrian's comment, though I knew it was a warning as much as it was an acknowledgment that he knew.

"N-no, my king," Tanaka said.

There was silence following the exchange, but after a moment, Daroc sat forward and spoke.

"Our problems seem related to me," said Daroc.

I met the general's gaze. "How so?"

He did not look at me as he answered. Instead, he stared hard at the table.

"It cannot be a coincidence that Ravena attacked us with the crimson mist, and two days later, we face another attack."

"Yes, but she got exactly what she wanted," I said. Ravena had killed innocent people before—namely her entire coven—but even that decision had been strategic. She gained nothing from killing a handful of villagers and farmers. "She didn't steal a spell book only to return and kill innocent victims."

That magic was meant for something far worse.

"Why are you assigning morals to our enemies?" This time, Noblesse Razan spoke. "They do not care who they kill so long as they win."

"Win what?" I asked. "You do not even know what she is fighting for."

"It does not matter. She has attacked our home, and for that, she must die."

I ground my teeth.

"How do you expect to find her if you do not know what she fights for?"

"You already said she wanted the spell book," said Noblesse Iker.

"The spell book is a tool," I said. "Nothing more."

"The woman wants power," Tanaka said. "I fail to see how that will help us."

"Men want power," Ana said. It was the first time she had spoken, and everyone at the table turned to look at her. "Women want to exist without fear."

"This is ridiculous," said Razan, offering a mocking laugh. "You have made this far more complicated than it needs to be."

"Then tell us how to find her," Adrian said.

The humor drained from Razan's face, and he fell silent, but Ana's comment had made me consider Ravena's fears. I knew what she feared most.

Me.

"Perhaps the focus should not be on finding her so

much as fighting her magic," I said. "As we learned with Ciro, though powerful, none of you are immune."

Silence followed my statement. None of them liked to be reminded that they could die so easily.

"How do you suggest we fight magic?" asked Daroc.

"You can't," I said, and for a moment, I stared at Ana, remembering how she had used magic when Gesalac attacked.

"Magic belongs to women."

"If that is the case, why do you not have magic?" Razan said coolly.

"Enough," Adrian snapped, and his voice echoed in the room.

I looked down at my hands, hands that had once summoned magic with a simple snap of my fingers.

But in this life, I was powerless.

I had no great ability.

I gave Adrian a mortal weakness.

"If you have nothing to offer, we have had enough of your council," Adrian said. "Leave us."

Chairs scraped the floor as the men pushed away from the table. As they rose, they bowed, though Razan lingered.

"My king, I did not mean—" he began.

"You were not invited to speak," Adrian said. "Though since you have endeavored to do so, let me be clear that your apology does not belong to me. It belongs to my wife. The very fact that you cannot see that is unforgivable."

He paled at Adrian's words, mouth pressed tight as he left the table.

Alone, Adrian's hand came to rest on mine, which were clenched into fists in my lap.

"I am sorry," Adrian said, thumb brushing over my knuckles. "Razan is a fool."

"A fool, yes," I said, my eyes burning, and I hated that the noblesse's words had unleashed such a reaction within me. "But he is not wrong. I do not know how to connect with my magic."

Adrian tipped my head back and I was forced to meet his gaze.

"Magic or not, you are no less valuable to me," he said, and he leaned in, pressing a lingering kiss to my forehead. I closed my eyes, forcing down these emotions I did not want to have around something I could not control.

When Adrian drew away, his gaze was troubled.

"What is it?" I asked.

"You said that with *The Book of Dis*, Ravena could resurrect the dead."

"The magic contained within that book is powerful enough, yes," I said. "If that is what she intends, I do not know."

He was quiet for a moment and when he spoke, it was as if he were confessing. "Sorin found the gravesite of High Coven yesterday. It was empty."

Empty? I straightened at his words, confused. "But… we were *burned*."

Adrian's jaw tensed. "I took what was left of the bones and ash and buried them in a single grave," he said. "I…couldn't leave you unburied."

I wanted to ask him why, but I didn't. He had said the grave was empty, that someone had stolen what remained of my coven…of *me*.

"What if Ravena intends to resurrect High Coven?"

I shook my head, a thickness gathering in my throat,

making it harder to breathe. Ravena had worked too hard to kill us only to bring us back. No. There was no reason to seek the remains of witches, save for one purpose—she wanted our magic.

I met Adrian's gaze. "Take me to the grave."

SEVEN
Isolde

Adrian did not question my need to see the grave.

I was not even certain why I needed to see it, only that I did. I knew it was not where we had died. It was only where we had rested the last two hundred years, and perhaps that was why, because every other place in this land reminded me of my death.

Nothing reminded me of peace.

I changed into boots and pulled on a heavy, fur-lined cloak before joining Adrian in the courtyard where he waited with Shadow. Though as I started to leave the castle, I found he was not alone but stood opposite Daroc.

I lingered in the shadow of the doorway and listened.

"Given yesterday's attack, I do not think it wise to venture into the forest alone," Daroc said, displeasure lacing his tone.

"Your concerns are noted, General," Adrian replied.

"And yet you ignore me in favor of what? Pleasing your queen?"

"How is it that you manage to continuously express both concern and disdain for my wife, Daroc?"

"My concern is for your queen. My disdain is for you."

Adrian smirked at his comment.

"If you wanted to play the role of a knight, then you should have come to her rescue during High Council."

"Razan is an idiot," Daroc said. "Arguing with him is a waste of time."

"What a coincidence. This too feels like a waste of time."

Even I felt the harshness of those words, and they were enough to convince Daroc to relent. The general turned and entered the castle, hesitating when he saw me. For a moment, I saw the pain burning in his eyes before he managed to call up his mask and harden his face. He continued past me, and I found that I could not breathe until he was out of sight.

Only then did I take a breath and join Adrian outside.

It was cold and the clouds, heavy with snow, made the day darker.

"You were unkind," I said as I approached.

"Daroc is used to me," Adrian said, holding out a gloved hand for me to take. He stood back as I mounted Shadow, and from my position on his horse, I stared down at him.

"He is not wrong to express his concerns," I said. "You could handle them with far more care than you did."

Adrian raised a brow. "You would have rather I agreed and declined your request?"

"No, but you did not need to tell him his concern was a waste of time. *That* is unforgivable."

Adrian frowned. "What would you have me do?"

"Apologize to him," I said. "He was merely cautioning you."

"He implied I could not take care of you," Adrian said, and his jaw tightened.

"You assumed that is what he meant. Could that be because you weren't here to care for me yesterday?"

Adrian's jaw grew even more tense, but he said nothing, choosing instead to mount behind me. He spurred Shadow on, through the courtyard and outside the gates where the treasonous dead remained, bodies anointed in snow, among them Gesalac, whose large body was already completely impaled by the spear—the pointed end protruding from the base of his neck, where his head would have been.

Adrian guided Shadow down the hill with slow precision. Parts of the path were packed with snow, which made them far more perilous. On the descent, I found myself leaning back into his warmth, and despite his frustration with me, he kept his arm secured around my waist.

As we approached town, my heart grew heavier.

The villagers had begun constructing a large, wooden pyre where the thirty or so bodies resting in the sanctuary would be burned later tonight. My hope was that no one else passed in that time. We had lost enough life.

Adrian's arm tightened around me.

We did not speak as we made our way through Cel Ceredi. Not even the heavy snowfall could hide yesterday's destruction. At least Adrian's soldiers helped with repairs, among them Miha and Isac.

"Killian?" I asked, spotting my commander with the villagers. He knelt at the corner of a home, repairing damage where an aufhocker had effortlessly torn away a wall to reach the family inside.

I swallowed hard.

Would I do something similar?

I placed my hand over Adrian's and halted our horse.

The commander looked up when he heard his name and rose to his feet. He wore civilian clothes—a brown tunic, pants, and thick-soled boots. I had not expected to see him like this, much less helping my people. He came forward and bowed.

"My queen," he said, eyes shifting to Adrian. "My king."

"Are you not cold?" I asked, frowning. He had no cloak, and his hands were red and raw from working in this weather. I felt far less a queen as I sat on my horse, having remained in the castle all morning in the warmth.

"No, my queen. This is hard work," he said and offered a small smile. "Where are you off to?"

"The queen wishes to gather lavender for the dead," said Adrian.

"Of course," he said and paused. "No guard?"

"We will not be long," I said, though just like Daroc, Killian was not pleased, yet he took a step away and nodded.

"I will look for your return."

Adrian spurred his horse on, and we continued toward the forest that loomed ahead, ethereal and ominous. I had never seen anything like it when I had first ventured through, and I had seen nothing like it since—full of endless trees that grew from barren ground and ghosts. There was usually no part of the earth I dreaded exploring, but these woods had memory, and they burdened all who entered. I could feel it weighing on my heart. It was the weight I carried for each of my sisters who had hung from these branches by their neck until dead.

"Are you all right?" Adrian asked. His voice was warm against my skin, and it broke the hypnotic hold of the forest.

I did not feel like discussing the forest. I knew what horror had occurred here, so instead, I asked, "Will we really gather lavender?"

"If you wish," he said.

"I wish it," I said as we were swallowed whole by the forest.

He waited until we had gone some distance before he spoke again.

"You should not feel guilty for not helping to rebuild," he said.

"Perhaps not," I said. "But I do."

I felt neglectful.

"You nearly gave your life to protect them."

There was a part of me that wondered if I *had* given them my life. I had come out on the other side of that fight as something different than what I was, and I still had no idea how it would change me. I thought about how I felt in this moment—what parts of my body were altered—but I was the same, save for these thoughts that reminded me I had turned into a monster.

Adrian moved my hair, exposing my neck, and pressed a kiss to my skin.

"I am sorry," he said. "For earlier."

"You'll have to do more than kiss my neck to apologize," I said.

"Earlier you did not desire my touch," he said.

"Earlier you were a bastard," I said.

Adrian chuckled, but his hold on me tightened and he spoke near my ear.

"I do not fear monsters as you do," he said.

"I do not want to lose my mind," I said.

"I have turned many mortals into my kind. Some are shifters and some are not, but none have ever lost their minds."

"You did not change me," I pointed out.

"I could," he said, and once more, I felt his lips touch my skin. "I would. You have only to say the word."

I held my breath, feeling a familiar heat stirring in the bottom of my stomach. It made me feel heavy and want to feel full all at the same time.

"How would you do it?" I asked, my voice hushed.

In truth, I had not let myself entertain the idea of turning for long, and when I did, I'd stopped myself, always with Lara on my mind.

Adrian smiled against my skin, and as he spoke, his teeth grazed my ear.

"I cannot decide. I have thought of it so often and in so many ways, but it always starts with you," he said. "With the moment you say yes, with the moment you beg to be like me."

I clung to each of his words and the way he said them. There was a desperation beneath and it called to me across lifetimes. This wasn't about the bite or the blood. It wasn't even about being like him. It was about loneliness.

Adrian did not want to be alone.

My hands tightened on his arm.

"So far, you have told me nothing about what I should expect."

It took Adrian a moment to speak, and I wondered if he was holding on to my words as well. There was an element of assumption in the way I spoke, as if I had already accepted my fate.

"I have changed my mind so often, I no longer know how it will happen, but if I were to take you now, it would be within the grove where I buried you, and I would draw out your pleasure until you were delirious with need, until your body was hot and your blood rushing, until you forgot all the horror it took to get us here, and only then would I enter you." He paused and his hand moved to my upper thigh as he whispered, "Are you wet for me now?"

"I would challenge you to find out," I said. "But I would like to hear the rest."

He chuckled, a warm hum that only succeeded in making me far more aroused.

"The rest is simple," he said. "I would fuck you to the point of climax and not let you come until I was ready to drink from you."

"So," I said. "It isn't unlike how you already take my blood?"

"Is that a challenge, Sparrow?" I said.

"Well, if you are going to make it memorable," I said.

"It will be memorable," he said. "You will never forget the first time you take my blood."

For the first time since he had begun detailing this fantasy, I stiffened and Adrian noticed.

"Are you disgusted with me?" he asked, and though

he tried, it was getting harder for him to hide his disappointment.

"No," I said. "I just cannot imagine it…what it will be like."

What it would taste like or how it would feel.

We rode in silence for a long moment, and I considered how many people Adrian had changed over his lifetime. He had not always turned mortals as strategically as he did now, and the result had been utter chaos. The power he had unwittingly bestowed on some mortals only illustrated the truth of humanity—when given the option, they would do terrible things, and terrible things they did, attacking villages only to rape the women and kill the men. Those who did not die were changed and left to handle their hunger alone, which led to more attacks.

"Have you ever turned anyone the way you plan to turn me?" I asked, a question that made me feel both embarrassed and guilty. I tried not to be concerned with who Adrian had fucked before me and should not care how he had turned anyone before me either, but it felt different. I knew by how he spoke that he valued this above anything, so why did it matter?

"I have never changed anyone in the way I will change you."

He spoke with such conviction, and the thing about his belief that he would change me was that I knew it was true too. But I needed time to process that I had become something I'd never planned for, a shifter.

"You once said these monsters who seek blood were creations of Asha," I said. "Are aufhockers any different?"

"No."

I was quiet, considering.

"Then is it possible that the aufhockers' behavior changed because of her?"

I could not see Adrian's face, but I could feel his body against mine, and as I spoke, he grew tense. He did not like what I was saying.

"Asha has no power on earth," he said, his voice tight.

"Dis does not either," I said. "Except for what she does through you."

Adrian did not respond, but he did halt Shadow, and as he dismounted, I scanned the snowy woods, frowning, seeing no sign of the grave he had spoken of.

"I wish to walk you there," he said, watching me. "It isn't far."

He helped me to the ground, my boots sinking into the snow as I landed. I let him lead, following in his footsteps, which made navigating the woods far easier. Now and then, I noticed how he would touch the trunk of a tree as we passed, fingers lingering as if he were collecting memories. Perhaps he was, or perhaps it was part of the way he remembered how to find the clearing that opened before us.

As I stood at its mouth, I was taken aback.

I had been unprepared for its solemn beauty.

A range of mountains created the backdrop to what Adrian had made my resting place. They sloped gently behind a forest of naked trees. These had thicker trunks, perhaps because they were older, and they seemed to reach endless heights, disappearing into a thick ethereal mist that nearly blocked out the red sky.

I stared so long at this otherworldly place that I almost missed the grave.

It was so simple—a large stone at the base of a tree—but it stole my breath.

I walked past Adrian, making my own way to the grave, and though I knew I no longer rested here, I touched the stone that had guarded me for so long. But the longer I stayed in this place, the more violated I felt. Knowing that someone had come here and disturbed our grave was even more painful.

It also made me sick to think that someone—possibly Ravena—was in possession of my bones and those of my coven. We had learned early on as witches that any parts of a body, be it hair or nails or skin, were powerful conduits—they were links to the dead, to their memories, to their power. With them, she could siphon our magic, and while it would not be nearly as powerful, it was still dangerous, especially because she possessed *The Book of Dis*.

I looked at Adrian, whose gaze moved from my hand on the stone to my face.

"Why did you choose this place?" I asked, and I could tell by his expression that he was remembering something long ago. Then he looked away, toward the mountains, and I followed.

"There was a cottage here long ago," he said, and as he spoke, something took root in my mind, and I thought I could see it and the way this place used to be before it had been drained of life in the same way my sisters had been drained of theirs—a forest crowded with commanding and verdant trees so lush, light only slipped through in pockets of gold. They made it nearly impossible to see the mountains, which grew rich moss and wildflowers in fertile crevices, and within that flora,

I could see the cottage, a collection of stacked and varied stones, a thatched roof, and a door made of oak.

I knew this place because it was where Adrian and I had fled when Dragos had made the decision to kill me. It was here we had spent our final night together, and it was here where we'd been captured. Where he had been beaten and I had lost my voice screaming for it to stop.

It was where Dragos had violated me, and Adrian had watched and raged.

It was where we'd witnessed the place we had called our home for a few short hours burn to the ground.

As the memories of that day came back, moisture gathered in my eyes and tears rolled down my cheeks. When I looked at Adrian, his face was haunted.

"Why did you choose this place?" I asked again, not understanding how he could come here when the terror had gone so deep.

"Because when I am here, I remember our final night together," he said, holding my face between his hands, thumbs brushing away my tears. "Do you remember the details of that night?"

I shook my head, and he smiled, though it was faint, and it quickly disappeared.

"We made love," he said. "It was different from all the other times...and it has never been that way since. I never want it to be because I knew that you were only saying goodbye. I knew it even when you spoke of our future."

"What did I say?" I asked.

I had no vivid memories of this night, but that was likely because it had been drowned in the trauma that had followed.

Adrian held me so close, I could no longer feel the cold around us, only the heat between us.

"You wanted a quiet life with me at the base of this mountain," he said. "We would have a farm and you would teach magic the way it was meant to be taught."

"How quaint," I said, managing to laugh despite how much I cried. The irony wasn't lost on me—the life I had wanted then and the life I had now.

"You named our children," he said, and the silence that followed his statement shattered my heart. They were the children we would never have.

"What were their names?" I whispered.

I knew he remembered, knew he clung to the memory of them though they never existed.

"Cora, for a girl," he said, and I swallowed something sharp and jagged in my throat, only to have it land uneasily in my stomach.

Cora. I thought the name was so buried, I could hardly recall where I had heard it, but once the seed was planted, a woman formed around the name. She had a proud face and stood stoic and still. Her eyes were dark, both humble and fierce. She was beautiful, and an ache settled deep inside me at the fact that I did not know what had happened to her in the aftermath of my death.

This was Yesenia's mother.

My mother.

"Cora," I repeated, and my brows lowered as I searched for the other name. Finally, I met Adrian's gaze. "Alek. For a boy," I said. "After you."

A ghost of a smile touched his lips but could not dim the pain in his eyes, and after a moment, he spoke. "I am sorry I could not give you what you wanted," he said.

"Adrian," I whispered. His words broke me in a way I hadn't been before. It had not been he who had taken away the future I had once dreamed of. It had been men. It had been Dragos.

I took his face into my hands, gaze falling to his lips as I spoke. "You are what I want."

He took my mouth in a searing kiss and gripped my hips, and though it was cold, it seemed important that we come together here within this place that had stolen so much from us. I did not protest as Adrian lifted my heavy skirts, seeking the heat between my thighs.

His fingers were cold at first but soon warmed, and as he moved inside me, his mouth devoured mine, trailing along my jaw and neck and over my breasts. There came a point when I could no longer stand, and I dragged him to the snowy ground with me, laughing as he hovered over me, the snow freezing my back.

Adrian did not leave me like that for long. He sat back on his cloak and dragged me onto my knees, his hands digging into my ass as he pulled me flush against his arousal. My breath caught in my throat, but Adrian gave me no time to exhale before he kissed me, devouring my mouth, while his hands moved between us. I shifted, rising until the crown of his cock was positioned within my heat. As I slid down upon him, a shuddering moan escaped my lips.

He wrapped his arms around me tight and helped me move.

"Yes," I whispered. "Yes, *yes*."

I spoke frantic pleas as I inhaled and exhaled, uncaring that I could barely catch my breath, only chasing this dizzy and euphoric feeling. When I was too tired to move, Adrian leaned back, his hands sinking into the snow as he thrust inside me. At first I remained close, hands pressed against his chest, holding still as he moved, but then I pushed away from him so I could watch his face—his hard expression, his determined stare which only seemed to ignite me more.

I let my head fall back as release roared through me, and before I could come down, Adrian's hands tangled into my hair and he kissed me hard as he came, his cock pulsing inside of me.

For a few moments, I stayed clenched around him, and in what remained of that breathless warmth, I asked for an oath.

"Anything for you," he said.

"Promise me the world," I said, breathing hard.

"It is yours," he said.

We gathered lavender. It lay crushed beneath a layer of snow, but Adrian knew where to look, so familiar with the woods.

When we returned to Cel Ceredi, the pyre was lined with bodies wrapped in black cloth. While Adrian and I placed the lavender we had collected among the dead, a heaviness grew in my chest, collecting in the back of my throat.

I hated this.

I hated that I had not been able to protect more than myself in battle, hated that I had barely managed that. I hated that whoever had done this—whether Ravena or some strange change in Asha's influence—only did so because Adrian and I ruled this land.

Perhaps Adrian was right about the benefit of my change.

When we had finished placing the lavender, Adrian took my hand, and we chose a place to stand before the macabre structure, with Daroc and Sorin on one side and Ana and Tanaka on the other. Killian, torch in hand, helped light the base of the pyre, which was packed with dried wood and hay. The fire caught easily and climbed, blazing viciously, and despite how far we stood from it, the heat still stung my skin.

I finally allowed myself to cry, and as the first tear trailed down my cheek, a woman began to wail. She was quiet at first, but soon she had the attention of everyone present, her cries so keen, they were impossible to ignore in the mournful night.

"This is the fault of our king," she said, twisting to face us. She pointed a crooked finger at Adrian. "You have brought this terror upon us!"

My heart raced in my chest as she spoke. I looked up at Adrian whose jaw was set, eyes hard and angry.

"You," she seethed, taking deliberate steps toward us—toward Adrian. "You will die by the hands of those you have murdered, and your queen—she will follow!"

I was surprised when Adrian stepped forward, drawing his sword, but the woman turned and ran into the fire. Her screams filled the air once more, guttural and violent, and as I watched her burn and her cries ceased, suffocated by the fire and the smoke, I wondered if her words were a threat or a prophecy.

EIGHT
Isolde

That night, I could not sleep, my mind racing with every-thing that had taken place in a matter of days. What stayed with me most were the words of the woman who had screamed her grief at us and how it had driven her to kill herself.

I had never watched anyone willingly burn, and perhaps it stayed with me so vividly because I had not had a choice in the way my life was taken. The more I thought about it, the more I recalled how the smoke had invaded my lungs and the feel of flames licking my skin. It was no wonder I had spent most of this life afraid of fire.

Restless, I rose from bed.

"Where are you going?" Adrian asked.

I looked at him, only able to make out the faint outline of his body in the dark.

"I cannot sleep," I said.

"Stay with me," he said, tugging me to him, and I

relented, resting against him while he threaded his fingers through my hair. "What are you thinking?" he asked.

I was thinking of many things—of Ravena and the attack on Cel Ceredi. I was thinking about how I had shifted in the water on that cold night and had not felt inclined to do so since, but was worried about when it would happen again. I was thinking about High Council and how Razan seemed to hate me just as much as Gesalac and Julian. And I was thinking about my home, trying to nurse the ache in my chest over Nadia and worrying over the frenzy taking root among the people there.

"I am thinking about how I must return to Lara," I answered finally.

Adrian did not speak, and I lifted my head to look at him, despite the dark.

"What are *you* thinking?" I asked.

It took him a moment to answer. "I am thinking about how I do not want you to go."

"You know that is not an option," I said.

"Send Killian," he said.

"Killian is not their ruler," I said, the burn of frustration heating my face.

"He is dispensable," Adrian said. "You are not."

His words shocked me, and I pushed away from him.

"He is not dispensable to me," I said. "And how dare you speak so callously of a man who fought for your people and helped them rebuild their village."

Adrian sighed and sat up.

"You are right," he said. "He has acted nobly, but I do not see why we could not send him to Lara in your stead."

"And I do not see why I cannot go."

"You think it wise to return to Lara alone as my wife

and give news of your father's death? Your people will believe I killed him."

"I will tell the truth."

"Your father played the role of a doting father well. No one will believe you."

My heart sank, hurt by his words, though I knew they were true.

"I have to go back," I said again, defiant.

"I will not let you go without me, and as of this moment, I cannot leave Revekka."

"I did not realize when I married you I would be required to always be at your side."

"Required?" he countered. "Is it such a chore?"

"You know that is not what I mean," I snapped.

"Then it seems we are both good at twisting words," he said.

Silence stretched between us, and after a moment, I took a deep breath.

"Do you agree that I will have to return to Lara?"

"Yes," he said.

"And if you come with me...when will we be able to return?"

"*When* I come with you," he said, "it will be when we feel safe in our own country."

I ground my teeth. I wanted to argue with him that Lara was my country too.

"And what about Nalani?"

I feared bringing up my mother's island, but I needed to know he had a plan for them.

"Isolde—"

"Tell me they are part of your plan," I said.

He was quiet.

"Adrian?"

"I am aware of what you want, Isolde, but I cannot give you everything you ask for all at once, no matter how I wish to."

"I am only asking to know more about them," I said. "You sent Sorin to scout the entirety of Cordova. Could you not send him to Nalani?"

"Say I did," he said, "and he came back with information you did not like. You would be restless to save them, but who do you choose? You swore to protect the people of Revekka and Lara. You never swore to protect Nalani."

"I swore to protect my people," I said.

"Can you even call them yours?" he said. "They do not know who you are."

I felt the heat drain from my face at his words and rose to my feet. Only then did he seem to realize what he'd said.

"I did not mean—"

"I think you should stop talking," I said, and he grew silent. "They may not know I exist, and I may not know their ways, but I still belong to them...more than I ever belonged to you."

I left and considered going to the library, but any research I attempted would be futile. I was unfocused and frustrated and far more restless after my conversation with Adrian. In many ways, I knew he was right. I had to be strategic about how I chose to help any of my people. I also wished he had chosen different words to communicate how he felt about my return to Lara and my concern over Nalani, because I was tired of his apologies in the aftermath of my pain.

I wandered the halls, wishing it were not so cold and snowy so that I could seek the solace of the gardens.

Instead, I lingered near the windows, staring out at Revekka's frozen landscape, wondering what horror Ravena planned to unleash on us next, hoping we would be prepared and knowing we wouldn't.

I moved on from the window, and as I made my way down the hall, I noticed I was not alone. Sorin lounged in an alcove, one leg propped over the other, a book open on his lap. He was dressed in a tunic and leggings and his feet were bare.

"I thought you didn't read," I said.

Sorin met my gaze, the serious expression he had worn while reading fading away into a sweet smile.

"I distinctly remember telling you I was kidding, my queen."

I matched his smile. "May I join you?"

He sat up straighter and closed his book. "Of course."

I sat beside him on the cushioned bench.

"What brings you out of your bed at this hour?" he asked.

"I needed a break from Adrian," I said, rolling my eyes.

Sorin chuckled, eyes glittering. "Exhausting, is he?"

"If you are referring to the words coming out of his mouth, then yes," I said.

Sorin laughed louder.

"And you? Why are you out here?"

"Ah, well," he said, smile fading, the cover of his book suddenly seeming far more interesting. "I am giving Daroc a break."

"I have a feeling it isn't his words you are tired of," I said.

Sorin shook his head. "The only time he speaks is when I've done something he doesn't approve of."

"I'm sorry," I said.

"I suppose you should be. It was your husband who put him in such a poor mood," he teased. Then he paused for a long moment, adding, "Sometimes…"

He trailed off and I waited but he did not finish his sentence.

"Sometimes, what?"

"I do not know if I should say," he said and met my gaze.

"If it is how you feel, it is valid," I said.

It took him a moment, but finally he spoke. "Sometimes I wonder if he is in love with Adrian."

I did not know what to say, and it took me a moment to find words. "Is it love or is it loyalty?"

He looked almost as though he were trying to make himself smaller as he sat forward, running a hand over his short, coarse hair.

"Maybe," he said and paused. "Perhaps I am only jealous."

I tilted my head to the side, studying him. "Or maybe you know a truth Daroc refuses to acknowledge because he also loves you."

Sorin covered his mouth and offered a single, disbelieving laugh and dropped his arms, letting his elbows rest on his knees.

"Enough about me," he said. "Adrian tells me you've turned into a beast." Sorin grinned, his dark eyes alight with amusement.

I glared. "Careful or I'll claw that pretty face of yours."

"You'd have to catch me first," he said. "And last I checked, aufhockers cannot fly."

I sighed. "I think I'd have preferred flying."

"There are few abilities greater than one another," he said. "It is all in how you choose to use them."

I met his gaze. "And you are the one to teach me?"

"It would seem so," he mused. "Let us hope Adrian does not come to regret it."

"Why would he?"

He shrugged. "Because he chose not to teach you."

"I don't think Adrian can teach me to shift, Sorin."

"Adrian can teach you anything," he said. "The only reason he doesn't is to keep parts of himself secret."

I frowned. Secret from who? It seemed that Sorin had more knowledge of my husband than I did.

The tracker got to his feet. "I shall relieve you of my presence for the night," he said and bowed. "I look forward to our training sessions."

I let him go without question, suddenly feeling very tired. I left the hall for my room and lay down in my bed, exhaustion settling heavily into my bones. I stared at the ceiling, though my eyes felt gritty and tired. It was cold in my room, and it made me hyperaware that I was alone, that Adrian was not asleep beside me, and that he had secrets he preferred to keep. I hated that it hurt so much.

I woke even before the sun began to redden the sky.

My room was cold, my hearth unlit, and while I could summon Violeta for the task, I wanted to be alone, so I pulled a blanket from my bed and wrapped it around me, choosing to sit at my desk. Nadia's letter remained folded, unanswered near my well of ink and quill. She had written long before my father had arrived for my coronation, long before I'd learned what he truly prized.

I considered responding to her. It would be an opportunity to lie, to tell her that my father was well and that we were enjoying our time together, but I did not think I could read her words again. It was bad enough that I could recall most of them on my own.

Think often of us, especially your father. He is lost without you.

Her words made my stomach churn, but I knew she believed what she wrote.

I also knew she believed I had a plan to kill Adrian.

Nadia had been the first to suggest it. She had put the blade in my hand, and while I had tried to carry out her wish, it had been impossible.

I had fallen in love with him, long before I even knew what was happening.

The body knows before the mind.

I wondered if news had spread across the courts, about how the former princess of Lara loved the Blood King, and I wondered if Nadia scolded anyone who dared speak such blasphemy about her sweet Issi.

But I had never been sweet.

And that had always been Nadia's greatest fault—refusing to see the princess she truly cared for.

"They will kill you," said a voice.

I turned to find Ana in my room, but it was not the Ana I knew—this one belonged to Yesenia's time. She looked just as beautiful, the only difference being her hair. Not a hint of silver showed in her golden tresses.

"I am going to die anyway," I said, and as I spoke, I carefully inked words onto the thick pages of a book.

"That is not funny, Yesenia."

I paused and met Ana's gaze. "Was I laughing?"

Ana paled. "So you plan to die and leave these spells behind. For whom?"

"You are using the wrong words. There is no plan to die, but I will die," I said. "And the spells are for me."

"I do not understand."

"You do not have to," I said. "All you have to do is hide the book."

A knock at the door made me jump, and I found I was alone in my room. Ana was not present, and the book I had been writing in was gone.

I'd had many moments in this palace where I had visions of the past, but this was the first one I'd had about *The Book of Dis*.

My heart beat heavily in my chest as I tried to process what I had witnessed, but I was once again interrupted by a second knock at the door.

"My queen?"

"Fuck," I said under my breath and rose from my place to open the door.

Violeta and Vesna had arrived to help me prepare for the day.

"My queen!" Violeta exclaimed as she entered my room. "Why did you not call for me?"

My lady-in-waiting collapsed to her knees before the hearth and began preparing the fire. Vesna remained near the entrance, arms folded, shivering.

"I did not wish to be disturbed," I said, letting my blanket slide from my shoulders and handing it to Vesna.

"Oh no, my queen. I couldn't," she said.

"Do not refuse my generosity, Vesna," I said, and she took the blanket.

Violeta climbed to her feet, dusting off her knees

as the fire roared to life. Once it was warm enough, I dressed in a black gown. The bodice was structured and dipped into a V that accentuated my breasts—something Adrian would admire. The collar was high and the sleeves long, embellished with silver beading made to look like flowers caught in moonlight.

I accepted whatever jewels Violeta gave me, eager to find Ana. All I had learned was that Ana had ensured the book survived two hundred years until I could return to claim it, but in those years, had she read it? Did she recall any spells? Perhaps we would be able to anticipate Ravena's next move.

Another knock came at the door, and I grew frustrated at having another visitor who would delay my search for Ana, but when Vesna answered the door, she curtsied immediately.

"Your Majesty," she said and stepped aside so Adrian could enter.

He wore all black, a long shadow, and he cast his darkness upon me though I could not deny that I wanted it.

He looked just as tired as I felt—pale, dark-eyed, and sad.

He had pulled his hair away from his face, and it exposed his beautiful, angled jaw.

"May I speak with you?" he asked.

I stared at him a moment, and then my gaze shifted to Violeta and Vesna. "You are dismissed."

When they were gone and the door clicked shut, Adrian approached, halting a few steps from me. I wanted to fill the void between us because I hated how it felt—empty and raw.

"I came to apologize," he said. "I was unkind in so many ways last night. I promised you the world, and when you asked, I took it away." He paused for a moment, looking away, his eyes becoming hard. "The problem is…I waited two centuries to have you in my arms again, and if I let you go, I fear you will never come back."

"Adrian," I said, whispering his name. His words made my heart ache.

"I came to let you know that I dispatched one of my soldiers to Nalani."

I straightened at his words.

"Her name is Ivka. She should return within the week with news."

I opened my mouth to speak, but no words came out, and the only thing I could think to ask was, "Why?"

He swallowed and answered, "Because I love you."

My eyes watered, and I had to bite my lip to keep my mouth from quivering. Adrian frowned and came to kneel at my feet as I spoke.

"You did not have to do this, but I am grateful you did."

He touched my face, and I covered his hands with mine.

"Do not cry, my sweet," he said, his lips close to mine. "This is likely the only honorable thing I will ever do in your name."

I believed him. He was the curse placed on this land when the first drop of my blood touched this earth. He had killed kings and ended bloodlines. He had conquered and would continue, and I felt a single sliver of fear at how unaffected I felt by such a thought.

Instead, I kissed him, and as my arms tightened

around his neck, he rose to his feet, and I followed. We stumbled back, knocking into my vanity, but Adrian did not seem to care. He only used it as a perch, guiding me onto it as he gathered my skirt, hands skimming my thighs before teasing my heat. I groaned, letting my head fall back, an opportunity Adrian took advantage of as he sucked hard on my neck, letting his teeth press against my skin as he did.

I grew frustrated with his playfulness and reached for his hand, thrusting his fingers inside me. Adrian said nothing, only kissed me harder. He kissed me everywhere—my mouth, my jaw, my neck, my breasts—and all I wanted was to open for him more, feel him more, but I was already wound tight, and my entire body felt like a heartbeat, pulsing and throbbing.

He kept his pace, a rhythm that had me breathlessly begging him to keep going. He pulled back to watch me as I came, and though quiet, the release left me shaking. Adrian withdrew and placed his fingers into his mouth before he kissed me deeply.

"Are you all right?" he asked.

"Yes," I whispered, and then we laughed together.

It was a beautiful moment, a brief second in our lives that felt simple and easy compared to what we faced outside this room—a life that would not wait.

Adrian helped me stand. "I will leave you to finish getting ready," he said. "Today we have court."

I could only imagine what stories we would hear. It was the first court since Ravena's attack, since the aufhockers' behavior had changed, and I was filled with an acute sense of dread.

NINE
Isolde

It did not take me long to restore my appearance. **I** smoothed my skirt and pushed my hair over my shoulder, hoping that it would help cool my heated skin, which was covered in a fine layer of sweat. I was slightly jealous of how quickly Adrian had pulled himself together.

I was still eager to speak with Ana and had time before court. I retrieved my daggers, fitting them to my wrists beneath my sleeves, and left my room in search of her, finding her in a smaller room down the hall from the sanctuary where the remaining wounded had been moved to finish healing. The room itself was long and narrow, more like a wide hall, with patients lined up in a row on cots.

When I walked in, Ana was rewrapping a leg wound.

"My queen," she said when she saw me, smiling softly.

"M-my queen!" The patient, an older man, seemed

to panic at my presence. He tried to push himself up onto his elbows, but I stopped him.

"Do not trouble yourself, please. I expect you to heal, not to bow."

"You are kind, my queen," he said as he started to relax, letting his head fall into his pillow.

"I am hardly kind," I said. It was the last word I would use to describe myself.

"You fought for us," he said. "You fought with us."

I did not know what to say because I felt very differently about how I had fought.

"All done, Petar," Ana said, patting his newly bandaged leg.

"Thank you, Lady Ana," he said as she rose to her feet. "Thank you."

Ana met my gaze as she came around the cot, wiping her hands on her apron. "I did not expect to see you before court."

"I hoped to speak to you first," I said. "If you have time."

"Of course," she said. "Would you like to walk?"

I hesitated. "I think we should find a more private place to speak."

Her brows knitted together, curious, but she did not question me, only followed as I led her to the great room in the library. It was where I did most of my research, and Lothian and Zann seemed happy to entertain my thirst for knowledge.

Once inside, we stood opposite each other and neither of us sat.

"What did you wish to speak about?" Ana asked.

I wonder if she could sense my anxiety and eagerness.

I took a breath. "I had a vision this morning," I said. "From...when I was Yesenia. I saw you, the way you looked two hundred years ago. You knew I was writing *The Book of Dis*. I entrusted you to hide it."

Her brows rose and she blinked, as if she were surprised by what I had told her.

"I...you did ask me to hide the book," she said.

"Did you read it?" I asked.

"Well, no. You had spelled it. It was blank."

"So you tried," I said.

Ana's mouth hardened. "I feel as though I am being accused."

"That's not my intent—"

"What is your intent?"

I sighed, frustrated. "I don't know," I said. "I thought perhaps...I had told you more."

"You never told me why you were writing it, only that it was for you."

We were silent, and I was frustrated that I had no other lead. Why had I been so intent on writing *The Book of Dis*? Of creating a book I had to have known Ravena would eventually steal?

"I feel responsible for this," I said. "For the damage Ravena has done and will do."

"You cannot take on this burden, Isolde."

"I can. I do. I had to have *known*," I said.

As Yesenia, I had been a seer. I had known enough to predict my own death and leave behind a book of spells that could raise the dead.

Ana was shaking her head. "You once told me there were few truths in the world. I cannot pretend to know what you saw in the future, but I know what guided your decisions, and it was truth, Isolde. You should find Adrian. It is time for court."

I found Adrian waiting for me in the great hall. The doors were still closed, and we were alone. He held out his hand when he saw me but frowned.

"Is everything all right?" he asked.

"Of course," I said and smiled, though I could tell by Adrian's expression he did not believe me, so I let my eyes wander to our thrones. I had always assumed they were the same since they were equal in size and dark in color, but now I stared with a far more critical eye. Bones lined the base of his throne, the careful arrangement of ribs looking like intricate woodwork, lacquered in shining black. Longer bones lined the arm supports on either side, and each was topped with a skull.

"You see it now," Adrian said.

"There are two skulls," I said. "If one is Dragos, who is the other?"

Adrian's fingers threaded through mine, and he spoke near my ear.

"His name was Branimir," he said. "He was my commander."

I did not remember him.

"Was he horrible to you?"

When he did not answer, I turned my head toward him. I could feel his breath on my cheek and his hand pressed against my stomach.

"Adrian?"

"No more than anyone else," he said, his voice low, and I took deep and steady breaths as his lips trailed my neck, his hand moving from my stomach to the bodice of my dress.

"We have court," I said, trying to turn toward him, but he held me in place. "Adrian," I said, growing frustrated, and he chuckled against my skin.

"Yes, my queen?"

"Do not pretend you do not know what you are doing."

"I'd rather you explain," he said.

"That you are making me furious?"

He laughed again. "I like your fury," he said, hand lifting to my neck. "Let me taste it."

Just as his lips crashed against mine, someone cleared their throat, though Adrian was in no hurry to stop his assault on my mouth until I pushed against his chest.

Daroc stood at the door that led into Adrian's study. His eyes were fierce, his face like stone. I thought of my conversation with Sorin and wondered if his frustration came from their fight or Adrian's obsession with me.

"We'll open the doors if you are ready, Your Majesties," he said.

"Does it look like we are ready?" Adrian asked, annoyed.

"You cannot have me in the throne room before court, Adrian," I said.

He raised a brow and I knew what he was going to say.

"That is *not* a challenge," I said, stepping away from him and heading for my throne. "We are ready, General."

Daroc nodded and closed the adjoining door.

As I turned to sit, I found Adrian still standing at the base of the dais staring at me.

"Yes?"

"Nothing, my sweet," he said. "I am only imagining

what it will be like when I fuck you on this throne before my court."

I could not help the smile that tugged at my mouth. I straightened my back and crossed one leg over the other. I was not sure how I felt about performing in such a way, though I knew those who attended Adrian's court had no qualms about having sex publicly.

"You would let your court look upon me?"

"Your body? No," he said. "Your pleasure? Yes."

He took the two steps to the dais and sat beside me just as the doors to the great hall opened. Adrian's noblesse entered first and took their places near the dais. I avoided meeting their gazes, especially Razan, whose expression was strangely smug. The guards entered next, stationing themselves around the room, fencing in the large crowd of people who followed. Not everyone fit within the hall, though they tried, cramming into the doorway and spilling into the foyer and beyond, into the cold and snowy courtyard.

They all looked tired and withered, their faces red and raw from the cold.

Adrian gave no signal to begin, and yet a villager came forward anyway. His hair hung at his shoulders and half was pulled back, exposing a wide forehead. He had prominent brows and a mustache that hid his thin lips. He carried a weapon, a bow and arrow slung across his back, and while he wore gloves, they were fingerless, exposing cracked and bloodied knuckles.

"Your name?" Adrian asked, expressing no irritation over his boldness.

"I am Oskar of Scarif, my king," he said, and I could tell by how he spoke, his breaths were shallow. He was working up his courage, and as he began, his voice shook and his eyes watered. "You cannot deny your people have suffered. We have been witness to the corruption of the crimson mist, the horror of the monsters in our woods, and now an illness tormenting our children. My oldest son was stricken first. He died an agonizing death, eyes bleeding, unable to stop screaming, and we were forced to watch. My wife and daughter also fell ill, but it was my youngest son I lost, the same as the first."

He spoke, emphasizing his words with his movements, jabbing his fingers and clenching his fists, and where before he had fueled his speech with grief, it now turned to anger.

A weight settled upon my chest as I listened to the man talk about the deaths of his children, and that dread slowly turned into fear as he continued.

"And I am not the only one. Many in my village have had similar deaths, all children, all sons. We have all met, and we can find no other common link between them."

My first thought was of Ravena and the crimson mist, but I had no certainty in making that connection. This illness could be something much more natural, and to assign magic to it would cause unrest.

Adrian allowed a beat of silence to pass before he spoke. He sounded both serious and emotionless. "Anyone else beyond the bounds of Scarif experience the same?"

"My son, my king," said a woman who raised her hand and stumbled forward.

"Mine, my king, mine!" said another woman.

A quiet murmur erupted in the hall, and it carried into the foyer and the courtyard.

"Silence!" Adrian ordered, and his eyes fell to the woman who had come forward. "You, tell me your story."

"I am Lina from Gal," she said. "My son was young and strong, healthy, but he came down with a fever we could not tame and then the convulsions started. When he died, blood dripped from his eyes and mouth."

"And you?" he asked the next woman.

"I am Mara, my king, also from Gal. She speaks the truth. My son died the very same."

There was silence after that as Adrian considered their words, but the crowd had become uneasy hearing these reports. They shifted on their feet and whispered, growing louder until someone shouted, "It is witchcraft!"

My heart raced, and suddenly this crowd had become the enemy as they raised their voices in fear and agreement.

Adrian stood, his powerful presence silencing the crowd.

"Bring forth the accuser," he said, and a guard pushed a man forward from the throng. He was short and bald, his round body draped in heavy wool, and despite how confidently he had called out his accusation, he looked frightened now.

"What evidence do you have to support your claim?" Adrian asked.

"You cannot deny that Revekka has been under attack. We have seen the crimson mist corrupt our people. Now it feeds our monsters. Is it so difficult to believe that it might also feed this plague?"

"Plague can be spread at will by vampires," I said. "And yet you do not accuse your king. Why witches?"

It was the first time I had spoken, and I felt Adrian's curious gaze on me, but I was angry. This man had already done irreversible damage. He had offered a way for people to rationalize illness, and the more it spread, the more hysteria would rise, and the only explanation any of these people would consider would be witchcraft.

"I would never accuse my king," said the man.

And yet you would accuse your queen, I thought.

"This illness could have been borne of anything."

"I acknowledge that we must consider more than one cause," he said and narrowed his eyes. "But it would seem you wish to rule out magic altogether."

"And you seem inclined to create hysteria."

At that moment, a man stepped out from the crowd. He was tall and broad and wore bronzed armor with a black cloak and gloves. I did not recognize the color combination as any from the Nine Houses, and he was far too regal to be from a Revekkian village.

"You appear eager to speak," Adrian said, directing his attention to the stranger, who took a moment to bow. As he straightened, his gaze darted to me, and it took everything in my power to remain still, not to shiver under his stare. There was something about how he looked at me, as if there were no depth to his eyes, that left me unsettled, and I found myself releasing my blade from its holder, seeking the comfort of its hilt in my hand.

"I believe I might be useful," he answered. His voice was low and deep. If there had been any other noise within the room, I wouldn't have been able to hear him.

"And you are?" Adrian asked.

"I am called Solaris," he said.

"Have you no country?"

"I have no allegiance," he said.

The villagers exchanged looks, seemingly just as confused as I was.

"Then why have you come to Revekka?" Adrian asked.

"To hunt a witch."

Chaotic chatter broke out at his comment, and I rose to my feet, gritting my teeth as I spoke to Adrian.

"End this," I said. "*Now.*"

He looked at me, his eyes passing over my face once before he turned back to the witch-hunter, but he hesitated as he started to speak, eyes narrowing. When I followed his gaze, I saw Noblesse Dracul pushing through the crowd. He was dirty and dressed in black; his clothes were weathered and worn. Something about the way he moved seemed wrong. He was staggering, almost as if he were drunk…but the longer I looked, the more I realized that he did not have dirt on his face.

It was blood.

Then a woman screamed, "His eyes! His eyes are bleeding!"

"It is witchcraft! We have been cursed!"

Panic ensued as those gathered rushed to put distance between themselves and Dracul while Adrian took a step forward, attempting to shield me as the vampire stopped before us.

"Dracul," Adrian said, but whatever he had intended to say was useless, because the noblesse was already dead. He tipped forward and landed hard on the marble floor, a pool of blood blossoming around his head.

A second passed and then Adrian lifted his gaze to Solaris.

"You have my attention," he said.

TEN
Isolde

I had gone horribly numb.

It took everything in my power to remain standing when all I wanted to do was collapse, my legs suddenly too weak to hold me up.

"Silence!" Adrian commanded.

"Allow me," said Solaris. He pulled one glove off, revealing a mummified hand, and turned toward the crowd, palm out.

Everything went quiet and everyone was motionless.

He had frozen all the villagers in the room.

Razan snickered. "What was it you said, Queen Isolde? Only women can possess magic?"

I glared at the noblesse.

"It is not magic exactly," said Solaris. "It is an ability granted to me by the goddess Dis."

"What did you say?" Adrian asked.

"I am no different from you," he said. "You were made to drain the blood of mortals, and I was made to kill witches."

Adrian's eyes narrowed. "Dis is the mother of witches. Why would she create you to hunt them?"

"Some mothers turn on their children," he said. "Especially when they misbehave."

"How do you know you were made by Dis?" I asked.

I hated to ask any question of Solaris, hated to draw his attention, but I wanted to know.

"The same way Lord Adrian knows he was made by Dis."

"I begged to taste the blood of my enemies after they murdered my lover," Adrian said. "Did you?"

"I held the bodies of my wife and child in my arms after Ravena's mist took their lives. I begged Asha to give them life once more. She never answered. Dis did." Solaris paused, his voice trembling. "You took your revenge," he said. "Would you deny mine?"

"I have no desire to form an alliance with a witch-hunter," Adrian said, and as the tension released from my body, I grew light-headed.

"Then make me a noblesse," Solaris said.

Adrian went very still. "Why would I make you a noblesse? You claim no allegiance to any kingdom, least of all mine."

"I will make a vow to you," he said. "And I will help you find Ravena. You cannot deny that I am useful."

Adrian took a step toward Solaris. "If I cut your hand off," he said, the words slipping between his teeth, "what would you have to offer?"

Solaris did not speak, but in the next second, the

great hall was awakened once more, a low murmur returning to life. Solaris's voice rose above it.

"You would deny my aid when I could save your people from this wicked witch?"

Adrian went still, and those gathered in the hall jeered with outrage.

"Our blood will be on your hands!"

"The Blood King will see us all killed!"

"Kneel," Adrian hissed, and the entire court hit their knees. He stepped from the dais, his boots echoing in the hall as he approached Solaris. "Prove yourself, then," Adrian said. "Find the witch. You have five days."

Adrian's words were like a blow to my stomach, and for one horrifying moment, I could not breathe. It was as if my lungs were full of smoke and my throat clogged with ash. I felt the fire against my skin; I could smell my burning flesh and hair.

I could not fathom that he would allow such a man to remain within our kingdom, so near to me—*me*, his lover, his wife, the one who had died at the hand of Dragos, the first witch-hunter.

I fled, leaving him on the dais alone.

I could hardly open the door, I was so frantic to escape. The air in this room was suffocating, too thick with the hate I could already feel brewing beneath the surface.

It will end us again, I thought.

A hand shot out, and I flinched, only to realize it was Miha. She turned the knob for me, and once the door was open, I bolted.

"My queen!" she called after me, but I did not stop, having no issue getting through the second door.

I was only halfway down the hall when Adrian called my name.

"Isolde!" His boots thudded against the floor in pursuit. "Isolde!"

He caught up with me and yanked my arm, forcing me to face him.

I slapped him, hard.

"How dare you," I seethed.

"What would you have me do?" he hissed furiously. He held my shoulders, bending over me. "Did you not see what was happening in that room?"

"You wax poetic about how excruciating it was to watch me burn alive. You begged to be a monster so that you could avenge me. You say you will not live another lifetime without me by your side, and yet you welcomed a witch-hunter into these halls."

I did not even recognize my voice as I spoke, and there was a part of me that knew he had no choice, but I could not handle his reasoning in this moment.

"Will you watch me burn again?"

"You aren't even a witch!" he yelled, his body shaking. "You have no power beyond driving me to the fucking edge of insanity."

I tried to hit him again, but he held me too tight, so I did the only thing I could to escape him—stab him in the heart. I shoved my hands against his chest and released my blade. The second it pierced his skin, he let me go, and I watched his blood darken the fabric of his tunic.

"Fuck you," I said.

This time when I left, he did not follow.

I raced upstairs and slammed my door shut. I could not contain my anger, so I let it rage. Books and candles flew, and I tore tapestries off the wall and my blankets from my bed. I threw jewelry and ripped my dresses from the shelves of my armoire. I was so careless in my frenzy, I froze in horror as my carved music box fell to the floor.

"No, no, no," I said, kneeling to pick it up. As I did, pieces of mother of pearl and wood chips were left on the ground, and the music it once played—a lullaby my mother had sung—sounded off-key and ruined.

"No," I cried harder, hugging the box to my chest.

This had been a gift from my father, and while that relationship had withered away, this—this gave me some connection to my mother, and I had destroyed it.

I wallowed in my sadness upon the floor, clutching my music box, and did not move until I heard a faint and muffled laugh.

It was light and pretty, and it only fed my fury.

Ravena.

I crossed the room and turned my mirror around, only to see my own reflection staring back, and it took the fight out of me. I rested the mirror against the wall and slid to my floor. There, I drew my legs to my chest, hugging them tightly, and sobbed.

I did not even look up when my door opened, or when Ana knelt beside me and drew me into her arms.

"Shh," she soothed, smoothing her hand over my hair.

"I hate him," I said. "I hate him, and I love him."

"Let's not speak of it now," she said.

So I didn't.

Instead, I cried until I couldn't shed tears any longer,

and by the time I sat up, my face was swollen and a little painful.

Ana reached forward, brushing away the strands of my hair that stuck to my tear-stained face.

"I am so tired," I said. "And I know that is not fair because you have lived this life longer than me...but I can't—" My voice faltered.

"You do not have to have lived a hundred years or even twenty. If your soul is tired, you will be tired."

A few stray tears fell down my cheeks.

"He has invited a witch-hunter into our home," I said.

I almost could not stand how Ana looked at me, as if she pitied my heartbreak.

"I know how you feel," she said. "I am afraid, too, but I also know why Adrian allowed Solaris to stay."

I rubbed my eyes harder, to the point that they hurt. I did not want to hear reason. I knew the reason, and I despised that it had to be this way.

"If he does not quell the hysteria...we are in even more danger," she said.

"I am in no danger," I said, swallowing hard. "As your cousin so graciously reminded me earlier, I have no magic."

"Do you really believe that?"

"I know what it is to have magic, Ana," I said.

She shook her head. "You are equating harnessing magic with having it. They are not the same."

We stared at each other and after a moment, I asked, "What are we going to do?"

"For now, you had better summon Violeta," she said. "Adrian has called for a feast."

"What?"

"While he conceded to allowing Solaris to stay, he

wishes to remind Revekka there is a price to pay for treason, so we are celebrating Gesalac's execution."

I was not so surprised given Solaris's arrival and Dracul's death—Dracul, who had been searching Cordova for Julian, along with his men. It would not go unnoticed that the traitor was still missing, and where were the rest of Dracul's men?

I could not help wondering if Julian might be responsible for Dracul's death somehow—but then, how did that explain how the villagers had died?

It made more sense that whatever this...*blood plague* was, it was somehow communicable.

"I know you are angry with Adrian," Ana said. "And you have every right to be, but I think you should attend tonight's festivities."

"I have every intention of going."

I had to go because I had made a scene running from court. Attending tonight would at least assure our kingdom that nothing could come between us.

Ana left to prepare for the evening, and I summoned Violeta and Vesna. Both gasped when they entered my room.

"My lady! What happened?"

"I have a temper," I said, unashamed.

Violeta walked farther into the room and started to pick up dresses from the floor. "We can clean while you are at dinner," she said.

"Do not bother," I said. "You should both enjoy tonight."

"What if you need us?" Vesna asked.

"I likely will only require help undressing, a task my husband is more than capable of."

Though I doubted he would be undressing me tonight.

Vesna blushed, and Violeta pressed her lips together to hide her smile, then cleared her throat. "What would you like to wear for the celebration?"

She continued to pick up dresses from my floor—full ones with lots of tulle and embellishments—but I wanted none of that.

"This one," I said, picking one from the pile.

Violeta's eyes widened. "My lady, I'm not so certain—"

"My husband will love it," I said.

She did not try to deter me, and I slipped into the gown, which fell over my skin like liquid gold. The neckline exposed the soft skin between my breasts while the two slits that ran down the front of the skirt bared my legs. The only embellishment was a cord-like belt that wrapped around my waist.

Violeta and I gathered up the jewelry I had thrown across the room, and I chose pieces as I went—gold earrings, a bracelet, and a delicate tiara. When we were finished, I sent my ladies-in-waiting to prepare for the evening.

No sooner had the door closed than a knock came. When I answered, I expected Adrian but found Ana instead.

My feelings were conflicted, as there was a part of me that wanted him to come to me. I also wanted to know that he was stewing over my rage. Ana must have sensed my disappointment, because she smiled a little.

"I am sorry I am not who you expected," she said. I opened my mouth to reply, but she continued. "I thought we could walk downstairs together."

"Of course," I said, taking her arm.

We made our way down the hall, and even from this distance, we could hear the revelry—loud chatter and laughs, screams and shrieks disturbing the night. The crowd was boisterous and likely reckless. I had no doubt our people would take full advantage of the festivities offered. We were all trying to escape the reality of the last week and the knowledge that tomorrow, when we awoke, we would face it once again.

The foyer was crowded with people. Some were drinking, some were dancing, others were fucking. The doors were open to the courtyard where a fire raged, and the air was full of smells, the strongest of which was the rotting flesh of the impaled bodies at the gate, though no one seemed to mind.

"My queen!" a man shouted. "Everyone, the queen is here!"

And suddenly, the crowd gathered began to chant, "Long live the queen!"

They were all drunk and happy, clearly forgetting my earlier departure from court, as Ana tugged me along into the hall.

It was far warmer here and just as crowded. I could only walk because the chanting from the foyer had carried into this room, and those gathered created a path for me—straight to Adrian, who sat at his high table. Daroc and Sorin were among those seated to his left while the chairs beside him were empty—one for me and one for Ana.

"Adrian may eat you alive," Ana commented as we approached.

I held his gaze, which was darkening by the minute.

What had he told me earlier? That he wanted to fuck me before his court?

Adrian stood to take my hand as he escorted me up the steps to my place beside him.

"You look beautiful," he said as we sat, and I did not speak. "Will you be cross with me all evening?"

Instead of responding, I took a sip of wine.

"So we have progressed to the silent treatment?"

Once more, I was quiet, though not speaking to him took far more discipline than I expected. I wanted to look at him and I had things to say, but none of them were for this space.

I thought that perhaps he had given up on getting my attention when he spoke again.

"Will you not eat?" he asked, and the way he posed the question—warm and gentle—I could not help looking at him. He leaned toward me, a plum in hand. The fruit was dark in color—a rich purple that promised sweetness.

Adrian waited, patient, and I took his hand and drew the plum to my lips, holding his gaze until the skin gave way beneath my bite. For a moment, I let myself wonder if this was how it felt when Adrian took my blood. My mouth was instantly flooded with sweet nectar, and as it dripped down my chin. I gathered it with a swipe of my finger.

Adrian snatched my hand and drew my fingers into his mouth, and as he sucked them, heat blasted through my body.

When he released me, he held my gaze and whispered, "Perfect."

This was his way of apologizing—but it was not the one I wanted.

The sound of breaking glass and shouting drew our attention to the crowd where a vampire stumbled back, hands clasped around a piece of shattered glass that was embedded in his arm.

"Bastard!" another vampire cried, another shard of glass in his hand. "How dare you drink from my vassal!"

He vaulted from behind one of the banquet tables and pounced, knocking him to the ground. The crowd cheered as the two men brawled, rolling around on the marble floor.

I looked at Ana.

"Are vassals not shared?" I asked.

"Some are," she replied. "Some aren't. It is a choice as personal as sharing a partner."

"Is the offense punishable by death?"

"Yes." It was Adrian who answered with a frustrated hiss, and he waited until I looked at him to add, "Though I suppose I am just speaking for myself."

The crowd grew louder and more disorderly as more people joined the scuffle. Before it got out of hand, Adrian signaled to the guards, who moved in, separating the two vampires and dragging them from the room. A crowd followed, still encouraging the fight, and in the relative quiet that followed, someone yelled, "Music!"

A cheery tune began and enough space was made on the floor for people to dance.

"Am I considered a vassal?" I asked, looking at Adrian. It was the first thing I had said to him all evening, and in the grand scheme of everything that occurred, it was meaningless—except that I was mortal, and by definition, a vassal was a mortal a vampire fed from.

Adrian returned my stare. A quiet heat burned behind

his eyes, and I noted how he sat, rigid and wound tight. If he was not attempting some semblance of control tonight, he likely would have held to his promise to fuck me on this table.

But he had no invitation, especially when I was not speaking to him, and so he remained still and answered simply.

"You are the love of my life."

It wasn't an answer to my question, but it was Adrian's answer to everything.

I took another sip of my wine, hoping it would help me relax, but sitting beside Adrian made that impossible.

I was hyperaware of every breath he inhaled, every slight move he made, and while I didn't look directly at him, I saw when his hand snaked out, how his fingers curled around his drink—slender and long, strangely delicate for the monster he was.

They were fingers that gave me pleasure, that had been inside me and coaxed me to come with an uninterrupted grace.

And no matter how many times he made me rage, no matter how many times we fought, attempting to navigate this quick marriage and this deep and intoxicating love, I never wanted us to end.

But this apology, he would have to work for.

I rose from my place at the table, surprised when Adrian reached for me. My eyes fell to where his hand held my forearm, and then I met his stare.

"Where are you going?"

"I am tired," I said.

He said nothing but shifted my hand, pressing a kiss to my knuckles before letting me go. I curtsied and left the dais, but as I navigated the crowd and dancers, I spotted Killian among the revelers, striding toward me. When I smiled at him, he grinned.

"Your Majesty," he said, bowing.

"Killian," I said. "I am glad to see you."

"I never thought you'd say those words again."

There was nothing hopeful within his eyes as he said it, and it seemed he finally understood I would never be his.

"Have you come to dance?" I asked.

He laughed, glancing at the crowd. "Only if you are offering," he said. "Though I understand if you wish to retire."

Despite our differences, there was a part of me that felt so comforted by Killian's presence. He reminded me of home, the good part, and he was fiercely protective, which was something I admired when it applied to the people of Revekka, whom he had effortlessly and selflessly adopted.

"One dance," I said.

He smiled and held out his gloved hand. We moved into the processional, choosing a place in line opposite each other. I laughed as I faced Killian, who looked out of place in his black uniform as he bounced on his feet and clapped to the lively music. We skipped to the center of the line to change places, linking our arms as we went.

"Please tell me you are having fun, Killian!"

"Of course," he answered, amusement sparkling in his eyes before we broke apart.

The song went on, an unending tempo that made sweat bead across my skin, and for a moment, I thought of nothing beyond the fun of this dance, something I had not felt in a very long time. Then a set of hands clamped down on my waist, and I was drawn back against a hard body. Fingers tightened on my jaw and my head jerked back as Adrian's mouth slammed against mine.

He was angry with me, though I did not know if it was because I had been avoiding him or because I had danced with Killian—perhaps both. I could feel it in his kiss, the way his tongue entered my mouth, viciously tasting me until I could not breathe, the way he held my face, hard, almost painfully. I pushed against him, and as he released me, his teeth bit into my lip. I stumbled back from his embrace, touching my fingers to my mouth. They came away with blood.

The sight of it shocked me, and when I looked at Adrian, I saw it shocked him too.

"Isolde," Adrian said, taking a step toward me, but I recoiled.

I did not think he could look any more devastated, and for the second time today, I ran from him.

ELEVEN
Adrian

I watched her go. The jealousy that had torn through me was extinguished at the sight of her blood, which I had no intention of drawing, and I felt none of the usual euphoria that came with tasting her, only shame.

My eyes shifted to Killian, the man who had been the recipient of her happiness tonight.

"You hurt her," he said, his mouth twisting in disgust.

And my response was no better. I was looking for a fight—a way to channel this deep and burning rage—

"She is mine—to hurt, to bleed, to fuck."

Though I had no wish to hurt her, no wish to be the source of her tears.

I hated that I was.

Killian's jaw only tightened. I knew he wanted to hit me. I could hear how he cursed me, but he did not move to strike. He left, a better man than I.

I felt Daroc approach.

"What do you want?" I snapped.

"I came to make sure you didn't kill the mortal," he said. "Your wife isn't the only one who is fond of him. The people of Cel Ceredi also have a soft spot for him after he aided them."

I glared at Daroc, but I was also grateful. I would have regretted any anger I took out on the man. I already regretted the words I'd spoken.

"She will hate me for this," I said. We still stood amid the crowd, though they kept their distance and no longer stared, uninterested in the interactions between a king and his general.

"For this?" Daroc asked. "You have done much worse."

I scowled. "I do not need your commentary."

"Then how about some advice?"

"Are you someone who should be offering it?"

His jaw tightened. "Never mind. Your wife is right to hate you."

Despite the dismissiveness of his comment, Daroc did not leave my side. After a moment of silence, he spoke. "I…did not mean that," he said and paused. "Isolde is seeking stability and familiarity because her world falls apart no matter the direction she turns. Today, during court, I saw her looking to you for safety because that is what she does—only, you did not save her. You pushed her into the fire again."

I wanted to say so many things.

I know what I did to make her angry. What else was I supposed to do?

Fuck.

But as I thought about Daroc's words, I knew what

he was trying to say—Isolde did not trust me to keep her safe.

And why should she?

I had not been able to save her all those years ago.

She feared history repeating itself.

"I must go to my wife," I said, but before I left, I met Daroc's gaze.

"Before dawn breaks, bring my sword."

Then, I went in search of Isolde.

It was not hard to find her. She never came to my bed when she was angry with me, but as I made my way to her floor, I found Killian leaving her chamber. I stayed in the shadows until he passed, frustration heating my blood, then I entered her room. She sat at her vanity, brushing out her hair.

She did not even look at me.

"Did you have a nice chat with your commander?" I asked.

"*Do not*," she said, turning toward me.

"What?" I goaded. "I saw him leave your room."

"He came to see if I was all right."

"Which warranted an invitation into your room?"

"Are you going to accuse me of fucking him?"

We sat in our anger for a moment, and there was something about how she looked at me that completely took my fight. I could not hold on to it now that I was alone with her.

"I know you are not fucking him," I said, quiet.

She turned in her chair, staring up at me, with her lip—bloodied, bruised.

Carefully, I clasped her chin. "I did not mean this," I said, whispering.

She swallowed, staring up at me, breathtaking. "I know," she said.

I leaned forward, hesitant, but when she did not move away, I kissed her—softer than I ever had—drawing my tongue over her wound. Even as it healed beneath my touch, guilt gnawed at my gut.

How would I ever apologize enough?

I felt that I had committed so many wrongs against her in just the last few days, I would never make up for them. I had failed to be compassionate when she had shifted for the first time; I had dismissed her worries and connection to her mother's homeland; and I had not been able to control my court long enough to prevent her harm.

I prayed for her, I begged for her—and yet, I could not take care of her.

I pulled back, running my thumb along her jaw, and we stared at one another. I could not place this look in her eyes, and her thoughts were more like static—a strange, unfocused tangle. She looked away and then stood, stepping around me to climb into her bed.

I turned to face her but did not follow.

She rested on her side, facing me.

"You hurt me today, more than you ever have before," she said.

I swallowed hard. She did not need to say it. I knew. I would never forget the way she looked at me in the hall or how hard she slapped me.

"I understand why you did it," she continued, her voice shaking and her eyes glistening. My heart and lungs felt like chaos, crushed and uncomfortable. I never wanted to be the reason for her tears again, and yet somehow, I knew I would be. "But in that moment, all I could hear were the screams of my sisters as they burned alive. All I could smell was their burning flesh. All I could feel were the flames licking my feet. And it isn't as if I don't already think of it all the time—relive it all the time—but suddenly, this nightmare that followed me into this life became a possibility as soon as Solaris spoke, and you stood there so stoic and cold and pretended that you had not watched me die because of people like him."

I clenched my jaw so hard, it ached. "You think I did not relive it while he stood before me?"

"This is not about you," she said, and her voice shook as she sat up. "You have never been hunted. Even now, you are hated, but no one can touch you because of your power. And then you callously reminded me that I have no magic."

I wanted to beg for forgiveness at her feet.

"Sometimes I fear you will not value me as much as you valued her," Isolde said.

That comment surprised me, and I felt a rush of anger that she would even say those words aloud. She had never expressed insecurity over this before, and it frustrated me that she would now.

"I value *you*," I said. "It is not as if you are two different people."

"But we are," she said. "You cannot refuse to see it just because you wish Yesenia had never died."

"How often must I assure you of your role as my queen?" I asked tightly.

"As often as I require," she snapped, and there was a flush to her cheeks that made me think she was either embarrassed or angry—perhaps both. "You know why I feel this way."

"I am not your father."

"Words do not heal trauma," she said.

"Then tell me how I heal this."

"You don't. You love me through the fear, even when my doubt hurts, and I will do the same for you."

There was a beat of silence, and I rose to sit beside her on the bed.

"I have loved you across lifetimes. Why would I stop now?"

She studied me with those beautiful dark eyes. I did not think she knew how deep they really went—how far I could see into her soul, how certain I was we were meant to be together.

"I am tired, Adrian," she whispered. "I am tired of fighting."

"Then let us not fight," I said.

She didn't speak, but after a moment, she rose onto her knees and drew her nightgown over her head. A rush of heat went straight to the head of my cock, instantly hardening as she exposed her gloriously naked body. I sat and admired her. She was perfect—her breasts were heavy, her figure full, and the warm light in the room made her brown skin glow.

I shifted onto my knees too, matching her pose, and kissed her, hands skimming along her waist to her breasts. I held them in my hands, moving away from her lips to take each one into my mouth, running my tongue over each nipple before sucking them into hard points while Isolde's fingers tangled in my hair.

I released her and kissed up her chest, her neck, her jaw, my mouth hovering over hers as I spoke.

"Let me make love to you," I said. "Let me worship you."

Her response was to undress me. She shoved my overcoat off and lifted my tunic, rising so she could pull it over my head. I stood to take off my trousers, and they were hardly off my feet before her warm hand came around my cock.

I inhaled through my teeth, hands going to her shoulders as I knelt on the bed. She allowed space for me but did not release me. I stayed on my knees as she wordlessly lowered her head, her mouth closing over the crown of my cock. I could not suppress a groan at the warmth of her mouth or the pressure of her tongue. She felt good and the blood rushing to my cock made me throb—not just where her mouth was but all over my body. I took her hair into my hands and held it so I could watch her work. She looked up at me, and I could not really describe the awe of this—of the attention she lavished on me and the way she looked at me while she did it. I had no power here. She held it all and she used it well as she kissed down my shaft, pressed her face into my balls, worked her hand up and down and over the crown. I could not help moving my hips, wanting to be consumed by her heat. As much as I wanted to thrust into her mouth, I grit my teeth against the need, trying to draw out the way she had decided to take me.

I only pulled her away when I felt the dizzying signs of my impending release.

She looked up at me, her lips still wet from sucking me, and I covered her mouth with mine, shifting her onto her back. I let my full weight rest on her. I took my time kissing her, enjoying the feel of her body against mine—how her breasts felt pillowy against my chest, how her hips moved, seeking friction, and the wet heat radiating against my lower stomach, teasing my cock as it lay between her legs.

She took a breath and spoke, quiet, as I trailed kisses along her jaw. "Is this how it will always be?"

"What do you mean?" I asked.

She pressed her head into her pillow, allowing me access to her neck.

"We always fight and fuck."

"This is not fucking," I said.

There was humor in her breathless voice. "They are the same for you, my love."

Her use of that endearment halted me in my exploration of her skin, and I met her gaze.

"What?" she asked.

"You have not called me that in a very long time," I said.

She had not called me that since the night she died.

Do not fight, my love. You are destined for this world.

I let my fingers drift across her cheek as I recalled that haunting and horrific night once again. I had never understood Yesenia's power, not even as she foretold my destiny, and I would not come to understand it for some time, but she had seen her death and my rise to power.

"Tell me," she whispered.

"When you died, you did not beg, you did not scream, and you did not speak curses into the world. You just accepted the end. I was so angry with you, and it would take years to forgive you, to realize what you had done—what you had *seen*."

I continued to caress her cheek.

"I grieve that I did not realize it sooner, that I spent

so much time feeling such resentment when I could have continued to worship your memory."

I had never admitted this aloud. I had barely let myself acknowledge that I'd had such feelings. They were what made me feel like a monster, what made me feel like I had betrayed her.

But if she felt that way, she did not say. She was quiet and took my face into her hands, pulling me to her.

Our lips crashed together, and once again she was the focus of my world.

I began my slow descent down her body, kissing every part of her—each dip and curve, each dimple and scar. As I moved along, letting my lips linger, my tongue taste, her body responded, tensing with anticipation and easing with relief. She made my cock pulse; she made my mouth water, and I was eager to taste her heat, knowing she would be warm and wet.

I pushed her legs apart even farther and took her swollen clit into my mouth, sucking and licking. Her breath caught in her throat, and she arched her back, pressing her hips into the bed, her thighs clenching around me. I dug my fingers into her skin, holding her in place as I licked at her entrance. She was slick and silken, and I suddenly preferred to drown in this.

"Sit on my face," I said, drawing myself up.

We switched places, and I grinned as she straddled me.

"Fuck." I looped my arms around her thighs. "Yes."

I buried my face inside her.

A guttural sound escaped from her mouth, and I watched her as she reached out to steady herself, gripping the headboard. Her breasts bobbed as she began grinding into my mouth.

"Ah, fuck," she inhaled, a hissing breath, and suddenly she did not seem to know what to do with her hands. They moved from the headboard to her breasts, squeezing as she sought desperate relief, and I was eager to give it.

Her moans gave way to keen cries and then her fingers tangled in my hair as her body seized and she stared down at me as she came.

She shifted to lay atop me, breathing hard, body sated and warm and perfect. Then she pressed a kiss to my chest and sat up, straddling my stomach, and my whole body tightened at the thought of being inside her. I thrust my hips, and she shifted down so her slick heat coated my cock.

She laughed and bent, her face hovering over mine. "Do you want to fuck me?"

I craned my neck to kiss her, grinding into her. "Fucking tease."

She straightened and took my hands. Lacing her fingers through mine, she drew them over my head. I liked how her breasts hung so close to my face as she stretched to hold me in place. She spoke near my lips.

"I am not teasing," she said and opened her mouth against mine, but she did not kiss me. Releasing my hands, she reached between her legs and grasped my cock.

I groaned and went to slip my fingers into her, but then she pushed the head of my cock through her heat before sliding down, settling deep until her ass touched my balls. She sat there for a moment, looking down at me, her hands planted on my chest, her breasts pressed together. I reached for them, squeezing as I lifted my hips.

"You are so fucking beautiful."

She laughed but did not speak. She was so dazed, and I loved it, loved that I could give her this high, that she could become so lost in me she could barely think.

She started to move, her heat enveloping my length, her wetness dripping down my balls.

I gripped her hips and helped her move, alternating between letting her grind against me and thrusting into her. At some point, I sat up, mouth colliding with hers as she wrapped her arms around me. I pressed my face into her breasts, taking her nipples into my mouth, sucking them until she gasped, my mind completely lost in the sensation of being inside her. My cock felt so full, my balls so heavy. I wanted to come inside her; I wanted to come on her breasts and in her mouth. I wanted to fill up every part of her.

I shifted her to her back and slipped into her again. We rocked together, hardly breathing, holding each other's gazes.

"I'm going to come," I said. My head was spinning, and my cock was pulsing. I gripped her, pulling her head back, exposing her neck.

"Bite me," she said. "Take my blood and fill me with your come."

I had no control. I bit into her neck, and she came, her muscles clenching around my cock. My release shot through me and I shuddered, allowing a guttural sound to escape my mouth as it filled with her blood. We stayed still, locked together, bodies flushed, drenched in sweat as I took long pulls from her, ceasing only when my cock grew soft inside her.

I kissed her neck and then her mouth, my body

melting into hers. She let me rest my head against her breasts, her hands smoothing my hair.

After a moment, she spoke, voice heavy with sleep.

"What will you do about Solaris?" she asked.

I lifted my head and looked at her.

"I don't like his name in your mouth," I said.

"I don't like his presence in my castle," she countered.

"Should I feel offended that you are thinking about him so soon after our lovemaking?"

"Is your confidence so lacking?"

I chuckled and then kissed her. After a moment, I answered her question. "I will kill him. When the time is right."

"When will that be?"

I stared down at her, sensing her anxiety.

"I won't let him hurt you," I said quietly.

Her eyes were dark. "Adrian," she whispered, shaking her head. "He already has."

Isolde's body cradled against mine, and for a while, I listened to her breathe, but I had one matter to attend to before daylight. I rose from bed, pulled on my clothes, and left her room.

I met Daroc at the bottom of the stairs.

Neither of us spoke; he only lifted my sheathed sword to show he had brought it. Together we headed for the courtyard where my noblesse usually gathered on celebratory evenings, drunk and laughing, amongst them Razan.

"Remember when our king would join us?" one was saying. "Now he fucks his wife and stays in her warm bed."

"You cannot blame him," said another. "She is beautiful."

"Ah, yes, but that mouth," Razan said, pausing to laugh. "If I had my way, I'd fuck her mouth every night, fill it so full of my come, she could barely breathe. Maybe that would keep her silent."

I entered the courtyard, my stride slow and calculated.

Razan's back was to me, and when the other noblesse went silent, he twisted around to look at me.

"King Adrian! Have a drink!"

He rose to his feet to face me, a wooden goblet in hand. When I did not respond, his dark brows lowered over his bloodshot eyes.

"You seem tense," he said. "What's wrong? You need me to teach your wife how to suck your dick?"

I reached for my sword, which Daroc had readied. The blade rang in the night like a bell, clear and cold, silenced only when it met Razan's flesh and bone.

His head hit the ground with a wet thud, rolling until it faced down on the stone ground.

In the dreadful quiet that followed his death, I stared at my blade, slick with his blood, feeling nothing beyond a sense of relief that he was dead.

Then I handed it to Daroc.

"Burn his head. Impale his body," I said and returned to the castle, to Isolde, where I lay beside her and slept.

TWELVE
Isolde

I would have to shift today. The thought made me nervous. The only part I liked about the idea was that I could spend time with Sorin, but before I met him for training, I decided to head to the library, uncertain if I would have the chance to visit later today.

It was early; the sun had not even brightened the horizon, and yet the staff were already busy, carrying armfuls of blackthorn branches, thistle, and baskets of garlic down the hallway, though they paused as I passed to curtsy or bow.

The items they carried were all used to protect against vampires in Lara on the night of Winter's Eve, which was said to be the night when all evil in the world gained control, but of that evil, vampires and vârcolaci, or werewolves, were said to be the most powerful.

"Are we preparing for Winter's Eve?" I asked, halting a maid as she walked by.

"Yes, my queen," she said with a smile. She seemed excited. "Do you recognize the holiday?"

"I do… Forgive me, but are we celebrating?" I asked.

I could not imagine. This night was the quietest in Lara. No one was allowed outside once nightfall came, and villagers kept their homes as bright as possible, fearing every creak or howl that disturbed the darkness outside.

We had truly believed in evil, and I never managed to sleep during Winter's Eve, though that may have been because Nadia insisted on staying in my room to recite protection prayers.

"I suppose you could call it a celebration," the maid said. "But I would call it more of a ritual."

"Why a ritual?"

"Well, if you are older, you believe this night gives rise to darker things," she said. "My grandmother says if we appease those things, our winter will not be so harsh."

"And what do you think?" I asked because the maid was young.

"I think it is all a fable," she said. "But we will use any excuse to have a bit of fun, especially during these times."

I was not surprised by the difference in views or that Lara and Revekka celebrated Winter's Eve so differently. Given that Adrian had ruled as king here for almost two hundred years, they had very little reason to fear the strength of vampires or vârcolaci.

I sent the maid on her way and continued to the library's great room, where the evidence of much of my research remained in haphazard stacks.

Only a week ago I had been trying to piece together a history via the journals of Revekkian villagers who had described the raw and unfiltered horror of Dragos's witch hunts. Now, I hunted for any mention of High Coven—my sisters, our magic, and spells.

"Do you have any books on illness?" I asked when Lothian and Zann entered the great room, each carrying a stack of books. They were so heavy, they had to bend back to hold them, and I feared they both might snap in two. They placed the books upon the table with a loud thud.

"Quite a few," said Zann. "What are you looking for?"

"At court the other day, several villagers said their men and boys had come down with a type of illness..." I began.

"Yes, we heard," Zann said. "A blood plague, we think."

"You already know?" I asked, surprised.

"We suspect," Lothian clarified. "We think the crimson mist is responsible, that it somehow morphed into a plague."

It was as I feared.

"We would have to experiment to be certain," Zann added.

"Experiment?"

"Well, we would need to bury the body of a person who died from the supposed blood plague. If they reanimate with the same characteristics as those who were infected by the crimson mist, then we can be certain of our theory."

I frowned. As much as I wished to confirm the truth, that was not a safe option.

"Of course, if we possessed other spell books, we might learn the truth and even find a way to banish it."

“But those were all destroyed during the Burning,” I said.

“Hmm.” Zann did not sound convinced.

“What?” I asked.

“There were rumors for a long time after the Burning that Dragos was collecting spell books, that he maintained a secret library somewhere here in the castle.”

“And you believe that?”

It was hard to accept that Adrian would not have found it by now.

“Do *you* really believe a king let that kind of power slip through his fingers?” Zann asked.

I supposed I didn’t.

I watched Solaris wandering through the snow-covered gardens. I did not like that he felt such ease within my home. He was an intruder, a man with no allegiance or home, and he was corrupting the one place I felt the most comfort.

“Well, aren’t we sullen this morning?”

Sorin approached, a lopsided smile on his full lips. He sidled up beside me, peering out the window. He was quiet once he spotted the witch-hunter.

“Do you believe he was created by Dis?” I asked.

“I think Dis grants powers as she pleases,” Sorin said. “We are nothing to her but pawns…even Adrian.”

Sorin glanced at me as he spoke, and I wondered if he was trying to gauge my reaction.

“Adrian conquers for himself,” I said.

“Perhaps he does now,” said Sorin. “But what happens when his goals no longer align with Dis’s?”

I lowered my brows. "What are you saying, Sorin?"

He shrugged. "Adrian bears the mark of Dis. You have seen it, the white ring around his eyes. He executes her will, even if he claims it is his own. It was the agreement he made when he asked that you be resurrected."

I did not know what to say or how to process this information, but I could feel Sorin's anxiety over it.

"He would never tell you this," Sorin said. "It is probably safer that you pretend you do not know."

"Is there a way to free him?"

"Do you not think he has tried?" He paused. "I think in some way...he hoped you would know."

His words made me feel guilty for not knowing how to help him.

"Are you angry?" Sorin asked, his voice quiet.

"I did not need another reminder that I have no value beyond the magic I once had."

"That is not true, Isolde. If anything, with your new ability, you will be the only one who can protect us when Adrian loses his fight with Dis."

Dread pooled low in my stomach. I did not like how he said it—as if it were an unavoidable truth.

"We should get to training," he said, and we walked together down the hall. "Do you think Dis likes dogs?"

"Sorin," I warned.

He chuckled and started to walk a little faster. "Maybe she would be more inclined to keep you around."

I tried to push him, but he took off at a run, cackling. I chased after him down the carpeted halls of the castle. The dread and doubt Sorin's words had inspired melted away as I ran after him.

"It was a simple question!" he said.

I ran harder and finally caught up with him, managing to jump onto his back. Unprepared for my weight, he stumbled forward and fell. I rolled off him onto my back, and he followed. We lay on the floor, staring up at the ceiling, laughing, and for a moment, I felt happy and unburdened.

"This is cozy," said a voice, and I looked up to find Adrian smirking. He stood beside Daroc, who did not appear to find any humor in the situation, and it was under his gaze that Sorin ceased to laugh. I felt his anxiety descend as he got to his feet.

"Let me help you," he said, holding out his hand, and I accepted.

"We were just on our way to train," I said.

"Obviously," Adrian said, an amused curve to his lips. "If it involves rolling around on the floor with you, perhaps I should join."

I pressed my lips together and glanced at Sorin. He was staring at the floor rather than Daroc, who seemed desperate to get his attention and frustrated that he couldn't.

"We'll leave you to train," Adrian said, and he stepped forward, pressing a kiss to the corner of my mouth. "I'll take you on the floor later."

As they passed, Daroc glanced at Sorin, but he still did not look at Daroc. As they disappeared around the corner, I started to ask Sorin about the interaction, but he stopped me.

"We should start," he said. "We'll run out of time."

He walked ahead of me, and I hurried to catch up with him.

"Sorin," I said. "Who knows about my ability?"

I was both curious and worried. I did not imagine Adrian would tell very many people, but since Sorin knew, I assumed Daroc also knew.

"Very few, I think," he replied. "This isn't something you want getting out until you have some control over the change."

It was going to be hard enough when it eventually became common knowledge. Not only could I shift into a creature that had killed a number of my people…there were a fair number who had been bitten just like me and given no chance at survival.

Sorin led me into a large, open room. The floor was stone, the walls brick, and there was a stretch of open windows high above my head. It was cold, even though a fire raged within the hearth.

"Since we must use discretion, we'll train in here," he said.

"What is this place usually used for?"

"Fencing, mostly," he said.

I was a little surprised and laughed. "I cannot imagine you following the rules."

"I never said I participated," he replied and faced me.

I knew it was time to begin, and I realized I had dreaded this moment because I did not want to be what I was. I did not want to face it.

"How did you shift the first time?" Sorin asked.

I paused, uncertain if I should be truthful. I still remember how I had woken up, desperate to fuck and so hot. "I…was having sex with Adrian."

"Huh," he said, an amused look in his eyes. "Have you tried that again?"

"You know, Sorin, turning into a dog is usually the furthest thing from my mind when I am fucking."

"It was only a question," he said. "Everyone has different sexual tastes. I am not here to judge."

I glared. "I will stab you. I have no qualms."

"No one knows that better than Isac," he said, and then he sighed. "I suppose we will have to do this the hard way."

I started to ask him what he meant by the hard way when he attacked.

I had not spent much time watching Sorin fight, but he was fast and nimble. I barely saw the flash of his sword as he brought it down on me, and all I could do was block it with the daggers I kept strapped to my wrists. They were a laughable weapon compared to his, but I managed to cross them and stop his blade.

"What do you think you are doing?" I seethed.

"What does it look like?" he asked.

He unlocked his blade, and I barely had time to escape, dropping to the ground to avoid his blow. I freed the hilt of my blade from its brace and swung, but Sorin jumped back. The distance allowed me to rise to my feet. I weighed my options quickly, wondering if it would be worth throwing my dagger, but I did not trust I would hit my mark with his speed.

"You have more than one strategy for defense," Sorin said. "Use it."

"An animal cannot hold a weapon," I said.

"You do not need to hold one," he said. "You are one."

"You cannot tell me you fight as a falcon," I said.

Sorin smirked. "I won't tell you then."

He lifted his blade as if it were a spear and threw it.

Once again, I found myself ducking as it zoomed over my head. It landed with a thud, the hilt vibrating, in the wooden mantle of the fireplace, and before I could rise to my feet to go after the blade, Sorin had shifted and flown upward, toward the high ceilings, and was now diving for me at a speed that made him nothing more than a blur in the air.

I bolted, but even as I ran, I felt his sharp talons in my hair. I covered my head with my hands.

"Sorin!" I screamed.

His answering call was a command—*do something!* But I felt no pull to shift, no indication that there was any other part of me than my human self.

Fear would not tear this creature from me.

Something stung my hand, and I knew Sorin's talons had cut me. Then he flew ahead of me, shifting as he reached for his sword, and by the time I was able to come to a stop before him, the tip of his blade was pointed square at my face.

I glared at him.

"You are a horrible trainer," I said, letting my hands fall from my head. I examined the wound he had made. It was a long and deep cut.

Sorin inhaled. "Adrian will not be pleased with me."

"I'll convince him not to cut you up if you promise to never do that again."

Though I was not as angry as I wanted to be. There was a part of me that appreciated facing Sorin and watching how he fought.

He frowned. "I truly am sorry, Isolde."

I sighed. "I suppose I cannot be frightened into shifting."

"No, but apparently you can be aroused into it."

I rolled my eyes. "Not funny."

Sorin sheathed his blade. "You have to admit, it is amusing."

I folded my arms over my chest. "How did you learn to shift?"

"I was thrown off a cliff," he said.

My eyes widened. "What?"

"It was early in my change," he said. "When Adrian was attempting to gain control over our population and numbers. Daroc and I were taken by surprise and captured by a few rogue vampires. They knew Daroc was important to Adrian and sought to torture him by throwing me off a cliff. I guess fear brought out my nature."

In moments like this, I realized just how much I did not know about Sorin or Daroc or even Adrian. They had lived so many lives since I had died.

"Can I ask..." I paused. "You don't seem happy... with Daroc."

His smile was sad. "That is not a question."

"I should not have said anything. I'm sorry."

"I am happy with Daroc," he said.

"Except that earlier, he seemed to steal your laughter," I said.

"That is not really fair to say."

"Then what is?"

Sorin was quiet for a moment. "I only worry that I am not good enough for him, that perhaps he now wishes for someone who is just as disciplined as him and the only reason he does not say it is because he knows he gave me this life."

"I do not believe that," I said.

"It is the only explanation I have for why he looks at Adrian the way he does."

"Does that…make you jealous?" I asked, wondering if we could finish our conversation from earlier.

"No," he said. "Maybe because I know nothing will ever happen. Daroc knows that too."

I wondered now if part of Daroc's coldness toward me was his anger that I had returned.

"Sorin," I said, quiet. "Are you still in love with Daroc?"

His eyes widened and he answered quickly, "Of course."

"I did not ask if you loved him. I asked if you were in love with him."

He was quiet and he swallowed hard, his eyes turning red.

"Whatever the answer, I just want you to be happy," I said.

He laughed bitterly. "No, you don't."

I flinched. "Sorin—"

"We're out of time," he said, dragging his sleeve over his eyes. "Have a good day, my queen."

He bowed and left.

I stood for a few moments in the quiet cold, stunned, regretting that I had said anything at all.

THIRTEEN
Isolde

I left the training room, stopping briefly to see if Ana was in her makeshift infirmary. The room itself was quiet, now only occupied with three patients, including Petar. Unlike the other two, he was awake, his injured leg resting on top of his blankets, propped up high with pillows. When he saw me, he straightened.

"My queen," he said, bowing his head. "It is good to see you again."

"Good afternoon, Petar," I said, smiling. "Are you feeling well?"

"Very well, my queen," he said, though I noticed he seemed hot. There was a thin sheen of sweat covering his face.

"You are certain?" I said. "You look…a little pale."

But pale wasn't the word. He looked…*green.*

"It is nothing, my queen. Only pain. Lady Ana

replaced my bandages. You just missed her if she is who you were looking for."

"And what if I came to check on you, Petar?" I asked with a small smile.

"I am not worthy of the honor," he replied.

"Of course you are," I said. "You fought to protect your people. There is nothing more honorable."

"That is kind of you to say," he said, bowing his head again.

That was the second time he had called me kind.

This time, I did not disagree.

I retrieved a strip of cloth from Ana's supplies and left the small infirmary. As I bandaged my hand, I glanced up and peeked into the old sanctuary, only to find Ana standing over Isla's body. She had drawn her shroud down, exposing her face to the grim light. I wondered how long she would let her lover rot in this dark cavern, but even I could not bring myself to ask when she might let her go. I had no right. I had not lost Adrian.

Ana's head shot up as I entered, and she dropped her hands from atop Isla's body. My face grew hot with shame—I should have never interrupted her. I hesitated a step and then spoke.

"I'm sorry. I should not—" I stopped talking abruptly and turned to leave.

"No, it's okay," Ana called, though her voice trembled. "I have been here too long."

I relented, facing her again. She had covered Isla once more and came around the stone altar, dressed in black. Her eyes blazed, rimmed red from her tears.

I took a step closer to her and spoke in a hushed tone. The weight in this room demanded it.

"Nothing is too long when it is goodbye."

She offered a slight smile and we walked together to the opposite end of the sanctuary, putting distance between us and Isla's corpse.

Though we had learned with Ciro that vampires who were consumed by the mist stayed dead, I could not help feeling unsettled so near a corpse. I had seen too many reanimate and rise, only to cause complete chaos.

"Did you need me?" Ana asked.

Our steps slowed until we came to a stop, and I studied her, wishing I could give her time to grieve before approaching this, but things had escalated too quickly, especially after court. I felt as though we had no time, but before I could speak, Ana's eyes fell to the hand I had crudely bandaged.

"What happened?"

"Nothing," I said. "Just…a small cut."

"That does not look small, Isolde."

The bandage was already soaked through with blood.

"Adrian can heal it," I said.

She did not look pleased with my response, but relented. After a moment, I took a breath.

"I hoped to ask you about your magic."

I did not think Ana could grow paler, but what little redness had colored her cheeks vanished. She could not be that surprised by my question—she had to know that I would ask her eventually.

"I would not call that magic," said Ana.

"What would you call it?" I countered.

Ana was silent, so I tried another line of questioning.

"Does Adrian know you practice?"

"He knows I study spells," she said, as if to correct me.

"You do more than study," I said, narrowing my eyes. "You speak them aloud."

It was one thing to read spells, another to provoke magic, and it came with its own set of consequences, even from those who were gifted. My eyes drifted to Ana's long hair, which was nearly white, leeched of color. Before I would not have thought twice about it, but Adrian's bite had opened a well within my mind from which I drew on Yesenia's knowledge.

"You lost the color in your hair after you cast a spell, didn't you?"

I thought of the Ana I had seen in Yesenia's memories, whose hair had been blond like Adrian's.

"That was not magic," she said. "It was men."

I stared, uncertain of what she meant, uncertain of what to say.

"Why are you bringing this up now?" Ana asked.

"We have to stop Ravena, Ana," I said. We had to stop her before the mist got worse, before the blood plague took the lives of more men and boys, before a witch-hunter created a killing frenzy...before Ravena managed to use my bones and those of my coven for her spells. "We need your magic."

"Isolde," she said. "I am not near powerful enough."

"Then we will make you. Adrian cannot battle magic," I said, nodding to Isla's corpse. It was a hateful reminder, and it made Ana even paler. "So we must."

She was silent.

"Do you intend to tell Adrian?" she asked, her voice quiet.

I narrowed my eyes, confused by her anxiety. Adrian was her blood, but even more than that, he'd always defended witchcraft. "Are you afraid of him?" I asked.

"I am not afraid," she said, and a strange hardness darkened her eyes as she spoke. "But I do not wish to be a weapon."

Internally, I flinched at her words, though I knew what she meant and why she said them. As Yesenia, I had been used in that way—as a weapon to criminalize witchcraft, to strike fear in the hearts of the whole of Cordova. I had been used to lift Dragos to the status of hero, and for that, not only had I died, but so had the whole of my coven—and thousands more.

And despite all the signs, I had still wished for peace. I had begged for understanding. I had believed that if only I could teach, they would see, but in the face of a vicious man, it had killed me.

I knew the truth of this world, and the only way to survive as a woman with power was to use it.

"Then become your own weapon," I said.

"If it were that easy, then I would," she said and paused. "Come with me. I have something to show you."

I expected Ana to lead me out of the sanctuary, but instead, she returned to the alter and slipped behind it. I followed, though the space was narrow, and watched as she pushed open a door.

I was not very surprised that something like this existed within the Red Palace. It was Ana who had shown me several secret passages throughout the castle.

"Come, I want you to go first."

"Where is it I am going?" I asked as I approached.

"You will see," she said, standing aside so I could enter the dark passageway. "Wait."

I did as she instructed, watching as she reached for something just inside the doorway—a torch, which she lit using the candles outside the entrance.

"Take this," she said, handing it to me, and then she closed the door, and the only light was what I held. Despite the warmth of the fire, the passage was cold. I could feel the frozen air seeping through my dress in spite of its thickness.

"I will be behind you," she said, and I started forward.

The tunnel curved to the left and then descended into a spiral staircase. I took each narrow step slowly, feeling the dust move beneath my feet. I kept one hand on the wall, which was also gritty and rough. The turn of the stairs eventually led into a room. Without the support of the stone wall, I felt as if I were floating, and it was dizzying. I exhaled slowly and deliberately as I continued down, inhaling the unmistakable smell of old books. It was a scent that clogged the air, making it thick with dust.

I held the torch aloft as I made it to solid ground and took in the room. It was a small, round library with shelves of books, and what did not fit was stacked on the ground or on the desk, which was large and crowded with papers and candles that had burned down to nothing but a pile of weeping wax.

"Are these spell books?" I asked, and when Ana did not reply, I turned to face her.

My hand trembled, a deep part of me overcome with a myriad of emotions I could not quite place. There was a side of me that felt almost joyful and a side of me that felt tortured by the symbolism of these books—one for each witch who had died.

"They are," she said and took the torch from me, using it to light others around the room before securing it within its own holder. When she was finished, she returned her attention to me. I tried to swallow past the thickness in my throat.

"Zann was right," I whispered.

The familiar feeling of shock ricocheted through me, but it was quickly replaced by anger. I curled my fists and turned to look at the many and varied volumes. Some were leather bound and some were stitched; some were rolled parchment. These were the spell books of powerful covens and the personal spell books of free witches, and they were all connected by their horrific and systematic murders.

"Ravena must not know," I said.

"I do not think she was as valuable to Dragos as you," said Ana.

"I was valuable enough to die."

"You were valuable enough to start a witch hunt," she said. "And that gave him power for years after your death."

I had yet to process how I had been used by Dragos, but the thought brought Ana's words to mind.

I do not wish to be a weapon, she'd said.

I understood what she meant, and yet *I* still wanted to be a weapon.

I touched the spines of the books with the tips of my fingers. Their energy was varied—some light and airy, others dark and heavy. I wanted to hold each one close to my heart. I wanted to mourn each one as they deserved, but neither of those things brought justice.

None of them allowed for vengeance.

"Does Adrian know about this?" I asked.

I turned to watch her reaction, but her expression remained stern.

"I…never told him," she admitted.

"Is it because you feared he would use you?"

"He would," she said. "Without question."

I frowned. I wanted to argue with her, but instead, I said, "I will not keep secrets."

She nodded, and while she seemed sad, she also seemed resigned.

"I suppose you will have to tell him if we are going to learn spells," she said, and my heart rose into my throat. It was strange to feel emotional about the thought of speaking a language, but this one was etched in my soul, and in truth, I never thought I would again. "I have been thinking about what you said, and perhaps we can find a counterspell for the crimson mist. It would be a first step toward what we really need."

"What do we really need?" I asked.

"To summon Ravena," she said. "And bind her magic."

FOURTEEN
Isolde

Leaving the small library felt like coming out of a cave, and when I emerged from its darkness, I felt changed in a way I could not really explain. I had stood among tomes that had belonged to witches who had existed before me, witches who had crafted their realities with words and intentions. I felt overwhelmed that so much potential was at our fingertips and deeply worried that I would not be capable of harnessing any of it—at least not in the way I'd been able to as Yesenia.

I just hoped Ana would be powerful enough to cast the spell.

I went in search of Adrian. Despite telling Ana I would keep no secrets from him, I thought of how she had worried that he might use her and found myself wondering if she was right to be afraid, given Dis's connection to Adrian.

Just how much influence did the goddess have over him?

The fact that I did not know made my stomach turn.

I headed for the garden. The castle bustled with activity as the servants prepared for tonight's Winter's Eve celebration. Blackthorn branches were draped over the threshold of the entrance to the great hall and the Red Palace, and thistle hung in the windows. As I left the courtyard, a fire blazed, smelling strongly of garlic.

I found Adrian in the snow-covered garden, at the edge of the pool where he usually stood and watched his fish swim. He had laughed when I called them his pets, but he visited them often, especially on days he sought peace. Except today, they did not seem to bring him the same comfort, because he stood with his hands fisted at his sides.

"Is everything…" I started to ask, but then my eyes fell to the pool where his fish were floating, bellies exposed and bloated.

They were all dead.

"What happened?" I asked.

"If only I knew," he said, not looking at me, jaw clenched. "If I had to guess, I would say someone poisoned the water."

Poisoned?

"You think this was intentional?" I asked, hoping instead that he was wrong and it was only a tragic, natural occurrence. But as I studied the fish, I doubted my idealist rationalization. They were all discolored, their gills bled, and red streaks ran down the soft parts of their bellies. There was a strange odor too, something acrid and sharp.

My thoughts at first went to my poisoner, who remained unidentified, but I had to admit that killing Adrian's fish seemed almost insignificant in comparison. This was something that only served to hurt Adrian, a fact I found appalling, though very targeted, and I wondered whom he had angered.

I reached for his hand, which was curled into a fist even at my touch, and kissed his white knuckles. He did not look at me, but his shoulders dropped and his hands flexed as the tension fell away from his body.

"We can bury them," I whispered, still holding his hand, still watching his face.

His jaw popped at my comment, but he said nothing. I knelt and began to dig into the snow and the earth, uncaring that it was cold or that the frozen dirt tore at my nails as I raked across it, trying frantically to break the ground.

I did not stop until Adrian knelt before me and took my bandaged hand into his.

"What is this?" he asked.

"It's nothing," I said. There were far worse things happening right now.

I tried to tug my hand away, but he did not let go. Instead, he pulled my poorly wrapped bandage from my hand, exposing the cut I had sustained during Sorin's training.

It was bleeding again, likely from my attempts at grave digging.

"Did this come from Sorin?" he asked. Finally his sharp gaze cut to mine, and I was frustrated that he chose this moment to look at me.

"You insisted he train me," I said.

"I asked him to train you to *shift*," Adrian said.

"He was."

"With a blade?"

"If you do not like his methods, perhaps *you* should train me," I said. "It seems right considering the only time I've managed to shift was with you."

Adrian raised a brow, a glimmer of amusement in his gaze, and while it irritated me that it was at my expense, I was glad to see it.

"That can be arranged," he said, the humor quickly fading from his eyes, and with it, my heart sank. "I do not like to see you hurt."

"Nor I you," I said.

He offered a small smile, but his expression had gone dark, distant. I wanted to call him back to me, but I did not know how. Still, he held my gaze as he ran his tongue over my wound, and my fingers tightened around his hand as it tingled, healing from the inside out.

When it was done, he brushed his lips against my knuckles but did not release my hand, though I tried to free myself and return to digging.

"Adrian—"

"It's all right," he said, but it wasn't. Someone had destroyed something Adrian loved, and it felt deeply personal. And yet as if he did not wish me to know how much it affected him, he added, "There will be other fish."

I frowned at him and he raised a finger, smoothing my frustrated brows.

"There is only one you," he said and helped me to my feet. "Come with me. I want to take you somewhere."

I was wary. This seemed too spontaneous.

"Where, exactly?"

"Let it be a surprise."

I hesitated, not because I did not wish to go with him but because I was anxious at the thought of leaving Cel Ceredi with everything that had happened since Ravena's attack.

"We will not be gone long," he said and hooked his arm around me, drawing me close, his hand tangling in my hair. "Please, Isolde. I want to see you happy."

My brows lowered, confused by his words. "I am happy with you."

He studied me for a moment, and I watched his lips as he strung his explanation together. "I have never seen you smile at me the way you did with Killian last night in the great hall."

I could not imagine that was true, but I felt as though he believed what he was saying, which made me sad. Did I scowl at him so much he forgot when I smiled?

"I want to be the reason for that smile," he said. "Let me try today."

I did not know what to say because I wanted to say so much.

"Just say yes," he whispered, reading my thoughts, and with his lips so close to mine, my resistance unraveled, and I relented. "Fine. Surprise me."

He kissed me, and when he drew away, he held on to my hand, leading me to the stables. It was a large stone building with a thatched roof, located on the other side of the castle grounds, a place I rarely ventured. It hummed with activity, having several grooms who ran about cleaning, feeding, and exercising horses.

Adrian had only to appear, and one of the working

men ran to retrieve Shadow. The massive steed snorted when he saw us, trotting beside its handler, who passed the reins to Adrian.

"Will you ride with me?" he asked, running his hand over the horse's shining coat. "Shadow would be very pleased."

I arched my brow. "Are you giving me a choice?"

"You always have a choice," he said. "Though I'd rather you ride with me."

"For my safety?" I asked, though I was already preparing to mount, one foot in the stirrup. The corner of his mouth lifted and his eyes glinted, and it seemed like he was not so far away now.

"There is no question," he said. Once I was settled, he followed behind me, adjusting the reins in his hands, and as he did, he spoke near my ear. "But today, selfishly, I wish to keep you close."

"It is not selfish," I said, and he kissed my cheek, lips lingering. Warmth seeped beneath my skin, to the very bottom of my stomach.

We rode out through the front gates of the Red Palace and into Cel Ceredi before heading east, descending into a snowy valley. Behind us, the Starless Forest loomed, a constant reminder of the horror Revekka had faced over the last two hundred years. It contrasted starkly with what lay before us—snowy valleys and misty evergreen forests. Several trails of smoke billowed in the distance, all marking villages and isolated cottages throughout the valley.

I realized I had not seen much of Adrian's kingdom beyond the path we had taken to get here, and I was eager to see more, despite the dangers we faced.

"Gal is nearby," he said, pointing northeast. I

recognized the name from court when two women had come forward to speak about their sons' deaths. "Cosvina is straight ahead." He pointed to a group of smoke trails nestled below in a valley. "And farther east is Cel Cera."

Ana's lover, Isla, was from there, and it was where she had been when the village was attacked by the crimson mist. I wondered how the people had fared since. There had been very few survivors.

"Your noblesse are responsible for various territories across Revekka?" I asked.

"They are," Adrian confirmed.

"What about the territories who have lost theirs?"

"The other noblesse split responsibility…until I can find suitable replacements."

"And you only choose people who are…*useful*?"

He chuckled. "Do you have an opinion, Sparrow?"

"Perhaps if you did not seek *use* but *loyalty*, we would not be in the situation we are now."

"Gesalac and Julian were once loyal," he said, and there was a bitter note in his voice that made me think Adrian was far more affected by their betrayal than he chose to show. I wondered what had shifted their loyalty and if it had begun before I arrived, because sometimes, I felt like the catalyst.

"Killian would be a great noblesse," I said.

"I am not in disagreement," Adrian said. "But would he turn?"

"Why do your noblesse have to be vampires?"

"I'd prefer they not die so quickly."

"He hasn't yet," I said, though the thought of Killian dying terrified me.

Adrian's arm tightened around me, as if he sensed

my sudden fear. I did not know if Killian would consider turning into a vampire or remaining in this land of red sun permanently. I was not even certain his perception of vampires had really changed. He helped the people of Cel Ceredi because I was his queen and because they were mortals.

"I killed Razan," Adrian said abruptly.

I went rigid against him. I wanted to look at him, to read his face as he admitted to murder, but another part of me was afraid of what I might see.

"Why?" I asked carefully, though I knew tension had been building between them since we had discussed Ravena at the council after her attack.

"He could not be silent," Adrian said.

We were quiet as we moved beyond the valley where the snow was not as deep. The landscape sloped down into a field that was split at the center by an emerald-green river that fed into a cluster of evergreens.

"It is beautiful," I said, breathless.

"Shall we race?" he asked, a note of excitement in his voice.

"Yes," I said and leaned forward, grasping tufts of Shadow's hair while Adrian took the reins into both hands. We started at a trot, and as we moved into a steady gallop, the ride almost felt like flying. Adrian's body tightened around mine, and the wind roared in my ears.

I smiled and laughed more than I had in a long time.

When Adrian slowed, I turned to look at him. He was grinning, a wide and beautiful smile I rarely saw, and then he kissed me, deep and long and hard.

He pulled away, leaving me breathless, and dismounted. I followed and he took my hand and led me into the trees, leaving Shadow to graze in the field. The snow here only peppered the ground, and the evergreens were so thick, it was hard to see what lay beyond the tree line, but the farther we walked, the more I noticed light—and not the muted tones of the red sky but true golden light.

I halted for a step, feeling an unexpected thickness gather in my throat, and then took off running, bursting through the thick line of trees into sunlight.

It was bright and brought tears to my eyes, but I closed them and turned my head toward the sky as warmth bathed my skin despite the cold. Then I began to twirl, spinning until I was laughing and dizzy. I was not sure how long I stood there beneath this sky, the one that had belonged to me as a princess and not a queen, but I soon sought Adrian, who waited in the shadows, leaning against the trunk of a tree, arms crossed over his chest, watching.

I had always thought he was beautiful, even when he was my conqueror.

Now, I loved him, and he was somehow more stunning.

I ran to him and jumped into his arms, his mouth closing over mine as he unclasped my cloak and his before laying them on the ground.

When he returned to me, our mouths collided in a feverish kiss as we knelt to the ground.

I guided Adrian's overcoat from his shoulders and ran my hands beneath his tunic, palms smoothing over his warm, hard stomach.

He shivered. "Your hands are cold."

I smiled. "I need them warm for what I want to do."

He raised a brow. "What exactly do you want to do?"

I rose higher onto my knees, my gaze level with his as I answered. "Suck your cock."

Adrian grinned and pulled me close.

"That mouth, Sparrow," he said, and his tongue parted my lips, twining with my own.

His hands pressed into my body as he ground into me, his arousal pressing hard against my stomach. With my hands warmed, I stroked him up and down as we kissed, smoothing beads of come over the crown of his cock until his fingers dug into my skin as he held me.

"You should sit back," I said as I pulled away. He did as I asked, resting his back against the tree. He gathered my hair into his hand as I bent to take him into my mouth. He was warm, and the come that had gathered at the tip of his cock was salty. I liked the way his breath hitched as I worked him with my hand and my tongue, the sting of my scalp as his fingers tightened in my hair, the bulge of his muscles as he dug his heels into the ground.

"Fuck," he groaned, his fingers pressing into my neck. He held me in place for a few seconds with his cock fully in my mouth before pulling me up and kissing me.

"I want to be inside you," he said.

I shifted forward, straddling him and sinking down onto his cock, my knees digging into the hard earth despite our thick cloaks.

"Do you like this?" I asked.

He laughed, hands on my breasts, squeezing every time I thrust my hips.

"Sparrow, I love this."

"Then tell me how it feels to be inside me."

"Warm." He paused, lost in his own pleasure. "Wet."

I laughed. "You are not very creative."

"Hmm," he said and let his hands fall to my hips. I was not certain if he was agreeing or if he could not form words. "You wouldn't be either if you were about to explode."

We grew quiet except for our ragged breaths, and I focused on the warmth spreading throughout my body, radiating from where we were joined. I widened my knees and Adrian's hand slipped under my skirt, using this thumb to slide over my clit. My muscles tensed and I held my breath, trying to prolong this feeling and let it build until I was light-headed and unable to contain it. I let my head fall back, my orgasm tearing through me as I came. I was left feeling drained, my body shaking as I collapsed against Adrian. He held me tight, one hand gripping my neck, the other on my ass as he thrust into me a few more times, groaning as he came.

We lay there for some time, uncaring that it was cold or that the ground was hard. I stared at the field where the sun still shone, turning tall blades of grass into golden wheat.

"I forgot how blue the sky was," I said. "I did not think that would ever happen."

Adrian's hands stilled, ceasing to run through my hair. "I am sorry."

I lifted my head and stared at him so he could see my expression as I answered. "I am not."

We rose to our feet and I walked to the edge of the tree line, right where the red sky faded into blue. Adrian came close, his chest flush with my back. One hand went around my waist and the fingers of his other laced through mine.

"What happens if you stay in the sunlight?" I asked.

"I burn," he said, and he lifted our entwined hands into the sunlight. I watched them, his pale skin contrasting brightly with my own. It took a few minutes, but soon blisters appeared on his skin, and those quickly burst, turning into red sores, and sizzled. My hand shook as he held it, and I jerked it from the light.

"Stop!"

I turned toward him, examining his arm, but it was already healed.

His laugh was breathless as he guided my eyes to his, tilting my head with his fingers.

"Do you worry for me, my sweet?" he asked.

"What a ridiculous question," I said.

This time his laugh was deeper, and he bent to kiss me gently before we returned to Shadow on the other side of the tree line. When we emerged, we found his black stallion quite a distance away, and when Adrian called to him, he snorted, pawing at the ground with his hoof.

"What is he doing?" I asked, glancing at Adrian.

His expression told me everything I needed to know—something was wrong. There was a part of me that did not want to know what Shadow had found. I wanted to live in the blissful moment we had created a little while longer, but we found ourselves moving toward the horse, who seemed even more unsettled the closer we came.

Then I noticed the acrid and unmistakable smell of death and my dread grew. Had we found what remained of Dracul's men?

Adrian reached for the reins, attempting to calm

Shadow, and my breath caught in my throat as I saw what lay at his feet. There was a ring where the grass was flattened beneath the mangled corpse of an owl.

Its feathers had once been white, but now they were flecked with blood, most of it dripping from its wide, round eyes.

I took a step back.

"What is that?" I asked.

I looked at Adrian. His eyes had gone dark, and his jaw popped as he clenched his teeth.

After a moment, he answered. "The correct question is who," he said, and then met my gaze. "Her name was Ivka."

FIFTEEN
Isolde

Adrian removed his cloak and gathered Ivka's remains. We did not speak on our return to the Red Palace, and anxiety tumbled around in my chest. I felt guilty that I was so afraid of carrying an owl home even though she was one of our own, but it was like bringing death to our kingdom, and I agonized over the consequences.

I had not considered asking Adrian what kind of shifter he had sent to scout my homeland, but if I had known, I would have refused to send her, too afraid of what might become of her—or even my people—on the mission.

I hung my head, heavy with guilt. No matter what kind of animal, Ivka was still one of Adrian's soldiers. She was one of our people, and I knew that not even my fear of owls explained why she had died.

Adrian was quiet when we arrived, and he waited for me to dismount before he spoke.

"I must take Ivka to her brother," he said.

I swallowed hard, nodding. "Of course. When will you return?"

"Sundown, likely," he said. "Before the festivities begin."

We stared at one another for a moment.

"I'm sorry," I said. "I did not mean for this to happen."

"I know," he replied quietly. "I do not blame you. It was my choice to send her."

But it was my insistence that had pushed him.

Adrian mounted his horse again, and as he took up his reins, he said, "This is not a night to venture beyond the gates. Stay within the castle walls."

Then he left, spurring Shadow down the hillside, disappearing from view, and I closed my eyes and spoke words into the air that I hoped were more of a spell than a prayer that he would be safe.

I found myself wandering into the kitchens, a place I had never been. Like many rooms in the castle, this one was cavernous. The doors, windows, and ceiling were all rounded, and a large iron chandelier hung over two long tables positioned before a great hearth that raged with fire. A man stood at one table, kneading loaves of bread. Violeta and Vesna sat at the other, along with Killian, who was the first to notice I had arrived.

He stood quickly.

"Isol—my queen," he stammered.

My ladies-in-waiting also stood and bowed, and the cook, who was a large, older man, whirled, face glistening with sweat as he clumsily bowed.

"My queen!" he said and began wringing hands. "I hope you have been pleased with your meals. Is everything to your liking?"

"Yes, thank you," I said and smiled. "What is your name?"

This time, he offered an exaggerated bow. "I am called Cyril."

I smiled at him, and then my gaze shifted to the table where Killian, Violeta, and Vesna sat, noticing a variety of strange supplies spread out before them—sticks, paper, twine, and berries.

"What are you making?" I asked.

"Lanterns," said Violeta. "To scare away the demons!"

Her tone changed, and I could tell she was joking. I admired the fact that she did not seem to fear Winter's Eve the way I had for so many years.

"May I join you?"

There was a part of me that did not wish to stay because I did not want to interrupt their fun. I recognized that my presence was not the most comforting, even to those who worked for me or knew me well. Still, I did not wish to be alone to worry over Adrian.

"Of course!" Violeta said.

After I was settled, Killian sat beside me and returned to his project.

"It appears your lantern has melted," I said.

"That's because he doesn't listen to instructions," said Violeta.

"Or you are really bad at giving them," Killian countered, smirking. I found it amusing that he was making lanterns. I had expected to find him training or in Cel Ceredi busying himself with errands.

"That is rude, Commander Killian," Violeta said, feigning offense.

"I quite agree," I said.

"You are not allowed to take sides until you try to follow her instructions," said Killian.

"Fine," I said and took up a set of sticks. "Instruct, Violeta."

She did, happily, using the sticks and twine to create a frame to which she glued a thin sheet of paper that she had dyed with colorful berries. When she was finished, she placed it over a lit candle on the table, demonstrating how it glowed.

"That seems easy enough," I said, glancing at Killian.

He stuck out his chin. "Let's see it then."

I took that as a challenge and started work on my own lantern.

"Why are you making so many?" I asked.

"We're taking them into Cel Ceredi to give them to the villagers to place in their windows tonight," said Vesna.

"I do not understand why you cannot just use candles," Killian said.

Violeta rolled her eyes. "Candles are hardly as decorative."

"Winter's Eve is not about celebration," he said. "It is about surviving the night."

She laughed. "Tonight is no different than any other. We have only given it a name."

"You are wrong," he said, his playfulness gone, and Violeta looked stricken by the sudden change.

"In Lara, this night is feared," I explained quickly, glaring at Killian. "We do very similar things—hang the blackthorn and the thistle. We even burn garlic and candles all night, but it is for survival, not celebration."

"What are you afraid of?" Vesna asked.

"Demons," I said.

After that, the jovial and carefree conversation was replaced by a grim silence. It weighed on me and gave way to thoughts I'd hoped to keep at a distance, at least until Adrian returned safe, but now I thought of Ivka and Dracul and his men we had yet to find. I thought of the mortals, all men and boys, who had died with bleeding eyes. There was no pattern to the plague, just as there had been no pattern to the crimson mist, which made me think that Lothian and Zann were right, and perhaps it had morphed into this deadly disease.

"Not bad," said Killian, drawing me from my thoughts. I had stopped working on my lantern, and I knew he had noticed. I was glad for his comment because it brought me back to myself.

"Superior work, my queen," said Violeta.

"You don't have to lie," said Killian.

"You are only jealous," I said.

"Yes, Commander," said Violeta. "And jealousy is not attractive."

When we were finished, Violeta and Vesna began to gather the lanterns by a string, which they had tied to the top of each one as they prepared to take them into Cel Ceredi.

"Lovely work," said Cyril, giving a toothy grin.

"And you, Cyril," I said, admiring the perfect ovals of dough he had formed on two large pans. "I cannot wait to taste."

"You shall have the first bite, my queen."

I smiled, though his comment made me shudder, and I hated that a discussion about bread made me think of aufhocker teeth sinking into my skin.

"Will you come with us to Cel Ceredi, my queen?" Violeta asked.

I hesitated, recalling Adrian's warning about staying within the castle walls.

"It is almost nightfall," Killian said, looking uncertain.

"Then we should hurry," said Violeta, undeterred. "Before the ghosts come out!"

"There are far more monstrous creatures to worry about, Violeta," I said, and her cheeks reddened at my mild reprimand. "Killian is right. We can go, but we must return to the castle before full dark."

With the lanterns gathered, we descended into Cel Ceredi.

Killian and I walked together while Violeta and Vesna moved ahead of us, arm in arm. Now and then, a burst of laughter bubbled from the lips of one or the other.

"Any word from Gavriel on Lara?" Killian asked.

"None," I said. "Adrian does not seem to be concerned."

The snow crunched beneath our feet as we walked a few more paces in silence.

"But are you concerned?" he asked.

I considered his question. "I fear I will never be able to return to Lara as their queen."

"What do you mean?"

"I mean that by the time I arrive, they will have turned against me," I explained. "And I will have to be their conqueror."

Killian said nothing, which I knew meant he agreed. There were so many factors that played into my return to Lara—my marriage, the death of my father, even the rumors of Asha's salvation. It was a prime environment for rebellion.

"Perhaps I should return—" Killian began.

"No," I said. I had hated it when Adrian had suggested it and I hated it now. "When we return, we return together."

We said nothing more on the subject as we entered Cel Ceredi proper. Though dusk was settling on the town in a crimson wave, several villagers were out and about, many milling around outside the tavern, drinking from leather tankards or wooden goblets. Their conversation was lively, and I assumed they had gathered to celebrate the eve of winter.

Violeta and Vesna worked their way through the crowd, passing out lanterns and exclaiming, "Happy Winter's Eve!"

I watched from a distance as the two women brought smiles to several worn faces, but I was anxious seeing so many outdoors, and I found myself studying the long shadows cast by the growing dark, wondering what would prey upon us next. I thought I may have found it when my gaze shifted to a hooded man sitting among the villagers, arms crossed over his chest, and while his eyes were hidden in the shadow of his cloak, I was familiar with his cold gaze.

Solaris.

"What is he doing here?" Killian asked, suspicious.

"Commiserating?" I suggested, my voice dripping with sarcasm, though I was not completely joking. I had no doubt this man had come here to gain admiration, and when he had not managed to obtain Adrian's, he sought it from our people.

He had yet to look away from me, and I wondered if he hoped to intimidate me.

"Oh, and our queen made these!" Violeta exclaimed.

A hush settled on the crowd following her announcement, and I could not discern if it was hateful, but I did not waver as I stood before them, waiting to find out, almost afraid. I had sacrificed some part of myself to fight for them against the aufhockers, just as I had done for my people when I married Adrian, and yet no one cared.

But then those who were seated stood and bowed—even Solaris.

"Rise, please," I said, not wishing for them to kneel so long in the snow.

"My queen," said a man as he got to his feet. "I saw you run to us when the aufhockers attacked. I saw you fight. We are all indebted to you."

"It is my obligation," I said. "Not yours."

"Nevertheless, we are grateful," said another.

"A happy Winter's Eve, indeed," said another. "Vesna, sing for us!"

"Yes, sing!" others chanted, and over the noise, Killian leaned toward me.

"It is dark. We should return to the castle."

I had not noticed because Cel Ceredi was so well lit with firelight.

"I would like to hear Vesna sing before we go," I said.

Adrian's warning echoed in my mind, but we would not be out far past dark. Killian did not argue and offered his arm. I took it as we walked closer to the crowd.

"Please, sit, my queen!" A villager hopped up from his chair. Gratefully, I took it, though I was very much aware I was now seated across from Solaris, who nodded at me.

"Your Majesty," he said.

"Witch-hunter," I replied.

I did not like giving him my back. I did not trust that, even in a crowd, he was safe. Yet I did not wish for him to know how uncomfortable he made me, and I very much wanted to watch Vesna as she sang.

"Enjoying your evening, Master Solaris?" Killian asked.

Silently, I thanked him. It was his way of telling me he was watching.

Vesna began to sing, her voice pure and icy, quieting the crowd. I closed my eyes and listened, letting her words caress my skin, coaxing chills, making me shiver deep in my bones. As she reached the climax of her song, I heard the unmistakable sound of galloping hooves.

I opened my eyes and stood, moving to the edge of the crowd. Vesna had ceased to sing, and the villagers were distracted as Adrian came into view atop Shadow, slowing to a trot and then halting altogether.

"My queen," he said, and while he did not speak the words aloud, I knew what he asked with his eyes. *What did I say about being outside past nightfall?*

"My king," I said. "We were just listening to Vesna sing. Will you join us?"

Adrian studied me for a moment, the corner of his mouth lifting. Then he dismounted and came to me, placing his hands on either side of my face as he kissed me.

When he drew away, we turned toward the crowd. They had all knelt.

"Rise," Adrian said. "Vesna, please, continue."

Her voice rose once more, and a shiver trailed down my spine, but this time, it had nothing to do with her singing. Adrian leaned in, his breath hot on my ear as he spoke.

"I shall very much enjoy teaching you how to obey me later," he said, his tongue teasing the shell of my ear.

"You may try all you like," I replied.

He was blatant in his affection, dropping his mouth to the crook of my neck, where he kissed and nipped at my skin.

"Adrian." I whispered his name fiercely. It was more a reprimand than encouragement, but a dreadful scream tore us apart.

SIXTEEN
Isolde

The sound sent my heart racing, and I looked toward Killian as he rose to his feet and came to my side. Violeta and Vesna also huddled close. Half the crowd was distressed, voices rising in fear. The other half looked on, curious, as we tried to locate the source of the screaming and the reason.

There was another wail, and then someone shouted.

"It's the blood plague! The blood plague has come to Cel Ceredi!"

No longer curious, the crowd began to disperse. Some were frantic to retreat indoors, while others tried to get a closer look at what was happening. Adrian and I pushed through the chaos to find a woman bent over a man who lay on his back in the snow.

"Please! I beg you," she moaned, rocking back and forth. "Someone help me take him to the king!"

"What has happened?" Adrian asked. He stepped

forward despite how hard I held him. If this was the blood plague, we did not know enough about how it spread to take chances.

It had killed two vampires, and yet Adrian still approached.

"My king! My king, please help! My husband is ill!"

Even as she spoke, the man on the ground before her began to convulse and blood leaked from his eyes, nose, and mouth. The woman shrieked, her shaking hands hovering over his body, as if she wanted to touch him but was too afraid.

Then he stopped moving altogether, and I looked on in horror as she began to scream his name. It seemed like the villagers drew nearer too.

"Efram?" she called, distressed and desperate. "Efram? No, please! Please wake up."

She took the hem of her dress and began to dab at the blood on his face. Killian approached, dragging her away from the corpse, and sat, holding her in his arms on the cold ground.

Though I admired his impulse to comfort her, I worried that he may become infected.

"Perhaps I can help," Solaris said, coming forward.

"He's dead," Adrian said. "You're too late."

The witch-hunter offered a cold gaze. "Are you saying I cannot try?"

Adrian did not speak, just gestured to the body.

Solaris knelt, taking the glove off his withered hand and holding it over the body—which took a deep breath.

The crowd who had gathered to watch gasped. I felt both shocked and sick. Adrian looked furious.

The man, Efram, who had died moments ago, began to choke. Solaris helped him roll to his side, and blood sprayed from his mouth onto the snow. Then he began to cough and spit mouthfuls of blood until he could produce nothing but clear saliva.

"Efram!" His wife had freed herself from Killian's grasp and crawled toward her husband while a steady rumble of voices began to rise behind me.

"It is a miracle."

"He is our savior."

"He has been sent by the goddess herself."

I clenched my fists against those words and stared at Adrian. I was not certain, but I thought for a moment that he might strike and murder the man Solaris had resurrected.

"Come, on your feet," said Solaris, rising.

Once they were standing, his wife threw her arms around Efram, but he did not return the hug, nor did he bear any expression, and I thought he seemed more like a revenant than a man returned to life.

If his wife noticed, she did not seem to care, because she turned to Solaris and exclaimed, "You are a god!"

Those nearby began to cheer as the man who had risen from the dead made his way through the streets of Cel Ceredi with Solaris by his side.

"They should be more afraid," I said, but the mist, the aufhockers, and the plague had all made them too desperate for a savior, and they had chosen Solaris the moment he had promised to rid the world of Ravena.

I had no doubt they would regret their decision, but it would be a hard lesson.

"Are you just going to let them go?" I asked, looking

at Adrian, who still stood near where Efram had lain, marked by his blood.

"What would you have me do when the people of Cel Ceredi think he is a god?"

"Exercise your rule as king," I said. "Bring Efram and Solaris to the castle, have them spend the night in the dungeon for observation."

I didn't know if he heard what I said. He seemed so focused on the villagers' retreat, but after a moment, he gave a sharp whistle, summoning Shadow.

"We should head back to the castle," he said.

I did not disagree, though I did so with dread, knowing no good could come from what had transpired here. Resurrection was the only part of necromancy, the magic of speaking with the dead, that High Coven never touched.

It was for the goddesses, we used to say, but I was not so certain it was for anyone. Even the goddesses brought people back wrong. The monsters we lived among were testament enough.

Adrian was in a foul mood.

I sat in bed, worrying over him, watching him.

He was across the room from me, his arm propped on the table, hand covering his mouth, silent. He had been like that since we had returned from Cel Ceredi.

We both knew the consequences of what Solaris had done. Our people would start to look to Solaris for protection and not their king. He had been smart to hide his abilities, to reveal them strategically, though I worried over that too. Who else would Solaris attempt to resurrect before we knew the consequences?

"We should have never let him stay," I said.

Adrian's jaw ticked. "Do you intend to lecture me?"

"It is too late for that, don't you think?"

He slammed his hand down on the table and stood. "Fuck!"

He began to pace, predatory in the way he moved.

"I will have to make him into a noblesse," he said.

I sat up straighter. "Why would you do that?"

"He has left me little choice in the matter," Adrian said. "At least if he is a noblesse, he is seen as part of my circle. If he remains separate, he is a threat."

"I thought we agreed that you would not take on noblesse based only on their usefulness."

"*We* agreed to nothing," he said. "You gave your opinion."

"Which you clearly did not value enough to consider."

"Value has nothing to do with it," he said. "This is political, Isolde. Solaris has publicly petitioned to become a noblesse, he has already created division, and tonight he illustrated an ability that goes beyond any power I possess. Our people will not understand why I would deny him."

"Your decision to turn him would be rash," I said. "We do not know who Solaris truly is or what he wants. He may claim to have powers granted by Dis, but there are always consequences to resurrecting the dead. If you wait, Solaris will destroy himself."

"And what do we do until then?" he snapped, standing. "Let our people follow like sheep to the slaughter?"

"You have had no problem waiting when it comes to my people," I said. "I suppose it only matters when your reign is being threatened by a man who has more power than you."

Adrian turned toward me fully, and the force of his anger took my breath away.

"You had better hope he is not more powerful than me," he said, and he took deliberate steps toward me, caging me with his hands on the headboard. "Because there is no one else here to protect you."

I tried to slap him, but he gripped my wrists, and I did not think I was imagining the white rim around his eyes flashing bright with malice.

"Not this time, my sweet," he said, and his mouth slammed against mine. His kiss was bruising and rough, and I tore away from him.

"I think you should stop," I said.

His hold on me lessened, but he did not release me and his eyes still had a faint glow. I had not been imagining it.

"You think?" he asked, voice low, body rigid.

"Let. Me. Go," I said through my teeth, and he released me, taking several steps away.

I stood and pulled on my robe, needing distance. I barely glanced at Adrian as I headed to the door, but the silence between us was heavy, and in a word, I could only describe Adrian as devastated.

"Isolde," he said.

I paused, my hand on the door, but did not look at him.

"I'm sorry," he said, and I wondered what was going through his mind and what exactly he was apologizing for—his words or the way he had attempted to work out his anger through me.

I turned my head a little and spoke. I could not see him, but I felt his gaze burning into my back, just as fierce as my turbulent feelings.

"Perhaps you should reflect on why you are always apologizing to me," I said. "*And change.*"

I left our room. Normally at this hour, I would return to my own quarters, but I was too wired, too shaken by what had taken place in Cel Ceredi and Adrian's rage. I decided to return to the secret library Ana had brought me to earlier. On the heels of everything that had occurred since she had taken me there, it seemed even more urgent that we learn how to stop Ravena.

When I arrived, however, Ana was already there.

She sat, bent over the desk piled high with open books and a set of notes. The candles were lit and had waned to almost nothing.

As I came down the stairs, she looked up, dark circles pooling heavily beneath her eyes.

"Have you slept?" I asked.

"A little," she said. "But I think I have found a spell for the mist."

"Show me," I said, approaching the table.

She turned the book toward me and tapped on a page that was beautifully illustrated. Whoever had taken the time to write these spells had also been an artist.

"This spell is for containment," I said. "Should we not look to banish?"

"If we banish it, we risk sending the mist to another plane. If we contain it, at least we know where it is."

"We need a vessel for containment," I said.

"I think one of us should be the vessel," Ana said.

I had never heard her be so sure about anything before.

"Ana—" I began, uncertain.

"You said you were preparing for war. Is the mist not a weapon?"

It was true that it was a weapon, but was it one we wanted to use? I had seen the horror it had created in my villages. Then again, the horror of war was no different, and I would bring it about to many people.

"Which of us will carry it?" I asked.

"You are queen," she said without question. "You should carry it."

I knew why she did not wish to contain such power. She did not want to be used as a weapon, but I did.

"It would be a waste," I said. "I cannot call upon power."

I had not even been able to shift since the night I was turned.

"You *can*," Ana said. "You will. You channeled power into your body once. You can do it again."

I sighed, but I could not deny the excitement that rose in my veins at her words.

"What do we need to cast the spell?"

"We need a water source to use as a conduit, and we must cast under the light of the first full moon," she said. "We will also need a third witch."

As Ana spoke, I began to recall some rituals for spells. A really gifted witch might be able to cast this containment spell, but we were learning, and it was best we followed the rules as closely as possible.

"A third witch," I repeated, and my thoughts turned to Violeta, who was the descendant of Evanora, another witch of High Coven. Her greatest skill had been binding magic. I wondered if the gift had passed to my lady's maid. If so and she was willing to help with this spell, then perhaps we would have a better chance at binding Ravena's magic. "I have someone in mind."

To my knowledge, Violeta did not practice magic, but I knew Evanora's death haunted her, and it was that kind of trauma that silenced witches in this age. Perhaps she was too afraid to try.

"Whoever you choose, she must be ready by the full moon, which is in two days," said Ana.

Two days.

That did not give us a lot of time to prepare or even teach but we had to try.

I thought of what had happened earlier, how that woman had screamed as she begged someone to save her dying husband, how she had tried to clean the blood from his face—as if somehow that might help bring him back to life. I hated that he had died, hated more that he had been brought back to life, and I dreaded that we still did not know the consequences of Solaris's actions.

Containing the crimson mist was the first step to countering Ravena's other spells, and I tried to imagine what it would be like if this was successful and we no longer had to worry about one element of her power. Though with *The Book of Dis*, I knew it was inevitable that something far worse would come.

Ana and I continued to plan, discussing where we would cast and why. I had first suggested the grotto, but it was not within view of the moon.

"There is a lake not far from Cel Ceredi," she said. "It does not freeze in the winter because it is supplied by a spring. I think it might work, though it is close to a village."

"Do you worry that we will be interrupted?" I asked.

"I worry that we will be hunted," she said.

It was a valid concern given what had happened during court. We had not been able to quell the hysteria over witchcraft, and Solaris was only making it worse.

Would we face another burning? If so, would I survive it this time?

SEVENTEEN
Isolde

I woke up in my room, though I'd had every intention of returning to Adrian's chambers after I'd left the secret library last night, except that he was gone. I was so unnerved by his absence that I left to check my own room, thinking he had gone there, anticipating my behavior, but he had not been there either.

I worried because it was unlike him. He never ran from my anger, though perhaps he was running from his shame, which, I had to admit, was justified. I understood his frustration, even his anger, and normally, I did not mind the way he wished to work through it. I could handle him, I could fuck hard, but the look in his eyes and the way he had held me even after I had said no—that had scared me.

As a result, my sleep was restless. Frustrated, I rose early and dressed before Violeta and Vesna arrived. The two looked tired and were far more quiet than they had been yesterday, the fun they'd had during Winter's Eve overshadowed by Efram's resurrection. While I hated to see them so subdued, I was relieved that they seemed just as disturbed by Solaris as I did.

"Tea, my queen?" Vesna asked.

My stomach turned at the thought of consuming the bitter drink.

"Why don't you each have a cup?" I suggested instead. Nothing tasted quite right to me still.

They thanked me, and since I was already dressed, we sat together while they sipped tea.

"Were you able to continue celebrating Winter's Eve?" I asked.

"It did not feel so much like a celebration after what happened last night," said Violeta.

There was a pause, and then Vesna spoke.

"Do you think that man is…actually alive?"

"No," I said.

I dreaded thinking of what may happen—what may have already happened. I was sure Efram's wife had realized by now that the resurrected version of her husband was not the same man.

"That man…Solaris," said Violeta. "He seems… cursed."

"How so?" I asked.

"It's as if he traded some part of himself for that hand," she said. "It is the only piece of him that seems to have any magic, though I hesitate to call it such."

I did not disagree, and it was one reason I questioned whether the man was truly a creation of Dis.

We sat in silence after that, each of us lost in our own thoughts, and shortly after, they rose to leave.

“Violeta, a moment?” I asked just as she reached the door.

She paused, her eyes widening, and I sensed she thought she was in trouble. She quickly collected herself and nodded. “Of course, my queen.”

She traded a look with Vesna before she closed the door, remaining near it like she was preparing to bolt.

“Please sit,” I said, directing her to the chair she had occupied before she had risen to leave.

She unclasped her hands, rubbing them against her apron before taking a seat.

“I wanted to ask you a question,” I began, strangely feeling just as nervous as she was acting. “Before I do, I want you to know there will be no consequences whatever you decide. I just want you to be honest.”

“If this is about Commander Killian, I can explain,” she blurted out, as if she could barely contain the words.

I was stunned. “What?”

An awkward silence followed. “Is that not what you wished to speak to me about?” she asked, a faint blush coloring her cheeks.

“It is now,” I said and could not help smiling. Then I added, “That is if you wish to tell.”

She fidgeted, twisting her fingers together over and over.

“It was just one kiss,” she said. “I did not mean for it to happen. It never will again, I promise.”

“I hope that isn’t true,” I said. “Unless, of course, that is what you want.”

Violeta looked surprised. “What?”

“Do you like Killian, Violeta?”

She hesitated and her blush deepened. "He is very kind," she said. "And brave."

My smile felt ridiculously wide and I giggled. "Then you should most definitely kiss him more than once."

"You are not...angry?"

"Why would I be angry?"

"I suppose I just assumed you would be, given that you are...close with Commander Killian."

"Killian is my friend," I said. "He is free to kiss whoever he likes, as are you."

She pressed the palms of her hands to her face. "It happened so fast."

"The kiss?"

"Well, no. The kiss was long." She paused and then hid her face. "We just got there sooner than I expected."

After a moment, she dropped her hands into her lap. I was still smiling at her bashfulness—a feeling I had never known. It was cute to watch, and I liked the idea of Killian and Violeta together.

"Commander Killian is a good man," I said. "He will take care of you...if you wish."

"Thank you, my queen," she said and took a breath. "Um, what did you wish to speak to me about?"

I took a moment, mourning that we had to make this transition, but it was important and urgent.

"Do you remember when you told me Evanora was your ancestor?" I asked.

"Yes," she answered warily, and I saw a hint of her fear—a spark of the trauma we shared deep in her bones.

"Do you have magic, Violeta?" I asked.

"What do you mean?"

"I think if you have to ask, then you likely know," I said. "I need your help."

"I am a servant," she said, and already I felt her building a wall between us.

"Ana and I are going to attempt to contain the crimson mist. It is possible the mist is also responsible for the blood plague. If that is the case, we have the chance to eradicate both," I explained. "But we need a third witch."

Violeta had stopped fidgeting, her hands now clasped tightly in her lap. It seemed this did not make her as nervous as kissing Killian.

"Are you asking me or ordering?"

"I will not order you to help cast," I said. "Your participation must be genuine or the spell will fail."

She was quiet, considering my words, and then she took a breath. "And what about the witch-hunter?"

"You have no need to fear Solaris," I said.

In truth, I no longer believed he was a witch-hunter at all. That was just a ruse to endear himself to Adrian's court.

"Magic will always be dangerous so long as women practice," she said. "No one wants us to be powerful. They taught us that once, and they will teach us again."

Her words filled me with dread and disappointment.

She was saying no.

"I hope you are wrong," was all I could say.

We were quiet, both of us observing the other, then she stood. "High Coven always tried to help people too. It got them killed."

"High Coven became docile," I said. "That is what got them killed."

She did not like my comment. Her nostrils flared as she took in a breath.

"One spell," she said. "I will help you with one spell."

"Thank you, Violeta," I whispered and then cleared my throat. "I will find you later. We do not have long to practice."

She curtsied, and when she left, relief washed over me, so intense, I burst into tears.

Sorin and I were back in the training room, but this time, we sat opposite one another, our legs crossed. I had not seen him since our last session, and I felt the distance between us. I wanted to say something, apologize for getting involved in his relationship with Daroc, but I did not know if he even wanted to approach the topic, so I stayed silent as he instructed me on how to shift into my animal form.

He was describing how it felt for him—how he always felt like his sternum was being cracked and ripped apart, how his ribs seemed to break and puncture his lungs, and just when he thought he couldn't breathe, he was flying—free.

I frowned. "Does it always hurt so bad?"

My body tensed involuntarily at the reminder of how awful it had been. How my bones had seemed to be breaking, rearranging, lengthening. How claws had burst from my fingers and fangs from my mouth. The process was bloody and awful, and the fact that it would continue to be made me dread this even more.

"You get used to it," said Sorin.

"This all seems more like a punishment," I said.

"You can choose to see it as a punishment, or you can choose to see it as a tool," he said. "A weapon."

I might have scoffed had he called it a gift. There was a part of me that was still angry with Adrian for how excited he had acted in the aftermath of my change when I had been so devastated, so frightened.

"I have yet to see the potential in this power," I said.

"You have yet to actually live in the skin," said Sorin. "All you have done is pout as if that can change what you have become."

"Excuse me?"

"I will not use caution with my words," said Sorin. "You will never reach your full potential if you continue to deny who you are."

His words made me feel defensive, and a rush of anger reddened my face. "I know who I am, Sorin. Need I remind you?"

"I am very much aware, Your Majesty," he said, his voice growing cold. "But in this room, you are my student. Do you know how hard it is to watch you mourn this change? To be given the luxury of time to accept it?"

"You act as if I should have expected to become a monster," I said, frustrated. "I never asked for this."

"I did not want to be *this* either," he said, pointing at himself. His voice rose as he spoke. "I did not ask to crave blood or live for an eternity or fight battles for causes I lost sight of long ago, but sometimes we do not get a choice!"

I stared at him in silence. I had always suspected this was how Sorin felt about being a vampire, but he had never confirmed his feelings until now.

"Sorin—"

"Fuck!" he said, letting his head fall into his hands.

I did not speak, did not really know what to say or to ask. When he looked at me again, his eyes were red and watery and he swallowed hard.

"Did you want to do this?" he asked. "To come back to this world?"

"I…don't know that I had a choice," I said, but I had never thought long about it.

Sorin laughed humorlessly. "I didn't either."

"What happened?" I asked, posing the question quietly, afraid that it might scare him away.

He did not answer immediately, running a hand over his short hair. "It wasn't even what happened," he said at last. "It was how."

I waited and finally he spoke.

"I didn't even know he had been changed," he said, and a sob burst from his throat. He closed his eyes and pinched the bridge of his nose.

I shifted onto my knees and held him as he cried. "You do not have to tell me," I said as he shook in my embrace.

"No," he said, taking a deep breath. "You need to understand."

Again I waited, and when he was able to speak, he continued.

"I did not know Daroc had been changed, and when he came to me, he was aroused and he touched me and caressed me and worked me into a frenzy. I liked it, wanted it—*wanted him*. I had not been ready for this before. We had never…" He paused. "It seemed right and then it wasn't. When he bit me, I screamed and pushed him away. He took a chunk of my flesh with him. I ran, naked, into the night, and Daroc chased after me. My screams drew the attention of other villagers. Their intervention cost them their lives."

I held my breath as Sorin described this horror.

"When Daroc caught up with me, I was barely conscious. He sobbed over me, he told me how sorry he was, and…he didn't let me die."

I did not know what to say so I stayed quiet.

"I do not wish to hold it against him. It's just that I will never forget."

"How could you?"

It was trauma, and it had happened when he had least expected, when he had likely been feeling emotions that far exceeded anything he'd ever felt in his life. At least I would have a choice when it came time for me to be changed.

"He hates himself for it, you know?" Sorin said. "And it has informed everything about our relationship. He treats me as someone he is responsible for, not as a lover."

I mourned for him, and Daroc too, though I did not think either would want it. So much about their dynamic and personalities made sense now. Daroc, quiet, stoic, angry, likely blamed himself for everything. Sorin, soft, funny, energetic, was just trying to hide his pain.

"Why do you stay? Why do either of you stay?"

"It is not as if I do not love him," Sorin said.

Silence followed and I struggled to remember how we had even gotten here.

He took a deep breath. "I did not mean to burden you with my problems."

"It is not a burden."

Once again we were quiet, and after a moment, Sorin

looked at me, changing the subject, likely not wishing to entertain any questions about what he had just told me.

"Do you remember how it felt when you first shifted?"

It had started out fine. I had not minded the fever or the desperate sex with Adrian. It was everything after that I hated.

I winced, recalling it. "Painful," I said. "It was… horrible."

"I understand why you would feel dread around shifting, and I cannot promise it won't feel like that again, but until you come to accept who you are now, what you have become, no amount of training will help you." I was surprised when he took my hand. "You are an aufhocker, Isolde, and monster or not, you have the potential to save far more of us in that form. So what do you want?"

Emotionally spent, Sorin and I ended training for the day, and I left with his words heavy on my mind. Of all Sorin's abilities, shifting seemed to give him an element of escape as the trauma of his change into a vampire far outweighed how he'd discovered he could turn into a falcon.

Still, his words filled my veins with an eagerness to truly know the monster I had become. I wandered into the library and found Lothian at the desk.

"My queen," he said and bowed. "Can I help?"

"I need information on aufhockers," I said.

"Of course," he said and came around the desk. "Is there…reason to believe there will be another attack?"

"I think there is always reason to expect another attack," I said, though I could not ignore the guilt twisting my stomach at his question. It was just another reason I needed to learn my potential when shifting.

"The thing that unnerves me about them," he said as we ventured into the stacks, "is that they take on various forms."

"What do you mean?"

"The shape they took to attack Cel Ceredi was just one iteration. They've been known to present as spirits, ailing elders—anything, really, to lure their prey."

I swallowed hard. Did that mean I too possessed that ability?

"I never knew," I said.

"Many do not," he said. "I think their forms have been given other names."

"What is their true form?"

"That is ambiguous," he said, and he stopped, choosing a book from the shelf. He checked the index and then handed it to me. "If I had to guess, I would say their original form was spirit, given that I think they can transform into just about anything."

I took the book, hugging it to my chest.

"Thank you, Lothian."

"Of course, my queen. If you need anything, let me know."

I watched him meander away, down the aisle and out of sight, before I sat on the floor amid the stacks and began reading. The book contained information on many monsters, and the chapter on aufhockers was short but it detailed Lothian's belief that their true form was spirit, which I had assumed was just energy, but according to what was written here, there was a difference.

Energy, it explained, *is something to be harnessed. Spirit, while a form of energy, is sentient. It has influence and can morph on its own*, which was even more unnerving considering how this book detailed their creation. *Aufhockers are believed to have formed from pieces of human souls.* Given that information, I was no longer surprised that they did not seem to have a solid form.

Over time, aufhockers seem to have chosen a primary shape, the most common being a large, black dog—or grim—due to its ability to successfully attack its prey. Once a solitary monster, these creatures can move in packs and act more like the vârcolaci—or werewolves—choosing a leader based on a show of their strength and ability. They avoid villages and tend to attack lone travelers.

At least I had been right about one thing: it was unusual for aufhockers to attack crowds, though that did not seem to be the case any longer.

I closed the book, needing to process the information I had discovered, though I had to admit, I was far more intrigued by my new ability and eager to learn if I could take other forms. If the aufhockers attacked again in their menacing grim-like form, could I challenge their leader for control? Could I lead them into battle?

That was potential. That was power.

I left the library feeling restless and eager to talk about my findings with Adrian, though I had yet to see him today. Usually, I at least caught a glimpse of him turning a corner, and I wondered if he had left the castle entirely. The fact that I did not know for certain put me on edge, but more than that, his avoidance hurt my feelings—and that frustrated me more.

Perhaps he was investigating Ivka's death, I rationalized. Or perhaps he had gone in search of the rest of Dracul's men, whom we all believed to be dead or also stricken with the blood plague.

I found myself in the east wing, walking down the mirrored hall where I killed my father. I did not know why I had come here; perhaps I liked being reminded of the pain because no other hurt compared. Even now, it didn't feel real, and sometimes I pretended it never happened at all, and that my father still resided in Lara. I pretended that he meant every word he ever spoke—*my gem, my treasure, my Issi, you are worth every star in the sky.*

I passed into the tower, and I climbed staircase after staircase, ascending in a dizzying spiral to the top of the roof. Memories from my past threaded together in my mind, and I recalled the first time I'd made this journey with Adrian so long ago as Yesenia.

"There aren't enough stars in your sky," I had said, staring up into the night.

I had wandered into the garden at night and he had followed, as he often did—my shadow, my protector. I was used to utter darkness, to a night where the only light came from the stars above, but here, there was so much light—so much fire.

Adrian looked up, exposing the long column of his neck, and I wanted to know what it would be like to kiss him there and what he would do in response. Would his breath catch? Would he grip me tight? Would he draw my head back to do the same to me?

Before my thoughts could spiral, his gaze returned to me.

"You aren't high enough," he said and then extended his hand. "Come, I'll show you."

I stared at his hand, hesitant. It was a strange thought, but I had never touched him before. I had been too afraid, knowing deep down, I would be lost to him forever after. But how terrible would that truly be? Even if I was to die, at least he would have a piece of me.

I took his hand, and it was warm and rough. I liked the smile he offered before he led me into the shadows of the castle where the servants' entrance was barely visible.

Inside, we were blanketed in darkness.

"Just a moment," Adrian said, and his hand slipped from mine as he stepped away, and for the first time since I met him, I realized how soundlessly he moved.

Without him near, I felt colder, and I wrapped my arms around me tighter.

"Adrian?" I whispered his name because I could not feel him.

I gasped when a hand touched my waist.

"Do you fear the dark?" he asked.

I turned my head, and the stubble on his jaw scratched my cheek.

"No," I said because it was true. "But I prefer the light. Nothing can hide in the light."

"So you fear what lingers in the dark?"

"I suppose," I said.

"Do you fear me?"

"No," I said, too quickly. "Should I?"

"Yes," he said. "But not for the reasons you think."

"And what do I think?"

A light flared and I turned fully to face him. We were

inches apart, and he brushed his fingers along my cheek, leaving a trail of heat that raced down my throat and into my stomach. I took a deep, shuddering breath.

He smiled wryly.

"You fear how I make you feel."

He stepped closer, until there was no space between us and I had to tilt my head back to keep his gaze.

I did not respond to his statement but instead asked, "What do you prefer? The dark or the light?"

"Neither," he said. "Evil basks in it all."

His words sent a trickle of unease through me and I shivered.

Adrian often seemed so carefree. In the few months I had known him, he had approached me with a smile on his face and a light in his eyes, but now and then, I sensed something darker beneath.

"We should go," he said. "You wish to see the stars."

He led me through the corridor and into the castle, and I found myself smiling and giggling as we navigated the halls, avoiding members of the court and servants, as if what we were doing was truly scandalous.

"There are a lot of stairs," Adrian warned when we came to the east tower. "If you get tired…"

"I am not like the women in your court," I said, because it was true. I had grown up in Aroth, where we had worshipped the earth—digging deep into the dirt with our hands to grow our food, hunting and trapping and gathering fruit. To these people, I was wild and untamed.

But when Adrian looked at me, I felt…like myself.

He chuckled quietly. "Noted, sorceress."

I took the steps first, and Adrian followed behind.

He kept pace with me, and I wondered how quickly he would scale them if I was not holding him back.

"Will you not be missed at your post?" I asked. I knew Adrian was part of Dragos's Elite Guard. They had a reputation for ruthlessness, carrying out his most personal orders, including, it was rumored, assassination.

"I do not have a post," he said.

At some point, we stopped climbing and came to a short corridor. Adrian secured his torch in the sconce on the wall before leading me through the door onto the roof of the castle tower.

He had been right.

As I stepped outside, I did not even need to turn my head up to the sky because we were already surrounded by stars. They stretched on for miles in clusters of colors, shining so bright, there hardly seemed to be any darkness in the sky.

Adrian took a few steps forward before he sat and lay on this back, hands behind his head.

"What are you doing?" I asked.

"How else do you stargaze?"

I tried not to smile and lingered on my feet for a few seconds longer before joining him. We were quiet, and while I tried to focus on the sky, it was hard with Adrian lying beside me. A warm tension grew between us, and I fought to keep myself from touching him. If I did, it wouldn't be fair.

I was not going to live for long.

"I know what you want," I whispered.

"What do I want?" he asked.

I took a breath, intending to tell him that nothing could happen between us—that it would end far faster than it began. I never fought the future, but I fought it with him because I knew that if we came together, we would only ruin the world.

But when I looked at him, no words left my mouth, and I understood that we were inevitable. Slowly, he kissed me.

For Adrian, that was our first night together, the start of something wild and passionate—the promise of a future he might build separate from the horror of his work as Dragos's guard.

For me, I knew I had taken the first step toward my impending death.

Two hundred years later, he had brought me here for the first time as Isolde to witness the fires lit across Revekka.

The night High Coven was murdered, the world looked just like this, he'd said. Then, those words had hardly fazed me. Now, they twisted through me, a thousand knives in my skin.

I thought he'd hoped it would awaken some part of me, but I had only pitied his quest for vengeance.

The roof was snowy and slippery, and the air was so cold, it stole my breath as I moved to the edge and looked down on Revekka. As before, fires burned across the land, but they were no longer isolated pyres; they surrounded each village, large circles of fire that would hopefully keep monsters at bay, though they had done little to keep the aufhockers from Cel Ceredi.

But maybe I could...if I could force myself to change.

I closed my eyes and spread my arms wide, focusing on the part of me that had not felt the same since the night I changed. It was a jumble of thorns, a chaotic mix of feelings I had not been able to confront but needed to untangle, and I knew, at the center of it all, was anger.

Anger that I had not had control.

It had started from the moment I drew my first breath and my mother died and only continued when Adrian walked into my life. From the beginning, I'd had no command over my body, which responded to him like it knew him, but once I came to love him, I'd only ever assumed I'd be the same kind of monster as him.

I was angry because I had once been able to see the future, and now I could barely navigate the present without coming away bloody and broken and bruised.

I felt my resistance give a little, and as I began to relax, an arm came around my waist. I stumbled as my back settled against Adrian's chest. His other arm crossed over my body, and he held me tight, his face pressed into the hollow of my neck.

It was an apology and I reveled in it.

We stayed like that for a while, silent and still. I was the first to move, turning in Adrian's arms to face him.

"I have something to show you," I said.

"I hope it is a good surprise," he said, smiling.

"I never promised a surprise," I said. "Or that it would be good."

"Quite the pessimist, aren't we?"

I smiled and led him inside, though I could not help feeling slightly nervous at the idea of showing him the library full of spell books. I knew Adrian was not opposed to magic, but that was before Ana and I had made a plan to contain the crimson mist.

"You are anxious," he said as we returned through the once-mirrored hall.

"Are you reading my mind?" I asked.

"Should I?" he asked.

"I don't like this room," I said, which was true, though it was not currently the source of my unease. Adrian said nothing, only held my hand tighter.

He did not question me when I led him to the former sanctuary, when I reached for a torch on the wall, or as I climbed onto the altar and squeezed into the narrow passage where the door to the library was hidden.

I did not prepare him as I led him into the darkness. I felt dizzy as we made our way down the floating stairs.

Adrian placed a hand on my shoulder, another on my waist.

"Wait just a moment," he said, his breath tickling my ear, and then he chuckled. "Breathe, Sparrow."

I exhaled slowly and deliberately, and when I took another breath, I inhaled Adrian's scent. He remained close, his presence a tangible thing that made me feel safe as we continued down the stairs to the small library.

I faced him but found his expression placid, not at all the surprise I'd imagined.

"I wondered when you would find this place," he said.

I blinked, shocked. "You knew this existed?"

He smiled faintly. "I did."

"Why did you not tell me?" I seethed.

"Because you were not ready," he said.

"Is that for you to decide?"

"When did you ever tell me you were interested in magic?" he countered. "I have only heard about how you do not have any and your fear that I will not love you without it."

I glared.

"Does this mean you have warmed to the idea of learning magic?"

"We do not have a choice," I said, still frustrated. "Can you battle magic?"

"You know the answer," he said, unamused. "How did you find it?"

"Ana brought me here," I said. He did not seem surprised by that either. "Were you aware that she has been practicing magic?"

"I wasn't...unaware," he said. "But I never told her I knew."

"What else do you know that I should also know?"

He raised a brow. "I could say the same for you. Did you not find all this out and keep it secret?"

"I am telling you now," I said. "As I always intended."

"I could say the same."

We stared at one another in tense silence.

"You never told Ana you knew of this place either?"

"No," he said. "But she is watchful."

I thought it odd that he did not say curious instead.

"Do you trust her?" I asked.

"To an extent."

"And what extent is that?"

"Ana has her own agenda," Adrian said. "It does not always align with mine."

"Are you worried she is working with Ravena?"

The thought had crossed my mind in the direct aftermath of Ravena's attack, but that had only been because I was surprised by Ana's magic. Since then, I had come to realize that she was only curious. Besides, she had been adamant about not being used as a weapon, and any alliance with Ravena would make her just that.

"No, even if she had betrayed us before, her loyalty would have shifted after Isla's death."

"And that does not concern you?"

"Not as long as she remains useful," he said.

There was that word again—*useful.*

"You do not like my answer," he said.

"I cannot easily forgive betrayal no matter how useful someone seems."

Adrian chuckled and took a step closer, hands coming up to cup my face.

"If it helps you obtain your greatest desire, then you will learn," he said and bent to kiss my forehead. My face warmed as his lips touched my skin, and when he pulled away, I stared into his eyes.

"Do you have your greatest desire?" I asked.

"Yes," he said, his thumb shifting to brush over my lips.

"Then what are you looking for now?" I whispered.

"Anything that makes us more powerful," he said. Then he kissed me, and I opened for him, his tongue plying my mouth as he bent over me before lifting me onto the desk. I reached for his hands as they gathered handfuls of my skirt, stopping him.

"I have more to tell you," I said.

"Does it involve how you would like me to fuck you?" he asked, kissing along my neck. I let him, allowing my head to fall to one side.

"No," I breathed.

"Then I do not wish to hear it," he said.

"I think you will want to hear this," I said.

Finally, he paused and pulled away, meeting my gaze.

"Ana and I are going to cast a containment spell for

the crimson mist," I said. "We have only a short while to prepare. We must cast tomorrow night."

He studied me for a moment. "Explain."

I told him about how Ana and I had arrived at our plan and how we needed to cast beneath the moonlight in the water. I also told him about Lothian and Zann's theory regarding the mist and how it might have transformed into the blood plague, which unsurprisingly he already seemed to know.

"Where will you cast?" he asked.

I noted how he spoke—as if he already approved.

"Ana says there is a lake fed by a spring."

"Galat," he said, pausing, as if he were recalling a memory. "We used to call it Green Lake because of its color. It is near Gal."

"Do you think it is safe?" I asked.

"The lake or your plan?"

"I suppose I wonder about both."

He tipped my head back. "I will not let you go to Galat without an escort."

"I did not expect to go without you," I said.

He seemed relieved, and I guessed that he had anticipated an argument, but I did not wish to do this without Adrian near, even though I would have Ana and Violeta.

"As far as your plan, are there consequences if it goes wrong?"

"It cannot really go wrong. It can just fail," I said, especially if we did not have enough strength between the three of us to call Ravena's magic to us. "But…if it goes right…then it is possible I will have the ability to control the mist, possibly perhaps also the blood plague."

Though, it was hard to say how the magic would work once it was contained.

Despite this, the thought still thrilled me, especially given Adrian's words the night before.

There is no one else here to protect you.

If I had Ravena's magic and learned how to shift with only a thought, I would never need protection again. I wanted that, desperately.

Adrian was quiet for a moment, and then he brushed his thumb over my cheek, pressing into me, still wedged between my thighs.

"I want that for you too," he said.

I met his gaze, and before I could confront him about listening to my thoughts, his mouth closed over mine once again.

This time, I did not stop him.

EIGHTEEN
Isolde

I could not remember a time as Yesenia that I felt uncer- tain about a spell, but I felt uncertain about this one, though we had done so much to prepare over the last two days. We had meditated, drawn warm energy into our bodies as we chanted, matching our words and cadence like a well-rehearsed song. The more we practiced, the more hopeful and confident Violeta and Ana grew.

On a technical level, we were ready, but the closer we came to nightfall, the more I felt like something was wrong. I did not share my feelings because I could not pinpoint why I felt this way. Perhaps it was only anxiety, but the dread inside me only deepened as the sun began to set.

I had just begun lacing my boots when Adrian entered my chamber.

He was dressed in black, his overcoat threaded through with gold, and he had tied his hair at the nape of his neck. The angles of his face were harsh in the warm light. His serious expression only added to my turmoil.

Perhaps I was just too desperate for this to work.

Adrian knelt and took over lacing my boots, his fingers working fast.

"How are you feeling?" he asked.

Frantic, I thought.

"What if this doesn't work?" I asked.

"Then we will try something else," he said, echoing my words, though I wasn't certain it was so simple. Even if we managed to succeed with our spell, would Ravena retaliate?

"What if we cannot stop her?" I asked.

It was likely that Ravena had the bones of my coven, and I knew she would use them for their magic, to heighten the strength of her army, an army that could literally be *anything*—another mist, another monster, another disease, or something we had yet to see.

"If you do not think we should do this…"

"I do not doubt the spell," I said quickly.

His brows furrowed. "Then what is it?"

I stared at him, trying to think of words to use to explain how I was feeling, but I couldn't.

"I don't know," I whispered.

Adrian's hand tangled in my hair, and his head rested against mine. "It will be okay."

Our lips met, and it was a simple touch, a soft caress. The second time was harder, the third deeper. A familiar and fluid heat gathered between my legs, and as much as I wanted to press them together, Adrian kept them apart, his body wedged between them as he kissed me. I pulled at his shirt as he buried his face between my breasts, kissing and nipping through my shirt. Then I stood suddenly, my fingers threading through his hair as he pressed his mouth into my heat, and I gasped at the feel of him sucking my swollen clit through the fabric of my clothes.

Adrian met my gaze from where he knelt on the floor, and I knew we were both unhinged. I could see it in his eyes—he looked the way I felt, but I had enough awareness to worry over this desperation. It was as if I would never have another moment like this in my life.

Adrian's grip tightened and he pressed a kiss to my stomach, then my hip, then my inner thigh. I kept my hands on his head, preparing to descend into a brief and utter madness, when a knock sounded at the door.

I froze, and even Adrian, who was not usually disturbed by the presence of another, went still.

"My queen," Violeta called from the other side of the door. "May I come in?"

Adrian and I stared at one another for a brief moment before he rose to his feet, pressed a kiss to my forehead, and turned his back to the door.

I cleared my throat and answered, "Yes, Violeta."

When she entered the room and I saw her expression, I knew she was just as anxious.

She curtsied.

"I am sorry for interrupting," she said.

"You aren't," I said.

Adrian cleared his throat, and I glared at him, but he wasn't looking at us. He had moved to the window and stared out into the fading twilight.

"I...wanted to give you something," she said.

She crossed the room and held out her hand. In her palm was a necklace. The pendant reminded me of a lantern, both in the way it was shaped and the filigree that framed a large, red stone.

"This was Evanora's," she said. "I read that if you have something to focus on, it is easier to call power to you. I thought perhaps it might help you tonight."

"Violeta, I—"

"Please, take it," she said, moving her hand closer to me. "Evanora would want you to have it."

I was not so certain about that, but she seemed so sincere, I took the necklace.

I had hoped that I might be able to sense some part of Evanora still attached to the jewelry, but there was nothing familiar about it save Violeta's energy. I closed my fingers around the pendant and, without warning, drew the young woman into my arms.

"Thank you," I whispered.

As she hugged me back, it was almost like I was embracing Evanora herself.

When Adrian, Violeta, and I entered the courtyard, Ana, Sorin, and Daroc were already waiting with our horses. Ana looked solemn and seemed lost in her own thoughts, though it was possible she was just focused on staying warm. The temperature had dropped significantly since this morning, and even dressed in heavy wool, I still shivered.

"It will snow," said Violeta, who stood beside me. When I looked at her, she had her head turned toward the clear sky and there was not a storm cloud in sight, though I did not doubt her prediction.

"Let us hope we will be home by then," I said.

"I'd rather not be caught in a storm, and we need the moonlight for this spell."

A blast of frigid wind roared around us. I drew my cloak tighter, dreading what would come once we made it to Galat Lake. The spell required us to enter the water and because of that, we planned to disrobe so we would not have to make the return journey in wet clothes.

I turned my attention to the rest of our company. Daroc and Sorin stood near one another, but they, too, seemed distant, both from us and each other. I wondered if Sorin had attempted to approach any of the issues he had talked about with me. If so, I had no doubt they were both hurting. "You do not seem to mind the cold like the rest of us, Daroc," I said.

"It is because he is already so frigid," said Sorin, and though I knew he was joking, Daroc's jaw tightened at the comment. When Sorin noticed, his smile faded, and an awkward silence descended.

"Ready?" Adrian asked, and I looked at Ana and Violeta, who nodded, but just as we were about to mount our horses, another galloped through the gates, bearing Killian. He was winded and his eyes were wide and wild.

"King Adrian, you must come with me," he said. "That man Solaris resurrected two days ago...he has killed his family."

I felt numb, and it had nothing to do with the cold.

"His family?" I asked.

Killian nodded, and there was a hollowness to his expression. Whatever he had seen...he would never be the same again.

"The wife and two children."

Bile rose in the back of my throat.

"Do we know where he is now?" Adrian asked.

Killian's features were hard as he spoke. "No. There is a search party following body parts into the Starless Forest."

"Fuck," Adrian said under his breath, and when I looked at him, his jaw was clenched.

"Go," I said. "We will be fine."

"You cannot go alone," he said fiercely, frustrated.

"I'll go with the queen," said Sorin quickly, and I wondered if he volunteered to avoid the horror Efram had left in his wake. "I'll keep her safe. I'll keep all of them safe."

Adrian was quiet for a beat, and then a chorus of screams sounded in the night. My blood ran cold.

"Go!" I commanded him.

Adrian reached for me and kissed me hard before he and Daroc mounted their horses and raced from the courtyard with Killian in the lead.

Silence followed their departure. The screams that had chilled me to the bone had ceased, and now the only sound was the howling wind. I watched until the darkness swallowed them and then turned and mounted Reverie.

"Come, let's go," I said, my words short.

I was afraid to think too long on what Adrian, Killian, and Daroc were about to face. If I did, I wouldn't want to go to the lake. This was something that would haunt them forever, and I hoped it meant that Solaris would hang.

"Violeta, ride with me," I instructed.

Sorin and Ana mounted his horse, Meri, and we left the Red Palace, heading east, following a snow-covered trail that glistened beneath the moonlight. Sorin was in the lead, and though I had taken this path with Adrian only two days ago, it looked and felt so different in the night. Perhaps it was because of the cold, though. Violeta's death grip around my waist did not help.

"Have you ever ridden a horse before?" I asked, hoping she might lessen her grip around me. It was the only thing I could focus on.

"No," she said, her teeth chattering.

There came a point when we descended into a forested valley which blocked the biting wind, and for the first time since we began this journey, I felt like I didn't have to brace myself against the cold, and relaxed, my fingers aching as I uncurled them from around Reverie's reins. I wished Violeta had felt the same, but she maintained her grip on me until we stopped within view of Galat Lake.

It was not a large body of water, which made it ideal for our purposes, and while trees surrounded us, none covered the lake, and I could see the moon reflected in its surface.

"I used to love this place," said Sorin.

"Used to?"

"We would swim here. Daroc, Adrian, our friends," he said with a note of longing in his voice. "That was a long time ago."

I tried to imagine that world for a moment, but there was no reason because it no longer existed.

"Violeta, you can dismount," I said, needing her to slide off the horse so I could too. With some effort, she managed to get her feet on the ground and I followed.

Then we approached the lake, staring into the still water. Behind us, light flared, and I turned, finding that

Sorin had lit a torch he had managed to stick into the ground.

"To keep warm," he said when he saw us looking. "I'll be in the trees, watching...not watching you all... standing guard, I mean."

I tried not to smile. "It's okay, Sorin. We know you like men."

He scrubbed the back of his neck and then shifted, flying into the dark.

Ana, Violeta, and I each took a side and began removing our clothes. Behind me, Sorin's torch still blazed, but I could feel none of the warmth as I slipped out of my cloak. The cold was brutal, and as I exposed each part of myself to the night, I felt even more dread at the coming ritual.

Once we were naked, we entered the water, stepping on sharp stones and slipping on slimy sand until we were waist-deep. I looked across to Ana, who did not seem to mind the cold. Her arms were at her sides, and her hair fell over her shoulders, covering her breasts. Violeta stood hunched, arms crossed over her chest.

"Ready?" Ana asked.

I was not sure but I nodded.

She closed her eyes and I followed, letting my arms rest on the water, palms facing up. I took a deep breath and allowed every part of my body to relax as I exhaled. I felt heavy and grounded and focused on nothing beyond me and the water touching my skin. I was surprised by how easy it had been to come to a place of peace within me so quickly, given how agonized I had felt up until this point, but that peace was quickly shattered by a familiar, vicious growl.

An aufhocker was nearby.

"Sorin?" I called, my eyes still closed, trying desperately to hold on to the calm that had entered my body, but I already felt as though I was vibrating, my adrenaline spiking.

"I've got everything under control," he called, though another growl joined the first, and the sounds of Sorin fighting filled the hollow.

I closed my eyes tighter and tried to focus. When Ana began to chant, Violeta and I joined, and the world seemed to fall away. We spoke in a language that had memory in my soul. I could feel the words moving around beneath my skin, twisting in the bottom of my stomach. I felt my magic roar to life—a stream of energy that tore me open.

I began to sob, to shake, to scream.

And then I was hit hard on the head, and I fell into the water, which was just as shocking as the blow. My hair was yanked back as I broke the surface only to hear Violeta's and Ana's screams.

I gasped for air as another two people grabbed my arms.

"Get her out!" a harsh male voice ordered.

I was dragged from the water, my ribs cracking against jagged rocks.

"Bloody witch!" another awful voice spat.

When I felt the earth beneath me, my attackers dropped my hands and began to beat my body. The first blow was a kick to my stomach. It stole my breath and made me nauseous, and as I rolled to protect myself, gasping desperately for breath, another blow landed on my back, knocking me flat to the ground. After that, it was a barrage of kicks to all parts of my body. I tasted blood and then I could not feel anything.

But that was not what scared me most; it was the peace that suddenly overcame me. I had felt it before when Dragos's men set fire to the tinder at my feet. My body eased, sinking into the ground. I could not feel pain. I did not even need to breathe.

I rolled onto my side, and as I did, I saw Ana only a few feet away, her battered face aglow in the torchlight.

Suddenly I was in another time, running through these very woods, the ground uneven beneath my feet, the limbs of trees striking my skin. My breath shuddered out of me, my lungs burning.

"Ana!"

Her name left my mouth, a choked cry. I hoped it would make her stop, but she only seemed to run faster.

"Ana!" I begged, wheezing her name. "Ana, please!"

She stumbled and fell and stayed where she landed, her body shaking with sobs. I fell to my knees and held her.

I had no idea what had happened. I just knew it was horrible because I had caught her fleeing the castle, battered and beaten. I didn't know how long we sat there, but eventually she sat up, her face swollen so badly, I didn't think she could even see me. There was a gash across her cheek, and her nose was broken, her lip split.

"Ana," I said, my vision blurred with tears. I wanted to touch her face, but I knew I would only hurt her, so I reached for her hands instead. They were bruised, her nails broken. "What happened?"

She tried to speak, but every time she started to open her mouth, a violent sob burst from her throat. I waited as she navigated this vicious cycle, and the more I watched, the more I wanted to carve out my own heart just so I would not have to feel the pain of it breaking.

"King Dragos keeps a pleasure house in the dungeon of the Red Palace," she explained. "He says it is for his lords, says they will perform better if they have a place to spill their seed."

She spoke with her bloody teeth clenched, her disgust barely contained.

"The lords are free to go any time so long as they bring a new boy or girl every month. They have kidnapped hundreds, and I have only helped a few escape, but tonight as I was trying to free a girl, I was caught."

Her voice broke and she shook, tears streaming down her face. She pulled her hands from mine and started to wipe her face, but I stopped her.

That only seemed to make her cry harder.

"They raped me," she whispered and then spoke through her teeth again, shaking with hate. "Every. Lord."

Tears spilled down my cheeks. I had no words.

There was no comfort for this—not even in revenge—because trauma was a nightmare that clung to its victims with an iron fist.

"Then they killed her," she said, and then she wailed. "They killed her because of me."

She collapsed in my arms, and I held her and cried with her until neither of us had anything left but rage.

NINETEEN
Isolde

I woke up crying.

At first it was because of my memory of Ana, and then I cried for myself.

Adrian lay beside me, and I turned into him, burying my face in his chest, weeping harder. He held me gently and whispered love to me while he kissed my hair.

It took me a while to speak, to form words beyond the sobs wracking my body, and I held onto Adrian harder, almost as if I feared someone would tear me away from him.

I don't know how long I cried, but what brought words to my lips was the realization that I still wore Violeta's necklace.

"How is Ana?...Violeta?"

When Adrian spoke, his voice was quiet, warm, and pained. "Ana is healed but she has not woken up yet."

"And Violeta?"

He was quiet and I shifted to meet his gaze. "Adrian." My voice trembled. "How is Violeta?"

He looked far more pale than usual, and he swallowed before he spoke, the words escaping his colorless lips in a whisper. "She didn't make it."

I shook my head. "She had to have."

If Ana and I made it, there was no other explanation. Why were we alive if she was dead?

I could not grasp it, could not accept it—wouldn't.

"Isolde," Adrian said gently.

"No—" My voice broke, and I dissolved into tears once more.

Adrian pulled me to him, and time passed in this turbulent manner—where I would cry and then sleep, overcome with exhaustion, and wake up once more in tears.

"How did you find us?" I asked.

He waited so long to speak, I didn't think he would tell me, but then he started. "Sorin," he said. "He found me in Cel Ceredi. He left you all in the grove, surrounded by villagers from Gal who thought they were doling out justice against witches."

A wave of nausea soured the back of my throat.

This was Solaris's fault.

"Why are you saying it like that?" I asked. "Why are you saying he left us?"

I felt defensive. I remembered hearing the low growls of aufhockers disturbing our casting, and the sounds of Sorin battling, but beyond that, I knew nothing because by then, we had been attacked. I wondered how the villagers had managed to slip past the monster or monsters attacking Sorin.

"Because that is what he did," Adrian said.

"He could not help it," I said. "There were…so many. It was almost as if they knew we were going to be there."

Adrian was tense beneath me. I did not think he blamed Sorin for having to leave for help, so much as he blamed himself for not being there at all.

"How is Sorin?" I asked.

"Devastated," Adrian replied, and I could tell he spoke with his jaw clenched. "He says he heard a growl and thought it was an aufhocker. Then he heard another and thought it might be a pack. When he shifted, he found he was surrounded by villagers, and by then, you had all been attacked. They were lying in wait."

If that were true, how did they know? We had told no one save our small circle about our plans to cast a containment spell for the mist.

A spell that we had not even been able to complete.

All of that work and time, wasted.

"What happened to the villagers?"

"Those who did not die that night will die today," he said.

I expected nothing less.

In the silence that followed, my eyes once again filled with tears. This time, I thought about how we had only been motivated to help our people, to protect them from Ravena's magic. But none of it mattered; all of it went unacknowledged.

Perhaps I was foolish to keep fighting for others and should only fight for myself.

At some point, I woke up again, and Adrian was gone.

I shot up from bed but found him staring out the window. When he heard me, he turned and crossed the room to me.

"I'm here," he said, sitting on the edge of the bed. He had dressed and looked every bit the deadly conqueror and regal king he was. His tunic was fine and delicately threaded with intricate designs. His hair was smooth, half pinned away from his angled face. His expression was severe, save for his eyes which studied me tenderly. Then he lifted his hand to caress my cheek and I flinched away.

His eyes widened and he dropped his hand quickly. As soon as I realized what I had done, I reached for him.

"I did not mean—"

"It's okay," he said quickly. "It's all right."

My throat was thick with emotion. I might have cried again if I'd had anything left to give, but I didn't.

Instead, I lifted his palm to the side of my face and closed my eyes, focusing on his warmth. Then he slowly let his hand fall away, and instead, threaded his fingers through mine.

I stared at our hands while memories and words spun in my head. Finally, I spoke. "I do not understand what happened at the lake."

"There is no understanding it," Adrian said. "Because it is hate, and hate can exist with no reason."

"It shouldn't," I said. "We were only trying to help banish the thing they feared."

"You were," he said. "And they did not deserve it."

Before tonight, I wouldn't have agreed, but now I was starting to think that the world did not deserve my blood or tears. "Do you know what was so terrifying?" I asked. I kept my voice low. Perhaps I thought that would lessen the pain of what I was about to say. "I got to the point where I was going to accept death," I said, and suddenly, I found the ability to shed more tears. "I could feel it. It blanketed my body, a familiar and warm embrace…and if I had succumbed, you would have too."

I had been closer to death than any other time before now, and that struck me hard. I was tired of being the weakest—tired of being the target for everyone's revenge against Adrian.

"Isolde," he said, my name a soft plea on his lips.

I knew he did not wish for me to think of this right now.

I released his hand and shifted onto my knees, wrapping my arms around his neck, but he did not touch me. Instead, he had fisted his hands and they rested beside him on the bed.

"Change me," I said, with more force in my voice than I had managed to use since I had woken up from this nightmare.

"Isolde—"

"You must! Before it is too late. You cannot be so blind. This will happen again."

"Not this way," he said. Now his hands had moved; they braced my body, as if he were prepared to push me away. "I will not change you this way."

"Because you have some fantasy attached to turning me?"

A shock of anger flashed in his eyes, and he looked away from me, his jaw clenched.

"I want to do what is best for you," he said. "You

have not even managed to accept or master shifting. You need time before you have to handle another change in your life."

"I cannot be responsible for your death," I said. "I can't."

"You won't." He spoke with a conviction I did not have.

He lifted his hand once more, slowly this time, to prepare me, and as he stroked my face, I leaned forward and kissed him. It was soft, barely a kiss at all, but the gentleness of it spoke to our pain, our fear, our love.

"I will call for a bath," he said. "We must prepare for the executions."

Adrian rang the servant's bell, and my heart rose into my throat when the first knock came. It should have been Violeta waiting on the other side, directing the other servants as they filled the tub with water. Instead, a string of people I hardly recognized entered, carrying pail after pail of hot water into the room.

"Where is Vesna?" I asked.

"She will be along after your bath," Adrian said, meeting my gaze. "I...wanted this time with you."

I did not mind spending more time with him.

When the servants had gone, I untied my nightgown and let it pool at my feet, leaving Violeta's necklace on, before stepping into the bath. Adrian watched me as I lowered into the water, but his gaze was different, not alight with desire but a strange intensity. I wondered if he was trying to prepare himself for the last time he saw my body—likely bruised and broken and bloodied.

He waited to approach until I was submerged in the water and knelt beside the bath.

"Is this okay?" he asked, and I nodded.

He lathered soap on a washcloth and began at my back, running the cloth over my skin in soft circles. There were places he touched that were sore, muscles that ached, and as he passed over them, I took a breath, releasing it slowly between my lips. When he moved to my shoulders and arms, his expression was hard, his mouth tight. I lifted my hand to his face, water dripping from my skin. I had no words to offer, but he met my gaze, eyes glassy.

"You should finish," he said, taking my hand from his face, offering the washcloth.

"It's all right," I said, voice hushed, holding my breath as I guided his hand over my breasts.

"Isolde," Adrian said tightly.

"Shh," I said and rested my forehead against his, moving his hand lower, down my stomach and between my thighs. His lips hovered near mine and his breathing grew ragged, but he did not attempt to touch me beyond my direction. I became frustrated, the heat between my thighs unbearable.

"Adrian," I whispered, and he squeezed his eyes shut. "I love you."

He kissed me hard, his free hand gripping the base of my skull. I wrapped my arms around his neck, and he lifted me from the tub, but when he pressed into my skin, I arched against him, a shock of pain escaping my mouth.

He froze, dropping his hands.

"I'm sorry. I—"

"It's okay." I took his face between my hands and forced him to look at me, but when I tried to kiss him again, he drew away and it hurt.

"I'll summon Vesna," he said.

"Adrian—"

"I will not be responsible for hurting you further," he said. "I can't."

I brought my hands to my chest, feeling strangely exposed and ridiculous before my own husband. I hated it. He crossed the room to ring the bell, and I sought my robe, desperate to hide.

Neither of us spoke, and when the knock came at the door, though I knew to expect it, I was not prepared to see Vesna. It was evident she had been crying; her eyes were rimmed in red and puffy. I crossed the room to her and held her tight. We cried together, even as she helped me dress, both of us very much aware that this was Violeta's role. Adrian sat and watched. His hands remained fisted, one on his thigh and one pressed against his mouth.

The dress was black with a lace overlay that pressed a pretty design against the collar of my neck. I chose to wear my mother's pearl tiara because I liked the weight of it, liked to pretend it was somehow her laying her hands upon me.

There were times when I wondered how my life would be different if she had been here. What would she have done in the aftermath of the lake attack? Would she have held me? Whispered her love to me as Adrian had done? Would she have felt just as vengeful as me?

Adrian brought me my cloak and clasped it at the front.

"Was Violeta right?" I asked. "Did we get more snow?"

Adrian nodded. "It is very cold, and we will be traveling to the Starless Forest."

I did not ask why because I did not need to. I knew what Adrian intended—to hang those who had hurt me, hurt Ana, murdered Violeta, from the very trees my sisters had hung from two hundred years ago.

We left our room for the courtyard where a crowd was gathered—mostly people who would attend the execution with us: Tanaka, what remained of Adrian's noblesse—Iosif, Vlad, and Iker—and Sorin, who did not look well. He was far too pale, the skin under his eyes too dark. I wanted to go to him, but he would not meet my gaze, and at our appearance, everyone bowed and remained kneeling until Adrian and I had mounted Shadow.

Then we made our way to the Starless Forest, and everyone waiting in the courtyard followed. Adrian did not rush, keeping a leisurely pace for which I was glad. The wind already stung without the momentum of Shadow's gallop.

Adrian cut through the center of Cel Ceredi, and the street was crowded with villagers who knelt as we passed. I could not quite place how this made me feel. I almost did not trust the pageantry of it because, while these villagers had welcomed me, especially on the night of Winter's Eve, they had also celebrated Solaris, the supposed witch-hunter, and fostered those who attacked us. More than anything, I blamed Solaris for what had happened at the lake.

Had the horror of Solaris's resurrection of Efram changed anything? I wondered.

"What happened last night? When you left with Killian?"

Adrian shifted Shadow's reins in his hand, and I took that as a sign of his discomfort.

"We found Efram and burned him," Adrian said. He did not try to elaborate, and I assumed it was because he did not wish to revisit the horror, so I only asked the question I wanted answered most.

"Where is Solaris?"

"Awaiting punishment," Adrian replied.

"Not execution?"

Adrian took too long to reply, so I spoke instead. "You still find him useful after what he did?"

"We should not speak about this right now," he said.

"Do you still plan to turn him?"

"I said I will not speak on this right now." His tone was firm, and it silenced me, but only because my anger was so great. I knew what he would say—the same thing he had before, that this was political, that he was being strategic, *that this man had use.*

We made our way under the eaves of the Starless Forest.

These woods carried the burden of hate. The trees were heavy with the memory of it, and unlike before when I could only feel it, today, I saw it—hundreds of spirits hung from these trees, hundreds of women of all ages. They were hardly visible, existing as ethereal, shimmering ripples of energy.

I wondered why I saw them now.

We passed beneath their feet, and I craned my neck to watch them, emotion gathering thickly in my throat.

"Can you see them?" Adrian asked after a moment.

"Can you?" I asked.

"No," he said. "But I hear them."

"What are they saying?"

"They speak spells," he said. "That's all they ever do."

We came to a small grove, and Adrian dismounted, helping me down. My boots sank into the snow, the cold seeping beneath my skirt, as we took our place at the center of the grove.

Daroc and several guards had already prepared the attackers for execution. Among those already present was Killian. Seeing him stole what little warmth was left within my body. His expression was severe, and when he met my gaze with those haunted eyes, they turned glassy.

I felt his emotion, and it welled inside me too. I mourned deeply for him and for Violeta, for what they had before she died, and what might have been had she lived.

There were fifteen prisoners, a mix of men and women. Their hands were bound before them, bodies bruised and beaten. A few glared at me through swollen eyes; others kept their gazes on their feet. I could not stop looking at them, feeling so many confused emotions tangling inside me. I wanted to demand answers, but I also did not wish to hear them explain their hate.

Each prisoner stood on a wood stump, and each had a noose around their neck, the knot secured before the ear and the lower jaw.

There was no fanfare—no words of warning, no shouts of protest—only silence as the guards and Daroc stepped forward to kick each stump from beneath their feet. The ropes creaked and the bodies swung, and there were a few strangled sounds, but mostly, there was silence as the bodies convulsed and jerked violently. Their faces swelled; their eyes bulged; their tongues jutted from their mouths. It was horrible to witness, and I watched until they ceased to sway.

When we returned to the castle, a pyre was being assembled in the courtyard in preparation for Violeta's funeral.

"Does she have to burn?" I asked Adrian, watching the progress blindly.

"It's safest," he said.

I knew that, and I knew why—buried bodies could rise again, and while I did not wish that for Violeta, it felt wrong to reduce her to ash and bone.

"How will I visit her?" I whispered, my vision blurry.

Adrian lifted my hand to his lips, and I looked at him, swallowing hard as he kissed me.

"Why don't we bury her ashes in the garden," he said. "Perhaps, when we return to Lara, you can bring a few of your mother's flowers."

More tears gathered in my eyes.

"I want to see her," I said.

Adrian froze. "Isolde—"

"You do not have to take me. I will go by myself," I said.

He stared at me for a moment. I knew his hesitation came from a good place, but I wanted what I wanted. I was not delusional. I knew seeing her would be difficult. I knew it would be how I remembered her for the rest of my life, but I needed to say goodbye.

Adrian took me to Violeta.

I expected her to be in the old sanctuary, but she was prepared for her funeral in her chamber.

"I did not want the entire castle to gawk at her," he explained, though I did not prompt him. And while I thought I could guess why, I still was not prepared when I entered her chamber. Though she was covered from head to toe in a black shroud, her body was bruised and swollen.

A dizzying wave of emotion brought tears to my eyes again and a tightening to my chest. I took a breath, but it left me in a huff, my mouth quivering.

I sat down at her side, staring at her face beneath the shroud.

"She died for nothing," I said. We never even managed to finish the spell. "I should have never asked her."

"You cannot blame yourself for her choice to help."

"Perhaps I should blame myself for thinking we could cast a counterspell at all," I said.

"Or you could honor Violeta and acknowledge that it was an incredibly brave thing," Adrian said.

I took a shuddering breath, and I lowered the veil.

I could not describe the physical pain I felt once I could see her injuries in the full light of her room. She did not look like Violeta at all, her eyes swollen shut, her cheeks cut and bruised, her mouth sunken and torn.

I thought I could kiss her goodbye, but I only had the strength to cover her face again.

I rose quickly and faced Adrian, brushing the tears from my face.

"She was brave," I said.

And while we had hung those responsible for her death today, the two I blamed most remained free—Solaris and Ravena.

"You said Solaris is awaiting punishment?"

"He is," Adrian replied, his expression growing hard. I knew he was preparing to argue with me.

"Let me execute it," I said.

Adrian stared at me, assessing. "Are you going to punish him or kill him?" Adrian asked.

I glared, and my anger burned my skin. I pushed past him and left Violeta's room.

"Isolde!" Adrian followed close behind and reached for my arm, turning me toward him. I jerked away.

"When will the value of our people exceed the value of your agenda? When will *my* value exceed it?"

Adrian flinched.

"Solaris might as well have been in that grove himself, striking and beating and murdering *us*. Will you stand aside while he inspires another witch hunt?"

Adrian closed the distance between us, his hands on my shoulders. He spoke between his teeth, eyes flashing with fury.

"How dare you," he growled. "How *dare* you."

They seemed to be the only words he could manage to speak.

Then he released me and took a step away, vibrating with his rage. "If it will make you happy, I will kill him today," he said. "But if what he claims is true, if he is a creation of Dis, you should know that I will suffer."

I studied him, his face red, the veins in his neck and forehead popping.

"What are you saying?"

"You seem to forget I was created by Dis," he said. "I am not completely free to do as I please without consequences. I do not want one of those consequences to be you."

I studied him and then narrowed my eyes. "How much control does she have over you?"

His chest rose and fell heavily, and I knew he did not wish to say, but after a heavy pause, he spoke. "More and more each day."

"Were you ever going to tell me?"

He said nothing. He had not wanted to admit this—he saw it as a weakness.

"How do we free you?" I asked, my voice a whisper, as if I could hide it from Dis.

He looked away, swallowing hard, and ignored my question. "Come, it's time for Solaris's punishment."

Adrian escorted me to the dungeons, into a chamber furnished with torture devices and weapons. I studied each, curious. There was a box lined with spikes, a triangular beam supported by two columns, a rack with straps for the wrists and ankles. Then there were smaller tools—a collar of spikes, metal bridles, and various sharp scissor-like instruments.

"Did these belong to Dragos?" I asked.

"No," Adrian said, though he did not elaborate.

When I turned to him, he was placing an iron rod into the fire.

"What is that?" I asked.

"A cauterizing iron," Adrian said.

"Are we cutting something off?" I asked.

"You are," he said.

"What am I cutting off?"

Before Adrian could answer, we were joined by Daroc and Sorin. They walked with Solaris between them, one gripping each of his arms, and they forced him to his knees in front of a round, flat piece of stone.

I expected him to look far angrier, but there was a resignation within his gaze. He stared up at us, waiting.

"You have used your power blindly," Adrian said. "You came into my kingdom and offered aid, but you inspired a witch hunt that nearly killed my wife, my cousin, and resulted in the death of a young girl. You used resurrection to present as a savior to a man who should have stayed dead. Now his entire family, and those who were brave enough to try to stop him, are dead."

As Adrian spoke, Solaris's head lowered in shame. Once again, I found myself surprised by his reaction. I had expected him to fight, to be defiant in the face of his punishment.

"For this," Adrian continued, "you must be punished. Do you have anything to say?"

Solaris lifted his head, his eyes widening a little. "I can only express I did not mean for any of this to happen," he said.

"Then what did you mean?" I asked. "Because from where I stood, your decisions looked very intentional. You came to court and announced you were a witch-hunter amid panic."

"It was wrong of me," he said. "I sought to be valuable, if not to you, then to your people."

"Why?"

"Because I want revenge," he said. "And not even against Ravena, though I would like to see her die. I want revenge against Dis. This hand… I did not know what she bestowed upon me when I begged for the lives of my wife and children."

I did not need to ask what he had done. I knew he had resurrected them.

"If you knew the horror of resurrection, why did you do it here?"

"I thought it might be different this time. It was dangerous and foolish." He paused, and then spoke through his teeth, voice shuddering. "But why? Why would this be the gift she bestowed? When all it brings is horror?"

"Your mistake was thinking it was a gift," said Adrian.

Solaris let his head fall; his eyes glazed.

"It might be hard to believe," he said. "But I had no wish to see that man turn into a monster."

"Intention does not matter here," Adrian replied.

Solaris nodded. "You asked when I first came, what I would have to offer if you cut off my hand. I have tried. It only grows back."

"Dis is a cruel mistress," Adrian replied, and then reached for an axe which hung among several weapons on the wall. It had a crescent-shaped blade and an iron handle.

He handed me the weapon, and I was surprised that it was so light.

"Take his other hand," Adrian said.

Daroc and Sorin cut his bindings. They did not have to force Solaris to lay his right arm upon the stone. He did it himself, though he shook. I admired his willingness to accept his punishment, and there was a small part of me that hesitated to go through with it, but sorrow did not atone for what he had knowingly done. I considered giving Adrian the axe to follow through, but given what he had said, I worried Dis might retaliate.

So I moved into position and let the axe hover over his wrist, adjusting my stance. Solaris's body was rigid, and air filled his cheeks as he tried to prepare for the pain.

I gripped the handle with both hands, and then I brought it down upon him. The blade was so sharp, it cut through his skin and bone effortlessly. Solaris had gone white, and a ragged groan escaped from his throat. Daroc and Sorin moved in, shoving him into the stone to keep him still as Adrian retrieved the cauterizing iron. As he pressed the flat, hot end to Solaris's wrist, his violent screams filled the chamber.

TWENTY
Isolde

Violeta was carried to the pyre in the courtyard, draped in her black shroud.

While I had felt some element of sympathy for Solaris earlier, it had dried up the moment I saw her again. I had no doubt that his arrival had inspired the people of Gal to attack us, and because of his carelessness, we were left with the fallout, with the grief, with the guilt.

Her family gathered opposite us, huddled together, sobbing. She'd had a mother, father, two brothers, and one sister. I saw parts of her in each of them. I tried not to stare, but I could not help watching, feeling responsible for every tear they shed.

There were others gathered in the courtyard—servants who had worked with her, villagers who loved her, and those who served closest to us, among them Killian.

We took turns laying flowers around her—lavender,

lilies, whatever had yet to die beneath the snow in the garden. I watched closely when it was Killian's turn. His features were hard, but his eyes were sad, and he lifted his hand, hesitating before he brushed his fingers against her ruined lips. His mouth moved, but I could not hear what he said, and at some point, it felt too intimate to watch.

I looked away until it was my turn. I placed my palm against her forehead. It was soft beneath my touch and bile rose into my throat.

"I am sorry," I whispered and bent to kiss her, my tears falling onto her face.

I drew back and returned to Adrian's side, and when they lit the fire, I lifted my hand to Violeta's necklace, squeezing it hard in my hand until it hurt, grateful now that it was her essence that clung to it because it would feed my vengeance against Ravena.

I sat with Ana for a long time after Violeta's funeral. She lay in her bed, in her small room, unmoving. I watched her stomach rise with each breath, fearful that at any moment, it would stop.

She was too still.

At some point, Adrian joined me, taking a seat on the other side of Ana's bed. He looked exhausted and worn; the lines between his eyes were deep and the hollows of his face shadowed. Our earlier conversation weighed upon my mind, and I wanted to ask him about Dis. I was frustrated that she added another complicated element to our lives, and I wanted it to end, but I knew it was not the right time to speak of her.

I focused on Ana instead. I was so tired of crying.

My eyes were raw, and my face hurt, but I could not stop, so I let the tears run freely down my face.

"Why won't she wake?" I asked. "You healed her. Why won't she wake?"

"I don't know," he said. "Euric says he has seen this before, and he believes she will come to, though it might be days."

Euric was the vampire who had bandaged my wound after I was attacked by a child possessed with the crimson mist. He had claimed not to be a healer, leaving the title for witches, though he was skilled in some of the arts.

We were quiet for a long moment, both of us watching Ana.

"Did you know about Dragos's pleasure house?" I asked.

Adrian kept staring at Ana.

"We all did," he said. "It was impossible not to know."

"Why didn't you do anything?"

"You assume I did nothing?" he asked, looking at me.

I supposed I had. "I'm sorry."

He shook his head. "I likely did not do enough," he said. "I was focused on killing Dragos. I thought if I succeeded, then every bad thing he'd done would go away. I didn't realize until after Ana's..." He paused and cleared his throat. "I didn't realize how awful it had become until...until then."

"You planned to kill Dragos? Even before my death?"

"It's the only reason I joined his guard," Adrian said. "It was not easy...pretending to be so loyal."

"What did he do to you?"

Adrian swallowed, and let his eyes fall to his hands, which he had clasped tightly in his lap.

"I blame him for destroying my family. Revekka was once very small, and Dragos wanted more land, more power. He declared war upon three other countries. They were called Bren, Kazan, and Oksana. My father was called upon to fight, and when he returned, he was not the same man. He was angry, and he drank, and that made him violent. One day, he walked into the woods and impaled himself upon his sword. I found him. I was only a boy. After, my mother, too, began drinking, and she whored herself around to sustain it rather than feeding me."

He paused a moment, letting his hands rest on the arms of his chair, gazing toward the window.

"One day, she didn't come home. They found her body in the river. I was old enough then to do something. It wasn't hard to find the man who murdered her. Everyone talked about it because no one cared that she was dead. Except me, though she did nothing to deserve my vengeance, save birth me.

"After I killed the murderer of my mother, I fled Revekka for Keziah. They are a vibrant and warrior-like people. I trained with them and only came to the Red Palace for the King's Tournament. Dragos did not care that I had murdered, not after seeing my skill in the ring, and he did not know that the only reason I sought to be part of his guard was so that I could kill him."

"I never knew," I said. "Why did you not tell me?"

"Once the truth is spoken, it always seems to find its target." He was quiet for a moment. "Once, though, a long time ago when I thought you and I could have a peaceful life under the mountains, my vengeance did not matter so much."

I recalled our conversation in the woods near the cabin where we'd spent our final night, when we had discussed a future that was so far out of reach, it would now only ever be a nightmare.

"Perhaps our mistake was ever thinking we were meant for such things," I said.

But Adrian shook his head. "I will never forget the times I spent with you, dreaming. Those are my brightest memories."

It was late when we left Ana's bedside. Usually, after executions and funerals, the palace was alive with celebration, but not this night. Tonight, the halls were quiet, a solemn memorial for Violeta.

I worried about returning to our room, thinking of how we'd left it this morning. It felt almost wrong to think about sex in this moment, but it was how I took control of my world, and no matter how dark or terrifying, I needed to reclaim it. "I need you, Adrian," I said, looking up at him.

He slowed and met my gaze. "I am here."

"I mean that I want you to make love to me."

His gaze softened. "Isolde, I—"

"Tell me you do not want me," I said, stepping closer, though we remained in the hallway, and nowhere near our room or bed. I placed my hands flat on his chest, smoothing them down his stomach, dropping one to touch his arousal. He took a breath, releasing it slow between his lips.

"It is never that," he said. "You *know* it is not that."

"I am well enough," I said. "The only way you will hurt me now is to refuse me."

It was not a lie.

He watched me a moment, not so much hesitant as he was discerning.

I rose onto my toes and pressed a kiss to his jaw, running my tongue and teeth along the column of his neck, nipping at his skin, sucking it into my mouth. He hooked a hand at the base of my skull and let me explore. I felt his control slipping. The tighter his fingers twisted into my hair, the harder he grew beneath my hand.

Finally, he broke and forced my lips to his, his other hand going to my breast, squeezing. I gasped, and he thrust his tongue between my lips, guiding me until the wall was at my back. There, his mouth explored me the same way I'd explored him, and I shivered beneath his touch.

I moved my hands around his neck, and Adrian's shifted to my ass, his arousal pressed flat against my lower stomach.

"What do you consider making love?" Adrian asked.

"Anything with you," I said.

He gave a strangled sigh and kissed me, holding me tight to him before turning me toward the wall. I planted my hands against it as Adrian lifted my skirts. His hand dipped between my thighs, his fingers sinking into my heat.

"Fuck," I breathed, my head falling back.

Adrian touched my breast with his free hand and kissed my neck, fingers moving inside me. Then he knelt, and his mouth was on me. I thought I might collapse from the pleasure.

"Adrian—" I warned, my legs shaking.

He rose to his feet and dragged me to him, my back to his chest, speaking against my ear. "Bedroom. Now."

He released me, and I turned to him, my body warm and lust-filled. I kissed him, sucking his bottom lip into my mouth before hurrying for our room. I walked ahead of him, teasing as I reached behind me to loosen the ties of my dress. Once we were behind closed doors, Adrian shoved my gown down and gripped the neckline of my linen chemise, tearing it in two before his mouth was on mine again. He pushed into me until the backs of my legs hit the bed and I sat.

He shoved off his overcoat and pulled his tunic over his head while I unbuttoned his pants. Once he was naked, I took his cock into my hand and kissed down his length before closing my mouth over his crown, sucking and licking. He groaned over me, gathering my hair into his hands while I coaxed beads of come from him.

At some point, he decided it was enough because he took my head between his hands and kissed me, moving me to my back, settling between my thighs. There was a wicked glint in his eyes as he taunted me with soft and slow kisses down my body and the sensitive skin between my legs. I twisted and arched beneath him, desperate for his mouth, the fullness of his fingers, anything that would free this pressure he had erected inside me.

When his tongue touched me again, I nearly came, but the relief was short-lived as he began once more, his fingers and mouth demanding my desperate participation. I curled my hands into the bedding, into Adrian's hair, dug my heels into the mattress, ground my hips harder into his face. I wanted him deeper, wanted the release I could feel coming. My body had grown too taut, the strain was too much—all it took was his consistent pace and I came undone—but it was far harsher than that. It was a complete break. A sudden rush that drained my body of all my energy. Suddenly, I did not have the ability to hold myself up—not even my legs. They fell open, knees on the bed, shameless.

Adrian did not mind as he stretched out over my body, a smug smile on his face. He kissed me languidly, our bodies radiating heat together.

"I like to make you sing, Sparrow," he said, reaching between us, guiding himself to my entrance, but instead of shoving inside me like I wanted him to, he let the head of his cock slide through my wet heat. The choice gave life to my limbs once more, and I wrapped my legs around him, heels digging into his ass. I drew him in until I felt his balls rest against me.

We both moaned, foreheads touching, lips hovering.

"I love this," I said, reveling in the weight of his body upon me, the feel of him inside me. "I love you."

I could not see his expression—we were too close—but all that mattered were his words. "All the stars in the sky, Sparrow."

He kissed me hard and began to move, alternating between shallow and deeper thrusts. Each thrust took my breath away and only gave a fraction of it back. I let my hands run down his scarred back, corded with muscle, and focused wholly on every part of him that touched every part of me until the tension in our bodies tangled. I held on, releasing it only when Adrian came.

TWENTY-ONE
Isolde

The next morning, I woke determined to summon Ravena and bind her magic—but with Ana still asleep, I needed help.

I found Lothian and Zann in the library. They were behind the round desk on the first floor. Lothian leaned against the counter, a book opened in front of him, while Zann stood close, his arms braced on either side of his vassal.

They both looked up when I entered, and Zann pushed away from Lothian.

"My queen," they said in unison, bowing as best they could with the desk in the way.

"We are relieved to see you so well," said Lothian.

I could only manage a quick, half-hearted smile.

"I require your assistance," I said. "Would you follow me?"

"Of course," Zann said.

The two followed me as I led them to the secret library. As we came down the floating steps, Lothian gave an audible gasp.

"I knew it," Zann whispered.

I stayed near the bottom of the stairs while they wandered into the small room. Zann's fingers drifted over a line of colorful spines. Lothian bent to read the titles of a stack of books on the floor.

"When did you find this?" Zann asked.

"Ana found it," I said. "I'm…not sure how long she knew about it before she told me."

I wasn't even sure how long Adrian had known about it.

"I need your help," I said. "I need to find a summoning spell and a binding spell. They need to be ones I can cast on my own, and they must be powerful."

"Nothing would delight us more," said Lothian, scanning the room. "I'll start in this corner."

We each took a part of the library and began to pore over books and parchment and long scrolls. We worked for hours, reading and deciphering handwritten texts, handing over those that were not in a language either Lothian or I understood for Zann to decode. All the while, my librarians began to organize the information, assigning categories and shelving accordingly. There were several scrolls that detailed laws for governing magic, rows of leather journals that detailed both the daily life of witches and quite a few spells. There were also extensive histories on members of High Coven and their respective covens.

"Can I see?" I asked.

"Yes, though it reads very subjectively," said Lothian. "Whoever wrote it was only an observer."

I scanned the page until I came to my name.

High Coven boasts a powerful seer, though she has yet to demonstrate her gift, given that a series of misfortunes have befallen Cel Ceredi. The people have become suspicious of the woman, who shows no propriety, given her earthly background. She has been known to wander away from the castle and gather herbs and flowers.

Rumors abound that she intends to make poisons.

She has wild ways, though such is the manner of her matriarchal tribe. Hers is the most prominent, the Xaneth. If she is any measure of the women they produce, it is evident we must act, for her defiance is a threat to the crown.

I rolled up the parchment.

"Do either of you happen to know the history of Aroth?"

"It isn't a good one," said Zann. "Are you sure you wish to hear it?"

"Yes," I said. I wasn't sure if anything would surprise me now, especially where Dragos and his lords were concerned.

"They were a tribal nation ruled by women. Their men were warriors and protective but not protective as in possessive; these men saw their women as sacred. As time passed, they faced threats from all sides, Vlasca, Zenovia, Elin, and of course Revekka. The younger generations began to think that the only reason they were seen as a conquest was because of the women who ruled them. There was a mutiny, and the men took control. I read two accounts of that day. One claims the ruling matriarchs were exiled, and one suggests they were murdered."

"When was the mutiny?" I asked.

"I believe it was about two years after the Burning."

"So many of us...murdered."

I was not even talking about witches anymore, but women. I lifted the rolled parchment to the flame. I did not wish for this information to exist about me any longer. "Strange that men claim we are weak when they are so afraid."

We worked well into the night. Each time Lothian and Zann came across a summoning spell, they added it to a pile for my review. I was not exactly sure what I was looking for, but I felt that I would know when I found it. I needed something that would draw Ravena to any surface I chose, something that could compensate for the potential that her power had increased since she had *The Book of Dis*. As for binding, I hoped to trap her wherever I summoned her.

At some point, I dismissed Lothian and Zann. They both hesitated to leave me, but I assured them I would be fine, and I only wished to read through what they had already found before we began again tomorrow.

Once they were gone, though, I could not focus on what I was reading, certain that I could hear someone sobbing, but it was distant and muffled. For a moment, I thought it might have been Ravena, coming to taunt me, but there were no mirrors here, no reflections in windows, no water to speak of. I followed the sound around the room to where it was loudest, and in the shadows, I found a door.

I turned the knob and pushed. It took a few tries, but it finally gave, groaning as it opened, powdering the air with dust. I found myself in a stone corridor. It was cold and dark, only a few torches hanging in sconces on the wall. They did little to light the long hall stretching before me, but I continued anyway, passing cells barred with thick iron. The crying that had been loud at first was quieter now, as if the person responsible had tried to muffle the sound. Still, I was able to follow it and came to stand before a woman in one of the cells.

She was naked and lying on her side, shaking. Her back was to me, the bones of her spine sticking out as if her skin had shrunk around it.

"Safira?" I whispered.

She did not move or act as if she had heard me.

She had been down here for almost a month, though Adrian had only ordered her to remain in the dungeons for a few days. That was after she had falsely claimed to be sleeping with him. I had approved of that punishment—but seeing her like this now made me feel guilty that neither of us had ensured her quick release.

"Guards!" I called.

"Keep your mouth shut!" a voice echoed in the dungeon. Whoever had called did not attempt to investigate. I wondered if that meant he was used to Safira making demands. I would not be surprised, but seeing her like this made me wonder if we had broken her.

"I command you, come this instant!"

"You little bitch," the guard growled, and suddenly, there was clamoring down the hall and heavy feet thudded against the stone floor. "You've a lot of nerve commanding me." He rounded the corner and halted when he saw me, though I was veiled in shadow. "Who the fuck are you?" he demanded, squinting to see me better.

"I am your queen," I snapped. "Open this fucking door."

"My qu-queen!" he sputtered, kneeling.

"I said open this door. I will not give the command again."

He scurried forward and fumbled with a set of keys.

As soon as the door opened, I swept inside.

Safira lay in the middle of the uneven stone floor. She was filthy, her hair matted, and her skin so raw in places, she had developed sores.

She also smelled like piss, and it burned my nose.

I wanted to get her out of here.

"Safira, come with me."

"Please just leave me alone," she said, still sobbing but quieter this time. She curled herself into a ball, knees to her chest. In this moment, she reminded me of Violeta—small and young.

My guilt blossomed anew. I knelt to the floor and the stones dug into my knees.

"I am not going to hurt you," I whispered. "I'm going to release you."

"To die?" Her voice shook.

"To *bathe*," I said.

She finally met my gaze, wary and confused. "Why?"

"I do not wish to leave you here," I said. "I should have protested this punishment. What you did…wasn't worth this."

She stared at me and then something dark came over her expression, and she reared back and spit in my face.

I had my answer—she had not been broken quite yet.

"You bitch!" The guard behind me started to move forward, but I held out my hand to stop him before wiping her saliva off my face.

Then I grabbed her wrists and hauled her to her feet.

"Listen and listen well," I said, my voice low and threatening. "I am going to give you one more chance to accept what I have to offer. If you refuse, I'll keep you here forever. Just like this. You'll grow old, naked and alone, and every day you will think about this night, when I offered you a world outside this cell. Now, what will it be, Safira?"

She jerked from my grip, and I released her, but her fight was soon gone. Her shoulders fell and she looked very tired.

"You are offering a bath," she said. "What else?"

My lips curled. "Are you bargaining?"

"If I am to trade this life for another, I want to know what I'm getting."

"Well, I would not mind another lady-in-waiting," I said.

She would never replace Violeta, but there was something very sharp about Safira. She was knowledgeable, and she had her pulse on palace gossip, which would greatly benefit me. Her brows rose. "Why would you want me as your lady? I am your enemy."

"A woman who wants to sleep with my husband does not make her an enemy, Safira. It makes her annoying."

She crossed her arms over her chest, resigned.

I took a step away. "Come along." I walked out of the cell, and Safira followed without protest.

Though late, I summoned a bath for her, and while she sat in the steaming water, scrubbing her skin, I read through one of the spell books I had brought from the library. It was one Zann had set aside for me, and it contained a set of geometric shapes that were said to channel various types of energy for different types of magic.

I traced one of them with my finger—a collection of triangles and circles.

"King Adrian has not yet turned you?" Safira asked.

My finger froze on the page.

"He has not," I said, without looking away from my book "Though, it is not from lack of wanting."

Although, last time, it had been me who begged Adrian to change me. I understood why he had said no in the aftermath of the lake attack. I had only recently come to accept the use of my aufhocker form, but that acceptance had yet to help me shift.

"Is it you who are not convinced?" Safira asked. "Do you not wish for immortality?"

I paused for a moment and looked up from my book. She had stopped scrubbing her skin and now hugged her knees to her chest. "I wish for invincibility," I said. "It seems more practical."

Though no longer guaranteed, apparently.

I set my book aside.

"Why don't you tell me who you are?" I said.

Safira straightened. "What do you mean?"

"You are angry like I am angry," I said. "Why? Where did you come from? How did you end up as a vassal?"

"I suppose I am like anyone who just wants to survive in this world," she said.

"What does that mean?"

She shrugged. "My family is very poor, and I thought I could come here and make money to send back. And I did, for a while."

"Will you seek to become a vassal once more?" I asked.

Her gaze returned to mine. "Am I allowed?"

"I do not see why you wouldn't. It is nothing that will interfere with your role as my lady's maid," I said.

She shook her head. "I still do not understand why you chose me."

"Because you have a use," I said and leaned forward in my chair. "Before my coronation, someone in this castle poisoned me. Only a few days ago, Adrian's fish were also poisoned. *Someone* within these walls is a traitor. I want you to find them."

I chose not to explain how Adrian and I suspected one of his four closest advisors of treason because I did not wish Safira to know of the bloodletting or its consequences. It was knowledge I did not trust her to have.

"Outside these doors, you are to gather information and follow any hint of treason. You are to report only to me—no one else. Not even Adrian. Am I clear?"

With anything of this nature, I felt the fewer who knew the truth the better. I thought of Adrian's earlier words—*once the truth is spoken, it always seems to find its target.* I expected her to question why I wished to keep Adrian ignorant, but that was not her worry.

"You trust me?" she asked. "To do this?"

"Not at all," I said, rising with my book. "This is how you earn my trust."

Safira finished bathing, and I gave her a nightgown to change into, sending her down the hall to one of the guest suites for the evening.

Once she was gone, I settled on my bed and began

to study the spell book, specifically, the various shapes I could use to summon and bind magic.

Each shape has a frequency, an assigned energy. Alone, a circle, an oval, a triangle, are sacred symbols. Together, they are a language that makes up a spell.

This language had a range of power based on how the shapes were layered and intertwined. With this type of casting, no words were needed. I found myself mindlessly tracing the shapes into the air while I continued to read—a circle first and several triangles within.

"A summoning spell," said a voice. "Well, aren't you quite the novice."

I looked up, locking eyes with Ravena who hovered in my mirror. I searched for changes in her—a difference in her hair color, aging in her face, a withered limb, signs that she might have performed spells from *The Book of Dis*, but she looked much the same—ginger-colored hair and narrow eyes, her skin stippled with freckles.

"You." My voice quaked, and I rose from my bed, snatching my blade from the side table. She laughed as I armed myself.

"I plan to build a throne from your bones," I said.

"Perhaps that is what I should do with yours and the rest of High Coven's."

"It makes sense that you would need our magic. You were never quite as powerful."

Ravena smiled, narrowed her eyes, and suddenly, I felt a grip on my neck and I was lifted off the ground. The impact against my throat made me want to vomit, but I couldn't even if I tried. I was slowly suffocating.

"I think you forget who is powerless now," she said.

I was still clutching my blade, and I lifted my hands

to my neck, hoping to stab at whatever magic she used to hold me. But there was nothing to grasp, nothing to pry away.

"You know this is what they wanted? All of us, divided, at war with one another. It's hard to reach a goal when everyone is fighting."

I could not form words; my mouth was full of saliva and my tongue felt swollen.

Suddenly, she released me, and I collapsed to the floor, coughing while simultaneously gasping for breath.

"It's no fun talking to myself," she said.

"Fuck you," I rasped, but the words were choked. "What do you want?"

"To restore balance to the world," she said.

I crawled forward and sat up, wincing as I swallowed, knife still in hand. "What does that even mean?"

"It means people have to die," she said. "Peace makes no one powerful, Isolde. Even High Coven knew that. It is what tore us apart in the end."

"*You* tore us apart."

"Vada tore *us* apart," Ravena snapped. "She was the one who sent us across Cordova to serve kings in their courts, all because *she* wanted power. That was the beginning of our end."

Vada was an elder. She had handed me off to Dragos dressed in red, though I'd begged her to let me wear another color. She'd frowned at me, too proud of her work.

"But you are beautiful," she'd said.

"This color is associated with depravity among my people," I'd argued.

"But that is not the truth in Revekka. You must respect their customs."

"Or they could respect mine," I snapped. *I* was the one with real power.

"Yesenia." Vada cupped my face between her cold and wrinkled hands. Her palms were softer than mine. They always had been. Vada had never planted her own herbs or harvested them. "We will not survive if we are not docile."

"Is survival worth it, then?" I asked.

"When you have someone to live for, no sacrifice is too great," she'd said.

But then we had gone on to give up our power, our autonomy, our lives, and we had lost those we loved anyway.

"You cannot believe that you have true power just because you sit upon a throne and wear a crown," said Ravena.

"Adrian treats me as his equal," I said.

"You do not know the man you married," she said. "Adrian sees a use for you just as he sees a use for everyone else he allows into his life. He just happens to fuck you."

"You don't know what you're talking about," I said, my fingers tightening around the hilt of my blade.

"You think Adrian wants to be free of Dis?" she asked. "What he really wants is to take her place."

"What's so wrong with being a god?" I asked.

"It's not becoming one that's the problem; it's who has to die for him to get there." She paused, and then said, "But you know he is dangerous. Or at least you did—he's why you created the book."

"You're lying," I said, but the shock of her words straightened my spine and I hated how truthful they felt.

She smiled and shook her head. “I am many things, but I have never been a liar, Yesenia.”

“Time changes people, Ravena,” I said, and I reared back and shoved the blade toward her, but unlike last time, the mirror only shattered under my blow.

Her laugh echoed in my room, and she was gone.

TWENTY-TWO
Isolde

I left my room for Adrian's.

I did not wish to remain there, not after Ravena's visit. Her words weighed heavily on my mind, most of all, what she had to say about Adrian.

You do not know the man you married…he's why you created the book.

I could not remember it, could not imagine it, and I did not believe her.

Clutching the spell book tighter, I entered Adrian's chambers, finding him sitting on the edge of the bed, his head in his hands.

I halted, immediately concerned. "Are you all right?" I asked.

"Just a headache," he said, but he did not look up.

I set my book on the table and crossed the room to the wash basin, where I soaked a cloth in cool water before bringing it to Adrian.

He looked up when I approached, squinting, and I pressed the cloth to his cheek and then his forehead.

"I am sorry you are unwell," I said.

"It is no fault of yours," he replied with a small smile. Then he tugged on my hand as he fell back against the bed, and I followed, landing atop him.

"Where have you been?" he asked.

"Looking for summoning spells."

The air hung heavy between us, and I knew it was because I had things to tell him, but I did not want to add to his troubles.

I adjusted the cloth on his head. "I have never known you to have a headache."

He touched the corner of my mouth, and I realized I was frowning. "It is nothing to worry about, my sweet. Did you find a spell?"

I rested my head upon his chest. "I found symbols," I said, and then paused. "What do you remember of Ravena?"

I was not sure what information I was really looking for, but I was curious about his observations.

"Not much," he said. "I only paid attention after your death. I watched her stand at Dragos's side until I invaded Revekka, and after I murdered him, I pursued her, but it was like she vanished from the face of the earth. I hadn't seen any sign of her until the crimson mist. Why do you ask?"

"I just wonder what motivates her," I said.

"I imagine what motivates most of us in this world," he said.

"And what is that?" I asked.

"Survival."

"I think it has gone beyond that," I said. "Has it not for you?"

"No," he said. "Why do you think I like what I am?"

A scream drove me from sleep. I sat up, heart racing, and the only reason I did not think I was dreaming was because Adrian was awake too.

"Did you hear that?" I asked.

Another scream.

We shot from the bed, searching in the dark for our clothes. I had just managed to pull on my robe and get the door open when I came face-to-face with Sorin.

"The castle's under attack," he said. "There are vârcolaci roaming the halls."

Vârcolaci were a type of werewolf. They were large and could rise onto their hind legs and fight using their clawed hands.

"How?"

"We do not know, but they did not come in by any usual means," said Sorin.

Adrian drew his sword, and I turned to look at him. He was shirtless, wearing only the trousers he'd managed to find in the dark.

"Please stay," he said, kissing my forehead. "Sorin, watch her."

Then Adrian was gone.

I stepped into the hallway long enough to watch him, the muscles in his shoulders tense as more screams sounded throughout the castle.

I looked at Sorin. "I think I know how they got in."

"How?"

"Ravena," I said, unwilling to completely admit that I had summoned her, that whatever connection I had established earlier had not fully closed. "We have to go!"

I took off down the hallway for my chambers.

Sorin did not try to stop me; instead, he followed, racing beside me. When we came to my hall, I skidded to a halt, finding the door to my chambers in ruins. Part of it hung off the hinges, part of it looked as if it had flown off and hit the opposite wall, and there were splinters of wood everywhere.

"Isolde," Sorin hissed as I crept closer.

I looked back at him and put my finger to my lips, glaring. My weapons were in the room, and I wanted them, but as I neared my door and peered through the wrecked doorframe, I saw that my room was still occupied by a vârcolac.

It must have sensed me because it turned its glowing, red eyes upon me and bellowed a scream-like roar.

I stumbled back, fumbling as I turned around.

"Run!" I yelled at Sorin as the creature exploded from my room. It used the wall as a springboard, flying through the air, landing in front of us, barring our escape.

Sorin lifted his blade.

"This would be a really great time for you to shift, Isolde," he said, gritting his teeth.

"Maybe if I'd had a better teacher," I returned.

The vârcolac roared again and rose on its hind legs, towering over us. He struck at Sorin, his razor-sharp claws tangling with his blade.

I raced back to my room to retrieve my sword, but just as my hand touched the hilt, another vârcolac rose from the shattered mirror on my floor.

"Fuck, fuck, fuck!"

There was no hesitation. The vârcolac did not even attempt to assess me as prey; it just pounced, a horrible growling coming from deep in its throat. I gripped my sword but knew the creature was too close for me to succeed in any kind of attack. I managed to jump out of the way, but just as quickly, the vârcolac whirled and charged.

This time, I swung my sword, gripping it with both hands. The blade cut into the vârcolac's paw but did not sever it. Blood poured onto my hilt and my hands, and while I tried to jerk my blade free, the vârcolac snapped at me. I fell to the ground to avoid its bite and crawled, but was flattened on the ground by a giant paw, its five sharp claws sinking into my back. I screamed and twisted, shoving my dagger into its arm.

It offered a loud shriek that rang in my ears, and I was able to stumble to my feet and run. I hit the doorframe, unsteady on my feet, and when I made it into the hallway, Sorin was facing two vârcolaci, the one behind me having also followed. I leaned against the wall, weak, and I thought of Sorin and our sessions. They moved through my mind quickly, and I latched on to a few words he had spoken.

This is magic, he'd said. *You just have to reach for it.*

I recalled how I had felt during the spell in the woods. How it had felt like my very womb had split open, and it had been full of light, full of magic, full of warmth, and it had given me hope—and then it felt as though it had been taken, snatched from me by hate.

But it hadn't. It had just been suppressed.

It was afraid, just as I was afraid now.

That was the design of oppression.

I turned my head toward the vârcolac, and a growl vibrated in my throat. It was the first time I'd witnessed the monster pause to assess me. I pushed off the wall and growled louder, the sound animalistic, primal. Then I took off down the hallway, my legs carrying me faster than they ever had before.

I felt my insides changing, and the pain was acute. It made me gnash my teeth, which had elongated. Blood spilled on the ground as my claws exploded from my fingertips, and as I changed, I launched myself at the two vârcolaci facing Sorin. He was bleeding badly, only holding his sword with one hand, the other arm limp at his side.

I went for the neck as I collided with one of the vârcolaci and bit down hard, yanking as we landed. The other creature slammed into me, and I flew across the floor, hitting the banister of the stairs, but I bounced back to my feet, a growl rumbling in my throat. I sprang, but so did the vârcolac, and we tangled in the air, biting and lashing at one another. We landed in a heap, continuing the close combat. The creature bit my shoulder, and its claws sank into my belly. I screamed in its face and then bit its snout and did not let go, my claws digging into its sides, and I only released the creature when I felt its hold on me lessen. Once it did, I tore out its neck just as I had the other.

Sorin's cry drew my attention, and when I turned to face the final vârcolac, the tracker had been thrown down the hall. His back hit the wall, and he slid to the ground, unmoving.

I snarled and shot toward the monster. Our bodies hit

hard, and it knocked the breath from my body, snapping my ribs. When I landed on my feet, opposite the vârcolac, pain shot through me, and yet I charged again. Our teeth sank into each other's shoulders, and as we landed, we rolled. I could not manage to get the upper hand, and I lay beneath the creature, its claws sinking deep inside me. And while I tried to lock my jaw into the monster, pain shot through me, roaring from my throat, and I released it.

But then there was a wet sound, and blood poured onto my body. The vârcolac lessened its hold and then fell, landing beside me on the ground. I turned my head to find Sorin, standing with his bloodied blade.

I wanted to call his name, but I could not speak in this form, and I had no idea how to shift back.

He looked down at me, and there was something horrifying about his face, a darkness in his eyes.

"I'm sorry, Isolde," he said and lifted his blade.

Shock left me immobile as his sword sank into my chest. I screamed, and as I did, I felt myself changing back. Tears poured from my eyes, and Sorin fell to his knees beside me, gathering me to his chest.

"I'm so sorry," he said. He was crying too.

I did not want him to touch me. I could not understand why he was holding me.

"Why?" I asked, my mouth quivering.

"Because he has to die," Sorin said. "Adrian will destroy us, Isolde. None of us can fight him. You have to understand. You once understood."

I shook my head.

"*The Book of Dis*," he continued. "You wrote those spells for him."

"How do you know that?" I whispered.

Ravena had just told *me*.

"I know a lot more than you think."

"You are a traitor," I said. "You are *the* traitor. You told Ravena about the bloodletting."

Sorin's brows lowered. "I am many things," he said. "A traitor among them, but I did not tell Ravena anything."

"I don't believe you," I said.

"I am not choosing one side over the other."

"Then you are weak," I said, and he winced, closing his eyes for a second. When he opened them again and gazed upon me, his treason only hurt worse because I did not see the hate I wanted to see. I saw regret and sorrow and deep, deep sadness.

"Adrian is becoming more and more a monster every day," he said. "Tell me you have not seen the signs. The flash of white in his eyes, the pain in his head. It is Dis taking over. It is Dis speaking to him."

"How do you know it is Dis?" I whispered, my mouth quivering. I did not know if it was from my anguish or shock.

"Isolde," Sorin said, shaking his head.

"Don't," I said between bloody teeth. "Do not say my name."

Sorin nodded and then spoke. "He'll hurt you one day, and then you will understand."

"He would never," I said with such conviction in my voice. I began to cry.

"I really do love you," Sorin said. "I wish you could remember…this is for the greater good."

Those words.

My father had used them.

"You wanted me to kill myself?" I asked, affronted. "For whom? For a kingdom of people who turned their backs on me for my sacrifice?"

"It is for the greater good!" he said.

"Get out," I said.

"Iso—"

"I said get out!" I yelled, blood flying from my mouth. "Get out!"

Tears streamed down Sorin's face, but he rose to his feet, took up his sword, and fled.

At some point, I must have passed out because I was roused by Adrian's rage-filled scream. I opened my eyes and stared up at him as he took me into his arms.

"Adrian." I whispered his name, lifting my blood-stained hand to his face.

"What happened? Where is Sorin?" he asked.

"Sorin did this," I said. "Sorin is a traitor."

"No." I heard another voice I recognized as Daroc's, but I could not turn my head to look at him.

My eyes were heavy, and my hand fell from Adrian's face, leaving a streak of blood. Adrian reached for it, pressing my palm to his cheek again.

"I will heal you."

"Adrian," I whispered, smiling at him. "Not even you can heal this."

Adrian's venom was powerful, but it had limits as we'd had learned with the aufhocker bite.

"Unless… You must change me," I said.

I recognized there were consequences, but none came close to dying.

Adrian's eyes passed over my face, as if he were

assessing just how much I wanted this. "You are certain?"

"It is either that or die," I said. "I no longer wish to be a sparrow."

There was no hesitation after that.

He positioned me so that my head rested on his shoulder, and he bit into my neck. At first, it felt normal, and then he sank his teeth in deeper, and it felt as though he had injected fire into my veins. But I did not scream; I only held onto him as tightly as I could.

"Drink, Isolde," Adrian said.

I was only half-aware when he placed something against my lips and a metallic taste filled my mouth. It was blood, different from my own. Stronger, somehow.

I did not know if I managed to drink, but there came a point when I felt as though I were floating, rising into a darkness pierced with stars.

TWENTY-THREE
Isolde

My throat was burning, and I groaned as I opened my eyes.

"Up," Adrian said gently, his hands on my shoulders, but any movement made my head spin. I buried my face in the soft blankets beneath me, squeezing my eyes shut.

"I can't," I said, my voice hoarse, and I winced at the pain.

"You must drink," Adrian said, and I moaned as I sat up, head swimming.

I felt horrible, and black spots marred my vision.

Adrian moved me. Bringing my legs on either side of his body, he pulled me against him and cradled my head in the hollow of his neck.

"Drink," he said.

And strangely, I needed no more encouragement than that. I bit into his skin.

It was easier than I imagined, but that was because of the fangs that had grown in behind my teeth.

“Fuck,” Adrian moaned, one of his hands tightening in my hair. “Yes, my sweet. Suck harder.”

As his blood filled my mouth and throat, the burning lessened, and my head cleared. I became aware of other things—how our naked bodies fit together, how Adrian’s full cock felt between my legs, and how aroused I was. I reached for him while I took long pulls of his blood, running my thumb over a thick bead of come, smearing it over his crown.

Adrian inhaled between his teeth, and then I released him and pulled away from his neck, rocking my hips against his length, my mouth closing over his. I had a strange feral need to fuck. It went beyond my usual desire. I could almost not describe it, but it rattled my bones and heated my insides, and it urged me to move, to fill myself up with more than just blood.

“No one has taken your blood?” I asked, my lips caressing his as I spoke. His hands splayed across my ribs as he held me, head tilted up to meet my gaze.

“Never,” he said. “I have waited for you.”

Our mouths collided again, and Adrian coaxed me onto my back, his hand cupping my breasts, squeezing, before he drew my nipple into his mouth. He shifted to the other, and my thighs tightened around him as my fingers scraped through his hair. When I could no longer reach him, I ran my foot along his cock. Adrian met my gaze, his eyes burning into mine.

“You want to touch me too, Sparrow?”

My mouth watered at the thought. “Yes.”

He held my gaze as he bent to lick me, and he sighed, a hum vibrating against my center. My muscles tightened everywhere, preparing for the pleasure his mouth would bring, but then he shifted, moving up my body once again, mouth closing over mine, his tongue stroking my mouth as he had done below.

When he pulled away, he said, "Suck me." He rested on his back, and as I started to take my place, his hands clamped down on my hips. "Not that way."

He guided my foot over his body so that I straddled him with my back to his face, and I rose onto my hands and knees, tongue sliding over the crown of his cock while his fingers parted my flesh. Now and then, he sucked my skin, and each time, a guttural sound escaped from my throat.

"Does that feel good?" he asked between each gentle pull.

"Yes," I moaned, unable to continue pleasing him with my mouth. All I could do was stroke his cock. I let my head fall against his thigh and ran my tongue over his balls before sucking each heavy sack into my mouth.

He hissed, forming words I could not hear, and suddenly he pushed my legs to the side, guiding me to my back, facing him. His body caged mine against the bed, his lustful eyes holding mine before he kissed me again. His hand swept down between my legs, and I was so slick, I could *hear* it.

"I need you," I said.

"Bite," he commanded, placing his wrist against my mouth. I held on to him as I obeyed, and when my teeth sank into his skin, he sank into me.

"Fuck," he groaned. "Fuck, you feel so good."

Adrian let me drink from him, moving his other hand to the top of my head, bracing himself as he moved, his chest to mine. His first few thrusts were slow and deep, and I felt every ridge of his cock, but then his movements became shallow, more concentrated, and a delicious friction began to take hold of me. In its grip, I could not control my body.

I released Adrian's wrist as a moan tore from the back of my throat, and just when I felt the tension in my body peak, he bit into the flesh of my neck.

I came, cursing, my fingers tightening in Adrian's hair, and he followed, filling me with warmth. I went limp beneath him as he finished feeding, and he pulled away, brushing strands of sweat-soaked hair from my face.

"How do you feel?" he asked.

I was still attempting to control my breathing, but I considered his question. The biggest difference had been when I had woken up with a burning in my throat, but since I had taken Adrian's blood, I felt the same.

"Are you asking if I feel different?"

He tilted his head, the corner of his mouth lifting, as if he found the question curious.

"I just want to know how you feel."

I answered on an exhale. "Exhausted, but not just physically...mentally too." I held Adrian's gaze and then asked, "How many people will betray us in the end?"

"I suppose we should expect that everyone will," he said.

"That is a sad existence."

"And yet it is ours."

He kissed me and then settled on his side, drawing me tight against him.

"Sleep," he said. "You will need it."

I considered asking him what he meant, but my body was warm and my eyes were heavy. I did not feel like talking, though there were so many things that needed our attention, and I let myself slip into darkness.

I was writhing—arching my back, my feet sliding against the bed, unable to find purchase. Hunger gnawed at the bottom of my stomach. Adrian was against me and he brought his wrist to my mouth again.

"Bite, Sparrow."

This time, I could smell his blood. I had expected it would have a different scent once I was changed, but it smelled like metal—sharp and bitter—and there was something inside me that craved it.

I took Adrian's wrist, but after a few pulls, I pushed it away and crawled on top of him. He was aroused, his length settling between my thighs, and the hunger I'd had for his blood dissolved into a desire for his come.

"What do you want, my sweet?" he asked.

"I don't know what is happening to me," I whispered.

"You are turning," he said. "You are hungry. You will be hungry for a while, until your change takes root."

"How long will that be?"

"To develop all your powers? Months."

Disappointment blossomed in my chest, and it unsettled me that I would not know my full potential for some time.

"Is this what it will be? Blood and sex?"

"Are you asking how frequently you will need to feed and fuck me?"

I glared at him, planting my hands on his chest. "It is a practical question, Adrian."

He grinned.

I liked his smile. I wanted it more often, but we did not have much to smile about outside this room.

He gripped my thighs and ground his hips into me.

"This will not last long," he said. "Though I will enjoy it while it does."

I reached for his hands and brought them to my breasts.

"You said no one has ever taken blood from you before. How did those you changed feed?"

Annoyance flashed in Adrian's eyes, but he answered, "I gave them my blood, but I drained it for them."

"And the sex? How many did you indulge?"

"Do you really want an answer to that question?"

In truth, I did not know. I could already feel the jealousy gathering in my chest, thick and hot.

"Did any of them try to bite you?" I bent over him, my lips hovering near his.

"Plenty," he said.

"What happened to them?"

He raised a brow. "I'd rather not answer a thousand questions about the hundreds of vampires I have turned in two hundred years."

Then he rolled, and I was on my back, pinned beneath his body.

"Suddenly I am no longer interested in fucking you," I said.

"No?" he asked, holding my gaze for a moment before his tongue swirled over one hard nipple, then the other. I could not help the way my body responded, tightening, widening, preparing. He chuckled and then sat back and flipped me onto my stomach. Dragging my hips up, he ran his palm over my ass before smacking my skin.

"Fucking beautiful," he said, his fingers diving into my flesh from behind. "Not interested in fucking me, hmm?"

"Adrian."

I wasn't sure why I was saying his name—it was half warning, half plea. He knew I hadn't meant what I said, and now he intended to teach me a lesson. I wanted it. I even widened my legs and he chuckled as he smoothed his hand up my back until he reached my hair, which he pulled, tilting my head back, my throat taut.

"So rarely under my control," he whispered. "I like you like this."

He withdrew his fingers and pressed a kiss to my lower back before he guided himself into me. He still held my hair, and once he gained momentum, he released me and placed his hand flat on my upper back, pushing me to the bed. His movements were rough and hard, and I loved it, wanted more of it.

I panted, ragged and raw, and the only thing I hated about this was that I could not see the pleasure on his face. He moved his hand to my clit, rubbing furiously, and then suddenly he was bent completely over me, my whole body resting against the bed. He bit me in the hollow of my neck, and I completely came apart.

When he was finished, he rolled to the side and draped his arm around my waist. I was too tired to move.

He kissed me and then nuzzled my neck in the spot where he'd taken my blood over and over tonight.

"You are my light," he said as I descended into darkness.

I was conscious that it was bright. I could tell, even though I had yet to open my eyes. There was a part of me that did not want to face the day, not in the aftermath of Sorin's betrayal. Today I'd have to talk about it and feel the pain—but it was not just my pain. It was also Adrian's and Daroc's.

"I know you are awake," said Adrian.

I opened my eyes, blinking up at my husband, who stood beside the bed, naked. His body was smeared with dried blood.

"I've had a bath drawn for us," he said and held out his hand.

When I sat up, my head swam, and I accepted his help as I rose to my feet. I looked down at my body and then back at our bed—it was all stained with blood.

Adrian offered a small smile. "New vampires are messy."

He walked with me to the metal tub, and I was glad for it because I did not feel completely stable on my feet.

I lowered into the water, steam curling around me as I did. Adrian followed, settling behind me. We spent a few moments cleaning the blood from our skin before I leaned against his chest, his arms crossed over my body, protective, comforting—and then he spoke, his voice soft and serious.

"Tell me what happened. Every detail."

I took a few moments to gather my thoughts, to decide how I would present the story of Sorin's betrayal. I was still confused by his actions. He had saved me from the vârcolaci only to stab me with his own sword. Had he had second thoughts? What about when we were in the woods on the night of the full moon? Had he hoped the villagers would do the job he ended up executing?

"I think I am responsible for the vârcolaci entering the castle," I said, pausing, but there was no change in Adrian's body, no hint that he was upset by what I was saying. "I…summoned Ravena via the mirror in my room, and when I broke it, I think I allowed the creatures in somehow."

"You don't know that," he said. "Ravena could have sent them on her own."

I did not acknowledge his comment, though what he said could be true.

"I realized what had happened, and Sorin came with me to my chamber. He fought beside me, even after I shifted into my aufhocker form."

At the mention of my change, Adrian's arms tightened around me.

"He saved me from one of the vârcolaci…and then… he stabbed me, and even after, he did not leave."

I was so confused, so tired of crying over everything that had happened to my people and to me. I hated that my mouth quivered now.

"He held me and tried to tell me it was for the greater good."

I *hated* those words.

You would be renowned, not just in Lara but all of Cordova, my father had said as he tried to convince me to die for something he'd called the *greater good*, which only meant a world where Adrian and I did not exist.

And apparently, Sorin believed the same.

Which hurt because I'd spent time with him as he'd recounted his trauma. I'd held him on the floor of the training room and mourned that his life had changed just as suddenly as mine. Maybe the most horrifying part of it all was that no one seemed to want me to die as much as they wanted Adrian to die—but I was the easiest target.

Well, no longer.

"What is the greater good?" Adrian asked.

"A world without you," I said, quiet and sad.

I gripped the side of the metal tub and turned around to face Adrian. He drew me close, my knees on either side of his waist.

"What is it that you want?"

"You," he said, trailing his wet fingers over my lips.

"Adrian," I whispered. "You know what I am asking."

"And I am answering," he said. "My goal has never changed. I will rule Cordova with you at my side."

"That is the destination. How are you getting there?"

He stared at me for a long moment and then answered, "You."

I jerked my head back, surprised by his answer.

"Me?"

"I cannot be...*free*...without you," he said. "Without your magic."

I stared, swallowing hard. I was conflicted. I wanted Adrian to be free of Dis, but I had never realized that he saw me as the key to that freedom.

"What do you mean?"

"Vampires cannot fight magic. You have said so yourself," Adrian explained. Then he whispered, as if he did not wish for anyone to hear, "But more importantly, witches are Dis's creations; you draw from her magic. Does it not seem plausible, then, that you could harness it against her?"

With my skills, it was not plausible, but his admission hurt me. It made me feel like there was truth to what Ravena had said—that I did not truly know Adrian, that he had brought me along because I had use—and I hated that she would be right at all.

"What if I had not had magic?"

He said nothing, but I knew.

"Ana," I whispered, and there was something about this that felt like deception. "Is this how I become useful?"

Adrian clenched his jaw, and his hands tightened around me, as if he feared I would run. I was still considering it. "I *never* said that."

"Is it not implied?"

"Do you think I would cast you aside if you could not do it?" he asked, angry.

I didn't, but it still hurt that he had not spoken of this before.

"Do you truly believe I want you for no other reason?"

"Why did you not tell me you needed my magic before now?" I asked. We had been so honest with each other about everything, why was this any different?

"Because you showed no signs of having magic, and why would I place the burden of my curse upon you?"

I bit my lip hard and looked away from him, frustrated with myself and with this situation.

"Ravena said I wrote *The Book of Dis* to destroy you," I said. The words were like blades scraping my throat, and yet Adrian did not seem at all surprised.

I felt his fingers against my jaw, forcing my gaze to his.

"I have no doubt that you did," he said.

"Adrian—"

I did not know what to say.

"If you do destroy me, it will be because of Dis," he said. "You'll remember that, won't you?"

"What are you saying?"

"I am saying I am no longer the favorite of the goddess's creations."

I started to speak, to ask for more, but there was a knock at the door, and Adrian permitted them entrance. I had expected Vesna and Safira, so I was mortified when Tanaka entered our room. I drew close to Adrian to maintain an ounce of modesty—an action Adrian apparently found humorous because he chuckled.

I could not tell if Tanaka was nervous or embarrassed or if he had merely overexerted himself in an attempt to reach our quarters. Either way, he was red in the face, and he paused to clear his throat.

"Your Majesties," Tanaka said, bowing. "Gavriel has arrived from Lara. He brings urgent news."

Despite my efforts to hide my nakedness, I pulled away from Adrian, straightening.

"What news?"

"I am afraid your country is under attack," he said.

"By whom?" I demanded.

"Alaric of Hela," said Gavriel, who entered behind Tanaka. He was clad in armor and dirty; even his hair, usually blond, looked almost brown. I was surprised by his sudden appearance in our room and crossed my arms over my chest. "They invaded in the night. I suppose they took your father's long absence as an invitation. Though that is not the worst of it."

"What is the worst of it?" I demanded.

"Alaric has been turned," he said. "And so has his army."

Adrian and I exchanged a look. We both knew who was responsible.

Julian.

Of all the kings to turn, I had not expected Alaric. He had never petitioned Adrian and had been vocal about his dislike for my father's surrender.

Adrian rose from the bath, water streaming off his skin.

"Give us a moment," he said. "As you can see, we are not in a state to entertain this news. We will meet you in the council room shortly. Summon Daroc."

"And Killian," I added.

"Of course, Your Majesties," said Tanaka.

They bowed and the old man cast a furious look at Gavriel before they departed.

"You are surprised," Adrian said as I got to my feet. "You did not expect this behavior from Alaric?"

"No, not in the least. He has never supported vampires of any kind. When my father decided to surrender to you, he was the most vocal against it."

"Sounds like Julian swayed him," Adrian said and grew quiet.

"Or forced him," I said. "Do you think Julian is using Alaric?"

"Yes. Hela is a large country with a large army. Likely Julian will allow Alaric to lead until he grows tired of him. Then he will kill him...but by then, he will have an army big enough to come after me."

I let Adrian's words sit in the silence between us. All I could think was that we had to stop him at Lara.

"What are we going to do?" I asked, though I did not expect a quick answer. Revekka was in a fragile state, not only due to Ravena's spells but the shifting loyalties of its people, who grew wary of our leadership day by day. Still, I had to defend my kingdom. Lara was mine by right, and I would be damned if I witnessed a king of the Nine Houses take what was mine.

Adrian looked at me, the tips of his fingers caressing my cheek.

"We will fight for your throne."

TWENTY-FOUR
Adrian

My gaze strayed to Isolde as we made our way to the council room. I worried for her and all the change she had seen in such a short time. I had been the catalyst for all of it, but she stood beside me, stoic and proud and beautiful, giving no hint to the internal turmoil of her mind, which I heard as her thoughts raced from Lara to Sorin, from Ana to Ravena, from her own power over magic to her power over shifting to when she would fully know her potential as a vampire.

She worried about me and she worried about Dis.

I could offer no comfort, save that I would not leave her side, but that all depended on how long Dis allowed me to be…me.

As I thought about the control she might leverage, my teeth clenched so hard my jaw ached. I could feel her influence now and then, teasing the edges of my mind.

That was how I knew she was unhappy with me—she had never attempted to control me before, but I had done something she did not like, though what exactly it was remained to be seen.

Gavriel, Tanaka, and Killian waited in the council room.

"I apologize for what happened earlier," said Tanaka as soon as we entered.

"It was not as if I did not invite you into our room, Tanaka," I said, my eyes shifting to Gavriel, who offered no apology. Clearly, he had enjoyed the sight of my wife.

"I merely thought the queen would want to know the state of her homeland as soon as possible," Gavriel said, his gaze lingering on Isolde. If Killian had not also been glaring at the vampire, I might have thought I was being overprotective.

"As urgent as this news is, I think we can all agree it is best given when we are clothed," I said. Gavriel swallowed and averted his eyes.

Before I could say anything else, Daroc arrived, and his presence halted all my words.

He looked devastated.

It was the only way I could think to describe him. His face was drawn with shadows, which pooled beneath his eyes and carved the hollows of his cheeks, but it was his expression that was most unsettling. He usually looked callous or angry, but there was a complete lack of emotion within his gaze that made me think he no longer possessed his body.

He approached us and was silent, but I was still watching him, wary, and I noticed the blood on his coat. He had taken out his aggression on something—likely a wall—and while the cuts had healed, he still bore the evidence of it on his clothes.

"Tell us what happened, Gavriel," Isolde prompted when I was too distracted to speak.

We listened as he detailed Alaric's attack on Lara. It happened three nights ago. It had been swift, and Castle Fiora fell quickly. I noted how Isolde exchanged worried looks with Killian.

"We were not prepared. And even if we had been, we did not have the numbers to fight such an army. Alaric is clearly out of control…there were women and children among his ranks."

"By the goddess," Killian muttered.

I could not help the disgust that curled my lip. I had never turned a child, and I had killed anyone who did. Becoming a vampire needed to be a choice. Sorin was my greatest example of that.

"How many strong?" I asked.

"At least seventy thousand," Gavriel said.

It was as I suspected. Alaric—or rather Julian—was building an army to take control of Cordova. But they had made a grave error and had not even realized it. Alaric and Julian had only thought of power when they had begun to create their army, not the consequences of thousands of new monsters released into the world. They had created chaos, and it was chaos they would not be able to contain.

I had no choice but to march against both vampires. This was more than a matter of freeing Lara.

"And our army?" Isolde asked, looking at me.

"I have one hundred and fifty thousand soldiers at my command," I said.

Some were already stationed in the territories I had conquered across Cordova—Jola, Elin, Siva, Lita. Some were left to maintain order, some to rebuild, and on the rare occasion the villagers organized to attack, they suppressed uprisings—but none of those rebellions had been vampire-led.

"How many can you send to Lara?" Isolde asked.

"Half," I said. "Among them, some of my most skilled warriors."

"You do not mean to leave Revekka, my king," Tanaka said.

I looked at my viceroy—the man who ruled in my stead. He was not a fighter by any means, but he was intelligent and wise, and I often appreciated his council.

"I do intend to leave Revekka," I said. "This is a greater threat, and I will be at the front of my army to face it."

"Revekka needs you," he argued. "What will your people do when they watch you march out of your kingdom when they are under such duress?"

"Perhaps rejoice that their lands will not turn into a battlefield."

"There is more than one type of battle, Adrian," said Tanaka. "And your people have been fighting it. They are afraid of it, and you are their only line of defense."

"Let me lead the soldiers to Lara," said Daroc. "I am your general."

Daroc was my general and second-in-command, but he was currently not fit to make decisions, much less lead an army.

"I am their queen. I will lead them," Isolde said.

"You have never led an army," I said and looked at her. "And you aren't going alone."

"I won't be alone. I will have Killian," she said.

"No. *I* will lead my army," I said, an ache forming at the back of my head, and with that familiar echo of pain came dread. Fuck. I was not ready for this. "I will decimate Alaric's army, and I will find Julian and skin him alive."

"And what are we to do about Ravena?" Tanaka asked. "What of the crimson mist and the blood plague? What about all these monster attacks?"

"We tried to banish the crimson mist," Isolde said, "and I was beaten within an inch of my life for it."

"So you would punish the rest of Revekka for the actions of a few?"

"I am not punishing anyone," she said. "As I have said explicitly before, the only way to fight Ravena is with magic. Do you have any, Tanaka?"

"Solaris does," he said.

"He does *not* have magic," Isolde said, her voice so severe, it echoed throughout the chamber.

"Whatever his power," Tanaka grated, shifting his gaze to me, "your people are turning to him faster than they ever caved to your rule, Adrian."

"I have handled Solaris," I snapped. My headache was growing stronger by the second, shooting pain to the front of my skull. Soon, I would not be able to see. "You will rule in my absence with my noblesse, and you will instruct our people to reinforce their homes, to build up great fires, to not wander beyond their villages. And when Ana wakes from the deep sleep she was beaten into by the very people she has cared for, you can ask her what she would do about Ravena. Are we clear?"

I took the silence that followed as acceptance.

"Tanaka, take my orders to the noblesse. Gavriel and Daroc, ready my army." I looked at Isolde, adding, "We march out at dusk."

I made it to my study before the first of Dis's attacks forced me to my knees.

"Fuck!"

I let my head hang and tried to crawl to my desk, hoping I could lift myself into my chair, but my head pounded, building pressure behind my eyes, and I could not see.

I heard her laugh in my mind—the sound like a chime, far too beautiful for her wickedness—and then she spoke.

"Just because you do not say my name does not mean I do not know what you are up to, my pet."

Another shock of pain lanced through my head, and I fell to the floor, unable to move.

"Tell me how you think you can be free of me when I created you," she hissed, and it felt as though she were in my ear. I turned my head toward her voice, and while I could see nothing, I knew she was here because she *was* the darkness. She was the night that fell upon the world and the inky sky between the stars. "I gave you everything, even your lover. Shall I take her back?"

"You wouldn't dare."

"I would dare," she said. "Do you think our pact means anything to me when you are plotting a way to destroy me? If she dies, she dies, and you will not follow. This world is your hell to live in, Adrian. You have created it."

"If you touch her..." I began, but my voice trembled, unable to carry out the threat I wanted to make.

"What?" Dis snapped, her darkness sinking into my hair, pulling it back. "What will you do, Blood King? Will you beg Asha for vengeance against me? I am afraid she has found her own path forward."

"What are you talking about?"

"I am not the only one who can create an incarnate, Adrian," she said. "Did you forget what you really are? My hand upon this world. What power do you have that I did not grant?"

I had no answer, and my hate for her deepened.

"Pray to me, Adrian, and I will let you go with a warning."

I gritted my teeth. I wished she were a physical body so I could dream of all the ways I'd kill her.

"Refuse and I'll leave a gift for your lover."

I rose onto my knees, my hands shaking.

"Say it," she ordered. "Say, 'I pray to thee, Goddess Dis, defender of my blood. Forgive my sins and guard against temptation, for you are my light in the darkness.'"

She had chosen her words to wound and likely hoped to provoke my violence, but I remained still, my nails digging into my palms, and I repeated her prayer, each word forced out between my teeth.

When I finished, she laughed again.

"Remember those words, Adrian. You will need them again soon."

She was gone and so was her pain, as if she had reached into my mind and pulled it free. When my vision cleared, I found that I was still on the floor and Daroc hovered over me.

"Are you all right?" he asked.

"Far from it," I said as I got to my feet.

I hated that he had seen me so helpless. I felt his eyes on me in the silence.

"Is it Dis?" he asked.

I did not respond. I did not like to say her name, much less hear it.

"You can tell me," Daroc continued.

"I do not want to talk about it," I said. Finally, I looked at him. "Did you need something?"

He opened his mouth to speak but hesitated, and I realized he'd come to talk about Sorin.

"I did not know," he began. "I swear to you. I—"

"I never thought you did," I said.

"I would like your permission to hunt for him," Daroc said.

I was quiet, studying him, uncertain this was the choice he should make so soon after his lover's betrayal.

"And what will you do when you find him?" I asked.

Daroc swallowed. His eyes were so red, they looked as if they were filled with blood.

"I will kill him."

"For me?" I asked. "Or for you?"

He opened his mouth to speak, but instead, he seemed to hold his breath.

"Would you really wish to exist in this world after you murdered your lover?" I asked.

I knew vengeance would come for Sorin, but I did not think it right for Daroc to take up the gauntlet, and I would never ask it of him.

"*Former* lover," he said, a bitter note to his voice.

"All the same," I said. "You love him."

His mouth trembled.

"I wish I didn't," he said through clenched teeth.

Because then I would not have to feel this pain. I heard what he did not say aloud, the words lodging in my heart like a knife. I knew a version of this desperation because I had felt it when Yesenia died.

"It's okay that you do," I said, and when he looked at me, I almost flinched. I had known Daroc for hundreds of years, and I had never seen him so devastated. And then he finally broke, a sob bursting from his mouth.

"He should have killed me," he said, falling to his knees, and another cry tore from his throat. "He should have killed me years ago after I turned him."

I knelt beside him and placed a hand on his shoulder. "I am glad he didn't."

Daroc remained on the floor for a while as wave after wave of emotion shook him. His mind was chaotic, and he vacillated between hunting Sorin and dying.

I could grant neither choice.

"I need you," I said. "For now, the answer is no, but after you have grieved a while, you may ask me again."

Daroc hung his head, defeated, though I knew he wavered, wondering if this would be the first time he defied my orders and went anyway. He rose to his feet first and I followed, holding his gaze.

"If I do not kill him, will you?" he asked.

"I suppose it depends on which of us sees him first," I said.

It would not be an easy execution, even with what Sorin had done to Isolde. For so long, he had been our source of laughter, of fun. He was the sunlight we never had in Revekka. Most of all, I had considered him a friend.

And this was why I had so few.

Isolde criticized my interest in use over loyalty, but loyalty was capricious. My empire was built on the usefulness of my armies and those who ran them. It was also built on the blood of those who had betrayed me.

"Do you think I will have a world to rule at the end of all this?" I asked.

Daroc's brows rose at the question. "Yes. What else are we working toward?"

I shook my head slowly and met Daroc's gaze. "Sometimes I can't remember."

TWENTY-FIVE
Isolde

I sat with Ana. She had made no progress and showed no signs of waking. I wondered if she would, if she might decide she no longer wished to face this life.

I could not blame her if that was her decision. She had seen too many horrors, and yet I did not want her to leave me. I hated that I was about to leave her. What if she did wake up and we were gone? She would have to face our trauma alone.

The thought brought tears to my eyes, and I leaned over her, staring down at her pale face, and whispered, "Please come back."

Then I pressed a kiss to her forehead.

As I rose to leave, I felt something beneath my foot. Stepping aside, I found a small, black book on the floor. I went to pick it up and place it on the table beside her bed, but as soon as I touched it, I knew it was a spell book. There was an unmistakable energy to it, cold and a little dark, which surprised me given that it had been in Ana's possession.

I started to open the book, hesitating a moment as I glanced at Ana. This almost felt like an invasion, but it was likely she had taken it from the secret library. I had taken books too, and perhaps she had found a few spells she felt worthy of trying against Ravena. I could not say I was ready to attempt magic again. I felt guilty and ashamed for what had happened with the mirrors, both my failure to injure Ravena and somehow leaving the portal open for the vârcolaci to enter the castle.

Still, I was curious.

I opened the book. It cracked as I did and revealed yellowed pages and faded handwriting. The first few pages detailed healing and cleansing rituals, but as I turned brittle page after brittle page, the incantations grew…darker.

It was the only way I knew to describe it. The words on this page had been used for something terrible, and it sent shivers up my spine.

The door clicked, and I slammed the book closed. I pressed it to my chest and looked as Adrian entered the room.

"Come to say goodbye?" he asked, his gaze moving from my face to Ana's. He stood at her bedside and placed a hand on her head.

"I hate that we must leave her."

"Tanaka will take care of her," he said. "He is like a father to her."

That was comforting, though at this very moment, I was not certain he was pleased with me. I was taking Adrian away from Revekka, and it was true that our people needed us just as much as mine did in Lara.

Adrian pulled his hand away and looked at me.

"I am bringing along Solaris," he said. "I'd rather keep an eye on him than leave him here to turn our people against us."

I did not like that he would be in our company, but I preferred that over leaving him in Revekka. His anger toward Dis was volatile and could be used against us.

"Perhaps his hand will be of use," I said, unenthused.

"Let us hope he demonstrates more loyalty to us," Adrian said. "Are you ready?"

"I have no choice," I said.

Adrian studied me for a moment, frowning.

"What will you do?" I asked. "If we cannot reach Lara in time before my people are turned?"

"If they are unwilling to conform to my rule, they will have to die."

The cold stung my eyes as I stood in the courtyard and watched our army assembling below—row after row of men and women, clad in red, gold, and black. At its head was Daroc, who gave orders; I could hear his muffled shouts but could not make out anything he said. I knew part of this ability was new. Prior to being turned, I'd have never been able to hear anything said on the field at the base of the Red Palace.

The development unnerved me a little. I wondered how much more my hearing would improve over the next few months, and my thoughts turned mostly to the evil that lingered in the woods and the monsters that attacked my people. Then I thought of Lara and how they would see my decision to change.

Traitorous, evil, weak.

I knew the words they would use, and each one burrowed deep, painful reminders of how they had shunned me the moment they realized I had not killed Adrian on our wedding night. Never mind that I had tried. Now that they had truly been overrun by a vampire army, I wondered if they would see Adrian and I as the lesser of two evils. Would they see our coming as a rescue or another siege?

I felt someone approach and looked to find Killian, who was dressed in Revekka's colors.

"Killian," I said in surprise.

He offered a small smile and straightened his jacket.

"Perhaps not the best timing," he said. "But you are my queen and I am your commander."

A thickness gathered in my throat. Sometimes I was so hindered by how I'd left Lara—without the blessing or praise of my people for a sacrifice I'd made to protect them—I forgot I still had support.

"Thank you," I whispered.

He smiled, but it was sad. He looked below at the massive army. "No need to thank me, my queen. I will always fight for you."

I knew Killian had never lost his loyalty to me as his queen, but this was different. Of anyone in my circle, he was my friend, and he had shown that time and time again.

I took his hand and held it. My action surprised him, and he met my gaze.

"I am grateful you are with me," I said. My eyes blurred and I took a breath to keep from crying. "I do not want to exist in this life without you, Killian. You and Nadia…you are my only family." I paused and then met his gaze. "I'd like you to consider becoming one of my noblesse."

He studied me, eyes searching, trying to figure out exactly what I meant.

"Are you asking me to become a vampire?"

"I am," I said. "I'll change you myself."

Killian pulled his hand from mine, and my heart fell.

"He changed you?"

I could sense his confusion and even his hurt. He felt betrayed.

"You don't…look different."

"I am tired of being weak, Killian."

"You are not weak," he said, angry. "Just because you are not invincible does not mean you are weak."

I smiled at him. "In this world, I am, and I am tired of being the one targeted for that weakness. At least now, it will be harder for them to kill me. I'd like it to be the same for you."

He was quiet, though as fiercely as he had reacted, I did not feel the distance I had expected. I knew he struggled over whether my change affected his loyalty to me.

"Think on it," I said. "You will be my first."

We marched out.

Adrian and I rode side by side, flanked by Daroc, Solaris, Killian, and Gavriel.

Miha and Isac lingered near as my assigned guards, minus Sorin, and I could feel their collective sense of betrayal and confusion.

Behind us, the villagers of Cel Ceredi had gathered,

and I wondered if they thought we were abandoning them as they watched us depart in the night.

If they had loyalty to Solaris, I thought, *at least he is at our side.*

As we continued, I found myself craning my neck, searching the sky for any sign of Sorin. Daroc was doing it too, but trying to be far more subtle.

"He is not here," said Adrian, and when I looked at him, he was staring straight ahead.

"How do you know?" I asked.

"Sorin isn't stupid. He knows if he is found, he will die."

"Perhaps that is what he wants," I said.

"If that were true, he would not have fled."

Adrian's comment left me feeling betrayed once more, and I realized that I had to consider all of Sorin's actions as deceptive, even his heartache over Daroc. It was like being stabbed all over again as I tried to decide what had been real and genuine and what had been a ruse.

Several scouts rode ahead of us, fanning out through the woods. They were sent ahead to search for signs of monsters, signs of Ravena, and decide where we would camp in the daylight. At some point, our position in line changed, and Adrian and Daroc led while I followed behind with Killian and Gavriel on either side. Miha and Isac were at my back.

I had yet to meet with Gavriel or learn the full extent of his observations while in Lara, and he took his time to speak.

"I have information for you, my queen," Gavriel said. "About the Sanctuary of Asha."

"Please, tell me," I said.

"The priestess who claimed that Asha had sent her a vision of their salvation is named Imelda. She says the incarnated woman has great power, matched only by that of the Blood King."

I knew Imelda. She was the head priestess of the Sanctuary of Asha. She had married Adrian and I, but outside that, my only interactions with her had been her attempts to berate me for not setting a better example as princess of Lara and sole heir.

"Your father worships the goddess, as do his people," she had told me one day. "Will you continue to set such a blasphemous example when you are queen?"

"You speak to the goddess, priestess?" I asked.

"Of course," she said, haughty.

"Then ask her why my mother had to die."

Imelda's expression was cold. "You willfully ignore Asha's plan for you," she said. "Perhaps your mother had to die so that you could be raised by your father, which will ensure you are a successful queen."

"What are you saying, Imelda?" I had stabbed a lot of men in my life, but never a woman—but I had wanted to stab her then.

"I am merely suggesting that your mother might have nurtured you far more than your father. It is no secret she was a gentle creature, hardly a woman who could stand among kings."

"It is good to know your opinion on my mother," I said, and the priestess bowed her head, as if she were pleased. "Perhaps if I had been raised by my mother, I would be more inclined to forgive you for it, but I was raised by my father, and like him, I am only interested in punishing those who slight me."

Needless to say, Imelda would do anything to see me fail to take the throne of Lara.

"She still claims the salvation of Asha has incarnated?" I asked Gavriel.

"Yes. There are rumors out of Vela that this woman walks the land there performing miracles."

"What kind of miracles?"

"Various things," he answered. "Some are simple like healing illnesses and giving life to dying land. Others are far more concerning. There is a claim that she was able to banish the crimson mist with only a few words, that she took life from a vampire with the wave of her hand."

My brows lowered. A few of those powers sounded much like Solaris's, but they were also things Ravena might do. Was her plan to act as a savior to the people of Cordova all along?

I worried and drew my lower lip between my teeth.

"And the people of Lara believe these things?"

"They have to," said Gavriel. "They are under threat now. Imelda has given them their only hope of survival."

It angered me that my people would turn to Asha when I should have been their hope. Even now, I was on my way with an army to set them free from the unjust rule of a power-hungry king. I should have had their praise. I was the one who had sacrificed my future so that they could continue to exist under the rule of my father.

But it was a sacrifice that would forever go unacknowledged. The more I learned, the less I felt inclined to fight for my people rather than only for myself and my right to the throne of Lara.

We rode hard and stopped near the border of Jola, a sea of black tents already erected by the scouts. Tomorrow, we would be beyond the cover of the red sky. It was something I had not had time to think about since becoming a vampire, but as we halted at camp, I stared at the brightening horizon. My time beneath the sun was over.

"My queen?"

I looked down to find Gavriel beside my horse.

"Are you okay?"

"Yes," I said quickly and swung my leg over, dismounting Reverie. I tensed, remembering how Gavriel had taken the liberty to touch me before and dreaded that he would attempt it again, but once my feet were on the ground, he took the reins.

"I shall water her for you," he said.

"Thank you," I said, and he nodded.

I watched him for a moment as he guided my horse away, uncertain how to feel about his helpfulness. Was this loyalty or something else?

I pulled off my gloves and entered Adrian's tent—our tent. He was already inside, pacing.

That was not a good sign.

"What troubles you?" I asked.

"When were you going to tell me about the priestess?" he asked.

I hesitated. "I...did not think it important until now," I said.

"How long have you known?"

"Since I sent Gavriel to Lara," I said.

"Fuck," Adrian muttered. He had yet to look at me, and I was growing frustrated.

"Why does this bother you?" I asked. "We do not know that there is any truth to it."

"There is truth to it," he said.

"How do you know?" I asked, narrowing my eyes. "What haven't you told me?"

He stopped pacing and finally looked at me. The white rings around his eyes had grown thicker, brighter.

"Adrian," I whispered.

"Dis has started to speak to me because she knows my plans," he said. "One of the things she said was that Asha had found her own path forward. I believe that means she's created an incarnate. I am an incarnate. We are their hand upon this earth."

"You have been here for two hundred years without an adversary equal to your power. Why send someone now?"

"If only I knew," he said. "Fuck."

He placed the palms of his hands against his forehead as if he were in pain.

"Adrian," I said, taking a step closer, but his hand shot out, halting me.

"Don't," he snapped.

I waited, watching. His eyes were closed, his jaw clenched tightly, and his hands shook.

"It's her, isn't it?"

He let out a harsh breath and then fell to his knees.

"Adrian," I whispered, taking a step closer. Then he looked at me, and the white had consumed his eyes and they glowed. "Adrian?"

"Run," he gritted out, the veins in his neck bulging.

I turned just as he lunged, but I did not make it far before I hit the ground. I rolled and tried to kick him, but he was already on top of me, holding me down, his fingers biting into my wrists.

"Adrian, please!"

I struggled against him, but he held tighter.

"You have done this to him!" The voice sounded like Adrian's, but I knew it was not him. Dis was in control. "He had no desire to be free of me until you returned—and to think I gave you to him as a gift."

I twisted and kneed him in the stomach. He loosened his grip, and I smashed my elbow into his face. It was enough to draw blood but not enough to push him off.

His hand went to my neck, and he leaned down and spoke against my ear, his blood dripping onto my face.

"How does it feel to know you will die at the hands of the man you love most?"

He tightened his grasp and I ceased to take in air. My face felt hot and swollen, my tongue thick. I struggled, attempting to free my hands, which he had pinned between our chests, but I could not move to stab him. This was what he meant—why he had not been surprised that I had created a book to kill him.

If you do destroy me, it will be because of Dis. You'll remember that, won't you?

The light from his eyes blurred with my tears, and then a shadow fell over us, and I was suddenly free of Adrian's attack as he went flying across the tent. I gasped for breath and was dragged to the other side.

"Isolde." Daroc's face hovered over mine, and all I could manage to do was cough and cry. "It's all right. I've got you."

He drew me into his arms and held me, crouched in the shadow of the tent. Across from us, Adrian's eyes had gone dark. He seemed to have regained control of himself, but I could tell Dis had ensured he was aware of everything that had transpired. I could not describe the expression on his face. I could only say that he was devastated, and when he rose to his feet, he raged.

TWENTY-SIX
Isolde

I stared at the light and shadow dancing across the tent roof, unable to sleep. I turned my head to Adrian who sat in a chair, his back to me.

He had not spoken since Dis had taken control of him earlier.

I had not either.

I could not bring myself to say anything—not even to tell him about the burn in my throat from hunger. I did not want him to have to hear my raspy voice, did not wish for him to hate himself any more than he already did.

I was still processing what had happened—how quickly she had taken control of him, how he seemed to have no ability to resist her actions. My throat felt tight and swollen, and it had nothing to do with what Adrian—Dis—had done earlier. It was the fear now that Ravena and Sorin might be right.

If Adrian could not control Dis, if he could not free himself from her, then he really might destroy the world.

I rose from bed, pulled on my robe and boots, grabbed my knife, and stepped out of the tent. I knew Adrian would not follow—at least not too closely.

Camp was still quiet, and though it was daylight, the sky was thick with clouds and the air heavy with the smell of rain. I was glad, at least, the snow had not reached beyond the border of Revekka.

I had left the comfort of my bed because I could not sleep, because I wanted to be outside of that confined space, because I wanted the freedom to cry without Adrian hearing. I could not stand the thought that he would have to listen to me, knowing he was responsible, though it was nothing he could control.

The air was cold and it filled my lungs, easing the burn of my hunger. I wandered around the black tents, nearing the edge of camp, when I noticed small, ghostly orbs floating in the distance. At first, I thought it was only mist, but they were too round, too compact.

They seemed to create a trail.

Normally, I would not follow, but I watched them sitting perfectly, whirling and churning, and I found myself stepping outside of camp, following them through the wood.

The leaves crunching at my feet were the only sounds as I made my way over the craggy earth. When I reached the first misty orb, it began to fade. I watched it until it was gone, and then I glanced back toward camp. It was still within view, looking ominous, a series of black pinnacles erupting from the ground.

Another orb drew my attention as it flew in a circle

around me. I followed and did not look back again, nor did I stop as each orb faded away.

I did not know how long I walked, but I came to a lake over which more orbs had settled. Their ghostly reflections led to the very center and then stopped.

I shed my robe and my boots, leaving my blade atop the pile before wading into the water. I expected it to be cold like it had been at Lake Galat, but this—this was warm, and from it, I felt an energy seeping into my skin. It felt dark but also light, no more dangerous than life itself.

The water was up to my shoulders as I came to the final misty orb floating at eye-level. It began to disappear as if it were smoke, and when the final tendril was no longer visible, I closed my eyes and dropped below the surface of the lake. Everything went white.

Someone was humming, and as the sound vibrated against my skin, I recognized the song—a lullaby my mother used to sing.

Moon above and earth below. I mouthed the words but did not speak them aloud. Then I became aware of fingers running through my hair. I opened my eyes and sat up, meeting the dark-eyed gaze of my mother.

I burst into tears and covered my mouth, but I could not contain the barrage of emotion that accosted my body. I shook, wracked with incomprehensible feelings.

This could not be. It had to be a spell, some form of witchcraft used to hurt me.

I shook my head, tears burning my eyes.

"Do not cry, daughter," she said in a smooth, balmy voice.

She held my face in her soft hands, brushing away tears. I wished she had been around to do this my whole life.

"You aren't real," I whispered.

"I am as real as any dream," she said.

"That is no comfort," I said, and she smiled.

She still held my face, and I latched onto her wrists, wanting to feel her touch always.

"I am so proud."

"Proud? I have done nothing to earn your pride."

"Know who you came from," my mother said, and her voice was stern.

"But I don't know who I came from," I said. "I know nothing of our people—"

She dropped her hands from my face and took mine into hers. "You are a strong woman from a strong line. Your roots go deep in this earth, and from them, you draw your magic."

I shook my head. "I don't understand."

"You are the daughter of witches, as all women are," she said, and she brushed a strand of hair from my face. "Magic is in our blood and bone; it is in the earth at our feet; it is in the very air we breathe."

"But I have barely been able to use magic at all." It seemed the only time I managed to do anything well was by chance.

"Words are spells, daughter, no matter how simple they may seem." She paused and then looked away from me and around.

Her expression was so peaceful, so happy. And she was so beautiful. She looked like me but also different—her nose was wider, her lips fuller, her cheekbones higher, her hair thicker, darker. I wanted to look more like her and less like my father.

"You brought yourself to this place," my mother said, and I blinked. I had been so focused on her, memorizing every part of her, I had not taken the time to observe where exactly we were.

The only thing I had noted when I had opened my eyes—other than my mother—was that we were surrounded by bright light. Now I realized it was only the sun beating down upon us, striking the surface of the fairest sand and the clearest water. Behind us was a curtain of dense forest, the greenery blazing against a blue sky.

"What is this place?"

"This is my home," she said. "Nalani."

Once again, tears blurred my eyes. "It is beautiful," I said, breathless.

"I always dreamed of bringing you here," my mother said. "And look, it has happened. Dreams are wonderful, are they not, my daughter?"

I met her gaze again and my heart sank, giving away to a profound and painful disappointment. "So this is a dream," I whispered.

Her smile was warm, but she shook her head. I was not certain if that was an answer to my question.

"Magic is not so serious," she said. "It is many things—an essence that gives everything on earth life and an energy. You can harness that energy if you remain aware enough, but you have become so caught up in spells, in words, in shapes. You need none of that to call upon your power."

"But…that is what I have always done," I said.

"No," she said. "You—no matter what incarnation—have always drawn upon the world with no effort. You only made spells to help women understand their potential when they could not *feel* it themselves."

I wanted to tell her I had no idea how to do what she was telling me, but she spoke, as if she heard me.

"Trust yourself, Isolde," she said. "Your soul has been speaking and you have not been listening."

I felt almost as if I were being reprimanded, but she squeezed my hands and I focused on her touch—soft and warm and real.

"It is no fault of your own," she said. "This world is afraid of powerful women."

There was no greater example than the Burning. Our trauma had crossed lifetimes. It was in our blood; it lived in the air and earth; it whispered in the dark.

It had silenced us for too long.

"Trust yourself," my mother said. "As I do."

I studied her dark eyes, wishing I'd had her forever.

"I have *needed* you," I said, my voice breaking.

She smiled, and though her eyes watered, I sensed she did not agree. She lifted my hand and placed a seed in my palm, curling my fingers tight around it.

"For when you return to your plane," she said.

"What is this?" I asked, but her hands were already loosening around mine and I felt a sense of panic rise within me.

"Don't let go," she said.

"Mother!"

I was torn from her and broke the surface of the water, surprised when I found I was alone. I had felt as if I had been pulled with such force—I was sure someone else had to be with me. I looked around the quiet wood, but there was nothing other than an unsettling stillness to the world, and I knew it meant we were about to be plunged into chaos.

My hand was clenched, and as I uncurled my fingers, I found the seed my mother had given me. It was the size of my thumbnail and felt like a weight in the palm of my hand. I nearly burst into tears once more.

She was real. I had actually visited her.

I left the water, dressed, and hurried back to camp.

When I returned to the tent, twilight was upon us, and Adrian was gone, though I noticed a wooden goblet on the table. When I checked, it was full of his blood.

My heart seized a moment, both at his thoughtfulness but also at the implication. He did not wish for me to touch him.

I did not drink it.

I stored the seed my mother had given me and changed into warmer clothes quickly, in case Adrian was in search of me. But I found him only a few feet from the tent, speaking with two of his scouts.

He sensed my approach because he went rigid. It was an observation that both hurt and angered me. If anyone should feel uneasy, it should be me.

The scouts ceased speaking and bowed to me.

"Good evening, my queen," said one.

"Good evening," I replied. "Is there news?"

I did not think there would be, given that it was just now nightfall, but I was curious and worried. The two glanced at Adrian.

"You are dismissed," Adrian told them, and my eyes narrowed, my face hot with frustration. The two bowed again, but I glared at Adrian.

"Are you going to dismiss my question as well?" I asked.

"I was only giving Sable and Lucia instruction," Adrian said. "They will be riding ahead to observe Lara. They will report back in the morning."

I did not think he was lying, but I did not like his coldness.

"Is this how you will treat me moving forward?" I asked.

Adrian's hard eyes found mine. It was the first time he had looked at me with more than a passing glance since last night.

"How am I treating you?" he asked.

"Like you blame me for what is happening to you," I said. My breathing was labored as I spoke because I knew these words would hurt, and they took every bit of my power to say. "Perhaps it is not Dis who is angry with me; perhaps it is you."

Adrian's eyes widened. "I am not angry with you," he said, though he sounded so now.

"What you are doing…" I said, staring up at him. "Shutting down, dismissing me, that is what Dis wants. She wants to drive a wedge between us like everyone else. Are you going to let her do that?"

"This has nothing to do with her," Adrian said. "I *hurt* you."

"I do not need a reminder," I said. Just hearing it made me feel sick. "But who are you going to be when you are not under her control?"

Adrian's jaw popped as he gritted his teeth.

"I will not pretend you did not scare me. I will not pretend that I am not devastated by what happened, but if you pull away now, then I will pull away too, and we will be doomed."

Adrian took a step closer and lifted his hand slowly, brushing his fingers along my cheek. It was a brief touch, and then he withdrew it.

"Kill me," he said.

My brows lowered. "What?"

"If she takes me again, if I hurt you again," he said, "kill me."

I started to shake my head. "You do not know what you are asking of me."

"I do," he said quickly. "Do not let me live with the guilt of having murdered you."

"So you would rather I live with it?" I asked. The words slipped angrily between my teeth. He said nothing, but I already knew his answer.

Camp was bustling with activity. Many of the tents had been packed away and the fires were nothing but smoking embers. I stood near Reverie, waiting for departure, but also using her as a shield as I studied Ana's small spell book. I still felt drawn to read it despite my mother's words about it being unnecessary to call upon magic with spells and shapes. In truth, I would likely need both tools until I became more confident.

"Are you well today, my queen?" Daroc asked.

I looked up quickly, closing the book.

He did not look any better than the day before—eyes

dark and hair a mess, but I was grateful for him. I did not wish to think about what would have happened had he not found us.

"I am...well," I said, though that felt like a lie. "You?"

"Well," he replied, and I knew that was a definite lie.

We were silent for a moment, and I shifted on my feet. Feeling awkward. Daroc had never held a conversation with me, much less started one.

"Thank you...for yesterday," I said at last.

"You do not need to thank me," Daroc said.

"Did you know?" I asked. I did not give any more context to my question, but Daroc knew what I was asking.

His jaw tightened. "I did not expect it to escalate so fast."

I swallowed hard and looked away, trembling.

"I am sorry about Sorin," I said, changing the subject, though this one was no better.

"There is nothing to apologize for," Daroc said. "You are not responsible for him."

I wanted to tell him the same thing. Sorin's actions were his own, but I knew it was too late for Daroc. It had been too late the moment he had turned Sorin. That was the day he'd decided to never let go.

Daroc bowed and left my side. I started to return to the book when I caught sight of Solaris who was slowly managing to pack his saddlebag. My feelings about the man were still mixed, but I walked toward him anyway.

"Would you like help?" I asked.

He jumped at the sound of my voice and glanced at me, managing a small, nervous laugh.

"Thank you, Queen Isolde," he said. "I could not ask it of you."

"I am offering," I said.

He looked at me, fully now, and I remembered how cold he seemed when I had first met him in the throne room only weeks ago. I recognized it now as a shield.

"I have to learn to do this myself," he said.

His words were not harsh, but they were dismissive, and a rush of embarrassment heated my face. Of course, he would not accept my help—I was the reason he struggled now.

"Of course," I said and started to turn.

"You know I wasn't lying," he said, and his voice called my attention back to his face. "When I said I was hunting witches. I am. But I would take any witch who might break this curse Dis has placed upon me."

I only nodded once and then turned from him, retreating to Reverie's side. I could not help thinking about his and Adrian's words. They both believed that a witch might be able to break Dis's hold on them, but such a spell would come at a great price—likely, a life.

We mounted our horses and left the campsite.

It did not take us long to reach Jola, and when we left the cover of the red sky, I looked up, frowning. The stars I'd expected to see were hidden by heavy clouds and the smell of rain was still thick in the air. Shortly after, it began to pour. I pulled up my hood, though it did little to protect me from the wet or the cold; my fingers were frozen around Reverie's reins.

We stopped once during our journey, and that was only because one of the rivers that cut through Jola and into Lara had risen due to the rain and was impassable. I was not certain if Jola had a different name for it, but we called it Argis.

I watched the speed of the current, and dread built within me at how close we were to my home. The air felt thick and heavy with the knowledge that when we woke at sunset, we would have to be going into battle.

"It does not seem real that this is how we must return to Lara, with an army behind us and battle before us," said Killian.

It felt very real to me, though I had never expected my ascension to Lara's throne to be easy, even before Adrian. Still, I knew what Killian meant.

"I am sure you expected something very different when you set out with my father weeks ago," I said.

"No truer words," he answered.

The rain showed no signs of stopping, so we made camp early. Despite the delay, we would still arrive in Lara tomorrow night. I stood near the tent opening, staring out at camp. I was cold and tired of being wet, but I looked for Adrian. He had yet to come inside since we arrived at camp. I did not know if he was keeping his distance despite our earlier conversation or if he was fighting for control with Dis. Either way, I felt his absence pull at my heart. I wanted to ignore it and focus on something, anything else, but it was impossible, and I hated feeling this way.

Sighing, I moved to the bed. I retrieved Ana's spell book from my pack and slipped out of my boots before curling into the warm furs of our bed.

I was starting to think that Ana had written this book herself. I was not yet sure what gave me that impression, but it had something to do with the cadence she used to speak spells. More...concerning to me, however, was just how much power was within this little book. There were spells for creating illusions and resurrection and manifesting portals, but not just to places on the earth—this provided access to other planes, including Spirit, Dis's realm.

I thought of my mother when she had given me the seed.

For when you return to your plane, she'd said.

Had I managed to wander into another world, and could I go back?

Was it possible to enter Dis's realm without dying?

I swallowed thickly, my chest tightening at the idea of seeing my mother again. I cleared my throat, forcing down the tears threatening my eyes at the thought, and focused on the book, pausing when I came to a spell that looked familiar. It was one Ana had taught us to chant on the night of the full moon before we had been viciously attacked. She had said it was a containment spell, but this…this detailed a resurrection spell.

I frowned, confused.

Perhaps I was mistaken, and the words were slightly different. As I began to compare from memory, Adrian entered the tent.

I closed the book and met his gaze, but he was not looking at me. Instead, he was focused on removing his gloves. He was soaked; water beaded off his clothes and his hair was plastered to his head. He looked beautiful to me, though severe, and while I knew he would be cold, I still wanted him near. I wanted to tell him about my mother and the things she had said, but there was something off about him. I could not help the element of guilt that came as I prepared to run if he looked at me with any glow in his eyes, but he sighed, and when he turned to me, they were as dim as ever.

"Are you okay?" I asked, setting the spell book aside.

"Sable and Lucia have returned," he said. "It seems Gavriel grossly underestimated Alaric's army."

"By how much?"

"They say he has nearly one hundred and fifty thousand soldiers at his command now," he replied—which was as large as Adrian's army, except we had only brought half.

"So he and Julian have turned more people?" I asked. "My people."

Adrian nodded.

I should have expected we would not reach Lara in time to save any of them. I wondered who had turned willingly and who had been forced.

"Do we have a chance against them?" I asked.

"Our army is far more skilled, and as you are aware, it takes time for vampires to develop their powers."

It was not the answer I was looking for, but I knew Adrian was right. I had barely developed powers since he had turned me. The greatest change was my thirst. I would be better off fighting this battle in my aufhocker form than anything else.

It was an idea I had been toying with since we learned of Alaric's invasion. I had gotten a taste of that form's strength and power when fighting the vârcolac and nothing compared.

"But you are still worried," I said.

I did not like when Adrian worried. He was usually so confident, overly so. He tapped his fingers against the tabletop as he stood near the fire, staring into the flame.

He did not respond to my statement, and he did not need to—I knew the truth. Instead, he began to undress, and as I watched him peel his soaked clothes from his wet, hard body, a delicious warmth simmered inside me.

Naked, he approached the bed, and as he sat, I turned toward him.

"We will each need to feed before tomorrow," he said.

"You say that as if it is a bad thing."

"It is not a bad thing," he said, trailing his fingers down the side of my face. "Are you afraid of me?"

"I have never been afraid of you," I said. "Even when I hated you."

I was lying, but only a little. I had been afraid when Dis had taken him over. But I had been afraid, too, when she had tried to take over the night of Efram's resurrection. I would not say those things aloud, and if he discovered them, it would have to be because he read my mind.

He smiled and leaned forward, resting his forehead against mine.

"I love you," he said.

I smiled and placed my palm against his cheek. "Why does it feel like you are saying goodbye?"

"I just want you to know," he said. "I want you to always know."

I knew what he was doing—it was not a matter of *just in case*, it was a matter of *when I lose control*.

I watched him a moment, wanting him—his come, his blood, his love. Those were the things that would make him mine, that he would remember in the face of Dis's control. I worked my shift over my head, appreciating the way Adrian's eyes darkened with lust.

Naked, I straddled him, and his hands dug into my ass as he settled me over his heavy arousal.

He tipped his head back to hold my gaze and I whispered over his lips, "Kiss me."

His hands moved up, over my back and to my shoulders, and as his mouth found mine, he ground against me, his tongue matching the pace at which I moved against him. I moaned and started to push him back, but he shifted first and pushed me into the bed.

His hand swept down my body, and I widened my legs, desperate to feel his touch. I was swollen and hot and completely void, and when he ran his hand over my heat, he moaned, breaking our kiss.

"So fucking wet," he said, and let one finger slip inside, then another. "Fuck."

He sat back, gripping himself as he curled inside me. As he watched me, I moved my hand to my swollen and sensitive clit, teasing him at first but soon becoming lost in the sensation as I increased the friction against it.

I dug my heels in. I threw my head back, a guttural cry leaving my lips, and then Adrian's mouth was on me while his fingers moved inside me, and with each thrust, each lick of his tongue, I felt myself breaking apart. I did not know how he could do this to me, how I could feel so grounded within my body, how I could feel the heaviness of my breasts and the heat inside me, the tightness in my muscles and the pleasure of his touch, but also have no control over my mind or the words and sounds that came from my mouth.

My fingers tangled into his hair, my nails scraping along his scalp as I pulled. I did not care that it might hurt; I needed something to hold onto as I rode this pleasure—until I came with a guttural sob. As my body relaxed, I became aware of how hot it was in this tent. I was covered in a thin sheen of sweat and my hair stuck to my neck and the sides of my face.

Adrian withdrew and kissed a path up my body before his mouth was on mine, and as he shifted to his side, positioning my back against his chest, he shoved his fingers into my mouth. I sucked them, shamelessly, tasting my come.

"I want this come around my cock," he said, and then he kissed me, and I had to crane my neck to reach him. He guided my leg over his, opening me wide, and the cool air did nothing to ease our heat. I moaned as he slipped his cock through my wetness, teasing until he slid inside.

My head fit into the crook of his arm, and he held my gaze as he moved inside me, touching my breasts and stroking my mouth with his tongue. I had no choice but to bend to his will—my back arched away from him, my head pressing into his shoulder. I fought to breathe as I writhed, lost in the pleasure he coaxed with each thrust of his cock.

I could tell when he was close because his pace changed, and he stroked my clit, which felt just as swollen as his cock. When he touched me, my lips parted on a silent scream, and he used the opportunity to thrust his tongue into my mouth once more. As he pulled away, he gripped my jaw, fingers splayed down the column of my neck, thrusting harder and faster—and as he erupted inside me, he bit into my neck.

This scream was not silent. It tore from my throat, a heady mix of pleasure and pain, soothed only when Adrian pushed his wrist to my mouth. We fed from each other until our bodies and eyes grew heavy and sleep drowned us in darkness.

Lightning lit the sky and rain fell in heavy sheets, but I could see through the curtain, between each drop of crystal rain, to the tree line where in the darkness, soldiers lay in wait for my army.

An arrow shot through the night, straight for my heart, and I caught it, but not before the tip could draw blood.

It was the start of the battle, and I raced forward, my legs carrying me at an unnatural speed—my bones broke and shifted, and my screams turned to howls as I transformed into my aufhocker form, my clawed feet tearing into the earth as I raced across the field toward the dark forest of trees.

My eyes were hazed in red, honed upon the dark between the trees where I saw men moving—I was so focused upon them, the shock of fire erupting around me did not register until it was too late. My hair caught fire and my howls turned to wails and then to screams as I faded into my human form only to wilt and die upon the ground.

I opened my eyes.

There was no transition from sleep to wakefulness—my body was alive, and I sat up, taking a moment to live within this energy which was so electric, it was magic.

The answer had come from my dream, a manifestation of what was to come and what I was called to do now.

I looked at Adrian, who lay sleeping beside me, and I bent to kiss him. When my lips touched his, all the heat in my body pooled between my thighs again. Insatiable. I straddled him and he woke beneath me, his erection pressing hard against me.

He groaned, his hands resting on my thighs, fingers gripping me I slid onto him.

"Fucking queen," he said as I rode him hard and fast, desperate to come as this storm built inside me. When it released, I would harness a different kind of strength that came with the confidence in knowing I could call to my magic and it would come.

As tremors shook my body, I slowly rose from Adrian and started to leave the tent.

"Where are you going?" he asked, a note of alarm in his voice.

I turned and looked at him over my shoulder, and something in my gaze must have told him to stay because he did not move from his place on the bed.

"I am going to summon an army," I said. "I will meet you at the border of Lara."

I stepped into the twilight, naked, drawn to the woods by an invisible force—a call from some deep place inside me. It was familiar but still distant, a part of my power I had not used in a very long time, and yet as I raced through camp, feet hitting the cold, soft earth, I knew this was right—I was on the path laid out for me.

I had *seen* it.

I shifted, the pain acute and biting as I took my aufhocker form and raced into the surrounding woods, a howl tearing from my throat—a call to others like me. As I sped along, I sensed I was not alone, and when I glanced to my left and right, the silhouettes of other aufhockers raced alongside me.

Their presence only made me run harder and howl louder, their wails joining mine. It was a haunting song that would terrify any human.

But I was no longer terrified of this form or what I might do with it.

I continued until I came to a rocky cliff that rose above me, walling off my flight, but at the very height of it, more aufhockers approached, baring their teeth. The sky above them was filled with flashes of blue-white lightning. It blazed behind them, only adding to their ferociousness.

I slowed and turned, surrounded by the same red-eyed monsters. My muscles rippled, my stride predatory, as I paced, waiting for my challenger. The pack was filled with tension, bodies vibrating with anticipation as their leader emerged from the dark wood. She was no bigger than me, but much older and tired. I did not know how I knew—but the knowledge existed in the air between us.

We circled one another, surrounded by a host of growls and keen howling, encouraging the fight. She snapped her teeth, nipping at my feet, and I snarled, instinct taking over as she tried to provoke me into an attack before I was ready. Our circle grew tighter, and she snapped, attempting to bite down upon my neck, but I moved and our mouths locked, sharp teeth clanking. It hurt, but only cut my mouth. We shoved away from each other and leapt together again. Our bodies slammed, and we fell to the ground, teeth locked, claws sinking into each other. Neither one of us moved, growls deepening.

Finally, she shifted her mouth so that she bit into my shoulder.

I howled and sank my claws deeper. We pushed away from each other, rolling in the mud, only to rise on our feet and circle one another again.

This time, I pounced, locking my jaw around her neck. She twisted and I fell onto my back. Suddenly her teeth sank into my throat. I screamed, though the sound came out more like a yelp, and I dug my claws into her ribs. She whined, and I was able to push her away with my feet.

The aufhocker flew and hit the stone wall, her head snapping back. She landed with a thud and did not move. I approached, nudging her with my nose, and I felt a pang of guilt having gone so far.

She was dead.

As I lowered to the ground beside her, it began to rain. I rested my head upon hers—it was a request for forgiveness and the only apology I could muster given the time I had and what was to come.

A chorus of howls erupted around me, growing louder and louder. They were mourning, but also welcoming me as part of their pack.

I was now their queen.

TWENTY-SEVEN
Isolde

My army was within sight of the border of Lara when I found them. I had heard them first, or more accurately, I'd heard the rain beating down upon their armor first, but now I saw them, assembled in perfect rows, armed and ready for the coming battle.

Even in this form, I felt dread.

The howls of my pack drew their attention, and many of them stiffened at the sound, raising arms, but as they turned toward me, I shifted, and an audible gasp left the crowd as I walked naked down the center of their ranks, straight to Adrian who had turned to watch me approach. His eyes glittered darkly, and when I was near enough, he dragged me to him, kissing me with a desperation I felt in my soul.

When he pulled away, he dragged a set of clothes from his saddle, and I dressed quickly.

"My blades?" I asked.

He arched a brow. "Can you carry those when you shift?"

In truth, I had no idea.

"Keep them, then," I said, knowing the priority for me would be to remain in my aufhocker form. As I turned to face the kingdom of Lara and the dark curtain of trees in which soldiers hid, I felt a mix of emotions. What Killian had said was true—it did not seem real that we were marching against my homeland.

I cast a glance to my left and right—the front line included Daroc, Killian, Miha, Isac, and Solaris.

"Their bows are ready," Adrian said. "And shadows move between the trees."

As he spoke, a row of infantry soldiers stepped from beneath the canopy. I could not tell how many, but they crowded together, their shields aligned to create a long, metal wall. Once they were in place, everything went silent, save for the sound of rain as it fell in lashing sheets upon metal.

We waited in the quiet, and then it happened—a single arrow cut through the air, straight for my heart.

I caught it, the tip barely touching my skin—just like in my dream.

I nodded toward the centerline.

"The field will erupt in fire," I said.

I felt Adrian's gaze upon me, but he said nothing.

There was another stretch of silence, and I broke from the ranks, walking to the middle distance.

"I am Isolde Vasiliev, queen of Revekka," I yelled. "I am of the House of Lara, daughter of Elvira of Nalani, sister of witches, and I have come to reclaim my crown."

And then I shifted. A wicked howl left my throat,

and the answering calls of my pack were like warning bells in the night. The shield line quaked.

Without delay, I charged and my pack followed. Just as I expected, a burst of fire exploded in front of me. It ignited so fast and so hot, my eyes watered. Some of the aufhockers could not pause in time before they ran headfirst into the inferno, but some managed to leap over the flames, and a chorus of pained shrieks and horrified screams sounded.

And it was to that terrible song that the battle for Lara had begun.

Behind me, Adrian gave commands, and our army raced forward. With them at my back, I circled and made a running jump over the fire just as hundreds of arrows rained down on us. One nicked me in the shoulder, but I landed with no trouble and dashed toward the infantry. Many of them had been plowed down by my aufhockers, and I could hear them in the forest beyond, tearing into flesh and mauling Alaric's army.

Or at least what I hoped was mostly Alaric's army. I had no idea how many of my people had joined him. I wondered how many regretted their decision already.

A line of men made their way toward me, swords drawn and shields up. I snarled at them and pounced, crushing two under my weight, swiping my claws at one, and sinking my teeth into another. When I looked up, one lone soldier stared back at me, eyes wide, shaking with fear.

He stumbled and then turned to run, but he was skewered by the blade of an approaching soldier.

"Deserter," he spat as he pushed him away, marching toward me.

I lowered, preparing to launch, but before the man could even lift his blade, he halted suddenly, and his head slid off the column of his neck. The blood from the blow that decapitated him splattered across my face, and when the rest of him crashed to the ground, Adrian was standing in his place.

"Take the castle," he ordered.

I held his gaze a moment longer, noting the fierce look in his eyes, hoping that what I saw was not the white of his irises glowing.

"Go!"

I bolted into the woods I knew so well, only to face the horror they had become—a sea of blood and gore. My aufhockers were locked in battle with vampires and mortals alike. There were dead in the trees and dead on the ground, and still arrows rained down on me. I tried my best to dodge them, but when one lodged in my shoulder, I faltered.

Then another came, and while I howled my pain, I kept running, my heart racing and my fear all-consuming. Then I heard the beat of hooves behind me.

"Isolde!" a familiar voice called. A wave of relief washed over me, and I returned to my human form at the sound of Killian's voice. I stumbled and fell, the arrows still protruding from my back.

"Stay still," he said, but I jerked when he pulled each arrow free, my growl of pain coming out between my teeth.

"By the goddess," he whispered, and I knew he was witnessing my wounds heal.

"She is not welcome," I said as I rose to my feet and stumbled toward his horse. "We have to get to the castle."

I mounted Killian's horse and he followed behind me.

There came a point when we left the thick of the battle behind, and when we broke through the wood and I caught sight of High City, tears pricked my eyes.

Home.

I could not help thinking it, though right now it was possible everyone within those walls saw me as the enemy. But as quickly as my heart rose at the thought of claiming my throne, it fell at the sight of hundreds of soldiers lining the walls of High City.

Killian did not lessen the speed of his horse as he made his way to the closest gate.

I expected a fight, to be slain the moment we were spotted. That would have been more reasonable than what happened. We were allowed into an open gate—a trap, likely.

"Killian," I warned.

"I am aware," he said tightly. "Just…be prepared to show off some of your new skills. Things aren't likely to go well."

Once we were through the gates, we were surrounded by soldiers with swords and arrows, both from the ground and from above.

"This is quite a welcome," I said.

"Queen Isolde," said a voice, and my gaze shifted to a guard I recognized—Nicolae. "We've been expecting you."

"You know, the army waiting for me at the border gave me the impression that you might be."

Nicolae smirked. "Still so arrogant in the face of your fall from power."

"A little presumptuous, as always, Nicolae," I said.

"Isn't that something," he said. "It is almost as if you presumed you could come back and be our queen after fucking the Blood King."

"I think you might just be jealous, Nicolae," I said.

"Jealous of a blood whore?" Nicolae scoffed. "Fu—"

"Enough of this," said Killian. "Take us to King Alaric!"

"You won't be seeing him, Commander," said Nicolae. "Neither will the *queen*."

The creak of taut bow strings sounded.

This was more than a trap. It was an execution.

"Now, Isolde!" Killian snapped, but I could not leave him. And I could not survive an attack of this magnitude even with my abilities.

But I soon realized that no one was moving. Everyone was still, frozen.

"Go!" Solaris shouted. He had just mounted the wall, and on either side of him, soldiers from my army followed, scaling the wall as if it were nothing.

Killian spurred his horse forward.

I managed to look back the moment Solaris let go of his magic. The arrows every soldier had drawn to kill Killian and I pierced Nicolae instead.

We galloped through the city, and as we went, our enemies raced behind us on foot. But Killian kept going, drawing his sword as we neared Castle Fiora. I could see the gates in the distance and a line of soldiers guarding it.

"Let me off," I said, and he slowed to a halt.

"Isolde," he said before I could turn from him. "I'll take you up on that offer. I would be glad to be your noblesse."

"Promise?"

"I promise."

I smiled. "Thank you, Killian. Now you can't die," I said, stepping away from him. "You promised."

I turned and sprinted, shifting as I did, while Killian turned to face those who had followed us to the castle.

I let out a piercing howl, running faster, and as I neared the guards who stood before my gates, I launched into the air, flying over them, landing on the opposite side.

I burst through the doors of the great hall.

I did not think being in this room would have any effect on me. I did not think I would freeze, but as I stood at the entrance where a blue carpet ran to my father's throne, I found I could not move.

The last time I had been in this hall, surrounded by its gilded mirrors and its blue banners, my father had claimed I was worth every star in the sky, and he had nearly gone to war with Adrian after he had asked for my hand in marriage.

Even as these thoughts raced through my mind, I could not look away from my father's throne, which was occupied by Alaric. He was a severe-looking man with long, dark hair and prominent, dark brows. His eyes were a piercing gray, and he sat with his large hands curled around the edge of my throne, dressed and crowned in black.

I was surprised that Julian was not here, but my attention was soon taken by Nadia, who stood to Alaric's left in the grasp of a guard who held her hostage, a blade to her neck.

I returned to my human form, my hands fisted.

"Queen Isolde," said Alaric with some surprise in his

voice, though it remained deep and menacing. "I have been expecting you."

"Everyone keeps saying that," I said. "You would think if that were true, you'd have made it easier for me to reach this point."

He chuckled. "You have proven very capable."

"You've just now figured that out?" I asked.

"I think you've had some help," he said. "An aufhocker bite, a vampire bite. You've turned yourself into a true monster."

"Not so different from you," I said.

He tilted his head, smiling.

"I suppose not."

I took a step forward, and Nadia inhaled, the guard pressing his blade into her neck.

"What is all this?" I asked. "A futile attempt to conquer my lands?"

"Futile?" Alaric asked. "I sit on your father's throne."

"My throne," I said. "My father is dead."

"No!" I heard Nadia say.

The mirrors on the walls began to tremble. I exchanged a look with Nadia.

My one and only thought was that Ravena was near. I expected the mirrors to explode, but instead, the floor began to crack and shards of mirror shot up from the ground. They were tall and sharp, and they surrounded us in a jagged circle.

Alaric stood, staring frantically at our surroundings.

"What is this witchcraft?" he asked and narrowed his eyes upon me. "You."

He started toward me, but then he began to seize and his eyes bled. He fell to his knees with crimson tears streaming down his face. The man who held Nadia followed, and as soon as he began to shake, she pulled his knife free and stabbed him in the chest.

"Nadia!"

"Oh, my Issi!" We ran to each other. She threw her arms around me, and I hugged her tightly.

"I missed you so much," I said, tears streaming down my face.

"I missed you, child," she said, and as she pulled away from me, she gripped my shoulders, then my face between her hands.

"My child," she whispered. "Tell me it is not true, what you said? King Henri is indeed…dead?"

A sob tore from my throat that I did not intend, and I nodded. "It is true."

"Oh, my dear." She hugged me to her. "What happened?"

"That is not a story for now," I said, and this time I drew away from her. "We must get you to safety."

But there was something in her eyes that made me feel uneasy—a strange look that set me on edge. My brows lowered. "Nadia?"

Her hand tightened around mine.

"My child," she said. "What have you become?"

I could not answer before I felt the sting of a blade slide straight into my heart. Blood pooled in my mouth, and the tears of joy that had streamed down my face became a mixture of pain and sorrow.

"Nadia." Blood spattered her face as I said her name. "Why?"

"You are no longer my child," she said. "My Issi died the night she had to marry that monster."

I covered her hands, which still held the blade in my chest. I realized she believed this would kill me, which meant she had likely never trusted that I would try to kill Adrian.

"You never were very good at reading people, Issi," she said.

With my hands over hers, I jerked them back, and as my wound healed, my claws burst from the fingertips and sank into Nadia's stomach.

Her eyes widened with shock, and as her legs gave out, I helped her to the ground.

"Issi," she whispered, a trickle of blood trailing down her mouth.

I held her to me, staring down at her pale face, watching as a single tear fell from her eye—it was all that she would shed for me.

As she took her final breath, I spoke. "No, Nadia. I am not your Issi," I whispered, though tears filled my eyes. I had no time to process the feelings that tore through my chest and ripped me open, but I felt raw and exposed and completely devastated.

This woman had cared for me and nursed me; she had stepped into a mothering role, and I saw her as such—and yet, when she had seen me shift, I had only become a monster in her eyes.

My breath became shallow, ragged, and I screamed until my throat burned, until my ears rang with the sound of it, until my wails dissolved into silent tears.

"Well, isn't this devastating."

I froze, lifting my head at the sound of Ravena's voice.

"First you lose your father," she continued. "And now the woman who treated you as a daughter."

My gaze fell to Nadia, whose eyes remained open and wide. I closed them, pressing a kiss to her forehead before carefully resting her upon the ground. Then I rose to my feet and turned, still surrounded by the mirrored circle, and faced Ravena.

She filled one of the large, jagged pieces of mirror she had called forth from the floor. I expected her to appear all around me as she had done in the hall of mirrors at the Red Palace, but she didn't.

"Why did you help me?" I asked.

"I have been trying to help you," she said. "I have warned you about Adrian. I have told you that we are fighting for the same purpose."

"You keep saying that, and yet you keep killing my people," I said.

"Men," she said. "I am killing men."

"Ivka was not a man," I said.

Ravena smiled, but it was sad. "An unfortunate sacrifice. I did not wish to see her die, but she would have distracted you, and Nalani is not your concern."

"Who are you to say?" I asked, gritting my teeth.

"You did not incarnate in this life to be Isolde of Lara. You incarnated to seek revenge as Yesenia of Aroth, and that revenge must be against men. They hurt you."

"You hurt me," I said.

"Not like them," she said, and there was an edge to her voice, as if she were insulted I had compared the two. "I know you sometimes mourn for the life you didn't live, but it was not just *your* life that was taken the night you burned."

My stomach roiled and I hit the floor, vomiting into

a chamber pot. My face was hot and my heart was racing in my chest. The feeling had come on so suddenly, I could barely stop my head from spinning.

The door opened and I looked up, realizing I was in my bedchamber at the Red Palace.

"Yesenia, are you okay?" Ana asked. She came to kneel before me, her golden hair spilling over her shoulders.

"I am okay," I said. I spent a few moments breathing through my mouth until the nausea passed.

"Let me help you," she said and took my hand. I got to my feet and then sat on the bed. Ana crossed to my nightstand, pouring me a cup of water. A sour taste still lingered in the back of my throat and on my tongue.

"What happened?" she asked as she handed me the cup.

It was cool to the touch, and instead of drinking it, I placed it to my head.

"I don't know. All of a sudden, I do not feel well."

"Are you with child?"

Ana's question shocked me, and I looked up to meet her gaze, which was soft and gentle.

"No," I said quickly and paused, going cold. "I can't be. I…"

I am going to die, I thought, though I knew there was a very real chance that I actually was pregnant, and if that was the truth, then I had just signed a death warrant for my child.

I stood, shaking.

"Ana, I can't be pregnant."

"You very well can be, Yesenia."

"You do not understand—"

"I know you've said it before, that you are going to die—"

"I am. Dragos asked if he would conquer the world, and I foretold that his attempt would end in his demise," I said. "He will *murder* me, Ana."

Her lips slammed together and her jaw tightened.

"Then you must flee," she said, as if it were that simple.

I shook my head. I had seen the future, seen my death at the stake, but why had I not seen *life*? My chest felt as though it were being ripped to shreds. I pressed my hands to my stomach and then hugged myself, tears streaming down my face.

"How did I not see this life?" I asked, my voice broken.

Ana rose and placed her hands on my shoulders. "You can change the course of the future, Yesenia. Perhaps you did so here."

I wanted to believe her, and perhaps stupidly, her words gave me hope.

"I don't know what to do," I said.

"Adrian will figure it out," Ana said. "But first, you must tell him."

Ravena came back into focus. She stood opposite me, and it was the first time I'd ever seen any kind of expression on her face beyond hateful smugness.

I remembered the rest of that night. Adrian and I had fled to the cottage under the mountains where we would spend a final night together. It was the same place Adrian had buried the bones of High Coven. It was where we had been captured, where Adrian had been beaten and where Dragos had raped me.

"I never told him," I whispered, staring at Ravena now. "I never told Adrian."

This revelation was a knife to my heart. There was a part of me that wanted to wonder what might have happened had we lived. Would I have had a boy or a girl? Would I have been able to use those names I had chosen?

"That is what Dragos took from you," Ravena said. "It is what *men* did to you because they feared you. Shall we give them something to truly fear?"

Ravena held out her hand, and while I had no real insight of what she wanted, I knew that I needed inside that portal if I was ever going to stop her.

I took her hand.

Entering the mirror felt exactly like running through glass. It hurt, as if a thousand pins were scraping over my skin, but once inside, I was awash in brightness. There was no floor or ceiling or walls. I existed in nothing, but I was not alone here. Only the woman opposite me was not Ravena.

"Ana?" I breathed.

I looked behind me to see out into the great hall. When I turned around, Ana was still there, slight and silver-haired.

"I don't understand. You're...aren't you at the Red Palace?"

"I have not woken up, but I will...after this." She smiled at me sadly. "Are you quite devastated?"

I could not speak, but the pieces were falling into place.

"Mirrors show the truth," she said. "I cannot hide from you in here."

"Please do not say it," I said, shaking my head.

"I wanted you to remember me," Ana said, and I closed my eyes against her truth. "*So badly*, but when you didn't, I knew I would be on my own."

"This whole time, it was you. Why did you create such havoc for *The Book of Dis*? You could have just taken it."

"I did," she said. "I have been using it for quite some time."

I shook my head.

"I have created a lot of monsters testing the spells you created," she said. "I often wondered what you were thinking, especially with the crimson mist."

The mist, I thought. *Isla*.

But that would mean that Ana had cast the spell that killed her lover.

Worse, though, was that I was the one who had written those spells.

"I don't understand. You are saying…I am responsible for the mist…for all monsters?"

"Indirectly," she replied.

"Why would I…?"

"Before Adrian was chosen as Dis's incarnate, she had chosen you. She fed these spells to you," said Ana. "You were to bring balance to the world, but of course, men got in the way."

"Dis hates me," I said.

"She hates you because she loves Adrian," said Ana.

"Then why did she allow me to incarnate again?"

"To keep him on her side," said Ana. "Though I think you know it is too late for that. That is why she takes control of him, to remind him that he is a pawn."

"And instead of destroying Dis, you wish to destroy Adrian?"

"There is no other way, Isolde," she said.

"I don't believe you."

"Isolde—"

"There has to be another way!" I screamed, my pain and anger tearing from my chest.

"Adrian *is* Dis upon this earth, and when we were powerful—when witches ruled the earth—we could keep the power in check, but too many of us are asleep."

"Then let's wake them up, Ana!"

She shook her head. "Look at you, one of the most powerful witches of our time, and you can barely wake up. You are so terrified."

"You do not want anyone more powerful than you," I snapped.

She shook her head. "You love him too much to see the truth."

"The only truth I see at the moment is how you betrayed me."

"One day, you will understand," she said. "And then we can work together to bring balance to this world."

"Is your idea of balance siphoning magic from the bones of High Coven?" I asked. "That does not seem like balance to me."

"Oh, but it is," she said. "I did not siphon magic from your bones for myself, Isolde. I used your bones to create the one monster who could destroy Adrian—Asha's incarnate."

No. I ground my teeth and charged for her, but I was hit with a blast of energy and thrown into the great hall once again. I landed on my back near Nadia, my breath knocked out of me. A horrible shattering sound filled the hall, and I rolled onto my side, covering my head as pieces of mirror rained down.

When it was done, I rose to my feet and stared at the ruined hall.

"Isolde!"

My eyes shifted to the open doors where Adrian stood, fierce and angry and beautiful. An ache filled my chest beyond anything I had ever felt before in my life. I wanted to tell him so many things, but all I could manage was a desperate sob, and just when my knees gave out, he caught me and held me to his chest.

I carried your child, I wanted to say. *We were going to have a child.*

The words crowded my throat and mouth, but I bit my tongue. I would have to tell him. I needed to tell him, but if I did, I risked losing him to Dis.

I risked losing him altogether.

AUTHOR'S NOTE

Today is September 6, 2022, and four weeks ago, I was seriously questioning my ability to write this book. I knew it would be hard—I knew there would be some devastating moments, but I did not expect so many. I am often asked if I know where a book or series is headed, and I usually have some vague idea; such was the case for *Queen of Myth and Monsters*.

But I was completely wrong, and everything took me by surprise.

I'm jokingly (and not so jokingly) calling this book THE ONE IN WHICH EVERYONE GETS A BACKSTORY because all of these characters I thought I knew (except Ana…didn't know her at all) had so much more hidden under the surface. Everyone in this book is suffering, and I think the hard part is trying to decide if you are really against anyone because they all have their motives—but that's the interesting part of being morally grey, and in a lot of ways, I hope you struggle to decide.

First, I want to be clear that Adrian as a character was not modeled after Vlad III. I did research on Vlad III's life and how he came to be in power because I wanted to study a ruler who was perceived by those outside his country as almost "evil" despite his people seeing him as a hero.

It's obvious that this book is heavily influenced by the myths and legends from Romania, Slovenia, Germany, and Russia, and this mostly extends to the lore around their monsters.

The vârcolac (or vârcolaci) is commonly called a werewolf, though apparently it is said to be able to shift into more than just a dog. Its origin also varies. In *Queen of Myth and Monsters*, I decided to make the creature into more of a werewolf-type monster, so it could stand on its feet. I wanted something that could mimic human movement to differentiate it from the aufhocker.

Aufhockers are also interesting. They look most like a grim (a black dog seen as an omen of death) but I do not feel like they act as one at all. The name is Germanic and means "to leap upon," which is what aufhockers would do to unsuspecting travelers. They were said to weigh down their victims until they caused their death or until they reached home.

Aufhockers can also appear in various forms, including as a spirit or a goblin-type creature. There is a version of it that is considered a vampire because it rips out the throats of its victims.

I had no idea Isolde would become a shifter in this book, and I fought it hard. I'm not sure what it is about werewolves, but I have never had an affinity or interest in them. That being said, I think the dynamic of the aufhocker is so interesting, and I love that later I can explore Isolde shifting into different forms other than a "dog." (I don't really prefer that term because I feel like…the form is so much more robust, but I don't know what else to use).

Another element I want to touch on is Winter's Eve. It's based on St. Andrew's Eve, sometimes called the Night of the Wolf, and is celebrated on November 30th. It is believed to be a night when magic is, essentially, at its strongest, which is part of the reason all types of monsters and the undead are able to wander around on this night. In particular, wolves are believed to be the most powerful, likely because St. Andrew is considered their protector. Several rituals were completed to prepare for the night, including hanging garlic.

Perhaps the most difficult element of this book was the magic—but this is also where I have the most to say.

I began reading a book called *Witch* by Lisa Lister, which detailed the rise of the patriarchy and, as a result, the oppression of women, their magic, and the demonization of witchcraft. I also began reading *When God Was a Woman*, which details the steady fall of a world that first worshipped women into a society that now seeks to revoke our rights—all because women are powerful.

We are powerful in the ways our world likes to undermine and silence us. Our intuition is often overlooked as only a feeling or being oversensitive. Our ability to give birth and control over our bodies are carelessly handled by men in government, who use religion as a weapon and reason when the Bible is only a myth constructed to oppress.

I always wonder what the world would have been like if humanity had chosen a different epic as the crux of its mainstream religion—which was one of the ideas that drove how the world of *A Touch of Darkness* unfolded.

I wanted part of the magic in the world to feel as though any of us can do it because I believe that we can. Magic comes in the form of intuition, that deep trust we have within ourselves to follow our instincts. Magic comes from the words we speak that can manifest a life beyond our wildest dreams. Magic comes from choosing to see meaning in symbols.

This is the foundation of the magic system in Cordova. Sometimes I felt like it was hard to pinpoint, especially for Isolde who has been trying to open herself to feeling and having this awareness after it was locked away due to her trauma.

I think this is the journey we are all on as women now. Some of us are waking up and others are asleep—either is okay. Trauma lives in our blood and crosses lifetimes. I think every day we wake up and live this life is progress toward healing.

Last, I want to talk about Isolde—my unapologetic queen. I hope I have given my readers, especially my BIPOC readers, a female character who makes them feel empowered and determined. Isolde is the character through which I have had to face the very complicated relationship I have with my heritage. As a "white" presenting member of the Muscogee Nation, I never quite feel Native American enough, and this is exasperated when others question my heritage.

Which happens all the time even in professional settings. I will never forget hearing that someone asked my team if "they are sure I'm really native." I don't know how else to say that we all look different—we are as diverse as our relationships with our tribes. Being Native American in 2022 looks different for every citizen, and that is the fault of our colonization—but it should not divide us.

I know my experiences apply to so many of you, and I wanted to confront those feelings with Isolde who, I feel, is a woman I aspire to be—she never apologizes for who she is; she doesn't bow to the will of men; she refuses to conform to society's standards.

She has had to survive like so many of us—I can't wait to see her conquer.

ABOUT THE AUTHOR

USA Today and international bestselling author Scarlett St. Clair is a citizen of the Muscogee Nation and the author of the Hades X Persephone Saga, the Hades Saga, *King of Battle & Blood*, and *When Stars Come Out*.

She has a master's degree in library science and information studies and a bachelor's in English writing. She is obsessed with Greek Mythology, murder mysteries, and the afterlife. For information on books, tour dates, and content, please visit scarlettstclair.com.